THE LONELY

The Lonely Duet

TARA BROWN

TARA BROWN

BESTSELLING AUTHOR

OTHER BOOKS BY TARA BROWN

The Serendipity Series
Fling Club
He Loves You Not

Blood and Bone
Blood and Bone
Sin and Swoon
Soul and Blade

The Puck Buddies Series
Puck Buddies
Roommates
Bed Buddies
Baby Daddies – coming soon

The Single Lady Spy Series
The End of Me
The End of Games
The End of Tomorrow
The End of Lies – coming soon

To Gitte and Jenny, Jagger-lip kisses and hugs!
This book is for you!

A NOTE TO THE READER:

This book has a trigger warning.

Thanks,
Tar

I

The front steps of any building you've never been in before always feel intimidating and seem larger than they really are. The entrance and steps to Speare Hall made me feel full of inspiration and anticipation the first time I saw them. It was spring and I was there to see where I would be living in the fall. The stairs were intimidating and exciting.

Spring orientation cured that feeling.

The cell-like cinder block room was not what I had expected—it was what I was used to.

But here I had expected romance and creativity in historic downtown Boston. I never expected blazing heat, lack of air conditioning, humidity, and a general sense of sterility. I looked around that first day for the cameras and guards, assuming I was on the set of the remake of *1984*.

Surely Big Brother was watching me.

Now, four months later, I still can't seem to get back that initial inspiration and excitement as I cross the threshold to start the year. I am stuck in the sterility and *1984*.

Today the school is alive with people and energy, just as it was on orientation, but today I see it for what it is. The building is strange and smells like prison, a familiar one. I know about the industrial smell of prison, all too well.

My excitement about being a freshman is long gone. Instead, I climb the stairs, gripping my belongings and trying not to make eye contact. I don't want my fellow students to see it—the fact I don't belong here, with them.

I glance at my watch and count the minutes until my saving grace arrives. I wish we'd managed to get flights together. But we did not, and so I am stuck with the responsibility of walking through the front door of our room alone.

I enter the gray dank room and dump my crap on the bed. The mattress is frightening with its plastic cover and the wooden desk in the corner is old and looks industrial. Everything about the small room is functional and wipeable.

I do like that; it feels like home, even if I don't want it to.

The floor is shiny like a hospital and the walls are white and stark. For a moment I think too far ahead and they close in around me. I almost bolt from the room, leaving my things and running the entire way home. The entire two thousand miles home.

Instead, I close my eyes and let Dr. Bradley's words fill my head. *Deep breaths in and out. Eyes closed. Body numb. You're at the beach and the sand is soft. The waves are small and make little noise. Slowly come back to the room you are in. Let the light of the room feel like it's blessing you. You are safe. You are grateful for the safety and the air and the roof over your head.*

I open my eyes and try desperately to let the light of the wide window bless me.

My heart is slowing and my mouth isn't as dry.

I've grown fond of Dr. Bradley's affirmations. At first they felt like weird juju you would hear in a room filled with women in their mid-life crises, but now they feel like a blanket for my heart.

I glance about, deciding to focus on the room instead of my insanity, but the room is blank. I need things, which means I need him. It is the worst part of being like *Little Orphan Annie*.

I hate needing him. I dread sending him texts asking for things— money. But I don't have any way of buying supplies on my own. He protests when I ask him for things, but at the same time I think he likes it, as he wants us in as much contact as possible. It's his rule. One of them.

I pull my phone out and sigh.

Can I go to the store?

Why do you insist on asking? Of course you may go to the store. I told you about this already. Don't ask stupid questions. What do you need? Is it anything I can help with?

Bedding and stuff. Remember I asked you before?

Right, but I told you to stop asking after the first time. I gave you the joint account. You explained your need for room essentials and I agreed. Decorate how you like. Spend it how you want. Make the room yours. The car will be there in 20.

KK. I don't mean it. I won't ever use the account without asking first. I don't like the fact that he gives me money. It won't ever feel like it's mine.

KK is a typo, not a send off. Please speak like an adult.

He's so snarky.

I sigh and look around the room. I can't unpack anything. I just can't. I need everything there to be able to do it, and I feel like I have nothing. No control. No peace. The room isn't clean, not like it should be.

I don't move. I just stand there and take it all in. I can't sit on the bed or touch anything. I never realized how bad it would be. The new place syndrome is almost physically painful.

I grab the wipes from the bag I carried up and I start.

It's a frenzy when it starts.

OCD isn't just a sickness; it's a way of life. I should have gone to school to be in forensics, instead of wanting to be in journalism. I'm sweating and moving in a way that would frighten a normal person.

Fortunately, the person who walks through the door understands. Her green eyes sparkle, but they're not surprised at the state of me, at all. "Em, did you do my side already?" Her voice is dripping with sarcasm when she asks.

I glance back at her, snapping out of my attack mode. I stop moving and look around. I barely remember entering the room—the room that now glistens far more than it did before.

"You know his car is sitting at the curb. His Hotty McNaughty driver saw me and asked if you were ever coming down."

It takes me a second to come back to the real world. I place the used wipe in the bin and dump pumpkin-spice hand sanitizer into my palm. She watches my face as she puts her bags down on the shiny mattress, which no doubt reeks of bleach.

I frown at the plastic mattress and our few belongings. "Don't unpack. Let's go to the store first. I forgot I asked him to let me get bedding."

She shrugs. "Kay."

When we leave I lock the door and walk away from the unfinished job. It's a step in the right direction for me to leave something before I've finished it. It will plague me, but at least I've done it.

His driver is playing with his phone when we walk up. His name is Stuart. He sighs and jumps out of the car to get the door when I try to grab it. I don't notice the way the people stare at the man in the black suit opening my door, or the fact I am leaving in a black Lincoln Town Car. What I do notice is the way Shell beams and tosses her hair about every time she sees Stuart.

"Try not to be too obvious," I whisper as Stuart gets into the front seat and starts the car.

"He's just so hot," she leans in and whispers back. Her lips smell like berry gloss. She always smells nice. Sometimes her clothes smell like food her mom cooked. That's my favorite. At least it was when we were in New Mexico. Now she smells like me. Lost smells of the many airports and taxis we've been in.

Stuart watches her in the rearview. I don't blame him. I doubted my hetero-ness until I realized I wasn't exactly attracted to *her*, but rather to the smell and the feel of her. Her clothes are always soft from fabric softener and her hair smells like garlicky Italian food. Her green eyes sparkle in a way I love—in a sisterly sort of way.

I want my eyes to sparkle like hers. I want my lips to glisten and smell like lip gloss. I want long, shiny dark-chestnut hair and a long, lean body. I want to be her most days. I'm not entirely sure if I'm her friend because I like her, or if it's that I want to be her.

Her nails are always long and polished. Her lips stick out from her face just enough that you can't help but want to kiss them. Even as a girl, I always wanted to kiss them. We tried it once. It felt wrong in my soul, but I liked the feel of her berry gloss against my mouth. Well, for all of six seconds. Then I needed it off me.

She flutters her eyelashes at me. "You think he'd go out with me?"

"Really?" I almost laugh at the question. "Do bears poop in the woods?"

Stuart looks at us in the rearview. "They do, and I'll pick you up from dorms tomorrow night at seven." He grins. I can't fight the grin that crosses my lips at seeing his.

"Oh, you heard that?" Her face flushes. "Okay."

She is ballsy. She always has been ballsy.

"You like Chinese?" Stuart is barely watching the road. It doesn't make me nervous like it should. He's an excellent driver.

Shell wrinkles her nose. "No. I like everything but. You're not Chinese are you?"

He snorts. "I'm American. Born in Wichita, but my grandma was of Japanese descent. I'm a quarter, I guess." His Kansas accent is so obvious it isn't even funny. Not to mention, he only slightly looks like he might have a touch of something exotic in his bloodline. He looks like every other Heinz-57 American, only he manages to look exactly like an Abercrombie model while doing it. I give her a horrified look.

She grins. "I love Japanese food."

I am dying inside.

"I know a place." He doesn't seem to mind that she is insanely rude.

I sit in the awkward silence of their rearview mirror-planned date and try to think of things to say. My filter denies every one of them. There is no recovering from the humiliation that's creating flames across my cheeks.

He pulls up in front of the outlet store.

"Thanks, Stuart," I say and grab the handle, but he's out of the car lightning fast and opening the door.

"I can get it."

He looks unimpressed. "I can get fired." His tone mimics my own.

"Sorry."

He shakes his head and climbs back in.

I elbow Shell on the way into the store. "Ass. Don't date his driver and don't ask people what nationality they are. It's embarrassing. He's born in Wichita. He sounds like he's from Kansas. You're a moron."

She isn't fazed. "He's nummy hot, and I get to see him naked tomorrow. I don't even care if he's related to me. It's on." She smiles her disgustingly naughty grin. She looks like she needs a scotch in one hand and to twirl her mustache in the other.

She pushes the cart and puts things we need in and I put them back. "I don't want to spend too much." She rolls her eyes and puts them back in the cart.

She snatches my phone from me and texts from it. I try to get it back but it rings. She passes me the phone with a smug grin as it rings.

"Hi," I say weakly.

His voice is quiet, but he still manages to be shitty, as always. "Buy whatever you want."

"I'm buying what I need." I'm getting defensive.

He sighs. "Either buy the nice stuff, or I will have the entire store delivered to the dorms. Better yet, I will order it all from some store no one but Paris Hilton can afford. You will be the most popular girl in dorms with your fancy espresso maker and fabulous couches." He sounds weird being so deadpan and saying fabulous.

"Whatever." My face is glowing red. I shudder, imagining the other students in my room.

"I've asked you repeatedly not to say that word. It's annoying." I hear the flipping of pages or a book in the background. He's working and I'm his annoyance.

"We done?" I ask saucily but he's already gone. I look at her and frown. "You shouldn't do that. He doesn't even want you to have my cell number, let alone touching it."

She sticks her tongue out and grabs the extra fluffy blankets. "At least you're getting your shit. Mine isn't arriving for like days."

I look down at my phone and send a quick text message.

Sorry to bug you again, but can I get her stuff? Her parents sent it, but it's not here and she won't have much anyway. They can't afford to send huge amounts of crap.

Yes. Stop asking ridiculous questions.

Thank you. I hate being nice to him when he's being a dick.

You are welcome. Please remind Miss Monkton that I would like her to go easy on Stu ;-)

Ok... I feel weird about the text. His winky face is strange for me. He has never been cheeky with me before. My response is to blush and stare at the winky face.

Also remind her my car is off limits for any extracurricular activities she has planned with him!! He never uses exclamation marks. For him it's like jazz hands—extra flashy. He really means it.

I scowl at my phone and text back, *No. Ewwww. No. Leave me out of it.*

She nudges me. "What's he saying? You're all flushed. Is he hitting on you?"

"Stop!" I frown at her. "I don't even want to know how he knows about the date, but he says go easy on Stuart and no nasty stuff in his car."

"Wow, he's good." She smiles deviously. "No promises though."

My heart stops. "I have to ride in the car. You know you can't do that in there, right?" My voice has the slightest hint of panic in it.

Her smile fades. "I know. I wouldn't. It was a joke."

I reach into my bag and fish around. "It's not here. It's not here." I see it in the back of my mind. I've left it on the desk in the room. I squirted some on my hands and placed the bottle down. My heart starts to race.

"It's okay. They sell it here." She tries to calm me down.

I'm almost shaking. "I don't have it."

"They have it here. They have it in the soap section." She grabs my hand and pulls me, while pushing the cart. She drags me to the aisle like a mother dragging a child across the store. She cracks open a bottle and squirts it on me. My breath regulates as the cold of it soaks my skin and the alcohol fills my nostrils.

She smiles and dumps some on her hands too. She puts the opened container in the cart. "See? Crisis averted."

I swallow and feel the heat on my cheeks. "I can't do this. I can't do school. I can't do cafeterias and bars and pubs and desks. Oh God, desks. I forgot about desks."

"We only have to tackle right now, Em. We don't have to take on anything else." She rolls her eyes when I sigh, and grabs my shirt, leaving indents in the cotton. "Come the frig on, nutbag."

I laugh nervously as she looks back and smiles. "You really are crazy."

She's the only person who can say it.

2

"You and Stuart were having eye sex in the car," I mutter, still cleaning the decorations before I can hang them up.

"Dude!" She laughs. "We weren't. He was just looking. He likes the merchandise." She puts up the last picture we bought, the one I called frivolous, and stands back to appreciate the work we've done. It feels homey. I knew it would. She's good at this.

"I like it."

She smiles at me. "You okay with all this?"

I nod and look around. "The clutter is a lot for me, but it feels like a room should. It looks lived in. Not like I'm hoarding and guarding everything like a dragon. It's weird to have everything out where we can see it and use it. But I like it."

"And you cleaned it all so you're free from worry." She crosses her arms and gives me a worried look.

I shake it off. "I'm going to the gym to run. You coming?"

She grins. "No. Stuart's coming over to go for a walk. I'm sure I'll get plenty of exercise."

"No my God. You're seeing his driver tonight. I thought it was 'I'm not Japanese' food tomorrow? How's there a walk already planned today?"

"His name is Stuart and you have to start calling him that. Face the facts, this is your life." She flashes her phone at me. "And he texted me." Her voice is high-pitched as she sings the answer.

I make a pouty face and walk out the door. "I hate you."

"YOU LOVE ME, YOU LITTLE SLUT!" she shouts at me as I close the door. The guy standing in the hall across from our door looks at me and grins. He's heard her shout that I'm a slut.

I furrow my brow, which only makes him grin harder. I scurry away quickly.

The walk to the gym proves one thing to me: the industrial feel of the building is wearing off. I see color and life everywhere now. Only one day of mass amounts of teenagers moving in and it's starting to come alive. Each door has decorations and personalized signs or covers. The handles have fun sayings hung from them like in hotels. A white towel is on the floor, making the shiny industrial flooring seem lived in. I plug my headphones into my phone and walk down the stairs and out into the muggy air.

Boston in late August is hateful. It's the only way to describe it. Hateful. I heard one of the Southerners say it and I agree. The way they say it is cooler though. *Haytful*. It's awesome.

The recreation hall is right next to our dorm, only a short jog and I'm there. I enter feeling overwhelmed, but I push it away and casually stroll over to the wipes, grabbing a handful. I take huge breaths and focus my mind as I wipe down the treadmill I choose. I use the wipe to wash the console on the massive machine and begin my stretches. I start the music and press the on button.

This is my thing.

I run.

I do it for fitness, but I do it for something else: I do it so I know I can. If anything goes wrong, I can run. It's a sick and twisted way to be, but I don't know any other way. I start light at a seven. I jog it for my five-minute warm-up. I put it up to an eight. I notice blue and red in my peripheral. I glance over, not losing my focus, and see a huge set of shoulders. The guy next to me is jogging too. I put it up to a nine and refocus my mind. My legs start to feel the press. They love the stretch and the pressure of the slight sprint.

My song changes and I put it up to a ten. It's the shortest of my intervals. Only three minutes at a ten. Then back to a nine for five. Then back to an eight for the rest of the run.

The ten is challenging me. I imagine the scene though.

I'm running in a dark alley.

They almost have me.

Their shoes make loud slaps against the cement.

The slaps get louder. With every step they get closer.

My legs start to burn but I push it harder.

I snap out of it and look at the time, only to realize I've been doing ten for four minutes. I drop it back to a nine. It feels easy for the first minute. But my legs are so taxed that the last minutes of running at a nine are brutal. I hit the slow-down button, almost panicking, and lower it to an eight. My legs relax. They like running at an eight. I notice something and glance at the guy to the right of me. He's talking to me. I pull out my earbud.

"What?" I say breathlessly.

"Are those Beats?" He's breathless like me.

"My time?"

He looks confused. "What?"

"You mean like, did I beat my time?" My heart is beating in my throat.

He laughs, slowing his treadmill down. He points to my earbuds. "The buds—are—they Beats? Dr. Dre, the rapper?"

"I don't know what that means." I pull one of them from my ear and look at it. "I think so." There is a sticker with his name on it.

"They're sick, huh? I have the full-ear ones. So awesome."

"Sure." I slow my treadmill down more, not certain if he's messing with my run because he's insanely attractive, or if I am just confused about the brand of headphones. Whatever it is I cant seem to focus on the machine or my feet at all. "You run fast," I notice as I speed walk.

He laughs. "Not as fast as you. If my legs were short like yours, I would be running half your speed."

I open my mouth, offended. "My legs aren't short."

"I didn't mean that your legs are short. I mean like—oh, fuck it," he says breathlessly and presses the cardiac-arrest button to stop the treadmill. "I mean that you're shorter than me. Like we run the same pace but my step is longer. So it's easier."

I laugh for the first time in a long time, maybe high on endorphins or how attractive he is. "I know what you meant. I just couldn't let you get away with that."

He wipes the sweat off his red face and wipes it on his pants. "Thanks. Sebastian Hollinger." He holds the sweaty hand out. My nose wrinkles when I look at it. He laughs and puts his hand away.

I bite my lip. "Sorry. I just have a thing with—"

"Some asshole rubbing sweat all over his hands and then touching you with them? Yeah, everyone does. Sorry about that."

"Emalyn Spicer." My name falls from my lips, almost desperate to change the subject and the focus from his sweat.

He smiles the most charming smile I've ever seen. My heart almost stops at the sight of him. He's got dark-brown hair, round sweaty shoulders, thick sweaty biceps, straight teeth, an amazing smile, and brown-hazel eyes. They're almost green and I almost sigh, but the sweat bothers me enough to keep me grounded. "Nice to meet you," I say softly.

He smiles. A lot. His smile broadens when he talks, "You too. Emalyn. I've never heard that name before. Where's it come from?"

I hate the questions about my name. It always comes up. I shake my head and push the heart-attack button too. "No clue." The treadmill comes to an instant stop.

He shrugs his huge shoulders. "Cool."

I want him to talk to me again, but I haven't flirted with many boys. I'm not great at flirting and playing around. I can count the boys I've flirted with and each time it ended awkwardly. But I know enough about being polite so I ask something common, "You from here?"

He shakes his head. "No. I'm from Northern Maine. You?"

I shake my head. "No. Long ways away." I don't want to say it but I do, "I'm from New Mexico." I wait for it. I know it'll start questions, it always does. Questions I don't like answering.

He frowns. "Wow, you're really pale and blonde."

"And I have blue eyes and no accent. I'm not Mexican. I don't think even half the population is Mexican or Hispanic. It's just a regular state. You know, regular percentages of regular people. Regular being a little bit of everyone. A mix of nationalities and races, so to speak."

He closes his eyes and shakes his head. "Yikes. I didn't mean to sound like I'm a Klan member. Jeeze. I meant like you're not very tanned. I always imagined New Mexico was warm and shit."

"You are actually worse at this than I am. That's saying a lot. This bit of tan is about all I get. I've never tanned well."

His red face loosens up a bit. "This is horrid. I'm way cooler than this, I swear. Can we just start over?"

I wave. "Hi, I'm Emalyn. White, extra white actually, and non-Mexican from New Mexico. How are you?"

He laughs. "You're funny. Funny and fast." He looks like he's struggling with something. "Wanna just have dinner with me? I promise it will be less entertaining than this." He points around us. "It's the workout, it's messing with me. I think I'm light-headed actually." His eyes twinkle, making me laugh again, that's twice now.

My face is split into a huge grin. "I'd love to."

I would?

My racing heart is saying otherwise. But I remind myself everything is about the new leaf. Freedom, adventure, taking risks—all are the new leaf that I so badly need.

"What are you doing in an hour?"

I raise an eyebrow. "Nothing."

Why am I still answering questions?

"Wanna meet at Chicken Lou's? One hour?"

I want to think about it. I want to say no. I want to be rational, but I don't. I smile and hop off the treadmill and grab a wipe. "Yeah."

"Great."

I wipe down the machine and wave. "See you in a bit."

He smiles his killer smile and makes my racing, panicking, and stressed-out heart stop.

Sebastian, Seb? No—Bastian? Maybe. Maybe just Sebastian.

My mind races and fills with terrors. Bad things. Fears and possibilities. By the time I get to the room, I've talked myself out of it.

Michelle is there getting all curled and dolled up and pretty. She smiles until she sees the look on my face. "What happened?"

I shrug. "Nothing." My voice cracks a little.

"Tell Shell-Shell what happened." She crawls onto my bed with her shoes on. My nose wrinkles involuntarily. She rolls her eyes and makes sure they don't touch the blankets that I still have to wash three times to get rid of the smell of the store. I have to wait for the weekend. The machines had waiting lists I couldn't bear. "Stop analyzing the dirt on the bedding and tell me what happened."

"I met a boy," I blurt.

Her eyes light up momentarily. "Cute boy?" Her face is panicked for a second. This is uncharted territory for me—us. She has always been the one with cute boy on her lips. Neither of us knows what to do about a cute boy and me.

"Cutest boy."

"Name."

I sigh when I say it, "Sebastian."

She makes a face. "What went wrong? I like that name."

"Nothing. He asked me for dinner."

She squeals and does a weird butt-hopping thing on my bed, before I can finish. "Where is he taking you? Oh my God, a real date. I could cry right now. You said yes to a boy and—wait—why do you look like that?" Her face drops.

I can't look at her. "Nothing. I just think it's super weird—he asked me out the first time he saw me."

"Oh my God. Em, you're never going to date and have a boyfriend and start this normal life you want so badly, if you don't actually go on a date. Yeah, so what? He asked you out. He likes what he sees and wants to get to know you and see if he likes more than what's on the outside." She takes my hand. "You don't have to do anything. It's just a date. No different than eating at the table back home, next to a boy. Dude. You got this. Bring the sani and have a meal. We did restaurants back home. You can do this. Wipe the cutlery down under the table."

"No." I gag a bit thinking about it and shake my head. "I just can't, okay?" I stand and walk to the showers. I stay in extra long. I try to stay in so it's too late by the time I finish. But I can't. I go back to our room to find she's gone, but the mirror has lipstick on it.

GO OR I WILL CUT YOUR HAIR OFF IN YOUR SLEEP!!!!

I shudder at the writing and pull on a t-shirt and some jeans. I look back at the red lipstick and rush to it. I'm wiping and cleaning in a frenzy before I realize it. I step back, horrified that the grease in the lipstick has permanently marked the mirror.

I pull my phone out and send a quick text. *I need a new mirror. Can Stuart bring one by later? Like a dressing mirror?*

Good evening to you too. How was the first day? Of course he can. What size?

I look at the mirror and shake my head as I text. *I don't know.*

…Take a picture! He's awfully saucy and impatient.

I hold the phone up and take the picture. It has me in it. I don't look like me though. Not the way I see me. The girl in the mirror looks normal. Blonde, plain, blue eyes that sparkle with fake life inside them.

I ignore my thoughts and slip on my Nike sandals and, of course, my running watch. I love that it's plastic and washable. I pull my hair into a messy ponytail and don't apply a drop of makeup. She's right; I have to do this. If I ever plan to get better, I have to do this.

I grab my wallet and leave, feeling weird. I start my chants, "It's just like eating beside a boy at home." I wash, rinse, and repeat this the entire way down the hall.

I send the picture when I'm on the stairs. I then send another text. One that I have been dreading since I agreed. *I'm going out for dinner.* I have to check in, it's one of his rules.

With whom?

Boy from the gym named Sebastian. Chicken Lou's.

My cell rings. I swallow and answer, "Hi."

He sighs into the phone. "Hi. So a boy from the gym? Alone? Already?"

He sounds annoyed and quiet. He's always quiet. I don't know what to say. "Yup."

It always sounds hollow wherever he is and his voice is a whisper almost, "I don't like it."

"Okay."

"I don't like it." His reaction throws me.

"Uhm, see I already told him yes."

"Did you tell him where you live or what your cell is?"

I shake my head. "No. You told me no one could know the number. I almost never even told Shell, even when you said it was okay but that you didn't like it."

"Call her Michelle, please. I don't like Shell. It sounds infantile. Message me from the bathroom when you get to wherever you're going." He hangs up. He always does. He never speaks to me nicely—well, he never really speaks to me. That's not what he's for. I hate that he called me infantile.

"Dick," I mutter and head for the restaurant.

Sebastian is standing outside when I walk up. He smiles and I forget about the weird phone call and the ruined mirror.

He looks the same as he did running. T-shirt that shows off his defined chest and arms and those shoulders, gah! His hair is shaggy and fluffy, most likely from being freshly washed and not styled. He has on baggy jeans and Toms. I smile when I catch a glimpse of his running watch.

"I didn't think you were coming," he says. I glance at the time and groan. I'm half an hour late and he waited.

He waited. I like that.

I smile back at him. "I'm sorry."

He opens the door for me. We walk into the chaos and madness. He walks past me when we get inside.

It's packed.

I freeze instantly.

He wraps his hand around mine and drags me through the crowd. There's an instant shiver up my arm. Not because his hand is warm and so big that it eats up my whole hand. Not because his skin against mine is making my belly dance. Not because I am sexually attracted to him like a—I'll stop there.

It's because HIS SKIN IS TOUCHING MINE! His bare hand is against mine. I can't imagine how many times he picked his teeth or scratched. I don't know him at all. I'm almost gagging. I feel the panic coming.

Someone bumps into me, knocking me. Another person touches my arm. "Sorry," they say. There is nothing but the sea of voices and chairs being shoved and waitresses shouting. People's skin is on mine, touching me. Rubbing their germs against me.

I close my eyes in the horde of people. I don't have any choice. They've surrounded me. I let him pull me along and drag me through the crowd. I start my affirmations silently. *I feel grateful for the light and air I'm breathing. I have hand sanitizer in my bag. I'm grateful for hand sanitizer and the fact I remembered it. Every mess can be cleaned.* I chant it. *Every mess can be cleaned up.*

He stops. I walk into his back and his arms wrap around the back of me, hugging me to him. My face is squished into his back.

"This is insanity." He shouts back at me, "Are your eyes closed?"

I manage to open my trembling lips, "Too-too m-many p-p-people."

He hugs me tighter to him. "Oh my God, Emalyn. I'm so sorry. I should have warned you. This place is nuts every night of the week." He is shouting loudly. It doesn't improve anything. He turns back the way we came in and pulls me out. He doesn't hold my hand. He keeps me hugged into him, like a two-person conga line.

I'm a moron.

I feel it inside, but I can't stop and be normal. When the fresh air hits I rip the sanitizer out of my pocket. I dump the cold gel across my hands. The smell of the pumpkin-spiced alcohol is therapy. I drag it up my arms and over the small amount of my chest that is bared in my t-shirt.

I know he's watching me. I can almost feel the crazed look on his face. I can definitely imagine it. I'm bathing in hand sani in the middle of the street.

I finish rubbing but don't move. My lip is trembling. I'm begging, pleading with myself not to choke up or freak out completely. I'm not too worried about the tears leaving my eyes, just flooding them. I don't cry. My tears always find their way to my eyes, but they never actually make it out. Instead, they make kaleidoscopes and change everything for me.

He doesn't even know me and I've revealed something so horrid. If he knew the rest, he would leave. He will leave. And that's okay.

I am seconds from pulling out the phone and sending the message for the car to come. I don't know if my legs can walk back to the dorm. They have the cement-boot feeling. The thick feeling they get. It's coming, it always does.

Through the kaleidoscopes I see his huge hand reach over and take the sanitizer like it's dangerous. He squirts some and bathes them in it then passes it back. But now that he's touched it, I have to do it again. It's insanity but it's my insanity. I bathe in it a second time and wash the bottle before I put it away. He takes my hand in his and walks me silently down the busy road.

"I'm so sorry," he finally speaks. His tone is one that suggests he might be traumatized.

Don't cry. Don't cry. Don't cry.

The tears are there in my throat. They are threatening me. I almost believe they will leave my eyes but they don't.

"I should have guessed. You cleaned that treadmill like it was your job." He laughs. He is smiling. I can hear it in his voice.

I glance up. "I get it if you want to run away as fast as you can."

He grins. "What? I have the cleanest date in town now. I've never felt so safe in all my life." He points with his free hand and I notice we are still holding hands. "I know a quiet place down the road. Very clean. Owner has OCD so the service is slow, but the place is immaculate."

"Okay." My voice cracks again. The warmth of his hand is nice. It makes the lonely go away. Maybe he's the cure. I sigh quietly.

He pulls me into pace with him. "So is it as bad as Howie Mandel's?"

I snort. "It's not what you think. I'm not just a germaphobe."

"What?" He looks confused. "You are so."

I shake my head. "I don't do it because I care about the germs. I was raised to be clean. I was raised with a lot of kids, and we were told we could ignite a plague if we weren't clean." I don't tell him that I've spent my lifetime trying to clean something up that I don't remember.

He makes a face. "Oh, one of those scary cult families where you get scrubbed with boiling water like *Mommy Dearest?*"

I laugh. "Something like that." The similarities are disturbing.

He shrugs. "My uncle Frank is a surgeon. I get it. He went through a vodka phase once. He had bottles of it in every bathroom, and we had to wash our hands with it." He steals a glance down at me. "The crowds are hard too. New Mexico is probably pretty quiet. Boston's not exactly quiet."

"What kind of surgeon?" We need to talk about him.

"Orthopedic."

"Wow."

He doesn't sound interested. "Yeah."

"You taking medicine then? Keeping it in the family?"

He looks down at me, laughing like I'm missing something. "No." His eyes are filled with a touch of something intense, but it's too far beneath the surface for me to see it. "I'm in business. What about you?"

"Journalism is what I want to do. I ran the paper at my high school. We did a lot of earth sciences pieces. Trying to be proactive about the environment. But I'm a freshman, so we'll see."

The Town Car pulls up as we round a corner. Stuart climbs out of the car he parks illegally. "You said you were going to Chicken Lou's." He looks pissed. His dark eyes are stormy. Shell is right, he's hot. Especially angry.

I don't want to explain the car or the driver to Sebastian. I scowl and shout across the street like a psycho, "Go home! I thought you were on a date!"

"Had to end it early." He's speaking through his teeth.

I roll my eyes. "The chicken place was too busy. Huge crowd." I pray he gets it without me having to explain.

Sebastian looks down at me. "Is that your—driver?"

I laugh nervously and shake my head. "No. God, no. Stuart, this is Sebastian. Stuart is a friend of my—uhm—family's. He's like a big—older—annoying brother." Stuart looks less than impressed.

Sebastian smiles uncomfortably. "Hey, man. We're gonna eat here. You wanna come?"

Stuart ignores him. "This is a bad idea."

"I'll call him. Now go away." I turn and pull Sebastian to the door. I almost grab the handle, but my hand freezes looking at it. Thankfully, Sebastian grabs it quickly. "Let me. Is everything okay?"

I look back at Stuart and nod. "He's really overprotective."

"Who are you going to call?"

"My—uhm—family." I laugh inside my mind. I've never said the word "uhm" so many times in my life—or "family."

Stuart doesn't get in the car. He watches. He always watches. It's creepy.

He isn't creepy, but his job is.

My phone vibrates the minute we get inside but I ignore it.

The restaurant smells great, and I can see the sparkle and shine in every corner. The servers are clean, with their hair pulled back and greased to their heads. Everything is white linen and immaculate. I almost sigh with relief, but then I notice how everyone else is dressed. We look like slobs. I look down at my chipped toenail polish and ugly blue sandals and grimace.

He must have seen the look in my eyes because he leans in and whispers, "Yeah, I forgot how fancy this place was. You okay here?"

I nod. "I'm starving. I don't care. I feel like an idiot, but whatever."

"Me too." We are still holding hands. It's weird for me to hold hands with anyone. After my panic attack it's nice. More than nice. He's like a hero. I feel rescued. The right way. Like he is a prince and not a dictator. My knight in shining armor. He might have cured the lonely.

3

"We ate and talked and ate some more. He eats a ton like me, so that's good. I didn't look like a pig." I'm nattering. It's a first.

Shell rolls her eyes as she applies my toenail polish. "I don't know how you eat that much and don't get fat."

"Sprints. But yeah, we ate and talked. He is so sweet. He never tried to kiss me or touch me, except the hand, and that was after he did the sani. I super like him." I'm gushing.

She scowls up at me. "One date and you're in love? I told you to have dinner. You girls are all the same. You hold out and the first boy you let in, you love him. You need to test-drive this shit and date a few others. This is too fast." Her tone is edgy. It hurts a little.

"It was just dinner." I'm getting angry.

"Are you going out with him again?"

I feel my face tightening. "No. I don't know. He doesn't have my number. You're the one who made me go. Why are you being a jerk about me liking him? You know how big of a deal this is to me. He saw the lonely and he stayed."

Seeing the look on my face, she lightens hers. "Sorry. Oh my God, I am being a bitch. Sorry, dude. I'm so happy for you. This is a huge step.

I'm just so annoyed with your Uncle Daddy Dude. He called like a hundred times when we were out. He was pissed that Stuart was on his own time. It was like eight at night. Like come on. You know?"

I nod. "Sorry." I say it but I'm still mad.

She laughs and blows her dark hair out of her tanned face. "No. It's not your fault. I should have known better than to fall for your Uncle Daddy's driver."

I laugh too. "He isn't my Uncle Daddy."

She makes air quotation marks. "Your *benefactor*."

It makes me feel weird when we talk about him. I don't like it either. I wish I had a mom and a dad and a normal life. I wish my clothes and hair smelled like food and not bleach and anxiety. She hurts me and she doesn't know it. It's not her intention to hurt me though. It's me reacting. So I keep my face pleasant. Until I feel it start. The room wobbles a bit and the polish bottles almost duplicate in numbers. They surround me. Each one has been touched. I swallow, looking at them all.

"I see you," she says, but doesn't look at me.

"No, you don't," I whisper.

"Just do it." She says it like it's nothing.

I reach over and grab the wipes, the polish remover, and all the little polish bottles she's touched. I feel sick wiping her off of everything that's hers. I feel sicker that she's okay with it.

She changes the subject back to my dinner, "So, he saved you and then bought you a dinner at an OCD restaurant? This guy is the real deal of sweet and romantic. He never even tried anything?"

I'm almost disappointed when I say it, "No."

"Wish he had?" Her glossy lips turn up into a grin.

I grin. "No." I don't sound convincing.

She laughs. "Stuart tried. Oh my God, that man is hot. No shirt and it's like wow. Wow. So beautiful."

"He's a ninja."

She arches an eyebrow and then looks back down at her work. "For real?"

I look at my toes and beam. "Thanks. Yeah, for real. He's like a badass ninja. He told me he was anyway. I mean he could be lying. But

I think he kinda looks like a ninja, ya know?" I flick her. "And not because he's from Wichita, crazy-ass racist woman."

She sticks her tongue out. "Are Japanese people even ninjas?"

"I think Sumo wrestlers." I furrow my brow. "He told you, he's not Japanese. He's from Kansas."

She wrinkles her nose in a cute sort of way. "I know. Have you heard him talk all twangy? It's so hot. I love him."

"One date and you're all in love with him?" I throw her words back at her and shake my head as I lie back on my bed, waiting for my toes to dry. "You're a dork."

"I'm a horny dork, Em. I needs me some ninja loving. You mind if I go get it on? You promise you'll be okay?"

I look at the ceiling and laugh. "Yeah. I got Netflix for the Xbox today, that you called a need and not a want. I'll watch that." My stomach hurts as soon as she says it, but I can't expect her to spend her entire year locked in here with me.

She jumps up and runs out the door. "Love you, smoochie."

My phone vibrates. I sigh and pick it up.

"Hi," I answer.

"You don't go to restaurants with boys that you haven't cleared with me first." His tone is harsher than normal. Not so quiet and proper.

"I didn't. You knew what I was doing."

His voice echoes a bit, "Don't play games with me. You won't win. You specifically told me you were going to a chicken place and then never went there."

"I did!" I shout and then swallow my words and anger as the memory of it all falls back into the forefront of my mind. "I'm sorry. I should have called and told you we were changing places. I just—well —I had an attack and had to leave the first place."

His voice softens, "Are you okay?"

I don't know why I feel so able to talk to him. Maybe because I never see him. "No. I had it right in front of him. It was humiliating."

"I'll call the doc. She'll want to see you."

I hate that. I hate that he goes for the doc. He never wants to talk to me. Even when I let him in and give him something, he shuts me down. He pushes me away.

"Whatever," I say.

"Don't say that. It's rude."

I don't say anything.

He clears his throat. "If you're going to date and Stuart is dating the ever-lovely Miss Monkton, then the rules are changing. You will not date on the same evening."

I frown. "What if we have a date planned for the same night?"

"Then he cancels his. You will remain in the dorms if he and Miss Monkton are out. Are we clear?"

"Yup."

"Yup is piss-poor English. Goodnight, sweet dreams."

He has never said that before. He was shitty like he always is, but he's never said sweet dreams before. He hangs up as usual, and I just stare at the phone.

Shell doesn't come home.

I don't sleep.

I don't sleep much on a regular basis, but the first night in a new place is always the worst. It's a guarantee that I won't sleep because of *it*.

I have an it.

I call it the lonely. It creeps up whenever I'm uncomfortable. It freezes me up. I feel it enter new places with me, like it's in the bag I packed. The broken bits of whatever it is inside me, the lack of trust maybe, have never healed. Nineteen years of life, almost twenty, and I can't get past it. It's part of who I am.

The difference between it and the phobias is that the lonely is genuine. It's been part of me always. The phobias were learned over time.

My phone vibrates as I'm lost in self-pity. I glance at it. *Go to sleep.*

I look at the phone, grinning. He always knows. I look around the room, wondering. How does he do it? How does he know? Maybe he is Big Brother and I am in *1984*.

When I pick up the phone, I can't even believe it's already three a.m. I text back smirking, *You first.*

I am sleeping.

I snort. He is making jokes now? My fingers almost tremble with anticipation and fear as I text my response, *What are you dreaming about?*

You.

My heart skips a beat. I have a fantasy. I can't lie. It's a deep, dark fantasy that I never let myself see. It mostly involves him being a duke or a baron who is bent on helping me, but like *The Phantom of the Opera.* He's troubled and wants to do anything to be there for me. He wants me. But he's ashamed of the hideousness trapped behind the mask.

I think there is a common dream with orphans about parents and benefactors. Not to mention, we are forced to watch more nun-themed movies than the average American, like *The Sound of Music.*

But with him it's so much more. I have a dream about him not being my parent at all.

I hold the phone and get a wicked grin as I text him back. *What am I doing? In your dream?* He might be a baron or a duke. He might also be that guy who sleeps with his dead mother in the motel movie. I shiver and push that thought away.

Sleeping and not annoying the living hell out of me.

My heart hurts instantly.

Night, is the last message I receive.

I leave it at that, telling myself it's what happens when you have an unrealistic dream about a man who isn't a character in a movie. The movies and reality are very different. I turn the phone off even though I'm not supposed to. It's one of his rules. I hate that I have to obey him, even when he's shitty to me. I hate needing him. I hate that he really is the only chance I have at a real future, instead of ending up as a waitress in New Mexico.

I stare at the ceiling and then try pacing. I watch another movie and then when I can't keep my eyes open a second longer, I do it. I turn off the TV and close my eyes. I let myself relax and try—just try to sleep. It creeps in and hugs me, wrapping me in fears and doubts. I remain there frozen until the sun comes up. I'm grateful we arrived a week early. I can't imagine trying to go to school as exhausted as I am. My eyes are crusty and my throat is dry when she bounds through the door with a smile that is unmistakable.

I'm grateful to see her. She is my saving grace.

"Oh my God, Em. He is A-MAZE-ZING." She thumps her back against the door and sighs. Her red face and dirty grin speak volumes.

My eyes won't stay open. I mutter, "The lonely," and pass out.

I wake as the sun is going down.

She is gone again but it's still light out, even if it's dusk. I yawn and stretch and turn the phone on. I climb out of bed and check underneath both of them and in the closets. The phone vibrates, undoubtedly with the messages he sent me while it was off. He's more than likely pissed that I turned it off. I ignore it and take my things to the showers. I'm taking a tiny stand for my dignity.

I'm mid shampoo when the shower curtain is ripped back, making me scream. My eyes open wide, getting only a flash of Michelle's stressed-out face and then close tight, taking loads of soap in. I cry out from the burning behind my eyelids, "Shit, Shell. My eyes. They're burning. Ass." I pull the curtain closed. My face is on fire and my eyes are scorching.

"Hurry up. He's going to come and get you if you don't answer that phone." She sounds panicked. "Seriously, Stuart just texted me. Uncle Daddy Weirdo is pissed. He's fuming."

"You think he's fuming?" I grumble.

I open my eyes under the water, but nothing stops the burning. I blink and bat them, but it still hurts. I wrench back the curtain and cuss under my breath some more. I pull on my robe and stomp across the bathroom in my rubber shower shoes. I leave my shoes next to the door just inside the room, as always, and slip on my bedroom slippers. I am so angry I could spit flames. If I had the slightest spark, I would have flames shooting from my nostrils. I wish I did have flames. I could use them to blowtorch things and sanitize like the kosher chefs do on TV.

I grab the phone off the bed and dial the number.

He answers in a rage, "YOU EVER TURN THAT DAMN PHONE OFF AGAIN AND I WILL COME AND GET YOU! NO MATTER WHERE YOU ARE! DO YOU UNDERSTAND ME?" His voice sounds so different I hardly recognize him. I wince, dropping the phone. I don't cry for other people. I don't cry unless I'm in pain—horrid amounts of physical pain. I refuse to allow myself the weakness of the tears forming in my eyes. I blink them back.

I shake, looking down. I take a breath and pick up the phone.

He speaks softly after I hold it to my face for a minute, "I'm sorry. I'm sorry. I was wrong to shout like that. You scared me. I have to know where you are." Again his voice is so altered, I almost don't know it. He is genuinely sorry. I can hear it. It doesn't change the fact that I am still genuinely terrified.

I don't speak. I cannot.

"I can hear you breathing. I know you're upset. Close your eyes. Just like Dr. Bradley says. Close them and find the peace and gratitude." He tries to talk soothingly but he can't. He isn't a soothing person.

"You're an asshole," I whisper. My eyes pop open when I realize what I've said. He laughs into the phone.

"Don't turn it off again, okay?" His voice is softer than normal.

"Whatever."

He sighs. "Come on. Work with me here. It's all for your benefit."

"Whatever." I'm angry. I never get angry.

"You mad?" He almost sounds amused.

"Yup."

"Good." He hangs up.

I put the phone down.

A text comes in instantly. *Ignore the bad messages, the early in the morning ones. Got a bit desperate.*

I ignore them all. Including the ones my eyes are reading out of habit.

I glance up at Shell. She bites her lip. "He gets so crazy. I'm scared of him. He called Stuart's phone and screamed like a psycho. Maybe you should call the cops."

I sigh, giving her a sideways glance. "And say what? I have a mysterious benefactor who insists on reaching me and keeping me safe? And then whine that in return I have to suffer through his bad temper, lack of social skills, and incessant need to have my cell phone on? The cell phone he gave me, for free? Along with the fact he's paid for everything for you and me?"

She crosses her arms. "Sometimes he's a bastard, dude. A nasty bastard. He's always watching you. It's creepy. We can go home anytime—you know that, right?"

I shake my head. "No, he isn't. He's like a dad or a big brother. He worries and overreacts. It's scary when he does it, but it's all in the name of keeping me safe. I went on a date with a stranger and then was unreachable. Your dad would be pissed if we were back home in Clovis. Besides, I don't want to go back. Clovis isn't my home." It never was.

She concedes, "Okay."

I distract her. "How was your date?"

"It was—" She beams again. "Oh my God. Oh my God. It was—oh my GAWD."

I roll my eyes. "Glad one of us has some 'oh my God' going on."

She flashes me a grim look. "Pretty hard to have any 'oh my God' when you hose every boy within a five-foot radius with seasonally scented hand sani. You never let anyone close enough."

I point. "I also don't have any STDs, pregnancy scares, or guys who won't stop calling, or guys who never call again. And smelling like pumpkin spice is a nice way to spend the day."

She rolls her eyes. "True dat. So are we going out or what? You put me in charge of the New Leaf Foundation here at college, and I think this is an excellent way to start it off. I heard there is a bar around that is fun with a capital T for trouble. And they keep the crowd to a reasonable level."

I laugh but she doesn't change her desperate expression. She pleads, "New leaf? I was kidding about the T for trouble. It's called Taboo. Supposed to be fun. The T is for Taboo. Okay, maybe a tiny bit of trouble. We can go somewhere else more mellow." Her voice rises with hope and sweetness.

I roll my eyes. "I don't do clubs."

"You'll have fun."

I look at her, astonished she actually said that.

"Please, try to have fun." Her attack is a pout and a soft smile.

"I don't want to go."

"If you hate it we never have to go again."

I cross my arms over my robe and tilt my head. "If I have a panic attack?"

"We can come home right away. I'll pack extra sanies and your paper bag."

I sigh.

She pleads and bats her eyelashes, "We can't drink. We're minors and not on the Mexican border. All we can do is dance and maybe score a bit of Ecstasy if we're lucky enough to find some."

I nearly stroke but she laughs.

I glower. "No. No drugs or I don't go." My brain is screaming because I don't want to go and somehow she has made me agree to it.

"Yay!" She jumps off the bed, grabbing my hands and hopping in an excited circle. I'm pretty sure I've just been had. She threw the drugs in to get me to agree and then was fine with the drugs leaving the table.

We change into club clothes; for me this is a t-shirt and jeans and strappy sandals but minus the running watch. I'm feeling bold. I laugh at myself in my head, but a thought about how crazy people laugh inside their heads floats through. So I stop and look at myself in the mirror, the new mirror Stuart installed. "Did you let Stuart in to change the mirror?"

"No, why?" She gives me a sideways glance in it.

"No reason." I shake my head, realizing they have keys to our dorm. I don't know if that bothers me or makes me feel safe.

Looking in the new mirror I realize I look like I do when I'm going to the gym, same ponytail and no makeup. She, however, dolls up.

I look like plain Jane next to her, exactly how I like it.

Crossing the parking lot, we run into a group of people. "Hey, Michelle," one of the girls calls out.

I look at Shell. She shrugs. "Stuart took me out last night. I met her in the seating lineup at a pub. Be right back." She runs over to where the girl is huddled with other girls. She makes friends everywhere. It's how I met her. She forced me to talk to her. I shiver and push away the memory.

I don't run over. I stay where I am and notice a couple of the guys in the group walking toward me.

"Hi." An amazing-looking guy nods at me. His grin makes me feel dirty. It's a bad feeling. "What's your name?"

I feel like I'm in trouble when he looks at me, but I don't say anything.

"Her name is none of your business. Now let's go." Shell storms back over and grabs my hand. She pulls me away just in the nick of time. Just as my hands start to sweat.

Her long, leggy steps are ridiculous in the four-inch heels. She drags me down the street. When we get to the bar Shell looks back at the girls behind us and grins. Three of them run up to where we are. They shorten skirts and plump breasts as we near the huge lineup.

One of the girls leans into me. "You should probably stand back with the dudes or tie your shirt up and pull your jeans down to the hipbones."

I frown and look at Shell. "Are you for real?"

Shell nods. "They won't let you in if you don't look hot. Smoking hot. Otherwise it's the lineup."

"You might have let me in on that before we left the house," I murmur.

"You wouldn't have come. Stop being a baby."

I look past her at the huge lineup and then down at my thin black t-shirt. I then look back at the hot guy with the scary smile. He winks at me.

"Oh, hell no." I roll my shirt up into my bra and reef on my jeans. They sit just above my underwear. I shiver and wrap my hands around my now-naked midsection. If sister Elizabeth saw me now she would flog me. I can feel the flogging if I let myself get too wrapped up in the fear of exposing myself like this.

My phone vibrates immediately. I know Stuart is probably spying on us and reporting back to the master. I take deep breaths when the bouncer gives us the greasiest smile ever, and pulls the rope aside for us.

A tall blonde points back at the guys, "They're with us."

The guys hustle through too. The creepy one is pressed into my back. His hands are near my sides. I can feel the warmth of him on my bare skin, brushing against me. I deep breathe my way through the ordeal, forcing chanting and other extremes.

We are rushed through to the club where the music pumps so hard I can feel it in my teeth. The panic starts to set in, but in the middle of it all something happens. Something that has never happened before.

I like the song that's playing and the room smells like something familiar, in a good way. I look around and no one notices me. No one is looking at me.

I let Shell pull me out onto the dance floor. I pull my t-shirt down and jeans up a bit. We start to dance. I've never been a big dancer so I'm surprised when I like it.

I start giving into urges, throwing my arms up and letting my hair down.

I'm having fun. I'm not the prettiest girl. The bar is full of them. The boys aren't touching me or trying to talk to me. The fears I have are numbed by the fact that I'm not getting the attention I feared I would.

Well, not until a tall guy in a light-blue shirt and dark-gray slacks walks up to me. He's dressed fancy for a bar in a college town. His face is handsome in a way that commands my instant respect. He looks like he should have supermodels on either arm, or be in a music video. He doesn't look older, just confident and dangerous.

He smiles at me and it's scary and cold. "Want to dance?"

I can barely hear him over the music. I shake my head. "No, thank you."

He smiles at me and looks down. He has dark hair in a fauxhawk and a dimple in his left cheek. I know him. I swear it. It almost scares me. His icy-blue eyes are so familiar, but like they're locked behind a haze.

"Do I know you?" I ask, almost like I'm in a dream. He looks at me with confusion mixed with a subtle hint of severity.

"I don't think so." He looks around. His cool demeanor and stylish clothes are catching the eyes of the girls around us. "I would never have forgotten your face." He's smooth and yet moody, compared to the other guys. He looks severe and harsh. I can't help but wonder why he's talking to me—the girl who looks like she might be the janitor, and not the girls who are almost naked and grinding up against each other.

It hits me like a ton of bricks and I know why he's talking to me. I ask inquisitively, "Are you him? Are you my guardian?" I am smarter than he gives me credit for being.

His cold blue eyes harden and he instantly looks more confused and less interested in me. "Him who? What?" He takes a step back and laughs, like he's confused but also mocking me. He rolls his icy-blue eyes. "I just wanted a dance, not ever after."

I frown as he turns and walks away. It stings a bit. Like I'm crazy for thinking he could be the man helping me.

I'm not accustomed to people being rude to me. Strangers are usually overly kind to me and all orphans. Growing up, we were always made to work hard and respect people. We were treated based on how we acted. I learned that quickly. I was never rude, nor treated rudely.

I reach into my back pocket and pour the hand sanitizer into my palm. I rub and close my eyes. The smell is therapy.

Shell must have seen it. Her icy-cold hands grip my arm and shock me. I spin wide eyed. "What?"

She looks over to where the guy disappears into the crowd. "Was he bugging you? You didn't fall for the crabby guy at the bar, did you? 'Cause that's a thing. They act all distant and grumpy, and we women can't help but want to fix them. It's like shooting fish in a barrel as far as girls are concerned."

I shake my head. But she eyeballs the hand sanitizer and makes her own conclusions. "This was a mistake. We should go." She looks worried.

I shake my head. "No. It's fine. I like it here. It's so intense and busy, I actually feel lost in the crowd. Like I blend. I have heard of this before, people feeling lonely even when surrounded by crowds of people, in cities like New York."

Her face splits. "Oh, man." She sighs. "I'm so glad. I was stressed about bringing you here, dude. I know it's my job to push the new leaf thing, but I was scared."

I shake my head. "Let's just dance."

She arches an eyebrow. "Wanna drink?"

I almost say no. I pause and give the question the moment it deserves. I nod. I'm not scared of the bar. I don't hate it. I wanted a normal college life. One drink is definitely normal. If it's not normal, it's new leaf for sure. And I can put the drink down. I don't have to keep it with me forever. It's temporary.

She comes back after a minute with two bottles of beer. She passes one to me and squeals, "The bartender thought I was twenty-one. He sold these to me." She widens her eyes in excitement and drinks. She brings it down and clinks it against mine. "To a new leaf," she shouts, grinning and looking around.

She is having so much fun. I love it. I can't help but wonder if I can suck some of the fun off her and force myself to be more outgoing. If I can force myself to not look too closely at the people around us, or the fact I am teetering on the edge of something bad.

I stand closer and compel myself to loosen up. I drink a gulp of beer. It isn't a big thing to her, but I've never drunk beer. It tastes sick, but I force myself to drink it. It's freedom and adulthood and a new leaf. Okay, it's a lot to place on one beer.

"Emalyn."

I look to where I've heard my name. My face instantly becomes happiness in a glance. My breath is caught in my chest. The pounding beat of the music and the pair of hazel eyes looking at me are making me happy. Divinely happy. It's a new feeling. "Sebastian." I had no idea how hot he actually was. Seeing him dressed up, not at all casual, is impressive.

His smile is bright. He looks at my beer confusedly. "Never saw you as a bar and a beer kind of girl."

I shake my head. "First beer and first bar."

He steps in closer so he doesn't have to shout. He smells so good my palms sweat, probably begging for hand sanitizer because he's pretty close. I fight off the urge. He leans down into my neck and speaks close to my ear, "You doing okay?"

I could love this guy. If my heart ever decided to open up to anyone, it would be him I choose. I nod.

His breath tickles my neck. "If you need out of here, you just let me know, okay?"

I smile into his shoulder and sigh. "Yup."

He stands back up. It makes some kind of cross breeze, and his cologne, that I must have missed when I smelled him earlier, is wafted back at me. It takes up all the sweaty air around me. In that moment, I feel it. The wall. The beer almost slips from my hands. I pass it to him. "Can you just hold this? I need to go to the ladies.'"

He nods. I point to Shell who I realize is watching me like a hawk, and then gesture between them. "Michelle, my roommate. Sebastian, the guy from the gym." I turn and run to the bathroom. The sea of people becomes thick and heady. I shove my way through. The cold air of the bathroom is a comfort. I take in gulps of it.

My shirt is soaked. I slip into a stall and pull it off.

I'm trembling.

His cologne made me freak out?

Shit is wrong with me.

Somehow cologne made the air dirty. It made a wall of sin and sick and twisted desires. It hurt deep in my belly.

Tears are flooding my eyes and I'm standing in the stall, waving my shirt back and forth, trying to dry it out.

With shaking hands and blinding tears that won't leave my eyes, I pull my cell from my pants. I can't text. The words don't make sense. I fat-finger the buttons in a panic. I delete the messages and hold the phone to my chest.

I start my affirmations in a breathy whisper, "You are alive. You aren't fighting the whole world. It's just a few people in a bar. They don't see you. Frig the bar. This is a tiny stall. It's a small room with a door and protection." I take a deep breath. My words feel thick with saliva and the distraught fear that cripples me.

My legs become heavy. I need to run before my legs become cement blocks. I pull the shirt on and storm from the bathroom, dousing myself in hand sani. I slip along the back wall. In the corner of my eye I see them.

Sebastian's laughing.

Shell pushes his chest.

He shakes his head, still gripping my beer.

They don't see me.

I slip outside. I am about to run but I see the car. I race across the street. I need the car. I need Stuart.

My lungs are getting thick. The air isn't coming the way I need it to. His face is stoic as he opens the door, barely registering me. He's so used to it all.

I'm breathless when I leap into the seat. The smell is like my hand sani. It's therapy. I take huge lung-filling breaths. I hold my trembling hands out. Stuart gets in and squirts the cold alcohol on me. "Where is Michelle?"

"Inside."

He sighs, "Okay. Home or drive?"

I don't look at him. I can't. I'm so ashamed. "Drive." My voice is weak and hollow. He doesn't say anything. He drives.

I open my eyes when I start to feel nauseated. My heartbeat is still crazed. The vibration of my phone brings me back.

I glance at it.

Where u go? It's from Shell.

Home, I type.

KK. Tell Stuart I said hi.

Tell Sebastian I said bye.

KK. Sorry, Em.

I shake my head and work at not feeling sorry for myself. *No. I am.*

I can't help but wonder if there was ever love and peace inside me. Was I always so filled with fear and pain? Was there ever a time when someone held me in their arms and made me feel safe? Was I always scared of cologne and touching?

I look out the window at the dark city streets and see nothing but places to hide.

When Stuart drops me off I climb the stairs and fight the defeated feeling.

"Look at it this way: You left the house, you went to a bar, you didn't run out after a second. You were in there for almost an hour."

I smile back at him. "Thanks, Stuart."

He shrugs. "It's cool. Tell Michelle to text me later."

"Night." I turn and climb the rest of the stairs. I let him be the one who's right, not the voice in my head that calls me a freak. That voice is always softly whispering my differences and flaws to me. It can take one night off.

Michelle doesn't come home right away. It makes me wonder. Is she kissing his lips? The lips I've caught myself staring at. Staring and wondering if they feel the way they look. Did she rub her lip gloss on them?

At least if they get together I can hear the details of what he looks like naked or feels like kissing. I can live through her, like always.

I'm almost insane by the time she comes strolling in the door. She shakes her head. "Sorry. Did I wake you up?"

"No. Did you have fun?" I ask. My tone is shitty. I know it is. I'm not sorry. I watch her. She pulls her phone out and sends a message.

She shakes her head. "Not so much. It was all right. That Sebastian guy is strung out on you though. Oh my God. He yakked my ear off. Like questions and trying to get your number and sweet frickin' God."

"What?" A smile forces its way across my lips. "Really? He didn't hit on you?"

"Uhhh, no. Dude. Hos before bros. You saw him first." She sighs. "But he did stop every other guy from hitting on me. He's huge and smoking hot. No one even spoke to me all night. But Stuart was texting me." That puts a grin on her lips.

Sebastian likes me? Even after he saw it? He gets it? I almost pinch myself but decide against it. Better to live in a dream world than no world. I roll over and fall asleep. I'm safe from the lonely and crazy excited for the gym tomorrow.

I wake the next day and race to the gym. I try to act casual, strolling in. I saunter over to the wipes and then to a machine, pulling my hair up into a ponytail. I clean and start at a walk, looking around, wondering if he's coming. Suddenly he bounds in and hops on the machine next to me. "Hey. How's it going?"

I shrug and grin like a fool. "Good. Sorry I bailed last night."

"Really, don't be." He shakes his head. "I get it."

I sigh. He looks yummy and he gets it. Seeing him makes me happy. He starts his machine. "Wanna get breakfast after this?"

"Sure. Can we get pancakes? I love pancakes."

He winks. "I know a place."

I melt.

I can't stop watching him and his form when he runs. I start my speed increases and constantly have to bring my eyes around. The way his pecs bounce and flex when he runs is horribly distracting.

I wonder what he looks like without the shirt. I laugh at myself. When it comes to boys and anything dirty, I'm all bark and no bite. I want to bite, but I shut it down before I even let myself entertain the thoughts. It's all I ever let boys be—thoughts, ideas, and dirty stories from Shell.

I finish my run early and get us both wipes. I'm grinning and waiting when he's finally done. He's sweaty, and in that moment I realize I'm seeing another person's sweat differently. It dawns on me that I don't consider him other people. That's huge for me. He is a friend now. Something not safe but not dangerous either.

It turns out, watching him eat pancakes is better than eating pancakes, or watching him run. I barely touch my food. Watching his jaw move and his eyes light up when he speaks is better than eating.

It's official.

He's my favorite person in the world. I've known him for a week and it feels like a lifetime.

Meeting for workouts and breakfast becomes an instant tradition. He doesn't try to kiss or touch me. He doesn't cross the lines that force the panic attacks. He stays a foot away and gives me my bubble, to the point I want him to cross it.

Two weeks later he asks me out on a date again.

Finally.

I do the butt-hop thingy that Shell does when I tell her about it. But then I glance at my phone and shudder. My fingers twitch when I drag them over the buttons, sending the text I have been dreading all day. *I'm going out.*

Him again?

I'm grinning when I send the next word, *Yup.*

Yup isn't a word. Where?

I don't know, it's a surprise.

You know how I feel about surprises.

I make duck lips and think about that. I don't like them either. I text, *I don't like them either, but I'm trying to be a normal girl and he makes me feel that way.*

I want to know where you're going when you do.

K.

K is a letter not a word!

I pause and then text with a huge grin. *O.K.*

It's okay. His reply makes me smile. He's such a crotchety bastard, and each one of those dots is his brand of annoyance being displayed for me. Maybe it means I can get under his skin a bit. The thought of that makes me smile the entire time I get ready.

My smile grows when I see Sebastian standing at the bottom of the stairs to my dorm looking dressier than normal. He's leaning against the railing in dark-gray dress pants and a matching dress shirt. His hair is styled with product and his face is completely clean-shaven. He smiles when he sees me coming through the door. He doesn't look like a college boy. It's like the night at the bar, only I don't feel like throwing up and sweating. Not yet.

"You look beautiful."

I smirk. I know I don't. I'm wearing black dress pants and a pale-green sweater. I look casual. I always look this way. Even in class, each day I am the only girl not overdressed. I am the only one, besides the professors, who is dressed down. "Where are we going?" I take the steps slowly.

He shrugs. "You are going to have to trust me."

I don't like that feeling, but I nod and take his arm. Touching his shirt feels nice. His bicep is strong and his shirt looks very clean and crisp.

He natters on about business and I ignore him. He is very intense with his courses. He's always talking about business, like he's already working. He manages to keep the details on the light side but still tells me tons. I watch his jaw move and the way his lips form the words starting with a W. They stick out, plump and kissable. Wednesday, water, workforce, watchdog. They all become my new favorite words. I sigh.

"So what do you think?" He's watching me. I've missed something crucial in the long-ass story. I have ignored a question of sorts and instead spent the long-ass time watching him.

I wince. "No."

He laughs. "No, you don't think it's smart to get a hybrid car for running around the city with?"

I'm confused—when did we start talking about cars? I shake my head. "No?" So glad I told him about the earth sciences articles I wrote.

He laughs. "Sorry. Was I boring you?"

"Not at all. I was just thinking about school. I have a big paper due." I laugh because if he knew what he was doing to me, he would think I wanted something other than dinner. Of course, my being all bark and no bite means we would both be disappointed.

We walk for a long time. He tries to pry things from me. I answer with the skill and precision I always do.

"So how many brothers and sisters do you have?" He nudges me as we walk up a hill, past some office buildings.

"Lots. I was raised in a huge family. Where are we going?"

He laughs. "We are there." He points to a glass door in an office building. He opens it casually, laughing about something.

I don't hear him. I just see the inside is a huge foyer with wide windows and a front desk. It's a new place. I twitch. My stomach starts to clench.

I never realized where we might have been heading.

I assumed a safe place in the public, a place like the OCD restaurant.

He walks to an elevator and pushes the button. He's still laughing and joking. He doesn't see that my hands are sweating. I force myself onto the elevator. When it starts moving, the walls slowly inch their way toward me. My heart rate is skyrocketing. My arms are sweating now. The elevator stops and my knees almost buckle.

He's nattering on about things I don't hear. He points for me to step off.

His hand is on the small of my back.

I'm almost hyperventilating.

I'm frozen.

He steps off, pushing me forward.

We walk down a hallway that I swear is getting narrower. He opens a dark-colored door. Inside is a glow, like there are candles or firelight. It's a huge space with high ceilings and walls that only go halfway up. Like each room has no ceiling.

The door closes with a click that sounds like a hammer pounding inside my head. I jump and look around. It's a house. A penthouse apartment with a view of the whole city.

I see another man in the corner of my eye and I'm gone. I've bolted for the door and raced down the hall.

He's calling me. He's running after me, but I get to the stairs, ignoring his shouts and heavy footsteps that slap the hallway and echo all around me.

I run as hard as I can. My legs have trained for this moment. I jump and run until I get to the bottom floor. I bust through into the foyer. I can hear the elevator moving behind me, but I push through the front door and out onto the street.

I am lost.

I run hard until I reach an alley. I lean my back against the wall of the building and make a call with trembling fingers.

✿ 4 ✿

My feet pound the treadmill with savagery. They're clawing at it. My heart is racing and my fingers are almost reaching for the handlebars. They don't, because I never touch the handles.

I don't know how long I've been running at this pace. I just am, until I can't. I need to feel something and exhaustion seems like a harmless thing.

I hate the way I am. I hate the pity and understanding in Shell's eyes when I bail on her new leaf trips and adventures. I hate the way Stuart notices my psychotic-ness, and yet justifies my actions and makes my excuses for me. He lets me do it. They all let me get away with it.

So I do.

I get away with not improving or changing.

The worst is that I see it. I ride on their understanding and the pathetic way they see me. I'm technically doing well. For people like me breathing, eating, and showering is doing well. I hate doing well. I just want to be normal. I want to be his.

I push it back angrily and drive my feet harder.

A flash of something takes me out of my raging run. The treadmill slows right down and stops. I'm gasping and heaving for air. I bend forward immediately.

"Wh-wh—what are you doing?" I ask in between panting and coughing.

Sebastian is in my face. "You trying to die?" He's angry.

"I was fine." I'm humiliated just seeing him.

I ran out on him.

His hazel eyes are greener than normal. Against his olive skin they stand out, as does the worry and concern plastered to his face.

I stand up straight and climb off the treadmill. He grabs my arm. I pull harshly. I stop myself mid pull and shake my head. "Sor—sorry."

He puts his hand in the air fast. "No. I'm sorry. But you looked like you were about to pass out."

I put my hands on my hips and pace. "I was." I laugh and cough. My breathing is ragged. I force myself to look at him. "I'm sorry."

He shakes his head. "No. Don't be. I shouldn't have grabbed at you." He still gets it. Even after my running out on him, he gets it.

"I mean about the penthouse." I clear my throat and notice it's not happy with me. It hurts like it's bleeding.

He nods, looking crushed. "Ah yes, the lovely dinner I had being made for you that you ran out on. Yes, I suppose you owe me an apology for that. The chef was at my place for five hours prepping. It was delicious. You missed out. Maybe next time?"

I pace back and forth. "I don't have an excuse. I'm just—well, I'm sorry." I could cry any second. I'm so embarrassed. I hate myself so much. I would do anything to make it okay, make me be normal.

He pulls hand sanitizer from his jogging pants pocket and holds it up. I burst into laughter. He smiles. "You've got me addicted." He pours some on my hands and then his. I rub them and walk for the wipe cloths. I tug a few out of the dispenser and go clean my machine.

He grabs my water bottle. I can't drink from it now, but it was nice of him to grab it.

He sees me eyeballing his hands on my water bottle. He holds it out. "Drink some." His eyes challenge me.

I look at him. "I can't." I can't fight the frown on my face.

He stands in front of me and shakes his head. "Do it."

I stop and look at the bottle.

He speaks loudly, "I've cleaned my hands. I never touched anything before I touched it. Just have some water."

If only he knew what he was asking of me. I shake my head and try to walk past him. He grabs my arm again. I don't pull away. He drags me into his embrace. He holds me tight to his chest. His shirt is damp with the sweat from his own workout.

I could die, feeling the cold, damp fabric against my face.

"Drink it, Emalyn. Please." His voice has become a whisper.

I whisper back, "How did you know I wouldn't have any?" He takes my hand in his and pulls me outside.

The fresh air is nice. It's not one-hundred-percent fresh with the humidity, but it's better than the recycled air in the gym.

I pull at his hand. "How did you know?"

His eyes say things he doesn't want to.

I jerk my hand free. "Which website did you check out?" I hate being diagnosed. He isn't the first person to do it.

He sighs. "I called my uncle. He recommended a friend. I told him that you saw the chef and that beautiful view and you lost it. Any normal girl would have died and gone to heaven for a guy to put that kind of effort in. But you had a panic attack."

Normal?

Of course he sees how not normal I am.

My jaw trembles. I point. "I never asked you to be my friend. I never asked for your help." I stomp away. I would run but my legs are almost crippled from the run I just did. It's a bad feeling. I ran so hard I can't run away when I need to.

I can hear his footsteps behind me. My heart races. I look back. "Just leave me alone."

He shakes his head and does the thing I asked him to do. He turns away and walks off. It disappoints me, which makes me mad at myself.

I hate being a predictable girl. I stop as I reach my dorm to find him standing on the steps with his arms crossed, breathing heavily. He has run around the other side of the building to beat me here.

"Didn't your uncle's friend explain about the paranoia that people like me get?" I ask, trying desperately to be funny. I joke, praying he will give up on the water thing. The worst part about being me is realizing how irrational I am. I only ever see it afterward. I know in an hour I'll be upset with myself.

Sebastian nods slowly. "He did. He also said that the only way to help was to force you out of your comfort zone, one tiny baby step at a time. He walks down the steps and holds my water bottle out. "Drink some."

I panic. "You've taken it with you. You could have done something to it," I almost stutter. I see the irrational behavior but am incapable of stopping it.

He shakes his head. "I sprinted around the building to beat you here. You know that it's impossible for me to have had even longer than a second to unscrew it. I would have missed you if I had. Drink some."

I snatch the bottle as my anger flares. "You're making a big deal about nothing," I snap at him.

"The date wasn't nothing. Baby steps, Em."

The new leaf.

I sigh and unscrew the cap. I look at the water and feel it—the anxiety and stress. I stall and lick my lips. When I look up at him it hurts that his eyes are hopeful. I can't stop the trembling hand or the twitching lips as I lift it to my mouth. The warmth of the plastic makes me sick. I almost gag but I tilt it back. He watches every tremble. Every motion and emotion.

I blank my mind and let the liquid pour into the back of my mouth. My throat wants to close and my lips want to clamp shut, but I take the control. I force myself to drink the liquid. I lower the bottle and screw the cap on.

"Happy?" My words are cold and dead. I'm angry, and I hate that it's not entirely him I'm mad at.

"Not even close." His voice is so hard and filled with disgust. I disgust him. I can see it. He walks away from me, leaving me standing on the stairs.

In the shower I spend a long time trying to talk myself out of the crazy way I am acting. I like him. I like him a lot, but the crazy side of me has made up her mind. She hates him. She hates the challenges he creates. She likes the safety and comfort of the routine. There isn't any point in arguing with her when she's like this. I shut my mind down and try to relax and not think about the communal shower I'm standing in. I have bleached it twice before showering so the fear is irrational.

I rinse off and wrap myself in my robe. I shuffle down the hall, looking behind me several times. I despise the communal showers. It's the worst part of my day. I have to drag travel-sized bottles of shampoo and conditioner and put them through the dishwasher afterward. Not to mention, the number of rubber shower shoes I've gone through or the fact I can't touch the shower curtain with my bare hand; I always have wipes next to me with bleach on them to wash down the shower first.

Shell looks up from her phone when I walk in. "You okay?"

I shake my head. "I'm tired of being a shell of a human. I would do anything to be a real girl."

She grimaces but snorts. "It's not that bad. You're getting better every day. I never would have imagined you would make dorm life happen and look at you. And we went to the bar. And you've eaten in restaurants. And Sebastian seems nice. Hot and nice."

"He is." I shake my head. "But I don't want to see him anymore."

She sits up on her bed. "Did he try something?"

I frown. "No. He's just like everyone else. He'll never see me." I lie back on the bed and close my eyes. She climbs on the bed and wraps herself around me. She smells like pumpkin spice. It makes me happy.

"I see you."

I nod. "I know."

Her warmth and softness are comforting. I imagine it's what a mother feels like.

I let her wrap around me and be there. Be the wall that separates the girl I am and the girl I want to be. I feel her fingers at my ears. We're sharing earbuds, like we did when we were little. Mine smells like sani wipes. It makes me smile and feel grateful.

Bon Iver starts singing and I forget everything. It's me and her. I don't need boys. I need her and earbuds, one for her and one for me. Mine has to be clean though.

My phone vibrates. I grab it.

Hi. Are you having a good day?

I'm confused. *Did Dr. Bradley up your meds? You seem cheerful.* It's brazen of me, but I don't care at the moment.

Funny girl. What are you doing?

Hanging out. Listening to music with Shell.

Call her Michelle, please. What are you listening to?

I grin. *Bon Iver.*

Bon Iver is a very talented group. I've been to four of their concerts.

No way.

Way! See how silly it sounds? Please speak like an adult.

I laugh. Michelle moans. "What are you doing?"

"He's being funny."

"Who?"

I grin. "Uncle Daddy Dude. He's been to like four of Bon Iver's concerts."

She laughs. "No way."

I grin at her. "Way." It does sound silly.

"He's not as stodgy as we thought I guess, huh?" She moans into my pillow and squirms into the bed to get comfier. I don't love her face on my pillow like that. My nose wrinkles involuntarily.

The thought crosses my mind and I send him a text. *You're cooler than I thought you were.*

Ah, so you see me as human now?

Just barely! I smile when I press send.

How's the guy from the gym?

I frown. *Not good. Bit of a wanker.*

My phone rings. I roll away from Michelle who sounds like she might fall asleep.

"Hi."

His voice is deep and relaxed. "I thought he was your dreamboat?"

"What?" I laugh. It's playful and resembles a giggle. "Who even says dreamboat?"

"Well?"

I shake my head, playing with the edge of the blanket I'm lying on. "No. Not so dreamboatish."

"Oh dear." He sighs and I'm not entirely sure it isn't in relief. "What happened? Did he hurt you?"

I press my lips together and nod. It takes me a minute to answer, "I guess so."

"How?" His voice is angry. The switch is fast and slightly creepy.

"He didn't—like—touch—me. He just made me do things I didn't want to do."

"Oh no, what?" He sounds panicked.

I moan. "No. He—like made me drink water from a sports bottle he had touched and made me dinner at a penthouse with a view of the city that he lured me to."

He laughs. I've never heard a full laugh from him before. It sounds like he's pulled his hands away and his laugh is an echo in the silent room.

He stops laughing. No amount of Bon Iver will fix the way he's mocking me. He's still chuckling when he speaks, "I'm sorry. I didn't mean to laugh. I very nearly made a phone call I couldn't take back. You scared me. I thought he'd done something to you."

"Well, he did. He's trying to fix me. He's trying to push me and I don't want that. Not from him. I just wanted him to see me as a normal girl. As a girl at school. Not a project to fix." I realize I've raised my voice and am sitting up staring at the cold floor.

He clears his throat. "Have you considered he may just see you as a girl. Not all girls are whole when you meet them. Sometimes you have to help them get there. Right now, you are a broken girl. That doesn't mean that you'll always be broken. That doesn't make you less of a girl." He clears his throat again. "I'll call the doc. She'll want to talk to you."

The tears in my eyes don't come out. They stay in there like tiny kaleidoscopes, trying to make the world the way I need it to be. My words don't come right away. I don't hear the click on his end when I whisper, "I'm not broken." But he isn't there. He never really is. He is the master of not being there.

Weeks have passed and I have not seen Sebastian.
I miss him.
I don't know what his number is or how to find him.
I can't find my way back to the penthouse.
I tried and got lost.

I even attempted to use his name and 411 but that is an impossibility. People only have cell phones, which are hard to track. I almost asked Stuart to help me track him. But I didn't. Who wants to be the girl the guy doesn't want?

Sebastian has evaded me.

"He's still an asshole?" she mutters it over her laptop.

I look at her and frown. "What?"

Shell smiles. "I saw the look in your eyes."

I shake my head. "Just tired. No look."

"Kay. I won't say I saw him yesterday then."

My heart almost jumps out of my chest. "What? Where? Did he talk to you?"

She nods with a sinister grin.

I throw my pillow at her, knocking her computer screen down and closing the laptop. She shoots me a blazing glare and points a bright-red fingernail. "That better not have done anything to that. I was done."

"What did he say? Why didn't you tell me yesterday?" I'm dying. Why is she being so sneaky? She opens the computer. I groan. "Shell, I am going to snap that thing in half."

She laughs. "He said he was good and asked me a million—no maybe a billion—questions about you."

"Like what?" I quickly grab my pillow and put it back.

"He said he missed you and wished things had worked out."

I scowl. "That's not good. Wished? Like past tense?" Shit, the only guy that ever got me. *Shit.*

She tilts her head. "No. Like he's picking you up in fifteen minutes."

It takes a second to sink in. "What? Why?" Then I get angry. "I don't want to see him." I know it's irrational, but I can't stop myself from being indignant. "He's a jerk. Why would he be coming here?"

She laughs. "Oh my God, for a girl who has never dated you have spun-out head case mastered."

I jump up and start grabbing clothes. I'm furious. "Why didn't you tell me? Oh my God. I hate you." I pick up all her dirty laundry, put it in the hamper, and wipe down the room again.

She laughs. "Because I knew you would find a way not to see him, and you've been moping around here nonstop. You're acting nuts, dude."

I'm ripping my clothes off and then pulling on new ones. I'm not even sure what I'm wearing. I just rant, "I cannot believe you would do this to me. I told you I have no desire to see him. He was a jerk to me." I can't stop my arms from dragging a brush down my hair or lip gloss from being applied. I look at her in the mirror as I draw on some eyeliner. "You are so selfish sometimes. You just want to go off and be with Stuart. You don't want to leave me with the lonely so you hired me a babysitter."

She shakes her head slowly.

I inspect myself and look back at her. "And for another thing, Uncle Daddy Weirdo isn't going to just let me go out. You've probably started a war now." I dump a ton of hand sanitizer on my hands and grab a wipe to open the door with. I glare back at her as I grab my cell phone and storm out.

"Where are you going?" she asks, stifling a laugh.

I snarl, "I have to go tell him to get lost. The nuns raised me better than that." I fling open the door and stomp down the hall.

A guy across the hall gives me a crazy look as he almost slides against the wall to avoid me.

I stomp down the stairs and fling the door open. Sebastian isn't standing at the bottom of the stairs. He isn't even there. I look at my cell for the time just as it vibrates.

I read. *Hi.*

I roll my eyes. *Not now.*

Don't be sassy. What are you doing?

Waiting for Sebastian so I can tell him to get lost!

If you leave the dorms message me!

Whatever. I already left. I'm out front.

Don't push me!

Whatever!!!!!!!!

I put the phone back in my pocket.

I jump when I hear a voice in the dark silence. "You look nice."

I glance up. Sebastian's staring at me from the shadows of the pathway. He's leaning against a post. He looks divine. How is it possible when he's only wearing faded jeans and a beige long-sleeve shirt?

"Why are you here?" I don't move. I'm terrified I will forget that I'm mad, because if I'm being honest, I want him. I want to be with him. More than I want anything.

"I needed to see you."

Need. That is a strong word.

"Why?" I still have acid on my tongue from yelling at Michelle and my words are filled with it.

"I needed to see you." He repeats himself.

I smile. I like that word, need. It's not want. He had no choice because it was a need to see me. I like that.

He pushes off the pole and walks toward me. His watch catches my eye. It's shiny and not his running watch.

"Why?" I ask again.

He climbs the stairs until he is standing just below me, down a couple steps. His eyes are at my level instead of a foot above me.

He swallows. "I'm sorry I researched your paranoia and OCD. I'm sorry I presumed to hire a chef to make you dinner. Mostly I'm sorry I challenged your comfort level and tried to get you to drink the water."

He melts all my irrational anger. I realize I'm more hurt that he stayed away so long. I lift my hand. It frightens me more than anything in the world, but I do it. I touch his face. His skin is warm. I can feel his stubble. He looks tired.

"Why didn't you come and see me?" I know the answer. Because I am a head case. Because I can't eat dinner or drink water.

He shakes his head subtly. "I thought I should stay away. I scared you. I didn't mean to. The way you looked at me when we were at my penthouse was so horrid. You were terrified. I never wanted to see you look like that again. I hated myself for making you feel that way. Not to mention, how angry you looked when I made you drink the water. I'm sorry, Em."

My fingers dig in slightly. I have the strangest urge. Before I can think my way out of it, I grab his face and pull him in. His arms wrap around me. He squeezes me. There is a tremor to his touch. Like he's panicked. I know I am.

His arms are fully encompassing me.

"I never meant to overstep my bounds." My hair in his face muffles his voice.

I shake my head. "It was my fault. I just don't trust people. You scared me."

"I know. I just want you to let me in."

I can't face him. I whisper, "You can't fix me, Sebastian. I'm not broken. I'm ruined." My brain holds all the reasons why I'm ruined behind a wall. I don't ever get to see them. But I know they're there.

I feel his jaw clench against my shoulder.

"You have to accept me for what I am."

He nods. "Okay." He lowers his hands and grips both of mine. He pulls back and presses his soft lips into my cheek. He stays there, breathing on me. It's disturbing and delicious.

He tugs my hands and pulls me down the stairs.

I notice he isn't wearing cologne. He's slowly becoming what I need to be comfortable.

He lets go of my left hand, but grips my right like he will never let go of it.

He looks down, grinning. "I just cleaned them when you were texting on the phone." I can smell the vanilla hand sanitizer in the air.

I look at him. "Shit. I need to text Michelle." I pull my phone out and send him a text. *Leaving Dorm. Not sure where. Text when I get there.*

He doesn't answer. I know he's pissed. I don't wait for him to call. I put the phone in my pocket.

"So what have you been up to?" I ask, desperate to just be normal.

He grins. "Not much."

Trying not to sound too much like a stalker I ask, "Have you been working out? I haven't seen you?"

He chuckles, looking down.

I frown. "What?"

His grin is bashful. He pulls me along the greens toward the OCD restaurant. "I've seen you tons."

I don't like that. I jerk my hand away. "You were watching me?"

He shakes his head. "No. I was genuinely at the gym the same time as you, but I stayed out of your way. I didn't want to upset you."

"I hate when people treat me delicately," I snarl.

He scoffs. "And you don't like help, and you don't want to talk about yourself. You have to give me something."

"I'm an orphan."

He looks at me sideways. "You said big family."

"Lots of orphans." He doesn't speak and for that I am grateful. The words roll off my tongue much easier without having to worry about the amount of pity he will give me. I'll hear it in his voice. Orphans always get loads of pity. "I was found at age six wandering the streets of a town called Clovis, New Mexico. No parents, no ID, no trace of where I came from. I knew my name, Emalyn Spicer. I was eating garbage and living on the streets. They don't even really know how long I was alone."

I can hear his breath. I can see his pulse in his neck, but he still says nothing.

"I was taken in by the Catholic Church and raised in an orphanage in Clovis." My voice doesn't waver. I have never told the story before. The words have never left my lips. I never had to explain it in Clovis. Everyone knew. Dr. Bradley knew. My benefactor knew. I have never had to actually explain myself to anyone.

The story comes so much easier than I had imagined it would. When I was little, I imagined I would one day be a famous writer invited on a talk show to tell the story. I never imagined I would be revealing it on the greens of a college in Boston. I never imagined it would be to a guy so beautiful and sweet that I couldn't imagine what I had done to deserve him.

"That's heavy, Em."

I nod. I am strong. I am if I let myself be. "Yup. The nuns had rules about how things were done. In the beginning I was such a savage. You see, if one kid gets sick, all the kids get sick. There isn't a lot of money and stuff. So they were clean. Really clean. Anyone who wasn't clean was punished."

His brow furrows, but I shake my head and hurry the words from my lips, "I don't blame them. They ran a tight ship. They had strict rules. But we were fed and clean and cared for. No one there hurt me —not in a way that couldn't be healed. But I have a germ thing. The germs were like Satan trying to get in and make us sick. Cleanliness is next to godliness."

He licks his lips and I smile through the pain. "If you're done with whatever friendship we have, I get it. I know how heavy this baggage is. I know what it weighs and what it means. I won't ever have children, and I won't ever be normal and have a family or any support or anything. I can hardly be in a room with more than a few people before I start plotting my exit. If I have to cross an area rug, my feet have to touch the same number of lines. I have to have everything even and balanced and controlled. I wash every surface I am near. I run so I can. And I'm okay with it because it's always been my reality. But I don't expect you to be." It kills me to say it, "I know what I am." The statement doesn't feel true. It feels forced because I don't want to be her. I would die or kill or do anything to not be her.

He spins me fast and lifts my chin. His lips press against mine. It's so much better than I ever imagined it would be. His lips don't hurt or crash or overstep. They're soft and sweet. He is delicate but in control. I'm not. It's weird, but I let his mouth explore mine. His tongue slowly slides into my parted lips and lazily caresses mine. His hands are soft, not holding me but embracing me. His movements are methodical. He pulls back. I open my eyes, which I didn't even realize I've closed, and grin. "My first kiss," I whisper.

He smiles and the world is okay. It feels like it grew a tiny bit. Like I let him into the small corner where I live. He grabs and squeezes my hand and kisses the top of it. "Now stop trying to scare me off with talks of having kids and area rugs and shit. I'm not going anywhere."

My heart skips a beat.

Maybe it is like Uncle Daddy Weirdo says, maybe I am a real girl.

The irregularly rapid heartbeat, combined with the warmth clawing around in my belly, makes me hopeful that I'm not ruined. Maybe I am truly just broken. Maybe I can be healed. It wasn't just a first kiss. It was hope and possibility; like the sky is dark and the air is humid, I am alive again—or maybe for the first time.

Either way, I am grateful.

❧ 6 ❧

His fingers brush along my belly, making a trail of heat and nerves. We've been kissing like we're fifteen for weeks. I pull away and shake my head. He whispers, "I just want to touch you." His lips call to me. I lean in and kiss him again. My head spins from the kisses. Somehow, I end up on top of him. His hands are dragging up and down my back, under my shirt. I sit up and push him away. I climb off backward. It's almost like a crab would walk, but faster and twitchier. He knows I need a minute.

This time is different though. I need more than that. I grip the cloth backs of my shoes when I pick them up and run.

The hallway of the penthouse feels like the one in *The Shining*. It's never ending and I expect ghosts to be here. I push the button for the elevator in a series of taps, like I'm sending it Morse code and telling it to hurry up.

I hear the door, followed by his voice, "Emalyn. Come back. It's okay. You're safe, Em."

Tears flood my eyes, though they never leave. Instead, they make the tiny kaleidoscopes to fix everything I see. I turn and run down the hall to the stairs when he starts walking toward me. The cold air in the stairwell is refreshing. I make it halfway down before I stop. He hasn't opened the door. He knows it feels like he's chasing me. I need the minute. I take a deep breath.

I whisper into the silence of the hallway, "The world is tiny. It's a small place where I have the control. I'm grateful. I'm grateful." I pull the hand sani from my pocket and wash my hands and lips. It stings a bit on my delicate, overly loved lips, but the smell is divine. It's caramel apple. I almost feel like Shell with her lip gloss, smelling so pretty. I put my shoes on the stairs and sit on them. My socks touching the stairs are freaking me out.

"I'm grateful for being such a weirdo." I smile. At least I can worry about the dirty socks I have to throw out and not the boy waiting for me in the building somewhere.

The pounding of my heart and the sweat on my palms start to diminish. The walls of the room back off. Things have color again. It's a stairwell, so there isn't much color, but enough to remind me that I am grateful I can see. I take deep breaths and stand up. I slip on my shoes and finish going down the stairs. I'm alone and I'm grateful for being alone.

When I push the latch on the door, he's standing in the foyer. His pants are still undone. I blush and remember it was my fingers that had done that. He chest stretches his t-shirt. I focus on that and not the pity and excuses he has flashing in his eyes. He's making them up for me. The poor orphan. If he only knew the truth. He wouldn't make excuses. He would walk away. I don't remember the truth of it all. But I know when my mind is quiet I still hear the echo of the gunshot and know it's bad enough that even my brain won't let me see.

I'm frozen in the doorway. The door to freedom and the outside isn't far from where I'm standing. I take a step toward him and not the door at all.

"Want to take a walk?" he whispers when he sees the choice I've made. I've chosen not to run. This time.

I nod. He grabs a sweater from the chair behind him and pulls it on. He tosses me a hoodie. It smells like him. I like the smell now. I grip it in my fingers. "Why?" I ask.

I can hear the smile in his voice when he speaks, "I needed to see you. I needed to make sure you were okay."

I shake my head, still frozen and gripping the hoodie. "Why are you putting up with me?"

"I like a challenge." He does up his pants.

I smile but I don't want to pull on the hoodie. I don't want there to be a second that I am not able to see him. It's the same reason I sit at the very back of the class and I don't sleep when I'm scared and alone. It takes over when I'm scared. He takes a step back. He sits in the armchair against the wall. He knows sometimes I need space. If he gives me space, I'll usually calm down.

He looks relaxed. I force my hands to work. I force the hoodie over my head. I lift my gaze to meet his. He grins. His hazel eyes scare me. I can see the thoughts he's thinking inside them. He's worried.

I walk to the exit. I hear him get off the chair. His steps are long, so when I push on the exit door and step out into the cold air he's behind me. Boston in the fall is cold. It's November and the air is chilly. I'm not used to it. The warmth of him behind me is reassuring just as much as it's alarming.

He takes my arm and loops it around his. He doesn't apologize anymore. He knows it isn't him. It's me. It's my reaction.

"Tea?" he asks and it feels like we move on and pretend we are normal.

I laugh and shake my head. "I hate tea. It tastes disgusting."

He stops and spins me to look at him. "Earl Grey?"

I nod. "Sick."

"Seriously?" He's snapping back from my head-case nuttiness faster than I am. "Orange pekoe?"

I wrinkle my nose. "Blech. Worse."

He shakes his head. "Em, that's a travesty." The way he says travesty is funny, as if my not liking tea is comparable to the travesties of war and famine.

"Ice cream?" I say.

He nods. "I know a place."

I grip his arm for a minute and then pass him the hand sani. He chuckles and squirts. "How does Michelle do it? My hands are so dry I can barely take it."

I laugh. "She wears nighttime moisturizer in a glove when she sleeps." I shudder at the thought of the creamy hands and wash myself and the container again.

I can't help but wonder if he notices the way I wash him off everything the same way I do Shell. We walk for a long time until we come to a place called Emack & Bolio's. He opens the door and puts his hand on my lower back. I'm a fan of that kind of touch. Even through the hoodie that's three or four sizes too big, I can feel the heat of his hand. It makes me shiver, in a good way.

"Be right back," I say and walk to the bathroom. I send a message when I am alone in a stall.

At Emack & Bolio's for ice cream.

Thank you for messaging me. Get the S'moreo. It's divine. And try paying for a meal too. No one likes a girl who doesn't pay for anything.

I gasp. *I don't have money. I have your money. So technically you're still paying and technically I'm not.*

We aren't having this conversation again.

Whatever.

He doesn't bite. He's gone.

I grab toilet paper for the door handle and head to where he's ordering. He smiles at me but not as hard as the girl behind the counter smiles at him. "What kind of ice cream do you like?" he asks.

I don't look at the girl. "S'moreo."

He turns and grins. "Can you scrape the top layer of the S'moreo off and get her two scoops of the stuff closer to the bottom?" He looks back at me. "Fudge sauce?"

I nod. He looks back. "Fudge sauce as well, please. I'm going to get the Almond Coconut Bar, also with fudge sauce, please."

She flutters her eyelashes. "Two scoops?"

He nods. "Please."

He hands her money and points to the small table in the corner. I sit and wonder if my face is covered in shock.

He frowns. "What?"

I shake my head. "Nothing. So, Almond Coconut Bar?" I inner sigh at my question and the amount of interest I place in it. I ask stupid questions when I get uncomfortable. The ice cream place is new.

He grins. "Love almonds and coconut." He makes a face. "S'moreo? What are you—ten years old?"

I laugh and look down. "A friend recommended it." I look back up at him. "You ordered my ice cream the way I would have ordered it?"

He looks confused. "It's not hard to guess. I watched you make a sandwich at my house. The mayonnaise was brand new and you opened it, took off the sealed protective cover and then scooped the entire top layer off. You pulled the meat out of the fridge and saw the seal was broken. I watched you. You put it back and cooked bacon for the sandwich instead."

I bite my lip and process it. "You watch me a lot." I wonder what else he's seen. It gets bad some days. I hope he hasn't seen those moments.

"I do. I like you. You won't give me your cell phone number because you say you don't ever use it. But you text Michelle a million times a day and tell her everything you're doing. You won't sleep at my house and never let me drive you home. You kiss me like you're trying to kill me, but back off and won't let me touch you. You always run when you've let me get just a little bit further with you."

I feel sick and panicked until he finishes his thought.

"You have me completely enchanted and bewildered and mixed up. I can't eat or sleep without wondering what you're doing. I watch you like a stalker would." He puts a hand out. "I am not a stalker, for the record." I laugh. He runs his hands through his hair. "But I'm addicted to you. I get excited every time we move just a bit further. I know something happened to you and your life has been weird and horrid in a lot of ways. I just want to be the good thing in it. I want to protect you and make you feel safe."

My face is on fire. The girl delivers the sundaes, but I stare forward and think about what he's said. He wants to be the good thing. He wants to be in my life. I haven't run him off. He sees it and still wants me.

Instead of focusing on the cute boy, my OCD catches a glimpse of the ice cream girl's gloved hands. I forget what he said and feel better about my ice cream. My natural defense is a well-oiled machine. It shuts down anything that makes me think.

She plunks them down and leaves.

I look at him and am speechless. His eyes search mine. When I offer up nothing, he leans in and mutters, "The service here is shit but the ice cream is delicious." I can see he's upset by the lack of response. I know I would be if I had just shared my deepest feelings and he had no response. I honestly have nothing I can share back. So I twirl the spoon in the ice cream and fudge sauce. "Thank you," I say after a minute.

"For what?"

I look at him and want so badly to say the million things I'm thinking. "For the sundae." I sigh.

"You're welcome."

I close my eyes and take a bite. The flavor coats my tongue. It's an escape. It always was. Once a month we would get ice cream. Always the huge tub of the cheap stuff, but it was ice cream and I was a kid.

I decide to give him what I can. It's not much, but if he knew the significance he would be excited. "The first memory I have is of ice cream." My voice is small, compared to the sound of the music in the restaurant and the few other people talking.

"Really? I think mine is my father taking me to the zoo." He bounces back so quickly.

I nod. "I was seven. I had been at the orphanage for a while, but I don't remember anything, before the ice cream. I just remember being walked to a table. The nun was pinching my arm—not on purpose, but she was mad and maybe a little rough because I had done something bad. I don't remember what. I sat down and there it was, a white bowl filled with bright-pink ice cream. The nun took it and walked away. I sat there, devastated obviously. I could hear the clanking and clinking of everyone else's spoons against the porcelain bowls as they scraped and spooned and ate. I could almost taste the cold ice cream. I knew what it was. I wasn't allowed any though. It was the last time I misbehaved. I made up my mind then that I would be the perfect child. I would do what they wanted. I wanted the ice cream so badly. There was a girl named Susan. She was perfect, always the best child. I watched her. I wanted to be her. So I did everything she did from that day on. So the next month, when we had ice cream

I got a huge bowl. More than the other kids. It wasn't pink. It was chocolate."

I have never shared a memory with another person. Except Dr. Bradley, but somehow she seems to know my memories better than I do.

He takes a bite and smoothes his mouth over the spoonful, leaving a mound behind. "That's the saddest thing I've ever heard, I think."

I shrug. "It wasn't sad though. It was motivating. It was like what your uncle's friend said: It was a baby step out of my comfort zone. Susan always got everything, and they treated her with kindness and respect because it was how she behaved. So I behaved that way too."

His eyes light up. "You should try to sleep at my house. Tonight." His lips play with a grin. He's trying to cheer me up.

But I panic. I drop my spoon in the bowl. It's instant discomfort and an increase in my heart rate.

He puts a hand out. "Slow down. Just stop and think. It's nothing more than sleeping. Nothing."

I shake my head. "No."

"Come back and watch a movie? Just snuggle?"

I laugh nervously. My heart is still thumping wildly. I nod. "Okay. Just a movie." I remind myself he might be the cure to the lonely, and chances are it's going to be a long night at my place if I go home. Michelle will leave and go be with Stuart.

I can't eat any more ice cream. I push the bowl away. I send a quick text, *Going to his place. Night.*

He doesn't answer me. He's still pissed about the whatever and the money talk.

"You done?" Sebastian looks confused.

I nod.

"Did I push you too hard?"

I nod again. "It's okay. I need pushes. You're the only one who challenges my quirks, besides Shell."

He smiles and stands. He takes my hand, without cleaning his. His hand is a bit sticky. I could die but I force myself to let him. He drags me from the restaurant. We walk back to his place quickly.

"Romance, horror, comedy, or drama?"

I shrug. "I don't know."

He smiles. "I have just the thing."

Back at his apartment I discover "just the thing" is actually a movie I've seen and love. I don't tell him. I let him turn it on and pretend to be surprised. I've literally seen like twenty movies in my life and he picks the one I love. It warms my heart, as does his reasoning for picking it. It's his little sister's favorite movie.

The movie is called *Amelie*. It's French and I adore it. It's romantic and fun and I wish I were her. She reminds me of Michelle in a lot of ways. She is alive with a zest for adventure and breaking the rules.

"Audrey Tautou is probably one of the most beautiful women in the world," I whisper as the movie starts. He pulls me in close to him. The hardness of his body is somehow comfortable. I love the feel of where our bodies meet. The heat that lies in the crease between us could light up the world.

"She's not as beautiful as you are," he whispers.

I smile. "Liar."

He laughs.

He tilts my face up and kisses me. In the flickering lights of the movie I forget who I am. I let his arms encompass me. I let his body wrap around mine. He pulls me in, kissing desperately. His hands move in a way that's new. They're driven and hungry. Like mine. We match for a change. His hand drags my shirt up my back. I moan into his mouth. He slides himself against me. The hardness of him is every-where. It's heady and rich. My hands are in his hair, pulling at him, dragging him onto me. It hits before I realize. I've pulled off my shirt. My bra and naked skin are rubbing against his sweater. He drags it off and that's when I notice it—the sickening feeling filling up my stomach.

The weight of him against me is too much.

I shove hard.

I roll off the bed, grabbing for the waist bin. I lose the small amount of ice cream and the pizza we had earlier. I gag, trying to be quiet. I leave my shoes and my shirt. I hug the bin and run for the bathroom. I close the door and sink against it. The weight of him and the feel of his skin were magical but they came with a flash of something else.

A dark figure.

There is someone else in our embrace. They are there in my memory.

I watched him through a tiny crack in the floor. He was holding someone, kissing them. The crack in the floor is big enough for me to see the bad things in the dirty house. I can't close my eyes because the image is in my mind.

My brain closes off before anything else comes up. I get sick again. There is nothing left inside me.

"What else happened to you, Emalyn?" He is beside the door. His voice is soft.

I shake my head. "I don't know."

"You do."

"I swear I don't. My mind won't let me remember." With the door between us I feel the best I ever have about our relationship. I love having him there but not able to touch me. All of the things I'm thinking come to a conclusion. "I can't see you anymore."

"Em. Don't."

I swallow and wipe my face, gripping the small garbage can. "I can't. I'm never going to grow past here. This is it. I'm always going to want to be where we are. Never moving beyond this. I was right, I'm ruined and not broken."

"I can wait. We've only been at this a short amount of time." His voice is desperate.

"It's cruel to ask you to hold out." Tears fill my eyes. They try to make the kaleidoscopes but I blink them back. I don't deserve a different view of things. "I'm never going to change." I stand and dump the pail into the toilet. I rinse it out with hand soap and dry it with a towel.

"Em, don't do this. You're doing so well."

The sentence stings coming from him. It shows me the truth.

"Do you like that I'm broken? Is it because you want to be my hero and my knight? You want me to need you to keep me safe," I mutter. I pray he didn't hear it.

I look at myself in the mirror. I see her still. The dead girl who never made it out of the scary house alive. I see her. I'll always see her. She is me. I am not the girl who lived and found food on the streets. I'll never be that girl. I'm the dead girl who didn't make it out. I've been living for us both, but I need to start seeing things for what they are. She is one of the only memories I have of the dirty house. She is the only one I need.

My dead-fish eyes stare back at me. I splash water on my face and let it come in and take over. I'm not afraid when I open the door. The look of terror and fear that was on my face has traumatized him. I know he won't touch me again, even if I beg him to.

He looks hurt and beaten down. I walk past him. I feel for my cell in my pocket and pick up my runners. I don't hunt down my shirt. I would rather be nearly naked and just in my bra, than collect my things and continue to see the look on his face.

I leave.

I don't say anything.

There are no words.

7

"He just wants to see you. Just once." Her eyes are shiny and desperate.

I shake my head. "Why? So I can look at him like he's a rapist again? So I can throw up when he touches me?"

She slumps on the bed. "Can't you just be his friend?"

I swallow down my bile. "No. I can't. He makes me think things. He makes me want things. But I'm not strong enough to have them."

She squeezes my hand. "Em, you are. We made it this far."

I smile. "I know. I'm happy about this far, Shell. I like it here. I want to finish school and have a normal life. I'm cool with my normal being what it is."

She shakes her head. "No. I don't believe it." She gets up and leaves the room.

There is a knock on the door after she is gone for a minute. I see her keys on the bedside table and moan. I climb off the bed and open the door. I can't breathe when I see him. He steps in and closes the door. His hands reach for mine. His skin burns me. His eyes are desperate and wild.

"W-what are y-you d-doing here?" I am almost frozen in fear.

Sebastian steps back and presses his back against the door, letting go of me. I too step back, making a large gap between us.

"I needed to see you."

I like that word need. I like that he needs me. I'm a selfish bitch.

"I needed to say goodbye in person. I never got to say the things I wanted to."

My heart aches instantly.

"I love you, Em. It's silly and fast and too much for what I get in return. But I do. You've got me on the run, chasing you all the time. You have all the cards and I don't even care. I'd chase you around the world." His voice drops off at the end and becomes a forced whisper.

His hazel eyes are shiny and complicated. "I've thought about nothing but you for the last couple months. And even if I see that you're right, I can't seem to make myself let go of you. Even though I refuse to see it all, the look in your eyes says the things you won't. I know, in my heart, you won't ever heal. You won't ever get past this. I can't force myself to give up on you. So I am leaving. It's about the only thing I can do. I need to sleep and not see your face every time I close my eyes. I hate that you think I want you broken and injured so you need me."

I sigh. He heard me say it. I wanted so many things from him and the acceptance that I'm a hopeless freak was never one of them.

"I can't force this between us, and I can't live with the look you give me that makes me feel like some kind of monster. I won't be at the school anymore. You don't have to worry about the gym or anything. It's all yours again."

I don't feel better.

He steps forward and kisses my forehead. His breath is soft air and devastating warmth on my face. He turns and leaves. He chooses survival over me. It's no different than what I have done. We are both just trying so hard to survive me.

I turn and collapse on the bed. I have schoolwork to do, but I curl into a ball and turn on the TV. I turn on *Amelie* and wish I were Audrey Tautou.

My phone vibrates.

Hi.

I drag my fingers over the top of it. *He left me. He left me broken. More broken than I already was.*

Do you need the doc?

I sniffle and heave. *Not yet.*

What do you need?

To be normal. I would die to be normal.

Don't die. Give Dr. Bradley a chance.

Next week.

I leave it at that and curl into the bed.

And weeks pass.

I don't run anymore. I don't need to. The running was for self-preservation. There is nothing left inside me to save. I study like mad and watch Netflix. I am ahead with all my work and acing all my classes, but I am more trapped in the lonely than I have ever been.

It's just before Christmas break and Stuart is driving me to the doctor's office. I avoided Dr. Bradley when I was seeing Sebastian. I didn't want her telling me how poor of a decision it was to bring another victim into my mess. Or to date so soon after a huge change like coming to college. I didn't want to see the truth of it all in her eyes. The truth that no matter how hard he tried, I would screw it all up.

I catch Stuart's eyes in the rearview. They aren't watching Shell, they're watching me. Shell nudges me. "We'll be right outside, okay?"

I nod. "Kay."

My phone vibrates. I answer, "Hi." I always sound impatient with him now. He annoys me by existing.

"You need to remind her that you're still not sleeping, okay?"

I shake my head and shoot Shell a look. "How do you know that? Maybe I am?"

He laughs bitterly. "I know you're not."

"How?" I ask softly.

"Do as you're told." He isn't laughing anymore. He's annoyed.

I wince. "Kay."

He sighs. "That is a letter. It's not a word. Can't you just speak like you have something of an education?"

"I'm doing fine in school."

"I know that. Nice work on the grades, by the way. I have to admit the straight A's surprised me. Between the whatevers and the K's, I figured you were doomed." His voice lightens. I don't know what the game is we're playing.

"Thanks," I say sarcastically. I don't even know how he knows I got all A's. I was so relieved to get good grades, with all the drama and heartbreak. It's one good thing about OCD—good grades.

He sighs again. "Call me when she's done. I want to talk to you about something important."

I hang up the phone and glare at Shell. "You told him I wasn't sleeping?"

She shakes her head. "I've still never spoken to Uncle Daddy Weirdo. Not even kidding. I don't know him."

My eyes find Stuart's in the mirror. He makes a face. "I don't know about your sleeping patterns. Jeeze. I don't even talk to him. You're the only one who has ever heard his voice."

I tilt my head in disbelief. "You've never met him or talked to him? Ever?"

He shakes his head. "Never. Not even kidding. Dude found me at my boxing ring. My trainer came up after a fight and asked if I was interested in a job. Said that the guy watched the fight and needed someone to drive for him."

I frown. "You took a job based on that little information?"

He snorts. "I get paid a hundred grand a year to drive your ass around. Hell yes, I took the job."

My stomach drops. "Who would pay that kind of money?" My brain whispers, *not good people.*

Shell giggles. "And my ass."

His stare leaves me and becomes deadly sexy.

Shell raises her eyebrows. "That's not all you're doing to my ass though."

I grimace. "Gross. Focus people. Jesus. So he hired you from a boxing ring? He clearly wanted someone who can handle himself. When did he hire you? I thought you were a ninja?"

He shrugs. "UFC. It's kickboxing. Same thing as being a ninja. He hired me at the beginning of the summer. He told me you would pick the city and that I would live there. I was pumped when you chose Boston."

"Where are you really from?" I ask, curious suddenly.

"Kansas."

I roll my eyes. "Well, duh. I know Kansas. I mean where were you fighting when he found you?"

"Wichita."

"He's from Kansas too?" I'm confused. "What was he doing at a boxing match in Wichita?"

He frowns and pulls the car into the parking lot of the doctor. "Not a clue." He hops out and gets the door.

I look up into his beautiful eyes. "A hundred thousand a year and you never questioned it?"

He shakes his head. "I was making thirty fighting and fifteen at the gym as a trainer."

"That is a disturbing amount of money." I walk away from them and pull my sweater tighter around me. None of this makes sense.

The door to the office feels like the door to Sebastian's building. I miss him in sick and twisted ways. Selfish ways.

I open it with a gloved hand. The only thing I love about winter, wearing gloves. Gloves in the summer make my hands sweaty, which freaks me out more. But gloves in the winter are my new saving grace. Gloves and Michelle.

I push the button on the elevator in a series of taps and take a deep breath. When the elevator dings and the door opens, her smiling face is there for me. She never makes me ride it alone. It's his orders. I like it though. I don't like taking elevators alone.

"How are you this week?" Dr. Bradley asks as I step inside.

"I'm okay. How are you?"

She presses the button and nods. "Excellent, thank you." When the door closes she turns. "He phoned only a few moments ago. He's terribly worried. Is there some stuff you don't want to talk about that maybe you should?"

The elevator stops at her apartment. We walk out into the huge open space. I hate it. It's too open and too white and too bright. I feel like I am under a microscope here, and she can see all the fine details I'm trying to hide.

I walk to the chair, where I always sit. It's the one with the back to the wall. I don't like chairs with their backs near windows or doors, and God forbid, open space. I shake my head and fidget with my fingers. "I'm doing good—well. I don't know what he's talking about."

She sits and sips from the glass of water she has. She always sets one out for me as well. It always has a cucumber slice in it and looks refreshing, and as per every other time, I've yet to drink it.

"He is under the impression you've had a bad break up. You're depressed a bit from it." Her deep-blue eyes and dark hair shimmer in the extreme light. The light that makes me feel exposed.

In it I can see her better though. She is mid forties and pretty, but like a mom. She reminds me of Michelle's mom. Pretty and clean. Only Michelle's mom always smells like food. I can remember the millions of hugs that smelled like spaghetti.

"He seems to think you are upset about the young man. Sebastian."

I continue to ignore her. I refuse to let her see that side of my soul. The dirty side. "There is something I want to talk about. My benefactor. I think he's a bad man. He's paying a hundred grand to Stuart to be my driver. Who does that? He hired him from a gym. He could be a serial killer."

She crosses her arms. "So you wish to discuss the possible previous career choices Stuart has made? Or that the man paying for you to get better, could be a bad man?"

I nod. "I'm going to bet mafia of some sort."

She doesn't grin.

I fidget my fingers. "Can we do the grateful thing again?"

She sighs. "Avoiding the conversation isn't going to make it go away. You know you're safe in here. Let's talk about the relationship. Do you feel like it was a wise choice, considering your feelings about people and proximity? Did you tell him everything?"

I snap. "What everything? My holey memory about a creepy house, blue eyes in a dirty hole, and a dead girl on a bed? What am I supposed to do with that? Oh, right—there was also a gunshot. Useful stuff."

Her lip plays with a grin. "Nice. I like that question. What do you think the answer is?"

I want to toss something. I might snap her head off if she asks me one more thing. I squeeze my hands into a ball. My nails are short, always. They don't leave indents but my fingertips start to get numb.

"He said you have been to the bar a few times. How was that? Seems like a big step."

I press my lips together and take in big breaths.

"Are you self-calming?" she asks and sips from the water again. I watch my glass. I'm so thirsty.

I decide I can play along with her. I shrug. "It was fun. The dancing was fun. I didn't like being around so many people, but they never really noticed me. So I felt invisible."

She nods and watches me. "Did you drink?"

"A sip of beer a few times. Nothing crazy."

"Did you buy the beer?" Her tone puzzles me.

"No. Shell did. She bought the beer and gave it to me."

Her eyes narrow. She sips the water again. I think she's doing it loudly to make me want some. "Was the lid off the beer when you got it?"

I frown and nod. "It was." *How did I not notice that?*

"Did you dance?" She changes the subject quickly.

"Yup."

"That's some progress, I think." Her voice lifts. I grin. I love her approval. Like I did with the nuns.

"Now the guy you met, was he there?"

I nod. My smile fades.

"Why did you break up?"

The words pop out, "I can't be that girl."

"Can't or won't?" She doesn't miss a beat.

I shrug. "Does it matter?"

She nods. Her eyes sparkle. "If you want to change and one day be free of it all, it matters. If you want to have a real relationship one day, of course it matters."

I look down. I need to change the subject. "I don't sleep much anymore. If Michelle isn't there I don't sleep. He asked me to tell you that." I'm dreading where she will take it.

She sits back on the chair, getting more relaxed. "Okay. What is that?"

"Before it was just the first night somewhere new. Now it seems to be all the time. It seems to be worse."

She drags her long, slender finger with a French-tipped manicure back and forth along the armrest. "Since the breakup?"

I nod. I'm close to her. I trust her. I relax and take a breath and remind myself of these things. She isn't the enemy.

"He broke up with you?"

I shake my head.

"Why are you so sad if you broke it off?"

I laugh bitterly; it's almost a sob. "I couldn't be with him."

"Sexually?"

The word makes my skin crawl.

"Do you want to talk about the house you've mentioned before?"

I almost crawl backward up the chair. "NO!"

She puts a delicate hand out. "Calm. Be grateful for the moments that matter. You are breathing air and are alive and the room is clean and free of germs."

I take a breath but my skin won't stop crawling and shivering.

"So sexually you can't be with him? Is it possible you feel guilty for wanting to?"

I'm up and walking for the door. "Thanks, Doc." I press the elevator. It opens immediately. She knows better than to chase me. The door dings. I walk across the foyer and out into the cool breeze. Michelle and Stuart are kissing in the front seat. I turn left instead of going to the car. I don't want to disrupt them. I have my wallet and phone. If I get desperate I'll call a cab.

I stroll down the driveway and out onto the street. The air is cold and crisp; it makes me feel clean. Well, clean-ish.

My phone vibrates. I pull it out and answer.

He speaks before I can, "Why did you leave the car?" He is moody.

I can be moody too. "Why did you hire Stuart for a hundred thousand a year to drive me around?"

He heaves a sigh. "He has a big mouth and my business with him is private. That just cost him his pay for a month. Why did you leave the car?"

I scream into the phone, "HOW DO YOU KNOW I LEFT THE CAR? WHERE ARE YOU? YOU FUCKING FREAK! STOP SPYING ON ME!" I'm trembling and at my breaking point.

"Are you finished?" He is calm.

I dry sob and feel bad for calling him a freak. It's a glass-house moment I'm not proud of. "Yes."

"Why did you leave the car?" He is so calm it scares me.

I laugh bitterly. "Why did you hire a UFC boxing champ as my driver?"

He laughs with me but says nothing. He is silent. I wait for it and then sigh. I am defeated. "I wanted to be alone. She made me feel dirty. I didn't want to be with them."

"Because I am a rich man, and if anyone ever knew that you were my ward, they would hurt you to get to me. I need to know you're all right. At all times. Stuart can protect you. I cannot. I am busy."

I am a burden suddenly.

I don't have anything to add to that. How can I be so angry that he wants to keep me safe? At all times. And I am a burden that costs him a fortune. I pause. "What? Wait—who wants to hurt you and me?"

"My business." His tone is getting edgy. I don't even want to know what he's talking about. I don't need new reasons not to sleep.

I pinch the bridge of my nose and take a deep breath. "Can you find Sebastian for me?"

"Why?"

"I need to tell him that I'm sorry. It's killing me inside that I made him feel so awful." I don't say that he is the only normal thing in my life and I need him. That I made a terrible mistake.

His voice is dead calm again, "Do you love him?" I spin around and look for him. He must be watching me.

I shake my head. "I don't think I'm capable of that."

I hear the car. He's gone. He's hung up again.

I turn and see Stuart. He looks savagely angry. He gets out and opens the door to the car in a rough jerk. Shell is scowling at me. I sigh and climb in, defeated. They don't speak to me or each other. When we drive up, Stuart doesn't get out of the car. He doesn't move his head. He looks straight ahead. I climb out. It's the first time I've opened my own door without a fight from him. I feel sick. I'm a moron. I know this. I walk up the stairs to the dorm. Shell stays behind in the car. I don't have to look back. I don't hear her door. I walk inside and feel the lump in my throat growing.

I sit on my bed and wait for the lonely, but even it doesn't come.

8

She packs the bag in a silence that feels heavier than the late August air we suffered through. She doesn't look at me.

"You sure you don't want to come? She is going to be pissed if you're not there. She says it feels like we're missing a member of the family."

I shake my head. I'm touched but her family's Christmas is huge. Italians at Christmas equal chaos, food, red wine, and kisses and hugs.

"My skin almost all peeled off last time I went. Remember, I ran out of sani and your poor dad had to go hunt for it on Christmas day?" Not to mention, I felt like a Dickens character. I was the poor orphan with no one, and they were the warm, friendly family with the smoking-hot sons. I think about my situation and realize it hasn't changed much. I am still fairly Dickens, only more like a combination of Miss Havisham and Pip rolled into Oliver Twist's life.

I sigh.

She glances at me. Her face hasn't changed much since I lost Stuart a month of pay by opening my big mouth. I knew better. Orphans always stuck together and never ratted anyone out to the nuns. No matter what. Even if it cost me ice cream.

"I'm sorry."

She shakes her head. "I don't blame you. He freaks me out." She kneels in front of my bed and grabs my hands. She doesn't do that much. Her eyes twinkle with fear and worry. "I just thought that maybe this would be a new start for you. No more nuns telling you to clean and telling you to hit yourself with branches. No more scripture and religious shit. I know you never believed so it was easy to walk away from the church." She squeezes and her voice wavers, "But Em, you haven't left. Not really. You're still in that damned orphanage. You're still alone in the world. You don't let me in. You ran off the most perfect guy in the world. You're running my perfect guy off. You clean when you don't have to, and you have meltdowns in the cafeteria, because the guy next to you has bad teeth and chews with his mouth open."

I look down. Shame and sadness are creeping around in my mind, bringing up old shit and bad memories.

She lifts my chin. I wish I could cry. I feel the tears there. I feel the pressure in my throat. But nothing comes out.

"Em, I'm not saying you don't have a right. You do. You have every right to be the way you are. You're doing well." Those words sting more than anything she has ever said to me. It's the Band-Aid I get slapped with all the time. The "doing-well" Band-Aid that's actually made at the "I hate to tell you how shitty you are doing" factory.

"Don't say that," I mumble.

She flinches as she hears herself. She knows how those words feel. "Sorry."

I shake my head. "I think it's good you're going for the three weeks. We need some time apart."

She backs up. "What? Don't say that."

I pull back too and look at my feet. "It's true. This is harder than I imagined it would be. Living together has been kind of horrible. You're too much sometimes."

"What?" She scoffs. "You are so ungrateful. Holy shit. I moved here for you. I'm in a city I don't like, going to a school I never ever dreamed of, and living with a girl who is a frightened little kid, trapped in an orphanage she never left."

My throat burns. My heart rate picks up.

She throws a bottle of hand sani at me. "Don't forget to wash up." She grabs her bag and leaves, slamming the door. I still don't cry. It's amazing but I don't. I wash my hands. The smell of the coconut-almond alcohol doesn't make me feel better. It smells like his ice cream. Dry sobs rip from my throat.

I stare at the wall for a long time. I snap out of it when my phone vibrates and I realize I'm sitting in the dark. I answer, "Hi."

"You okay?" He cares. I can hear it in his voice.

I shake my head, making an ugly-cry face. It doesn't feel genuine though without the waterworks. "No."

"Get dressed and go downstairs. Look nice. I have something for you."

I shake my head. "No, thanks. I'm going to order pizza and hang here."

He sighs. "Don't try my patience. Outside in half an hour." He hangs up. I don't want to go. I don't want to face Stuart. I've managed to not get a ride since I last saw him at the doctor's office. I've walked for everything I had to do. As penance. I'm good at penance.

I watch the clock, feeling the nerves building inside me. I'm taking a stand. I'm not going. I've had the worst couple weeks ever. I don't have to do everything he says.

My indignant attitude lasts twenty-three minutes. Then I jump up, rip a brush through my hair, and pull on dress pants and a pale-blue sweater. I smear lip gloss on my lips and wash my hands three times. I race out the door, throwing on my parka. I make it to the front door in exactly thirty minutes. I'm huffing from not running at all in weeks.

Stuart looks sad when he sees me. He's sad for me. He feels sorry for me. His pity burns a hole in my already battered chest.

I climb into the backseat. He closes the door softly. It hurts more that he's not being an ass. I'm not worthy or strong enough for him to treat me like shit.

I keep my eyes down.

My phone vibrates. I answer, "Hi."

"I'm running late. The limo is stuck behind an accident. Tell Stuart not to take you to the place until I message him." He hangs up.

I frown and look up at Stuart. I clear my throat. "Uhm, he just called. He wants us to just drive around until he messages you." I barely finish the sentence when Stuart's phone plays a song. He looks at it and answers, "Hello?" He makes a weird face and nods. "Yes, sir." He hangs up and shrugs. "Guess he was ready now."

I point. "Has he ever called you before?"

He shakes his head. "Not so much. A couple times to scream at me but the directions are always texts."

I can't help but feel weird. But the look on Stuart's face catches my eye in the mirror. "I'm so sorry." My words are soft. They have no strength.

He shakes his head. "I know you didn't mean to." His eyes narrow. "He's just a weird rich guy. He messes with people. He likes controlling us. We gotta play the game, Em."

I swallow. "Is she very mad at me?"

"She's sick right now. She almost didn't get in the cab. She hates herself for what she said."

I clench my jaw. "Me too," I whisper and look out the window.

"As soon as she lands you know she'll be messaging you."

I nod and fight the feelings roaming my insides, making them cramp up.

He drives into an old part of town where we sit in a parking lot. He waits a minute and then climbs out. I get out and hug my parka. Mid December is cold. The wind is bitter and the snow is annoying. Boston is not my favorite place to be for winter, except for the wearing gloves part. Stuart walks with me toward an old brick building. He looks around. He's never walked with me before.

"Do we go inside?" I ask.

He shakes his head. "He was supposed to meet us in the parking lot. He said he was taking us somewhere by helicopter. We were going to like it." He looks around and hugs his pea coat to himself. My stomach hurts. I've felt this pain before. It reminds me of something.

Stuart must feel it too. He stands really close to me. He pulls out his phone.

"Was this the address?" I ask. My nerves are on high alert.

He nods. "This is where he said on the phone."

I think about what he's said to me about Stuart protecting me. I stand closer. The parking lot is bare, beyond the dried, crusty snow-drifts. The snow is barely covering the ground. We crunch around, walking and waiting. Stuart dials. He holds his phone out. "Crap. No service."

An SUV pulls into the driveway. It's not a limo and it's not a helicopter. I look at Stuart. "He said he was in a limo and you said we were going somewhere by helicopter. What if that's not him?"

Stuart looks at me. "Stand behind me." His face is tense and angry. I don't know what's going on. We both feel the tension. Everything feels out of place. I glance at my phone but there is no service. I shove it down the back of my dress pants and into my underwear. I remember the talk from eighth grade. If anyone ever snatched you, you were to press 911 and then shove the phone down your pants. Wherever they were taking you, they weren't taking your pants off till they got there. I never had a phone before. I honestly never thought I would need to do it, regardless of how much it scared me.

"I wish we never got out of the car," I mutter.

Stuart steps forward when a man steps out of the backseat of the gray SUV. He has on a huge fluffy coat and sunglasses.

The guy looks like a douche.

Sunglasses?

I know it isn't him. Uncle Daddy Weirdo is way too cool to wear sunglasses in the winter, like this douche. Sunglasses or no, he freaks me out. I step closer to Stuart. I look down at my Ugg boots and grimace. I wish I wore my runners. I start tensing my legs as two more men get out of the car.

"Who are you?" Stuart asks.

The man laughs. "Just give us the girl. That's all we want."

I take a step back, certain I have misheard them.

Stuart looks back at me but doesn't take his eyes off the men. "Run," he says flatly. I don't need to be told twice. I turn and bolt.

Over my footsteps I hear men grunt and slapping sounds. I leap at the chain-link fence. My fingers claw at it, dragging myself up in frenzied panic. I reach the top but my boot is grabbed. I jerk and kick but I'm pulled hard. I kick again and get loose. I pull myself up again and scramble to the top. I swing over and start to clamber down the other side. My assailant's sunglasses meet my eyes mid fence. He smiles. "I like when you run, little girl."

I gag. His voice is creepy and sadistic. I jump, feeling something pull in my ankle. I run hard. I hear him land with a grunt. I push my legs harder. They are just starting to warm up so I dig in.

There is no way he will catch me. No way. I run around a building and through a parking lot. I round another building and push it down an alley. I'm completely lost. I end up in another parking area. I slide between two vehicles and catch my breath. My ankle burns and my lungs hate me and the cold air.

I almost cough but I hold my breath. I hear his footsteps. He's still running. My back is against the cold, hard car. My muscles are trembling from the crouched position and my vision is fuzzy. Lack of oxygen and too much adrenaline.

"I know you're here. I'm tracking your cell phone." He has an accent. It's English. No Australian. I glance around and think of what to do. If I pull the phone from my pants he won't be able to find me. But then neither will Stuart. I decide to risk it. I fish my phone out of my pants and check the signal. I have a bar. I text as fast as I can.

HELP! BAD GUYS! PLEASE COME FIND ME!

It delivers. I hear a ping in the parking lot. My stomach sinks. I close my eyes and wonder if he *is* the bad guy or dead at the hands of the bad guy. Has he been conning me all along?

My breath is gone. My legs become concrete. His footsteps get closer. I slowly place the phone on the ground and back up silently. I am fighting the paralyzing fear as the lonely starts to take over.

His feet crunch the old dry snow. I'm trembling. I back up. My exhale makes mist in the air. I try not to breathe. I hold my mitten over my mouth. It makes me sick, but I don't have any other choice. It all feels familiar. The mitten and hiding amongst the cars. I start getting lightheaded.

I lean into the car more, needing the support.

I need to keep backing up.

"Emalyn Spicer. Such an odd name for a girl who was raised in a Catholic church. Don't they usually name you after a saint?" His voice is like nails on a chalkboard. It burns and hurts. He isn't my benefactor.

I would know his voice anywhere. This is a bad man who wants to hurt me to get at my benefactor. Just like he said they would. I was foolish. Why didn't I listen? Why didn't I stay with the car? I had to walk and be stubborn because I didn't want to see Stuart. Stuart who is now fighting for me. No doubt outnumbered and hurt. My heart is aching.

I'm panicking as his steps get closer. I can hear him stepping in between the cars next to me. I look around. There is nothing. Nothing I can see. I count to three and jump up. I sprint behind the cars and jump over a small barricade. His shoes slap the hard road behind me. It's the moment I've trained for.

What I haven't trained for hits me in the butt cheek with a stabbing pain. I slam into a building. The lonely comes fast and hard. My feet won't move. They're concrete boots. It's like I'm wading through the water, clutching the side of a building. His feet are crunching on the crusty ground behind me. I fall into the cold snow. My knees scrape on the hard crust. I'm still dragging myself when I see shiny dark-brown leather shoes walking up to me. I see his shoe come back, like he's going to kick me. I blink but my eyes don't open. The shoe connects with my stomach. I grunt and cry out. I hear it but it doesn't feel like it comes from me.

I feel something woolen being pulled down over my face. And then I'm out.

9

The dark is a quiet place. Reflection and contemplation are the only things to do in here. Well that, and imagine the worst things possible.

But I don't have to reflect or contemplate on any of those things. I know what the worst things possible are. I know about the things that hide in the dark. Insanity is the least of them.

I am curled in a ball in the back corner of the room.

It's stressing me out that I don't know where he is.

Him or Stuart.

I don't have my phone. The thing I never imagined loving, now feels as if it's an appendage that's missing. I miss the feel of it, when it vibrated and I knew he was there. He was always there for me. I pray they're both okay.

I hear a scream cut through the silence. My heartbeat quickens. It sounds like Stuart. He screams again. My back is pressing harder into the concrete. His screams worsen. He is brought closer to my door. He is sobbing. I cannot imagine the horrors he has seen, or the pain he has experienced to make him sob. But he sounds like a child. Weak and fragile. They have hurt him badly.

My jaw is trembling. The sounds are gone again. It is my heartbeat and exhaling breaths that keep me company in the dark.

The darkness keeps me awake.

My butt hurts, my heart hurts, my throat burns from the tears in there, and my eyes burn from the lack of sleep.

The door opens.

The light is harsh and white. I squint to see a hand rise in the open space. A gun is lifted. I don't have time to flinch or cry out. The dart is sticking out of my arm, and I am sliding down the wall.

The door closes again.

My throat gets thick and my limbs feel like they're getting fatter. When I hit the floor I cannot move. My eyes flutter and then close.

When they open again I am still alone in the dark. I put a hand down on the cold concrete floor and rub it back and forth. I dreamt I was back in my dorm. The cold hard floor tells me otherwise.

I push and lift myself up. My arms tremble and shake. I'm weak. Hunger and thirst are brutal. I push myself back into the corner again. I hate how dark it is. It feels like a vast empty space.

When I rub my eyes I feel like my hands are bonier than they were. I don't know how many days have past. My stomach is pulled in, and I can feel my ribs when my arms sit on my belly.

I was already thin from the sprints, but now I am skinny. It has to have been at least seventy-two hours to get me to this point. No food. No water. I am going to die soon. I want to cry out. I want to beg. But I don't. I sit and wait. I don't wait long before the screams happen again.

My hands shoot to my ears, covering them.

I know what it is to sit, scared and in the dark, and listen to screams. This is not the first time in my life this has happened.

I sob along with him. It's Stuart again. He cries out words. I don't know what they are but he is begging. Pleading. It sounds like they're ripping his fingers off. Maybe they are. I sob dry heaves and shake.

"Please, God. Please save him. Please, make them stop," I whisper into the darkness, desperate to drown out his screams and pleas. I have never begged God for a single thing, believing he never saw me as worthy. But I beg now.

A movement catches my attention. I almost crawl up the wall backing up. "Who's there?" I whisper.

A chuckle lets loose. It fills up all the air and space. It's a man. He's inside the cell with me. I crawl to the farthest corner and hold myself, clinging for dear life. "Who are you?" I wonder for a second if he's real. I could be so hungry that I'm hallucinating. I'm starving.

"Emalyn Spicer. Such a interesting name."

It's the man who chased me. I think my stomach still hurts where he kicked me. I cling to myself and turn my face away from where he is.

"What do you know about your life before Emalyn Spicer?"

I hate the way he's saying my full name.

"I know who you are. It's all very fascinating. I know you aren't Emalyn Spicer, are you? Fascinating indeed." His voice is harsh and cruel.

A loud bang breaks the quiet of my harsh breaths and his soft chuckles.

The door opens.

The bright white light is there.

I see something in the gap of the door and the frame.

It's Stuart. He's unconscious and being dragged by my room. His hands and face are bleeding heavily. I cover my eyes quickly.

The slapping footsteps fill the gaps between my shuddering breaths. They draw closer for a second. They're right in front of me. I avert my gaze and tremble. He bends down. I can hear everything he does. He grabs my face softly and turns my rigid head to face him. I can't see his face. The light behind him ensures that. It still stings my eyes.

"Such a pretty girl. I'd hate for you to not be pretty anymore." He laughs, standing back up.

His footsteps slap back across the floor.

I hear a scratching sound. A hand shoves a tray of something in as he leaves the room.

The door is closed.

It's dark again.

I don't wait. The smell of the food invades my space. I scramble across the floor to the tray. I reach out, savagely. There are no utensils. No napkins. I lift the small tray off the larger one. It's a hot dinner. Maybe a TV dinner. I lick from the tray, without using my hands. The weight of it makes my arms tremble. The first taste is gravy. It's divine and salty.

I don't think. I revert to my old ways so quickly. I lap at the food like a dog. Like before the orphanage. Mashed potatoes and gravy. I get a piece of meat in my mouth. I chew the grizzled meat and choke a bit when I swallow before I'm ready.

I get a mushy pea in my mouth. I almost gag but I force it down. I force it all down. Mushy peas and meat and gravy. I lick the tray until there is nothing left.

I reach out into the dark for the drink I swear I saw. I knock something with my hand. It sloshes. I grab it and gulp back the liquid inside. It's stale and funny tasting, but it is amazing. It's fluid. I finish the drink and realize what it is. Iced tea. Unsweetened iced tea. I shiver from the flavor. I place it back at the door and scramble back to the corner.

I can't help but wonder what it is all about.

Is it Emalyn Spicer they're looking for?

I sit there and wonder how—how he knew I wasn't Emalyn Spicer. No one but Emalyn and me knew that little secret.

It dawns on me he wasn't asking me about my life before the orphanage. He was asking about my life, before Emalyn Spicer.

I close my eyes and try desperately to remember the memories I have blocked out.

There is nothing but blue eyes peeking from a hole where tiny fingers reach. Sunlight glinting off blonde hair. Everything else is shut down.

I know I told them I was Emalyn Spicer. I know who she is; I know who she isn't as well. I can see her face staring at me. Her blank stare haunts me. She is me.

I've lived for her. I had to. I owed her that. I remember the gunshot. I remember the debt, but I don't remember the cause of it.

I look down at the floor and laugh.

It's hysterical and demented. It takes away so many things. It's the kind of laugh I have never had. I laugh harder. Tears form in my eyes. They don't come out. They never come out. I can't even cry for me, or Emalyn.

I think it's days before I get a tray again. I'm starved and sick. The smell of my own urine and shit in the other corner is making me sick. I'm dying from the phobias and the nervous ticks the nuns gave me.

They bring a tray, but when I reach it I discover the food is in a bowl. My hands are filthy. I can't eat with them.

I heave dry sobs and hold the bowl. I try tilting it but the food is thick. It won't come out.

Finally, I put it on the floor and hold my long greasy, stringy hair back. I eat from the dish like a dog would. My nose rubs in the food. It doesn't smell good. It's a stew but it smells gross. Like it's old and freezer burnt.

My body doesn't care. I eat. I gobble. I gag from swallowing too much and not taking my time. I stretch my tongue as hard as I can to reach the bottom of the bowl. The bowl is too deep.

I grab for the glass of tea and dump some in the bowl. I swirl it around and drink the last of the stew mixed with the tea. It makes me gag but I do it. I need the food. I drink the tea down and wipe my face off with my shirt. My tattered and filthy t-shirt.

The lock in the door turns. I turn my head like a feral cat. I scramble back to the corner. My old ways are all back—my ways of living on the streets like a feral cat. They were always there, hiding under the surface. I just never knew it. I never knew I could go back so easily. I'm in dirty pants and a filthy shirt. I stink in ways I don't remember being possible.

The door opens. The blinding light is too much. I squint my eyes. The man walks in. I would know the slap of his shoes anywhere.

"We have a deal to offer you today. One of you is going to be tortured. It's a live feed for your friend—well, benefactor. I suppose he never was your friend. Now, Stuart has had his fair share. He has volunteered every day to spare your life."

That hurts me but only a little. My survival skills are something to be proud of.

"He has been beaten, cut, flogged, whipped, burned, and has

endured water torture. We are offering you the opportunity to take his place."

His accent sounds like he should be offering me a picnic or reading a children's story. He should be saying happy jolly things to me. Instead, he is offering me the chance to save my friend.

I don't answer him. I watch his silhouette in the light of the door-frame. He turns and leaves the room. He's closing the door when I speak, "I will."

He pokes his head back in. "You will what?"

"I will take the torture."

He snaps his fingers. "Clean her up. I want to see her skin blush when I strike it."

I'm about to change my mind when men come barreling into the room. I fight immediately. There is no point. I won't win. But I fight anyway.

They drag me out into the white hallway. It's stark and bright. I'm carried down it. My feet drag. They can't walk. I didn't have much fight in me.

I'm shoved into a room.

A girl with dark hair and pretty gray eyes is waiting for me there. The men leave me in a heap on the floor. I realize how disgusting and filthy I am when I see how clean she is. She wears a long white dress. It's weird. Like she is an angel. She smiles. Her teeth are bright white against her dark-red lips. "Hello," she says softly.

She takes my dirty-brown hand and lifts me off the ground. I stand on wobbly legs and let her pull me to a huge steel tub. Steam lifts off it.

She pulls my shirt off and tosses it into the bin. I can see myself in the mirror. I've never looked more like the dead girl from the house. Not ever. She pulls my pants down. I should gasp and grab them. I should leap away from her.

I'm too exhausted and sickly. I do nothing. I let her pull me into the tub.

The water burns my skin, it's so hot.

"You're cold. It's not that hot," she says when she sees me flinch.

I step in, wincing and sucking air. My skin burns but my legs collapse into the tub. I sit as she washes me. It's the most frightening, and yet amazing feeling I've ever had. She washes my hair, scrubbing my scalp. She pours buckets of the hot water over me.

A disgusting film starts to sit on the water. She lifts me out and grabs a shower nozzle. She sprays me down. My hands cover my breasts and I cross my legs hard. I can see my nakedness in the mirror. I look weak and hungry.

She pulls me out and wraps me in a huge robe. It's soft and fluffy. She takes my hand and leads me down a different long white hallway. It's freaking me out. The hallways are baffling. But it feels like that is the point. I'm completely disoriented. The floors are dark slate and the walls are bright white.

She holds my hand tightly and drags me down the long, wide hallway to a huge dark-brown door.

I glance out the windows and wonder if I'm still in the city.

"Is this Boston?" I ask in a dead voice. The windows are glazed in a way that makes them blurry. I can't see anything out of them, but the bright light can get in.

She ignores me and pulls me through the doorway.

The room is large and warm. There is a fireplace and rugs in the middle of several couches and chairs. The floor is wood and warmer than the slate. The walls are a pale-blush color. It suits the furniture. There is a bed at the back of the room.

I gulp.

It has a massive canopy.

My stomach twists when I see the Australian man is sitting in a chair. He grins and my heart beats wildly.

His face—I know it.

The woman curtsies and leaves the room, closing the door and clicking a lock.

My eyes are wide. I'm clutching the robe.

He doesn't stand. He smiles. His dark-gray pants and pale-blue dress shirt look almost exactly the same as they did the night in the bar.

He smiles and flashes the dimple in his one cheek. His dark hair is in the same fauxhawk.

My heartbeat picks up. The room is completely silent except for the dripping of my wet hair on the wood.

"Go sit by the fire, warm up." He points. His Australian accent is gone.

Was he even the Australian or are they two different people?

Am I hallucinating?

"Go," he demands.

My feet back up. I'm not turning my back on him. He doesn't move from the chair.

He sits so relaxed, it's almost cocky.

"Go to the fire." His tone lowers menacingly.

My stomach twists more. I step back again. I walk around the couch opposite him and drop to my knees slowly. Thankfully, there is a fluffy rug in front of it. I sit there quietly. I don't know what to say or do.

He watches me. His grin is sick and twisted. "Anything you want to talk about?" he asks.

I swallow. "He will come for me."

He grins. "I'm counting on it."

I shake my head. "Why?"

"We have business. Is it warm enough in here?"

I nod and look down at the rug. His cold icy stare is freaking me out.

"Are you from Australia?" I ask, still looking at the thick fluffy rug.

"No. But I didn't want you getting your hopes up if you recognized me. I'm good at accents."

"That's why you asked me to dance in the bar?" That at least made sense. I never could figure out why a sexy well-dressed man would ask me to dance. At least not whilst I was wearing my running watch.

"I wanted to see if you were the mess the files said you were."

Files? I glance up at him, confused, and yet relieved. He knows me as a broken orphan who lied about her name. I smile; it's a sickened bitter smile. "Well?"

"You are much worse than they know."

My back starts burning from the heat of the fire. I take a deep inhale.

"I have a second offer." His voice is honey sweet.

I shiver. "No."

He grins. "You don't want to hear it?"

I shake my head and clutch the robe. I'm feeling exhausted. The fire is relaxing me, and from the bed in the corner I would expect that is his hope.

"I'd be willing to forgo the beating if you were nice to me."

I cringe and shake my head.

"You'd rather be beaten? Am I so repulsive?"

I gag again but manage to swallow it down. The stew was the worst meal yet, and the fire is so relaxing.

I can see his plan. Gross me out and make me feel sick, but relax me into submission with the fire. Unfortunately, it's working.

"You would still rather have a beating, than have Stuart beaten?"

I nod.

He stands and puts a hand out. "Okay then."

I look up at him. I don't mean to turn it on; my eyes naturally do it. He shakes his head. "Those long lashes and pretty blue eyes won't work on me. Come here."

"No." I swallow and hesitate. "I'm not coming with you. You're going to beat me either way."

"That's right." He nods. "I am. But it will be much easier if you just come willingly."

I look into his icy-blue eyes for the truth. I push myself up and walk on shaky legs to him, to stand close to him. He jerks his hand, insisting I take it.

I lift my hand into the air and drop it into his. He closes his around mine gently.

Terror isn't the right word. Paralyzing fright isn't either. I don't know that a word exists to describe it, but I feel it as he pulls me along to the bed. He's gentle. My heels start to dig in and his grip tightens.

"No, no, no, no, no no!" I chant and pull back.

He stops and looks at me like I'm a child. "It will be much worse if I have to drag you."

A sob rips from me. There are no tears. He pulls me along. He stops moving when he's alongside the huge bed.

He pushes me down on it. "Remove the robe and scoot down to the bottom. Hang your feet down off the end."

I stare at the floor. My body is convulsing in fear.

"What is your name?" I whisper.

"Does it matter?" He sounds dry.

"Yes. I need a name to hate you properly."

"Then you must call me Eli." His name makes me twitch.

I let the robe slip from my shoulders as I climb onto the huge bed and lie back, swallowing hard again. The bed is soft and luxurious. The black blankets are soft and velvety against my skin.

My eyes feel like there is sand in them. I wish I could cry. I wiggle so my feet hang off the end.

I stare up into the canopy. It's dark like the bedding, so I pretend it's the night sky when I feel his hands touching my feet. He moves them over my feet and ankles softly, like he's letting me get used to his touch.

With a soft jerk he pulls me down to the bottom of the mattress to hang my feet off the end as he commanded. His shoes slap against the floor when he walks around the room. I don't see his hands near my face when he puts the blindfold over my eyes.

The heat from his face and hands makes goose bumps along my body. I grip the bedding.

His hands touch me again when he slides something down onto my legs. I can't move them. My feet are forced to flex out the bottom. Something is hooked around my toes. I can't move them at all.

"I don't want to mar that skin. Not yet. I'm going to start the film now. Please feel free to be extra loud. It's better for the footage." My stomach is in agony. I'm desperately gripping the bed. I want to cry out before he's even done anything.

"At anytime you can ask me to stop. Stuart will be punished then."

I bite my lip and wait for it.

He's by my face again, his fingers on my chin. He slides something into my mouth. I spit it out.

"Unless you want to bite your tongue I suggest you keep that in." I shake my head but he forces it in again. "I will tie it on."

I don't spit it out. I moan and cry, shaking my head. The terror is everywhere. The pain is going to be bad. I know it will be. I've been punished before, though I hardly recall it.

Wind rushes past the paddle, before I feel the first strike. I scream and bite down on the wooden piece in between my teeth. The shocking pain is brutal and stings long after the paddle is gone.

The wind rushes again, just before the smack but the loudest sound is my scream before he even makes contact. The searing pain rocks me.

Tears shoot from my eyes. It's bitter sweet. My eyes stop hurting but the rest of my body tenses. My legs are on fire. He's paddling the bottoms of my feet. He's going to cripple me. I'll never run away again.

❧ 10 ❧

My feet tingle.

I don't have any choice but to lie on my back on the hard concrete and keep them in the air. Any contact sends me over the edge, but it's bittersweet somehow. I suppose I had imagined he would rape me, and that would be the first time I ever had sex. A beating on the soles of the feet is far less scarring than that.

In the dark I hear my heart beating, my shaky inhale flowing from me, and a dripping noise that at first drove me insane. Now I hear a beat to it. It's musical and delightful to have company. I am less alone with the water.

The door opens and the tray scrapes along the floor. I don't look. As long as I don't hear the slapping of the shoes against the floor I'll be okay.

What does it matter anyway? I saw the daylight, I sat at a fire, I've eaten and drank, and had a bath. I laugh and realize it's almost like being at a spa. My first time.

The room takes my laugh and gives it back in an echo. It feels like there is another person here and she's laughing with me. I stop laughing when I realize there is actually another person here with me. There always is. She has never left me.

My laugh has faded, but the room still feels more alive for having been filled with it.

"Em." A whisper slips into the dark with me. I ignore it at first. It's no big deal. The dark has whispered my name before.

"Em. Did they hurt you?"

I frown and look around the room. I feel vulnerable on my back now. I sit up and wince when my feet touch the floor.

"Em. Over here." The whispered voice is coming from the corner across from me. It's so dark I can barely find the direction.

"It's me, dude. Stu." His voice is less of a whisper. I roll onto my knees and crawl across the room in the dark, with my feet dragging behind me.

"Where are you?" I put a hand out and feel for him.

His hand swipes across my knee in the darkness. It feels funny. I crawl back toward him. His hand is sticking out through a hole in the wall near the floor. Like a mouse hole.

The touch of him isn't disgusting. I don't need the sanitizer. I need the warmth of him. I lie on my belly by the hole, gripping him for dear life.

"Where's your phone, Em?" he whispers.

I shake my head. "I put it down in a parking lot. Are you okay? Are you badly hurt?"

He squeezes harder. "They said they want your phone. They need to reach him."

I shake my head. "That doesn't make any sense. The man with the fauxhawk—his name is Eli. Before he caught me I texted for help, but I think my text went to Eli—like the guy holding us hostage is your boss. I sent it and then heard it deliver at the same moment to his phone when he was chasing me. I think your boss is Eli." I'm not sure I'm making sense. I'm also not sure Stuart is really there. I've had this before. Daydreams in the dark.

He sighs. "Well, frig. I don't know then. Maybe he is the dude. Maybe fauxhawk is Uncle Daddy Weirdo. Eli seems like a weak name though. I always imagined he was cooler than a douche in sunglasses in the dark." His voice is weak, but he forces a chuckle.

"I'm sorry."

He chuckles and coughs. "Em. What did you do that could possibly have made this happen?"

My stomach twists. I shake my head. The tears block my throat up again. Emalyn's name pops up in my mind. I don't know what it means. "I'm sorry you're hurt."

He laughs again. "I fight for a living. This ain't no thing. Trust me, I got this. I can take pain like it's nobody's business." His twang is thick. I close my eyes and grip to his warmth for dear life.

We are silent and have been clutching to each other for a long time when the door to his room opens.

In the light the open door makes, I can see in his room for the first time. Through the small mouse hole, I see two men walk in and grab his feet. They pull hard. I grip to him but his hand slips from mine in a jerk.

"I'll take it. I'll take the punishment. Don't hurt him," I cry out. Stuart's face is beaten and swollen. He shakes his head. "Take me." His voice breaks.

I slap the concrete. "Take me. Please, I'll do anything." Stuart looks at me with severity. "Shut up, Em. I got this." He winks but I shake my head. "I did this."

He frowns and looks back at the men standing over him. "Ignore her." They drop his feet and walk out. He jumps up and rushes at the door. His screams fill the cell, but I can barely hear him.

The blood pounding in my head from my racing heart is blocking out the sounds, or dulling them at least. I start to sob silently when the door to my cell is opened. The men come in.

Stuart reaches through and grabs for my hand. "EM! DON'T DO THIS!" His pleas are desperate.

It's the first time I've cried in fear since I was a small child. The tears blind me. They rip from my eyes so hard and fast that they make it impossible to see anything but the blurry light. The kaleidoscopes are desperate to save me.

Hands grab at me. They carry me, struggling, out into the white light. Their hands grip and tug at me. I kick and fight but it's useless. I'm brought to a small room. It's not nice like the other one was. It looks industrial, like a bathroom or a kitchen, but without anywhere to cook. There is a huge sink and table. I stand there frozen. My feet burn but they've started to go numb. The pain of standing is too intense.

I'm shivering and freezing. I'm wearing the robe. It's not white anymore. It's dirty and damaged, like me.

The room is silent.

The cold floor feels shocking against my hot feet.

The lock turns in the door. I can't move. I can't step. My feet burn. I can't run, I have to face whatever it is.

Eli walks in. He looks the same. A silver dress shirt and black dress pants. His shoes are matte black leather with very square tips. He crosses his thick arms and smiles at me. His cocky, shitty face is the one in my nightmares. It will be there for the rest of my life.

He leans against the closed door, watching me. He is huge. I feel like a child compared to him in the small room. He runs his eyes over me. "I hear you chose to be punished, saving Stuart again?"

I swallow and watch his cold blue eyes. "Why are you doing this?"

"You need it." He shrugs. "And I like to." He pushes off the wall and walks toward me. "Don't look so horrified. Everyone enjoys the feeling of making another person feel something. Everyone."

I shake my head in jerks as he circles me.

He leans into my neck. "Even you. You like the fact that I find you attractive. You like having that power over me."

"You're insane," I whisper.

He laughs and leans in closer. His breath hits my neck, making shivers everywhere else. "I think you like that about me. We match, you and I." He runs his hand down the front of my robe, tugging at it. I whimper and grab at the cloth, clutching it together. He stands back. "I have several choices for you today."

He walks over to the large industrial sink and turns the tap on.

"We can do a little dunking in this sink."

I shudder. I can't imagine the horrors that lie in the sink.

He turns and smirks. "I can paddle your feet again. I am really hoping that's the choice you make." I cringe, but my brain is crying about the sink.

He talks louder over the rushing water. "I can go get Stuart and put you back in that comfy little cell." I shake my head on that one.

"No to Stuart then? Okay. And last offer, you can be nice to me." He licks his plump lips and lets a slight grin lift one side of his mouth. "Really nice." His cold blue eyes land on my chest. I'm hyperventilating. The sound of the sink is fogging up my brain.

I lift my hand and point at the sink.

He looks surprised. "The sink? Really? More appealing to put your face in my cook's dish sink than to let me make love to you for the first time? I could make you a woman."

I close my eyes. The shows I've seen on bacteria and dish sinks are playing a highlight reel in my mind. I nearly—very nearly—ask him to make love to me. But the idea of his body pinning mine to the bed makes me sick. He starts to roll up his sleeves. I see hints of tattoos sticking out the bottoms of the rolled sleeves. They don't match the look he has.

"Remove the robe." He sounds disappointed.

"No. Please no."

He instantly walks to the door and taps and shouts, "Bring her back and bring me Stuart!"

I spin. "NO!"

He turns back and watches me. With trembling fingers and sobbing tears streaming my burning cheeks, I pull the robe away. It drops to the floor and I swear the sound echoes. He licks his lips. I shudder again.

He walks to the sink and holds a hand out. I slouch and shuffle on my burning feet to where he stands.

He grabs the back of my neck and shoves me forward. His fingers bite into my neck, pulling at the hairs. I see things being stirred up in the water. He turns the tap off. Looking in I can see stains and old residue from whatever else has been in the sink. His hand tightens.

"Wait," I say. I don't know why. I have no intention of letting him do anything else to me.

"Yes?" His voice is hopeful.

My lip trembles. The filth in the sink is going to kill me. At the least I will be horribly ill. I shake my head. "I'll do whatever you want."

"Do you want me to make love to you?" he asks softly.

I shake my head but answer with my lips, "Yes."

He leans in. My body is on fire with shame and hatred. "I don't believe you."

His hand tightens again and shoves my face forward into the water. I scream into the dirty water for what feels like an eternity. I'm clawing at the edges but the shiny metal is slippery. His hand is strong. I run out of air and suck by accident. The dirty water fills my mouth. I don't want to inhale it. I swallow. It's cold and tastes of metal. My lungs scream.

He pulls my head up. I cough and seize up. "P-p-please." I'm panting and gasping. My stomach turns as the cold water makes its way down my throat and breasts.

His hand tightens on the back of my neck. I take a deep breath and hold it tight as the cold water sucks my face into it. I don't scream this time. I wait it out. I keep my eyes closed. I start panicking when the air gets old and my body is screaming for new oxygen.

I start the clawing again. My feet connect with his leg. I kick and claw at him. He pulls my face up. He's laughing. The edge of the sink is digging into my stomach and hipbones to the point I think they're bruising. My lower lip trembles again.

"Are you going to cry for me?"

I shake my head.

He presses his face into mine, brushing his lips against my cheek. "I want you to cry for me. Please cry."

I fight it. I fight him.

He shoves my face back into the water. I decide to be calm this time. I won't cry for him or anyone.

Something brushes against my ass cheek. I start to struggle again. His fingers caress my naked skin softly. Patting playfully. I'm freaking out. My body had fought before, but now I am thrashing and raging. I've run out of air and am sucking it in.

He lifts my head, laughing. "Well, seems like we found the magic button." He steps away from me. "Thank you for crying."

He grabs the door handle and knocks once. His cold stare will haunt me in that cell. He grins and leaves the room.

I'm humiliated and choking on the filthy water. I grab the robe and pull it on. I can't stop the tears. I can't get away from the filthy feeling that's covering me. Some of it's the water, but a lot of it is his hand roaming freely.

I grip the robe and hobble back to the room on the arms of the men. The darkness of my cell is a comfort. For the first time ever I am relishing being alone.

"You okay, Em?" Stuart asks from the hole between our cells.

I shake my head in the blackness of the room. I can't form words. I know he will understand. I suspect he's felt the same a few times. God knows what they've done to him.

I close my eyes and sleep. I'm safe and grateful to be alone. I never imagined I would ever feel that way. But I do. I become one of the things that hide in the darkness.

The door opens. The light doesn't bother me anymore. I don't fight them when they come for me.

I stand and walk proud. I refuse to limp or cower. I won't let them have the satisfaction of knowing my pain. My pain is private. It's the only thing I have left that is.

His hands have touched me, beaten me, and tried to drown me. I will never cry for him again. I have decided this in the dark.

I walk past the blurry windows, noticing I've stopped caring about what city I'm in.

There is nothing left inside me. I've drank sink water and sat in a room with my own waste. I've eaten from the floor like a dog. I have nothing left.

I'm not even a shell of a girl anymore.

Even the dead girl is gone, left me in the dark at some point. I think I was sleeping when she snuck off. I woke and I knew she wasn't there. I've slipped so far down, that there isn't anything left.

I'm taken to the bathroom and cleaned. I don't cower or fight the girl. I stand there, hollow and alone. She cleans me quickly, softly. She has delicate hands. I hate the mercy they show me and the pity in her eyes.

I'm given a new robe. I look at the filthy one being thrown into the bin and feel like I'm leaving a friend behind when we walk out.

She walks next to me, not holding my hand or touching me.

She opens the door to the room with the fireplace.

My belly aches. My feet clench on the hardwood when I see the bed.

He's sitting on the couch with his legs wide, like he always does. He looks striking and harsh, exactly what he is. I don't cower for him. There is nothing left for him to do to me.

She leaves and I stand, terrified but stubborn.

His cocky grin creeps across his lips. "I've seen that girl before." His eyes are lit with flames and excitement. "You ready to wrestle?"

My right eye twitches. The fear inside me is real. No matter how much I hate him or try to hide it, the pain is going to be real.

"Go sit by the fire." He points.

I turn my back on him and walk to it. I kneel on the warm rug and wait.

He pulls out a book and starts to read. It's *Dracula*. Bram Stoker's *Dracula*. My knees start to hurt but I sit. He turns the pages slowly, like he is savoring the feel of every word and maybe even the texture of the pages.

He drinks from the glass next to him. I lick my lips. The water looks refreshing. He glances at me. "Want some water?"

I watch him. He shrugs and chugs back the drink. He sighs at the end and nods. "That was good. Hint of lemon in it."

I hate him.

He lifts the book again and continues. My feet feel like they're going to explode so I sit on my butt. My legs are crossed and pulled in tightly. I don't want them even an inch closer to him than they need to be.

The fire is burning my back, but it's better than sitting near him.

"Is there anything you want to know?" he asks over the edge of the book.

"Why am I here?"

"I like you here. I like to read and know you're close by. It's comforting."

I watch his eyes; they're so familiar. "Do I know you?"

They squint into a smile. "Do you think you know me?"

I shake my head. "I'm confused. You act like you hate me and want me to suffer, like this is personal, but you have Stuart convinced it's about his boss."

He lowers the book. "Maybe it's both."

"No." I shake my head. "It never was about him. It's me. This is personal. You are doing this to me for a reason."

He folds the book closed and crosses his arms. "What reason could there be? You're Emalyn Spicer, right?"

I flinch.

He laughs. "I guess we both know that's not your name, is it?"

I hate him. I hate that he says her name. He has no right. My heartbeat is picking up. Just when I think I have a steady calm and can control the moment and my emotions, he pulls something new out of the hat.

"Why do you care what my name is?" I whisper.

He stands and walks to me. He puts a hand out. I hesitate and then lift my hand and put it in his. He wraps it tightly around mine and pulls me to the bed.

"Which is it?"

I glance at him.

He raises his dark eyebrows. "The feet or you let me have you."

My stomach aches. My feet and brain are both begging me to just let him do it. I shake. "Feet." My voice is gone. My body disagrees.

I undo the robe and let it fall to the floor. I climb onto the bed and lie back with my feet hanging over the edge. I don't care about the nudity or the blindfold that is placed on my eyes. The pain I'm about to experience is killing me. My whole body is tense and twitching. My legs are locked into position. I hear the air brushing the paddle as it's swung.

"STOP!" I scream.

My hands are balls of sweat, clutching the blankets.

"I will let you have me," I say in desperate gasps. "Just do it."

"You want me?" he asks. He's breathing heavily. "Say it!" he shouts at me.

My lips tremble. "I want you."

The paddle drops to the floor, making loud noises. My feet are freed. I lift my hands to the blindfold but he barks, "Don't move." I freeze and lower my hands. I'm shaking.

"Slip back up the bed to the pillows and lie there." His voice sounds weird. I do it. I notice everything. The room smells like the fireplace and a subtle cleaner or essential oils. The bed is soft and more comfortable than anything I've ever slept on. The air is warm against my naked skin. I feel more naked suddenly. I don't know where he is. I don't hear him at all. I lick my lips and wait. It's more torture than anything in the entire world.

My body is a tense ball of nerves.

I wait for what feels like an eternity but he doesn't touch me. A small hint of curiosity disguised as worry niggles around inside me.

Was he waiting for me to ask him to do it and then not going to? Is everything a game or is this waiting the punishment today?

In the silence of the room I hear something. It's the flipping of a page. He's reading.

I'm lying here naked, alone, and terrified, and he's reading? By the fire? I don't know what to say or do.

The blindfold across my eyes itches a bit. The comfort of the bed feels wasted by the fact I'm stuck lying in one position.

The air is warm but I'm shivering with expectancy. I hear a page slowly turn again. He pours himself more water. I can hear the echo of it in the glass. He drinks. I lick my lips again.

He has me fixated on the water and the fire and the book. I never wanted to lose my virginity this way, or any way. But he's got me so confused I forget that fact. I forget to focus on the fear of what he might do because I am so thirsty.

I feel something I'm not sure I've ever felt before, frustration. I'm not sure where it comes from, but it's deep inside me.

Stockholm syndrome might be setting in. I'm disappointed the man holding me hostage is drinking water and tormenting me, instead of just doing the thing he threatened, and then giving me some of that delicious sounding water.

I've officially lost my mind.

He drinks and I can imagine the glass of water against my lips.

Something is happening to me. I'm about to ask for the foot paddling just so I can have a drink, when I hear him get up. He walks softly in my direction. His shoes are gone. His steps are soft.

His weight on the bed starts my stomach burning. He grabs my right foot and starts to rub softly. I part my lips, about to beg for water but I don't. I know what's about to happen is going to be the most horrible thing that can. It isn't worth a glass of cold lemon water.

I notice the way he's pulled my leg, separating it from the other. My breathing is faint and jagged. His is even.

His hands traipse their way up my calf, still rubbing and massaging. Something warm and soft brushes my leg, just above the knee. When it's gone the spot feels cold.

It was his mouth.

I tremble as his hands work their way up to my thigh. I'm about to burst with a terrible scream, begging him to stop and just paddle me, but I don't.

His mouth is on my thigh. I gasp. It's not just in horror. It's in shock as well. He chuckles and I feel sick again.

He is gone and air is all there is between my legs. I don't feel his clothing pressing against my naked skin or his warmth. I don't feel his weight on the bed at all.

"Are you ashamed of yourself?" he whispers.

I shake my head but it's a lie. I am desperately ashamed.

"What's the worst thing that can happen right now?"

I need him to stop talking. My eyes are squeezed shut. I don't want to answer him. I know the answer but I can't say it.

"What's the worst thing?"

"You rape m-m-me," I mutter into the darkness.

"You asked me to do it. Doesn't that change things? You said you wanted me," he says softly.

I feel my lips curl into a sneer. I did. I asked him to. I offered myself up for water.

The air is cold somehow, even with the heat. I shiver. He places something on me. I feel with my fingers. It's the other side of the blanket I am lying on. He's wrapped me up.

I hear his silent footsteps and the door. I am alone. I curl into a ball and grip the covers. The tears start. I pull away the blindfold.

He is there beside me, sitting in a chair beside the bed. His face is sad. I stop crying, scared of what the next thing is. I didn't hear him come back in. Maybe he never left. Maybe I'm hearing things.

"Why are you crying?" he asks. "You don't know, do you?"

I shake my head.

He leans forward. "I would never have hurt you like that, but if I had, it wouldn't have been the end of you. I need you to see that. You've survived everything else. So much more than any human can fathom. You think one act can destroy all the strength you have? You think being raped in a hole can ruin a girl? You think being beaten can destroy the strength inside you? You truly believe that there is no worth in you because of the filth you still feel upon your skin?"

I shudder from the tears and the heaving sobs. I shake my head.

His blue eyes burn suddenly. He climbs onto the bed and wraps himself around me.

He's insane, but I think I am too because his words make sense to me.

❧ 12 ❧

I wake up in the cell. He's moved me somehow and I didn't notice.

"Stuart," I whisper.

He doesn't answer me. I crawl along the floor, slightly disoriented. When I reach the hole in the wall my arm bumps against something.

It scratches on the floor and scares me. I jump back. I reach out slowly, terrified of what it is.

It's flat. When I get a grip on it I sigh.

It's my cell phone. I push the button to turn the power on. It shows the apple and makes a dim light in the cell.

I'm more scared with the light there. It makes shadows. I see my white robe in the light. I never even noticed it was there. My comfort in my skin is different than before.

I turn the phone when it comes on and shine the light in the hole to the room next to me. There is a bed and a toilet. His cell is much nicer than mine. I'm not angry. I'm grateful he has those things but worried that he isn't in the room.

I scuttle back to my corner and tuck my feet under me. My phone starts to vibrate like mad. Seventy-five messages. My eyes widen.

I start reading Shell's.

Em, I'm so sorry. I shouldn't have said and done that. I'm so glad I came with you. Please don't be mad.

Dude, I said sorry. What do you want blood?

Em, why aren't these delivering?

Did you for-reals turn the phone off?

I saw Sebastian today. It's been like a week since I got home and you aren't texting me. I told him your number. I don't even care if Uncle Daddy Weirdo gets mad. Sebastian is a mess, dude. Destroyed. He is so upset. He flew all the way here to find you. From Maine, dude.

I CAN'T BELIEVE YOU'RE BEING SO SEFLISH AND PETTY AND IGNORING ME! DO YOU HAVE ANY IDEA HOW HARD IT IS TO TEXT AND HOLD THE CAPSLOCK?

Emmmmmmmmmmm, don't hate me.

I miss you.

Now you're making me scared. This is fucking bitchy, dude.

Oh and Merry Christmas, Asshole!

I lower the phone. My heart burns and hurts. I start to cry.

I look around the dark and feel more lost than before. I start to feel rage burning inside me. I tilt my head up and shout, "I want out." I scream, "I WANT OUT YOU ASSHOLE. ELI, YOU SICK MOTHER FUCKER, I WANT OUT!" I sob and lean into the wall. I almost throw the phone but I stop myself.

No one comes. My tears dry and I start reading the texts again.

Emalyn, you are being so mean. I'm scared. Please just text and tell me you're okay.

The next message is from me. *She doesn't have this phone now. Please stop texting.*

YOU SICK SON OF A BITCH! IF YOU HAVE DONE ANYTHING TO HER I'LL KILL YOU WITH MY BARE HANDS!

I'll let her know you messaged her.

FUCK YOU!

I snort.

I go back to the menu and find Sebastian's. I assume they're his. They have only a number and no name.

Em? Is this you?

Sorry but I found Michelle yesterday in Clovis. I got your number. I hope you're okay with this.

I just wanted to say sorry. I never should have left. I've tried coming by the dorm but you're never there. The guy at the gym said he hasn't seen you and Michelle said she hasn't heard from you. I'm getting worried.

You're that angry? Michelle is getting scared. She phoned the police yesterday. You're officially a missing person. My heart is broken I think. I have so many things I need to tell you.

You've been missing for two weeks. I'm coming for you. I will find you.

She doesn't have this phone anymore. Please stop texting.

Who is this? Where is she?

I will let her know you messaged her.

Where is she? If you have her or hurt her I will kill you.

I don't want to read the hopelessness in their messages. I look around in the dark and start to plot. I guess it's another thing about the dark. It's perfect for plotting.

When I realize my plotting is petty and entirely based on super-heroes and the desperate hope Sebastian is one, I sigh and give up. I open my conversation with Eli. I can see the little writing thingy. He is messaging me as I look at it.

He is watching me. It's *1984* in so many ways.

How are things?

I shake my head. *I hate you. How could you do this to Stuart and me? Why did you do this?*

I need you to hurt and cry. I need those things from you.

The answer is as messed up as everything else that's happened. I shake my head. *You're sick. I'll never cry for you again.*

Don't make promises you can't keep.

I dial 911 but the service is cut. The texts are working because of the Wi-Fi. I feel like an idiot. All this time he was there for me and helping me, but it was all to what end? This? Alone in a cell, flogged, beaten, humiliated? I don't understand.

I crawl to where the hole is and lie on my side. I reach through and pretend I can feel the warmth of Stuart's hand against mine. There is no defense for the stupidity I am guilty of. The words of Sister Elizabeth bounce around in my head, *Nothing is ever free, Emalyn. Nothing. At some point you pay for everything.* I have a horrid feeling I might be paying for things I can't remember.

I fall asleep with my back to the open air of the room and my hand in the hole. It's huge for me. I have nothing left to lose. No one can hurt me more than I have already been.

My sleep and dreams are restless and chaotic. I wake with my face against the cement. I move my hand and have a small panic attack. It brings something with it from a place I've sealed off in my mind.

The hole.

I have the strangest feeling like I'm in the hole. I move my hand like I'm reaching for the sunshine. The cold cement and the darkness make me shiver. I can feel the bugs crawling on me. I scramble up and begin brushing my body off.

I hated falling asleep in the hole. My skin is crawling.

My whimpers and cries fill the darkness.

I back up, scrambling and swiping at my robe. Pressing my back against the wall, I take gulps of air. I feel the walls of the corner and feel better.

"I'm not in the hole. I'm not in the hole." I shake my head. The hole had no corners.

Whatever is attached to the hole memory is fuzzy and bad. My brain shuts down. It doesn't let me see any further behind the curtain than that.

I clutch my cell phone and press the power button.

The Apple sign and the light make me feel better. I'm exhausted and done. I open our conversation and text.

I want to go home. I don't want your money and help. I just want to be free.

Where will you go? His response is fast. Like he knew I would text him.

My stomach hurts when I think about it. *Women's shelter? Convent? A suburb where I can make a new life for myself. Anywhere I can to get away from you.*

That's hurtful, considering I am the only person you have in the world.

I would laugh. If I weren't sitting in the dark smelling my own piss and feeling disturbed and disgusted at the thought of what you'll do to me next. I look at it, read it over again, and press send. My stomach hurts being so sassy. *Whatever it is, you can't hurt me anymore.*

The phone vibrates with a FaceTime call. His call. I take a moment and answer it.

"Hi." He's acting like we are friends again. The anxiety is killing me. His face is bright and clean. "Where will you go without me?" He sounds different than before.

It's Eli, but it's not the voice of my benefactor who has talked to me all this time. I'm so confused. I'm scared that Uncle Daddy Weirdo is hurt and Eli has captured him as well.

I can't stop staring at him, plotting. "I need to go. Please. I can't do this anymore. Can you just finish torturing me all at once so I can be free?"

"Go to the door and wait. I will come and get you. It's almost New Year's Eve." He looks at me one last time and then the screen freezes.

I put the phone down, confused. There is no way it's only New Year's.

The door opens.

I see his hand.

I stand on my shaky legs and walk to him.

He drags me down the hall. It's toward the bathroom. He opens the door. It's light and bright and empty.

"Clean up." I look at him, checking for the joke or the twist in the plot. He steps back. I walk into the bathroom and close the door slowly. I watch his face in the gap as I close it. I click the lock and sigh.

I climb into the huge shower and turn it on to hot and let it scald my skin. There are things that try to flash into my mind in the shower, but I push them back. Something about his face is there still, picking at me.

I wash myself and shave everything and triple rinse. I was feeling like a wooly mammoth. I climb out, pruned and beet red.

I pull on the clean robe that's folded on the counter and leave the bathroom. He is standing in the hallway. "Were you there the entire time?" I ask.

"I was."

"Scared I'd get away?"

He laughs and shakes his head. I catch myself noticing his dimple.

"No. I stayed in case you were scared of being alone." His kindness puts me off.

"I am alone." I hate him. No one has ever inflicted the kind of pain he has on me. He tried to drown me. I need to remember that. I am dead inside because of him.

He holds his hand out. I take it. I don't know why. He walks beside me, still leading. He opens a door to a hallway I've never seen. I look around. "Is this place like a whole floor of a building? It's weird with all the hallways."

His eyes sparkle. He brings me to a room with a dark-purple bed and regular furniture. He turns and leaves. I'm confused.

The bed is big and inviting. I climb up onto it and rest my head on the oversized pillow. I'm so tired my eyes burn. They flutter, and in the flashes of light I see him again. I open my eyes. He crawls onto the bed with me and smiles, but he looks different now. He looks kind. I don't know what game we are about to play, but I am too tired to fight it.

"There is something important we need to talk about." His being nice scares me. I'm prepared for his behavior when he's acting like a psychotic serial killer, but his kindness is alarming.

"I think you're bipolar. You need help. You can't act like a serial killer one moment and then a nice person the next. It's disconcerting." I shake my head. "And I'm too tired to be this confused. If you're going to kill me, just do it. I don't care anymore. I'm done."

"You're prepared to die?"

"Yes." I nod and swallow. "I am dead. You have killed everything inside me."

"Have you ever feared I would kill you?"

I shake my head. "No." I'm too tired to lie, but I manage to squeak that one out.

"Liar."

I smile and think about Sebastian. I would die a thousand deaths to be in his arms, in his penthouse, eating that damned meal the chef prepared. If I ever get out, I'm hunting his ass down and forcing him to repeat that night. I need a do-over.

Eli lies beside me and sighs. "If you had one wish, what would it be?"

"I don't know. To be normal, I guess." There is no guess. It's been my wish since I was tiny.

He kisses the top of my head. "You wanted to know why I cared what your name was?"

I nod against his soft lips pressed against my forehead. I'm too tired to panic.

"My sister was named Emalyn. Her last name wasn't Spicer though. The Spicers were the couple that kidnapped us both when we were very small. They took us to a farm where they had a feral little girl."

I close my eyes, trying to hide from the words but I can't. They rush in, pushing me and forcing me to see. The silent tears burst from my eyes, and no matter how hard I press them shut, I break my vow to never cry for him again.

The memories start slowly and build quickly. "You are the boy in the hole," I whisper, terrified. "From the dirty house. Eli? That was your name?"

He nods against me, trembling.

"You saved me," I whisper again. I feel like we are in my dark cell, both of us trapped there. "I was the feral little girl. I killed your sister."

The words force the curtain down. The floodgates burst, bringing everything with it. Every memory is running forward and backward, until I am stuck with only one image. It's him standing in the room with the dead girl, holding his hand out to me. It was the first time he had ever done that to me. It was the first time anyone had ever done that to me.

I curl into myself and cry until I sleep.

᪥ 13 ᪥

My eyes flutter a bit. The warmth of him is still there.

I'm frozen. Not in the darkness but in genuine fear.

The tables have turned on me. I am the one who wronged him. I am the one who owes him. I am the one who broke him. I deserve every injury he inflicted upon me. I deserve so much more than what he has done to me.

I have done this to myself.

I murdered his sister.

His name is Eli and he saved me, even after I murdered his sister. He held his hand out and took mine in it. He pulled me to safety with my hand that was coated in his sister's blood.

I glance up to find his eyes closed. In his sleep I see the face of the boy so clearly, I can't believe I missed it.

He blinks and looks down on me. He smiles and it breaks my heart. My nose wrinkles involuntarily.

He laughs softly and squeezes me. The dimple. Of course I remember the dimple. The dimple, the icy-blue eyes, the dark hair, the hand reaching for me.

He moans. "We haven't slept beside each other in fourteen years, and it still feels the same." He says it so softly and sweetly I could be sick.

I hate myself in a thousand different ways.

He kisses my forehead. Slowly he works his way down to my cheek. He kisses and moves on to my nose. I close my eyes, making a single tear creep down my face. He kisses my tear. "You're safe now," he whispers.

I don't know what that means. I can't speak. I don't know why he's touching me or what sick moment this is we are having, but I want out.

"I never blamed you. I saw what was happening. I saw you make the choice to try to save her."

I shake my head.

I'm so ashamed. "I can't do this," I mutter and curl into him, trying desperately to hide. I'm craving darkness and being alone. "Put me back in the cell," I say quietly. "Just kill me."

He holds me to him. "No. You need to tell me the things you remember. I know you remember them now. I can see it."

I'm aching in every place I can. "The Grand Canyon," I whisper. My tears are leaving dark spots on his dress shirt.

"What else?"

"The dirty house."

"What else?"

I squeeze my eyes shut. "My name."

He holds me tight to him. We are almost one person, we are so close.

"Do you see why I brought you here?"

I sob.

"Why?" he demands.

Heaving sobs leave my lips, "To punish me for helping them. For killing her. For stealing her name and pretending to be her. You want revenge and you deserve it."

He grabs my face and lifts it. "No. No you're missing the point." His voice cracks as he climbs off the bed, looking savagely angry. He paces like a madman then looks at me and shakes his head, bewildered. I don't know what I've done wrong this time, unless the anger is left over from everything else. Then it's justified. "Don't you see? All of it is so obvious?"

I shake my head.

He grabs the footboard and shakes the bed. "GODDAMMIT! I'M TRYING TO SAVE YOU! I'M TRYING TO FREE YOU!" He takes a breath and calms himself, but when he speaks again he sounds completely exhausted, "All of this has been planned to free you. You were never going to get better."

My breath has reached a new level of ragged despair.

"You were always trapped in that house. You never left it. You took her life and never lived it. She would have wanted you to live, Sarah. You've hidden it all away and punished yourself for something that was never your fault. Don't you see that?"

My name hurts me.

I pull the blankets up to my lips. The kaleidoscopes in my eyes make angles and sharp points in the bright light of the room and the severe look on his face. I realize he has never said my name before. He has never ever called me Emalyn. All along he knew I wasn't Emalyn. This is the first time he has addressed me by a name, and it's my real one. Confusion and darkness make my heart beat in my throat and my stomach threaten to spill.

He points at me. "You will tell me the story. Now you choose how you want it: by the fire, in the dark cell, in the tub, or in the bed." His voice is demanding and desperate.

"The dark," I whisper.

He nods and holds a hand out. I climb from the bed and stumble to his hand. He grips me tightly and drags me to the door. He pulls and jerks my hand until we reach the cell. He flings open the door and drags me inside. He slams the door shut, making an echo in the dark.

I creep to my corner and sit. Stuart doesn't try to talk to me. I press my back into the corner and slip down the wall. I'm scared of where he is. Eli is insane. His sadness and grief and torment have made him crazy. Not that he doesn't have a reason. Now I'm the one making excuses, giving him the "doing-well" Band-Aid and pity.

I can hear his feet on the floor. He's pacing still. His breath is ragged.

I close my eyes and see it all. The sunshine and the way it made her blonde hair glisten. The smile on her sweet face. I feel sick. I'm crippled by guilt and pain and sorrow. I look down and feel the tears drip onto my hands. My hands that I have tried so hard to clean, and yet here they are, still covered in her blood.

My voice is blank when I speak, "I think they—the Spicers—had been doing it a long time. I don't know if I was theirs or if they had taken me too. I don't have very many memories before you came. I don't remember a family other than them. I remember other kids at the house though. They would stay for a short time and then be gone, and Randy would start to get edgy and angry. I remember I was in the hole for days before we met you and Emalyn. At least I think it was days."

I whisper my next words, "I can see the picture so clearly—the way the hole skewed my view of the world." I know he knows what the hole is. I remember seeing his bright-blue eyes looking down at me through the gap between the board and the ground. His desperate blue eyes.

I'm grateful I can't see his face now as I continue to confess to the darkness and the pacing footsteps. "Laura, my mom, pulled back the lid and dragged me out. Said we were going for a car ride. I was shaking, I was so hungry and thirsty. I would have done anything for water, just water." My voice breaks with sickening guilt and harsh pain. I'm dying inside. My brain is working against me, changing the memories. It is my own desperate attempt to push it all away and make everything tidy again. But I know what I would do for a glass of water.

I cringe and speak softly still, unable to raise my voice with strength or bravery. My shame is too heavy for that. "We got to the Grand Canyon the next day, but I never got to see anything. I remember there were crowds of people, and I could just make out the canyons through their legs and bodies as they walked. It was all I ever saw of it all. Laura dragged me around the whole time. Pulling me after them. He picked her—he picked your sister. He knelt down next to me, and he whispered with his whiskey breath that he wanted her. He asked me if I wanted her too. I did. I said I did. I didn't want to be alone anymore. I never saw you, just her. She was shiny and pretty and clean. So clean. Then they dragged me back to the car. Laura took me back the next day. I got to see the canyons through the legs and sea of people for a second before she made me go play in the sand with your sister."

My voice wavers but I force the next part out, "The next day we were home you guys were there with me at the dirty house. At first I was in the hole. I remember your frightened blue eyes. You were screaming something at me and wouldn't calm down. So they took me out of the hole and put you in it. Your sister was allowed to play with me for a couple days. I shared my bed with her and my dolls, but she didn't want them. She cried. She cried all the time." My throat gets thick. I can't say anymore. I just can't. I want to retch. I would cut out my tongue before I would say any more.

I twitch from the horror crawling around on my skin, like the bugs in the hole.

His voice breaks the silence and he continues my story. He is the only other person who could know it. "They put me in the hole. He kissed Em and made her cry and you didn't even notice. I remember you. You played alone and quiet in the corner. Always in corners. You acted like you didn't hear the screaming or the crying, but I saw you. The panic and the denial. It was all over you. Emalyn wouldn't stop screaming. You put the toys down and I saw you go inside. I heard the shot and the screams. I couldn't get out of the hole and you were screaming. Laura was screaming. I finally got the board off and scrambled out of the hole. When I got inside, Randy was hitting you and Emalyn was dead on the bed."

I can't cry.

I'm stuck in the moment.

My voice wavers, "I missed. He was so big and fat and I missed. Somehow I hit her. She was so little compared to him." I can see her face looking at me from the bed—the way I see it every time I look in the mirror. Her dead-fish eyes see through me.

"I grabbed the gun from the floor and fired the shot you had meant to. I turned and fired another shot. Laura dropped to the floor. I dropped the gun." His voice is soft and scared like mine.

I whisper, "You saved me. I tried so hard to save her and I couldn't, and even then you still saved me."

He crosses the floor. He drops to his knees in front of me. He grabs my hands and holds them tight. "But don't you see, you did. The thing he was going to do to her would have been worse because afterward he would have killed her anyway. He killed all the others, Sarah. All of them. We lived. We made it out. And nothing they ever did to us can change the strength inside us. We aren't victims, we're survivors."

"But I missed him, somehow. Somehow the bullet hit her." I cry and pull my hands from him. "I'm so sorry. I'm sorry." I cover my face and cry harder than I ever have.

He wraps himself around me and tries to shelter me from it all. All the memories. He kisses my head. "We ran and hid. We stayed together in that barn for all those days, remember?"

"I went to sleep and you were gone. Where did you go?" I ask softly. I'm out of tears too quickly and lost in the sickness of the things I have done to survive.

"I went for the police. I told them everything. I tried to come back for you. I tried to find you. But you were gone." His voice is dull.

"Did you tell them about how I shot her?"

He nods. "I told them what you were doing and what was happening. They saw it all. The other bodies. The hole. Everything."

I feared the prison cell they would put me in more than anything. "I have to turn myself in," I whisper. I no longer fear cells. I no longer fear anything.

He shakes his head. "They know who you are, Sarah. You're the only one who doesn't."

I start to freeze up. The dark isn't as comfortable with that statement hiding in here with me. "Who am I?" I'm not sure I want to know I am the daughter of serial-killing rapists. I blocked it out for a reason. My lip trembles and I can't breathe, but I manage the sentence I need to say, "Eli. I am so sorry I stole her name. I didn't want the police to know who I was. I didn't want to be the girl who left Emalyn for dead. If I was her then she got out. I left me there on the bed. Sarah died and Emalyn lived."

He puts a finger on my lips. I almost pull away but I don't. "You were a six-year-old. You were barely alive when I met you." He kisses the top of my head and turns, pulling me down the hallway. He walks toward the door. He drags me through, and in the light I see him differently. He is the boy who saved me. He looks like he did then. He doesn't look mean and angry. But he has to be crazy. He tortured me. That's not normal. I have to remember that.

I tug on his hands to get away.

"You are not a bad person. Trust me, I know you better than anyone." He turns and looks down on me. "Is it me you're scared of?"

"You hurt me. You don't know me. I know I hurt you first and so you owed me that, but the fact remains that you hurt me—you could hurt me."

"It's not what you think." He shakes his head. "I will explain. I swear it." He smiles and I see clarity in his eyes that I don't understand. He is crazy, but he isn't a shell of a human like me. In some way I want to be him. I want to be better than him. I want to be whole again.

He pulls me down another hall I've never seen. He opens a tall, narrow door to an office. It's cluttered with documents and books everywhere.

He moves some papers and turns a large leather chair for me and pats it. I grip my robe and sit down. I'm shaking and scared.

He walks around to the other side of the desk and sits. He rifles through some things, wriggling his lips until his eyes brighten up. He grabs a paper and holds it for me to see.

I glance at the headline.

"Two-year-old Sarah Mastermen missing from Chicago Hospital."

I frown. "Me? I sort of assumed I was a Spicer like them."

He shakes his head. "No. You had some teeth removed and filled, and they stole you from the hospital. It was a simple surgery. Your parents were in the waiting room."

I read the article and look up at him. "Do they know that I'm—?" What am I? A murderer and a psychotic mess?

He nods his head slowly. "Yes. They know the basics. You're alive and not ready to see them. We needed to crack the memories before we risked telling them anything else. In case they came looking for you, before we had the chance to do all of this."

"They wouldn't want me back. I'm a murderer," I mutter. "I'm responsible for luring those kids."

He slides one of his huge hands along my cheek. "You are so close, Sarah. So close to fixing it all. Stop going backward."

I glance at the wall behind him. It has my name on it with a list. I frown. "You were tracking the things wrong with me?" I ask, walking to the wall.

"Dr. Bradley is the best in memory recovery and PTSD. She helped me. She deals with extreme cases of hostage situations or kidnappings —people like us who need to learn to see the world again. Who need to see that the things we've done aren't who we are. Sometimes you're made to do something you don't want to. That doesn't make you guilty of it."

I look at him. "You knew where I was all along? You've been watching me? You left me there all this time?"

He crosses his arms. "No. I didn't know where you were. You made it to Clovis before the police could find you. I searched high and low for you."

I narrow my eyes. "How? How did you find me then?"

"Random luck actually. Or fate, rather. Emalyn is a pretty rare name, but combined with the name of the people who ruined my life. It was a breeze once I saw it. When you wrote that article in eleventh grade about wastewater management, it came across my desk. Someone in one of our companies thought it was an interesting article and take on things from the perspective of the youth. I almost died of a heart attack when I saw that name. The combination. I flew out immediately."

I look around the room and shake my head. "My article? From school? What do you do?"

"I'm a business man. I work with my family. This isn't our office. It's Dr. Bradley's."

"How are you so rich? None of this is making sense. Not that it ever has."

"I was born rich, Sarah. Emalyn and I were with our parents that day because they were telling us they were getting a divorce. It was our family's first outing together in months. We were so excited. We didn't know they had brought us there to tell us the bad news." His eyes twitch with the memories.

I close my eyes. He touches me, making me flinch away from his hand. He grabs firmly and pulls me into his embrace.

"I spent a couple years watching you. Studying you. I know everything about you. I know what you hide and who you are. I brought your file to Dr. Bradley, but she was fearful that you were completely submerged in the Emalyn Spicer character you had made. The life of the little lost orphan you had created. We created this abduction and reality to help you."

I push him away. "You tortured me and hurt me to help me?" I ask incredulously.

"Yes. It was the only way. We thought maybe the relationship with Sebastian would help trigger things, but when you ended it we knew. There was no other way. Studies have shown that victims who are at the brink of death and lose everything, find peace all over again. They gain a coping mechanism and a new outlook on life. A new life. The new leaf you wanted so badly. The freedom you were willing to die for."

I feel sick and horrified, and yet still deserving of everything he did to me.

His blue eyes watch me. "I have things, quirks if you will, that are left over from the things that happened to us both. My quirks prevented me from living a normal life. Even close to normal. Sometimes they still do." He swallows and takes a moment before continuing. "The nightmares were brutal for a long time. My uncle knew Dr. Bradley. He knew I needed help. No one believed me or that you were real. No one. The Spicers were sick people who tortured and murdered little girls. They never left one alive. You were my imaginary friend to everyone else. The girl who shot Emalyn. Everyone thought I had made you up to deal with the fact that I had accidentally shot my own sister while trying to kill the Spicers."

I gasp. I never thought he might be blamed. I still see him as the little boy in so many ways. I can't imagine him trying to explain me to them. The hopelessness he must have felt.

He brushes my hair from my face. "You ran so fast and so far that we couldn't find you. Not even a trace of you. When you did get caught living on the streets, they never imagined you were tied with the Spicer file. It was so far away. No one clued in that you were a girl missing from Chicago because you weren't close to where you had been abducted from, and it had been five years. You looked so different. No one had any idea of who you were and no Emalyn Spicer was missing. You were missed in the system."

I get lost staring into his blue eyes, reliving the horror of it all. "I climbed into the back of a truck. I thought you had left me. I didn't blame you. After what I'd done I understood." The memories are there like they were then—fresh and I'm still covered in blood and filth. He is looking down and shaking his head.

He glances at me through his lashes and grins. "When I found you, they all had to apologize. All of them. I am crazy, but I never imagined you. And I never forgot you."

"Why did you do all this?" I ask. It's the question I should have asked all along. "Why do you even care if I'm a mess?"

"You wished to be normal more than anything in the whole world. You were so broken and no one knew how to help you. The orphanage didn't know how to help you because they didn't know what you had been through. But I do. I get it."

"How did you know what I wished for?"

He runs his hand down my cheek again. "I watched you nonstop for two years. There isn't a thought in your mind that I can't read on your face." He bends and brushes his lips against mine so softly. The kiss is intimate. I'm scared of intimacy but I'm not scared of him. Not anymore. I don't understand why he kissed me. Why he does anything. I want to go back into the dark of the cell.

"What do we do now? Where do I go?" I ask. I feel lost and overwhelmed. I don't know how to find normal from where I'm standing. I've never felt more broken.

"You go back to school and start over. New year, new leaf, new you."

I shake my head and snuggle in closer to him. "I don't want to. Can I stay here?" I don't want anyone to see me or know the things I've done. "Can I go back in my cell?"

He chuckles. His laugh reminds me of the creepy guy kissing my thigh. It makes me shudder. I push it away and just see him as he is. I don't want to think about the things he's done either.

He clears his throat. "Sarah, you are a master of denial. No one is as good as you are. I don't want you wasting this. You need to work on you for a while."

"No." I don't want to face a world where I did any of those things. I shake my head.

He lifts my chin. "You have to actually live that life you want."

"I can't." I glance up at him. "I don't know how to live with what I've done."

He nods. "You will. I want you to start figuring things out. It's a long road from here but you can do it. You know the truth now. No more pretending."

I don't believe him. It might be that I don't want to. I want to bury my head back in the sand.

14

The doctor's office feels different. So do I.

It's been weeks of pacing the office and processing everything. While some things have improved, many things have worsened.

"You're sitting in a chair with your back to the window," Dr. Bradley says and sips her glass of water. I look behind me and notice I am.

I turn and look back at her. "I guess so."

She smiles. "That's an improvement."

I nod. "Yup." Her smiles and approval don't measure up to what they did before.

"Is the lonely still coming?"

I shake my head. "No." I don't tell her that it abandoned me in the dark.

"Do you feel more free?"

"Free?" I bite my lips and do an inventory of feelings. "In some respects. I'm not scared if that's what you mean. But that's because I don't care. If I die tomorrow it won't matter. Nothing can hurt like it did before. Nothing can ruin me the way my past has."

"You know that's not true. You have friends and a family you need to meet. If you died you would never meet them." She is still testing me.

I sigh and nod. "I guess. I just feel so stripped bare. One good thing though is I don't feel like washing my hands all the time. It doesn't matter if I do or not. They won't ever come clean." I lean forward and take the glass of water in my hand. Her eyes widen. I sip from it and even stick my fingers into the water to fish out the cucumber slice. I take a bite. There is a moment where it's hard to chew, but I force myself. I want to show her I am strong. I don't know why.

"That was a bold statement. But you know that's not true. You aren't tainted with the death of Emalyn." She nods.

"No. I don't know that. But I do know I don't have to worry about the germs because that was never what I was trying to wash off. It's the same as the corners. I don't need them. I'm not in the hole. I'll never be there again."

She watches me. "You don't seem happier, Sarah."

I grin and laugh. "I'm not. My brain was forgetting those things for a reason. You and Eli made me remember them, and now instead of dealing with them slowly, one at a time, they're all in my face. I don't know where to put them all. I can't make them go away so I'm numb. It's like I'm refusing to look. Like I know the facts, but I don't want to feel them." The words sort of fall out dramatically.

She folds her arms. "That's excellent. The way you described that was excellent. You are still trying to put things in their places then? Make things tidy?"

We have had the same conversations for weeks. I'm almost ready to attack her. Instead, I laugh and have another sip of the refreshingly cold water. "I am. I'm better in some ways, but I can't get rid of thirteen years of training and discipline." Sometimes I miss the simplicity of the cell and the beatings.

She taps her fingers on the sofa and smiles softly. "Well, my thoughts on that are that you were living in a false reality. You weren't dealing with the things that happened to you. You can't ever heal and move on if you don't know that you're damaged and why. Let's move on. Have you been seeing Mr. Adams since you were freed a couple days ago?"

"Who?"

She smiles softly. "Eli? Eli Adams. Your benefactor."

My inhale tugs in my chest. It catches on something like a sweater on a nail. I shake my head. I know my face is obvious so I just say it, "No. He won't take my calls or speak to me. I don't blame him. I know it's my fault. He's texted me when he had to. I don't think I can face him anyway."

Her eyes narrow. "How does that make you feel?"

Anger flares. I want to snap at her but I take a breath. "Not good." My voice is soft. I can't make it louder, not without screaming.

"Why?"

My head snaps up. "WHY?"

She jumps at my snapping at her. But it doesn't stop me.

"WHY? YOU FUCKING LOCKED ME IN A CELL AND BEAT ME AND TRIED TO DROWN ME AND HE TOUCHED ME AND MADE ME—made me think things." My voice drops off and gets stuck in a heaving gasp. I'm ashamed.

"Get it out," she challenges me.

I rock on the chair and hug myself. "I shot her, and I swear I can't drop the gun." I cry so hard I can't breathe. My tears and words are silent. "It's stuck in my hand and I can feel the weight of it."

"What would have happened had you not? Had you just stayed outside and played with the toys?"

"H-h-he would have hurt her like the others and then killed her."

"How many kids did he leave alive?"

I don't answer or look at her. I just hold myself and shake.

She answers for me, "None. He left none alive. You saved her a much worse fate."

"But if I had shot him she would be alive."

"There is no if. You have to look at the choices and the circumstances. You were six years old. The only thing that ever saved you was that you were hers. Not his. Randy Spicer wasn't allowed near you. But even with Laura protecting you, you were alone in the world."

"I still am," I whisper, still squeezing my eyes shut. I can't do the light of the room with the things I've put out there in it. The light feels too bright for a second. It shows too much. "Can we do the grateful thing?" I whisper again.

She stands. I open my eyes to see her offering me her hand. I take it.

We walk to the mats. She lies down and pulls me with her. I lie back and close my eyes.

Her voice becomes the soft pillow my fears rest their weary heads upon. "You are alive, Sarah. You made it out of the room and the house and the orphanage. You have air and space and someone who loves you so much he would hurt himself to break down the walls you have built. You are grateful for the simple facts of friendship, air, and freedom. If Emalyn were here she would tell you she was grateful for the freedom you gave her. The life you gave her. The air she breathed and the space she got. But you need to be strong enough to let her go."

My eyes are closed. I see it all. I see it the way she says it. I can't make Emalyn grateful though. I think they're right. I did what I could. It was the wrong thing, but it was what I could do. I was a child. I tried. I failed but I tried. I need to let myself see that.

Eli's words come back to haunt me. He said that if he had raped me that the one act wouldn't ruin who I was. I was stronger than that. In my heart of hearts I believe that. Pulling the trigger and freeing Emalyn cannot ruin me forever. I need to get past it or, at the very least, accept it.

"Be grateful for the things that you can control. They are there for you to control. You choose the ways you live and love. You control that. Letting go of the other things, the things you can't control, is easy when you feel like you control the life and the love."

I nod. I believe her. One day I will control the way I live and love.

"You are grateful for Mr. Adams and the way he takes care of you and loves you. He is your family and you are grateful he chose you. Family is rarely a choice and he chose you. As an orphan that is a great feeling."

I don't understand how or why he loves me. I don't accept that. I killed his sister. Even if I didn't mean to, I did. I take the breaths as they come, slow and steady, trying desperately not to feel the weight of the guilt upon my chest.

"In reality you are only as guilty as you were old. The weight of what happened to you is an accident committed by a child, a six-year-old child. So the weight of the guilt and pain can only be as big as it was at six. You cannot stand there as an adult, holding a gun on a little girl. That is not the way it happened. And only when you let go of the control and blame will you be free." She lies there next to me and doesn't speak after that. It's the quiet reflection time.

I take a mental inventory. I am grateful for Eli. He is, in some twisted way, like a member of my family. I'm not ready to meet the Mastermen family who I was taken from. I'm not ready for all of that. I am grateful he and Dr. Bradley have agreed to let me take some time before I see them. I can't bear the thought they will see me as the broken girl I am. I always imagined if I had a family, I would be perfect when I met them. I just want to be normal.

And Dr. Bradley is right that the sin I committed was as a child, and I view it as myself as an adult holding a gun. But she's right; that wasn't the way it occurred.

I open my eyes but they flutter in the light. I'm not scared anymore of what will be there when I open them. I'm not scared because Eli took my fear from me.

He gave me hope in return.

I suspect he took the lonely too.

But I am neither healed, nor better in the way I want, nor forgiven, and I don't believe I will ever forgive him.

Instead of the lonely, I have a broken heart and a sickening case of something I refuse to name but cannot avoid feeling. It's the memory of being beaten and tortured and forced into degrading situations.

My stomach convulses. I sit up and vow never to forgive a moment of it.

"Done already?"

My face is flushed. I nod. "I need to go." I walk away and press the elevator button like a madwoman, as always.

I ride down alone. I'm so lost in thought. I don't notice the man standing in the doorway when it opens. I step out into him and jump back. "Oh sorry," I say before I see it's him. It's Eli.

He steps back and lets me out, swallowing hard and looking to the side sharply. I glance up at him. "What are you doing here?"

He points. "I wanted to see her." His eyes are different now. They avoid me.

"Did you know I was here?"

I can see the answer in his face. "No. I expected you to still be in session. I was going to wait in the other offices." I feel my face pinch, thinking about the other offices. The ones with the cells and the kitchen sink. The intense role-playing therapy offices. He sees my reaction and fakes a warm smile. "How have you been?"

I look up at him, even though he avoids my eyes. "Since you messaged me this morning and told me to stop being a pain in the ass? Good."

"Excellent." He chuckles nervously and runs his hands through his dark hair. My insides are burning with conflict about him. I cannot help but see the boy who saved me and not the man who hurt me. He doesn't scare me the way he should.

The doors have closed, so he leans past me and pushes the button. The proximity and the warmth of him heat up my face. "I need to talk to you," I whisper into his arm. I don't even know why. I have nothing to say to him. Perhaps it is the fact that he is the only person who truly knows me, including me.

He steps back and I see his answer before he speaks, "Just call if you need anything."

Anxiety builds inside me and I label it Stockholm syndrome. I brush past him and walk out into the frosty January air, worried about my sanity. I grip my coat and walk to the car. Stuart waves.

I take a relaxing inhale and let go of the conflicting feelings inside me. Eli is a head case too. He's the male version of me. It's no wonder I can't shake the haunting look in his eyes.

Stuart opens the door and I catch a glint of something in his look. "Wipe the smug grin off that face," I say as I climb in. He's looked this way all week, like he did something amazing by pretending to be tortured and hurt to scare me.

He chuckles and gets in. The car is started and warm. "I still cannot believe that shit worked. Look at you, touching doors and shit. You were the toughest nut to crack, girl."

I snort. I look out the window.

"You know you're a different girl, right? Sarah, you look different, you talk different, you walk different. No more Little Orphan Annie." I meet his dark eyes in the rearview. I see myself differently in his eyes. He nods. "It was worth it. It might not feel like it today or next month, but it was. One day you'll be strolling down the Riviera and you'll see that. When you lose control, you lose the cage you built trying to maintain it."

I pull out my cell phone and notice the messages I've missed. I still have to have it on at all times. I still have to answer his messages. His rules are still in place, but I obey them now for a different reason.

You're right. I think we need to talk soon.

I shudder. The last time he sent a message like that I ended up in a cell. I don't get how he can talk to me in text but not to my face. I wonder if it's the same as me and Sebastian separated by the bathroom door. Things are said easier when the world cannot see us.

The whole thing is a mess and while I asked to speak to him, I'm not sure I can meet him.

I sigh and stare out the window, remembering Shell screaming at me over and over when I spoke to her. I should have called the cops. She was right. I should have called them.

The realization brings back a thought. I glance up and look at Stuart in the mirror. "She comes back today. You excited?" I ask.

"No. I know she is gonna kick my ass for taking part in it all."

"Yeah. She is. She still thinks I should call the cops. She's pissed and I haven't even told her anything yet."

His eyes flinch. "I know."

"I believed you were hurt, Stuart. She is going to hate that fact. That you tricked me."

"I know."

I shake my head. "I still can't believe you tricked me."

He puffs up his chest and misses the heartache in my eyes and the point I am making. "Three years of theatre." He looks proud of himself.

"Are you even from Wichita?"

He shakes his head. "Nope. Detroit. Dr. Bradley said I should be from a Southern state because studies show women feel safer with men with Southern accents. They're more calming." He drops the Kansas accent.

I feel sick. "Is your name even Stuart?"

"Yeah."

"How did you get into this?"

His eyes narrow. He watches me for a second and then looks back at the road. "Dr. Bradley—she's my doctor too. I've helped on a couple now. All the people there were either doctors, or patients who have survived and come back around. No one else would get it. It's extreme and harsh, but it's the only way sometimes."

I doubt the authenticity of the story for a second, but the look in his eyes isn't something anyone can fake. It's the look a person gets when they remember something they'd rather forget.

"Do you ever just wish it had been you that didn't make it?" I ask and stare out the window.

"Every day." His words are hollow like mine. "But then I remember I was given a second chance by Dr. Bradley. I was given a second chance to live. Not everyone gets that, Sarah."

Those are the words that save me.

Emalyn didn't get a second chance. I am living it for us both, and I have yet to do the task justice.

🐾 15 🐾

The door bursts open. Shell leaps at me. She hugs and examines every inch. Tears have claimed her face and mine. She wraps around me and pulls me into her. I can't hear anything she says over the shriek in her voice. I feel like I'm in a melodrama.

She stands up and kicks the door closed, wiping her face. She's huffing and puffing. It takes her a minute before she speaks, "Did they hurt you badly?"

I lick my lips and nod. I don't have the ability to lie to her.

"Sexually?"

I grimace and shake my head.

"Beatings?"

I avert my eyes.

She breathes through her flared nostrils. "I'll kill him. I'll friggin' kill him."

"Just sit."

She paces and rants, "I will peel his goddamned skin from his body. How are you so calm? Goddamn. I was so worried." She sighs and sits beside me. She drops her dark head into her hands and shakes it back and forth. "You scared me."

"Scared me too."

She turns her head and frowns. "You seem different."

I laugh bitterly. "That was the point."

"Just start at the beginning and tell me every detail."

"Are you sure?"

"At the beginning." The fierceness in her eyes suggests I better not miss a second of it.

I sit back on the bed and let it flow out of my mouth. I watch her expressions as the words roll off my tongue. She cries and shudders. It no longer feels real to me. I've been combing through it in my therapy detox for a week. I'm exhausted thinking about it. But for her it's new and real and painful. She looks horrified, and when I finish she doesn't speak. She curls into a ball and cries. I pat her hair and rub her back. I comfort her.

"I don't mean to be selfish. I-I-I'm so sorry." She heaves. She lies there for a long time. The sun starts to go down.

"Are you scared you'll never get past this?" she whispers into the muted dusk light.

"Yes and no. Sometimes I think it will never go away. I still have moments where I can't feel anything, or I feel too much and get over-loaded. Dr. Bradley has been helping me. I started heavy sessions with her. Eight hours a day of intensive therapy. I am so talked out. It's not even funny."

"I hate that they did that to you and you're so calm."

"I wasn't calm. I cried for a long time. I couldn't talk. They made me look at hundreds of photos of her. They made me see her the other way and write her letters. I begged to go back to the cell." I hold out my arm, where a bandage covers the scab. "I smashed a window and cut myself on the glass."

She turns and looks at me. "You?"

"Yeah. It just doesn't feel real. It's like a movie I don't want to watch because it makes my tummy hurt."

She frowns. "It makes my tummy hurt too. I can see you, all little and scared in the hole."

I frown at her. "Don't try to see it. It already ruined the person I would have been. Don't let it in."

A single tear makes its way down her cheek. "It's hard. When I think about it I want to go on a rampage." Her lip trembles.

"New leaf?"

She laughs. "We need to plant a new tree to get a new leaf. The old new leaf plan isn't strong enough now. We need a new tree in a different country. Not just a new leaf but a new everything."

I laugh with her. It feels nice to laugh. For real.

She plays with my hair. "How is he so rich and hot and normal?"

I shake my head. "He's rich and hot, but he's not normal. There is a sickness in his eyes. They're broken like mine. Like a mirror with cracks in it, but none of the glass has fallen out of the frame."

"Spooky."

I stare out the darkening window. "Yeah."

"I feel so bad for him. I mean I feel bad for you too, but he knew his life before. You know?"

I nod. "I hate that his life is this. That I was part of the reason it became what it is."

"Em, you know you didn't do it—" she grimaces, "—Sarah. Sorry."

"I can't get past it either. I've been Em for so long. Em the orphan."

She sits up. "Why did you lie about it? Why did you make your name Em?"

I shrug. "I just remember loving her name when I met her. She was so pretty and clean. I named my Barbie Emalyn the day they got there. When the police found me and asked me my name, it just burst out. I didn't want to be Sarah. Sarah was the name of the girl who killed Emalyn. She didn't deserve to live on."

She grabs my arms. "You didn't kill her. The circumstances did. No six-year-old who lived the way you did can be blamed for that."

"I know. It's just hard. I can feel the gun in my hands. The facts are the facts. My statement is being given to the police. Eli's parents will see it. They'll know it wasn't him, for sure." That gives me a sense of peace.

She snuggles into me again. "You didn't do it. Killing someone is taking the gun and shooting them. Not missing him and hitting her. It was an accident."

"It hurts the same either way."

She squeezes my arm. "I love you, homie. Sarah or Em or whatever. I love you. You're the same to me, no matter what. I know your heart. I know you couldn't hurt a fly."

I feel a sickening amount of relief. Tears slip from my eyes. I was so worried she would hate me. I was terrified she wouldn't understand. Like she would see the gun in my hands, the way I do.

She looks around the room. "It is different in here. It's dirty and there isn't a variety of hand sani on every counter or shelf." She has avoided eye contact with me for a few minutes, but then she looks at me. "What do you remember?"

I twitch my foot. I don't want to answer. "All of it."

"You remember the shootings and the Spicers?" Her voice is soft and scared. "You remember him hurting you and the other kids? It's not just a story that Eli convinced you to believe?"

"I remember every second."

She looks down. "I feel so bad for you both. They made him go in the hole? He was a little boy? I don't even know what to say, Em —S-Sarah."

I laugh bitterly. "Me either. It's cool if you call me Em. I'm still that girl in some ways."

She smiles. It doesn't look real. It's broken and devastated. "All the good ways. But I think you should be Sarah now. Let Em rest." Her green eyes shine. "She has earned her peace."

My own eyes shine as they fill again with tears. "Yup."

She pretty much pulls me down on the bed and wraps around me and pets my head. "We can get a second opinion if you want. Like if you don't want to see him anymore."

I clear my throat. "I don't—mind—seeing him. I can't seem to think of him in the monster sort of way."

"But he is a monster."

"I know."

"Well, if you need anything I know Mom and Dad will help. We talked about it at Christmas and they're not comfy with him paying for our shit anymore. And that doctor is a quack." She is getting snot and tears on my shirt.

I laugh. "Dude, it worked. I drank sink water, ate from a dog dish, was beaten and violated, humbled, and humiliated, and everything was taken away. But all the crazy went with it. All the fears and despair and pathetic Emalyn Spicer. I feel new. I feel brave and fearless in so many ways. Dr. Bradley is a quack, no doubt. But she is a genius quack." I glance over at her and wink. "I haven't made you wash your hands or asked you to pick up your bags or made you take your shoes off."

She laughs a wet giggle and sniffles. "You still noticed it?"

"Yeah. Old dog new tricks. But I have never been this free. I'm free. I'm able to feel guilty and horrid and sad, but at the same time I feel excited and I have lustful thoughts. I smelled a guy yesterday with cologne and I just enjoyed it. He smelled nice. And that was it. I wasn't scared of him. He didn't even glance at me."

She nods as though she accepts it all. "Okay. I agree. If you smelled cologne and my shoes are on your bed, she might be onto something. But, I still question those methods. Harshly."

"Yup. She's freaking nuts."

We both laugh.

I sigh. "Tell me about Christmas. Is Joey still hot?"

She nudges me. "He's a player piece of shit. Never date Italian men —dude—ever."

"I'll never date anyway." I stop laughing and turn and face her. "That's not true. I want to date. I don't want to let any of the old stuff define me anymore. That was old me talking out of habit."

A slow and steady smile creeps across her lips. She nods. "You are better."

"I'm on my way. And I've made my peace with some things. Things I never want to lose."

Her eyes sparkle. "You should call Sebastian. He messaged me when your—er—Eli messaged him. He was so mad. He's good for you. He's so normal and nice and vanilla."

I bite my lip and wonder if I can. I want to. That is the difference in me. I want to try to move past it. Not give up and die in the hole I'm not really trapped in. If I'm totally honest I want to forget again. But that's not likely. And by forgetting I am not honoring Emalyn and the death she had.

We fall asleep the way we are, holding each other with the lights on. She has her shoes on and I try to turn my mind off.

School starts back the next day, and it's hard sitting in a classroom knowing what I know about the world.

We spend the first week back to school in each other's constant contact. Shell hardly lets me out of her sight. She's like a stalker, a chatty one who doesn't try to hide the fact she's worried.

She doesn't see Stuart and I don't hear from Eli. We don't get texts or messages or phone calls. It's weird, and I can't help but wonder where he is. When I see Stuart he's joking and laughing, but doesn't know anything about Eli.

They both feel like they are part of me.

I see Dr. Bradley every day for the whole week, doing the same things and talking until I am blue in the face. On the ride home the last day of the week I lean forward, resting on the seat. "Have you talked to Shell?" Stuart shakes his head. His eyes wander a bit. He doesn't want to talk. So I mutter, "I miss you."

He smiles in the rearview. "Me too."

I wave bye when we get to the dorm and I run across the greens to the door. I don't know what I expected with Eli, but for some reason radio silence wasn't it. I walk into the usual inquisition. "How was it?" Shell is against my therapy completely now. I barely make it out of the room without her in tow. I think Stuart being the driver is the thing that saves me.

"Fine."

"Was she mean to you?"

I roll my eyes. "No. How many times do we have to go over this?"

She snarls and hands me a menu. "Which pizza do you want?"

I point to the Margherita and slump onto the bed next to her. We watch two movies, *Sleepless in Seattle* and *You've got Mail.* We are halfway through the last of the pizza and the second movie when my phone vibrates.

Stuart will be there in fifteen.

I glance at it and feel the fear instantly building inside me. I didn't see how messed up Eli was at first. I thought he was a gangster or a mob boss. I never imagined he was as sick as he is. I see it now. And yet, in some sick, twisted part of me, I still want to see him. Even if the voices in my head are begging me not to.

I fear strange things like him, not the things I should fear. I don't want to walk into him wanting to play victim together and get some kind of gratification from our injuries and sadness. I desperately want to believe that when he talked about me getting better, he was sincere. And I'm concerned he hasn't been able to get better himself in fourteen years. It makes me sad. I want him to be whole too. Not just save me but save himself. And I don't want to talk about this for the rest of my life. It has eaten up enough years already.

I get up and pull my shirt off. "I have to go meet him."

"Eli? Well, I'm coming." She is defiant. I knew she would be. If it were her, I would be too. I look back. "Okay."

"Why are you changing?" She sits up.

"Oh, uhm, I did therapy in that shirt. I get sweaty and stinky."

Her jaw drops. "Oh my God. You're changing to go meet him?" She is disgusted. "What the actual fuck?"

Trying not to look horrified or guilty of her accusation, I sneer. "No. I just don't want to be sweaty." I don't truly know how I feel about seeing him, but romance is not my intention. I want to understand how he could have hurt me.

She crosses her arms and tilts her head. "Is this that Stockholm syndrome where he holds you captive and beats you, and you feel like you deserve it, so you love him?"

"No." I sigh and lower my gaze. "Maybe. I do like him. I can't seem to shake the fact I see him as the boy I knew. But he doesn't see me beyond the science experiment and lifelong project. I have a horrid feeling it's just left over from before. Like he has to keep saving me to save himself." Her face is growing in horror and fear. "And I need to know why he was able to hurt me like that. I need answers and I don't have an explanation for it."

"You want that? You want those answers?"

I shake my head. "I just want some of the damned control back. I want my answers. Why he could hurt me, and why he helped me but kept his distance from me. I want to know exactly what has gone on because it seems like there was a lot that happened behind the scenes."

She stands up and grins. "Well, then I suggest you go there and make him uncomfortable for a change. You want control back? The best way for a girl to have the control is to dress in a way that will make him uncomfortable. I can't wait to see the look on his face. Wear this." She grabs a red slutty dress from the closet.

I arch an eyebrow. "Let's try to stay in the realm of possibility and not be totally obvious."

She grabs a black one that's worse.

I back up, slightly shocked. "Whoa. Easy. I don't want to be part of some game play. I just don't want him to have all the control. He never answers my questions."

"What if he abducts you again?" she pauses and asks when I turn to grab the brush off the desk.

I stop and think before I shake my head. "What can he do that he hasn't already done? What can anyone do to me that hasn't already been done?" I turn and face her. "I don't have any walls left, Shell. I'm like a single tree standing in a field for everyone to see. There is nowhere for me to hide."

She raises an eyebrow and passes me a pale-pink cotton dress that doesn't match the season at all, but it's longer and more my style. It is designed with a wide neck to hang off the shoulder, but at least the entire dress is there. "Sometimes having a couple things you keep to yourself isn't such a bad thing, Em."

I take the dress and smile. She is never going to stop calling me Em. I don't mind it though. It's like Emalyn isn't completely dead and gone. Like a small spark of her lives on in me. But not the bad stuff.

I pull on the dress.

"You have to take the bra off, dude. Off-the-shoulder dresses look slutty with bras sticking out. She passes me a white thing. "Bandeau."

I tug my bra off and slip the bandeau on. I slink into the dress and look at myself in the mirror. I run my hands through my blonde hair and wriggle my lips back and forth. I make duck lips and nod. "It's too much. I look like I'm going there for a date. I don't want that." I slip on my Uggs and turn to face her.

"Dude, my issue is the Uggs." She gives me the duck lips of disapproval.

I shake my head. "I like my boots. We are not having this conversation. I want a different dress. Or pants. Sweat pants."

"What do you call a girl in a dress and Uggs?" She giggles and mocks me, not listening to my protests.

I frown.

"Eski-ho." She bursts into laughter and shakes her head. "You're wearing a dress. He's going to expect your usual homeless attire. This will throw him off, trust me.

I roll my eyes and she gathers herself to do my makeup. She lightly dabs makeup on, still snickering at her own joke. "Okay, I am a believer in Dr. Doom. This is my makeup. My germs. You didn't even blink."

"I cannot get dirtier than I am." I shrug, not wanting to think about it.

"It isn't bugging you that I've touched it to my face?"

I open one eye and frown. "Trying to make me stress about it?"

She laughs. "Just testing." She spins me back to the mirror. "You look pretty."

I do.

I look innocent but still pretty enough. It's a good look for me because you can't see the makeup. I shrug on a sweater over the dress, and then haul on my huge white down jacket, pocketing my cell phone.

She slips on her coat and opens the door. I look back at the apartment and cock an eyebrow. It's a swamp.

She grimaces. "I might miss you cleaning all the time."

"Me too." I sigh and we walk down the stairs. I glance at my phone. We are crazy late.

Stuart and the car are sitting in the snow across the street. The cold wind attacks my skirt and legs. I moan, "I hate Boston. I hate winter. I hate dresses."

She links her arm into mine, which I barely feel with the down jackets. Stuart has the door open when we get there. He looks desperately in Shell's direction. She ignores him completely and climbs in. His jaw tightens. He looks at me apologetically. I put a hand on his coat sleeve and shake my head. "We cool? Me and you? No more lies and weirdness?" Hoping Shell is seeing this.

He nods but still flashes a concerned look. "You forgive me?" I nod as he closes the door.

I nudge her. "You okay?" She looks pissed.

I know that if the hostage heels had been on the other foot, I would never forgive him. Never. But I can only hope for the sake of the car rides and the tension levels, she lets him beg for forgiveness. He is so damned sexy and she is such a sexual person, I am betting they'll be back together in a day or two.

"Give him a chance to explain at least," I whisper just as he gets in.

She scowls. "Screw that. You may have Stockholm but I don't."

He puts the car in drive, inching along in the snow. He looks at us in the rearview. "I think I'll be bringing the SUV from now on. I just didn't want to change it up before I told you."

"It's cool. Probably better in the snow." He's still treating me with kid gloves.

His eyes dart to Shell in the mirror. "Welcome home."

She gives him the cold shoulder. True Italian woman. And she's only half.

He drives us to a building in the heart of downtown. We could have walked. He pulls up and hops out. I feel silly having him open the door. I look at him. "After the cell this feels strange."

He nods. "I know. I need this job though, Sarah."

"I won't say anything."

He blushes. "Thanks." His eyes dart to Shell.

I wink at him and look back at her. "Just wait here till I see what he wants. I'll message you."

She scoffs and scoots along the seat toward me. "Yeah, right."

I put a hand out. "Dude. I want to be strong on my own. I swear, Stuart isn't going to let anything happen to me."

She looks homicidal for a second and then nods climbing back in. "I expect a text every minute."

"Done." I turn and run for the building. I know I won't be texting her. She'll be busy. He's got some groveling to do.

I run to where a man opens the door under the awning to the fancy building.

"Good evening."

I duck my head. The entrance is stunning. I stop and stare. It's incredible. The man at the front desk looks like a bellhop. "May I help you?"

I look confusedly at the room and walk to him. My bare legs are freezing. It looks like a hotel, but I don't think it is. I blow on my hands and speak softly, "Hi. I'm a guest of Eli Adams."

He lifts the phone and speaks quietly, "Go on up. Tenth floor."

"Which room?"

He smiles at me like I've told him a lame joke. "The entire floor." He rolls his eyes and goes back to whatever he was doing.

I frown and sigh. I hate the building already. I cross the shiny floor and press the elevator button.

The doors open, but I'm not prepared for him to be there. I flinch seeing him.

He smiles. It's the same fake smile he gave me at the doctor's office. "Sarah."

My air is sucked out of my lungs. I feel like I'm drowning for a second. I calm myself and smile back. "Hi." He steps back. "Come in."

I hesitate but force myself inside. This is the test. It's the practice run for any other guy. For Sebastian. I remind myself I wanted to see Eli. I wanted my answers and here I am.

"How are you?" he asks.

I frown and look at the stainless steel wall. "Since I saw you a few days ago? Fine."

"Right. Of course."

I look up at him. "I'm fine. Really."

He looks tense.

"Are you waiting for me to fall apart?"

He watches my face and nods.

"It won't happen. It's different for me than you. I was already pulled apart. The memories suck, but inside I already knew they were there. Your eyes and her face have haunted me for the entire fourteen years."

He doesn't look convinced. "I'm afraid you're still so fragile."

"I'm not. You can't tie someone up, beat them and make them

sleep next to their own shit, and then call them fragile. I was fragile before when I lived in that little hole."

"Duly noted," he says softly.

The way he's treating me is insanely off-putting. I can't help but contemplate on what kind of person he is. My mind takes detours, but I snap out of it as the elevator dings to his floor. He holds a hand out. I take it and step off, instantly noticing how open and incredible his home is. The lights of the city are unbelievable from his windows. His hand squeezes mine. "I'm glad you came."

I nod but I don't have a response. It's all too weird.

We walk in silence to the far side of the room, where one entire wall is made of windows. The place feels cold and lonely. The only light comes from the dimly lit kitchen.

"Tell me what you're thinking."

"That I didn't grow up like you."

He sighs. "You did not, indeed."

I glance over, narrowing my gaze and hugging myself. "Was your life hard though? Even though you had all those people who loved you?"

He nods but says nothing.

"Hard enough to make you tough?"

He nods again.

I bite my lip for a moment, contemplating it all. "Mine was hard and I might have been tough if not for all the limitations. I didn't have a mom and a dad and Dr. Bradley to help me."

"Trust me when I say my world was no easier."

"Just more beautiful." I lean forward and stare out at the city. It feels like it's his.

"The view has never mattered to me." He leans against the window and watches me. "May I be candid?"

I give him a look. "When are you not?"

"It just feels like you're not dealing with this. It took me months to get to where you are now. Years even. I'm scared you're walling up again and not really letting it all sink in."

"You were a little boy dealing with it. I'm an adult, sort of." I unzip my coat and pull it off. He looks down on me like he's battling with something. I sit on the long leather couch and cross my legs. I glance at the glass coffee table and huge fluffy white rug and laugh. "Your life was filled with things like this." I tap my Ugg against the glass. "And therapy."

I turn and look at him. "I had people but they didn't feel sorry for me. I was just another orphan. The people in my town felt sad for me and treated me with tons of kindness and pity because they all assumed I had been abused and brutalized. What kind of kid is wandering the streets at six years old? A kid who doesn't have loving parents. It was no mystery that I was tortured or beaten or molested. But the nuns and priests taught me that nothing is easy or free, and hard work is what everyone does to get by. No matter their lot. They taught me that bad shit happens to everyone and no one in the world is exempt from horror and pain. So I guess, sitting here right now, I can't help but see all their words clicking into place. I never understood them before, but I do now. I'm no longer hiding so I can hear them."

He still avoids my eyes. "But they didn't know what you went through."

I shake my head. I feel sick thinking about it. I push it down and smile. "No. But there was a girl who was taken from her parents. Her mom was her sister. She lived in that house till she was ten. Her name was Beth. She's the same age as me. She's becoming one of the sisters. She shakes if you raise your voice around her and pees the bed at night, still. God knows what happened to her to make her that way."

"So you feel like you are actually coping with it all?"

"I do. I didn't have a choice. You forced me to see it all and face it all and hate and love and fight it all. And now I'm sorting through the pile of things I feel. Some I don't need to feel and others I do. But I came here tonight to ask you how and why. How you could do those things, and why didn't you ever reveal yourself earlier?"

He furrows his brow. "We can discuss those things when I feel ready to talk about them."

"Why did you want me to come if you don't want to talk about it?"

"I wanted to be sure you were actually taking this as an opportunity to free yourself from it all."

I narrow my gaze. "Have you freed yourself? From me and from the whole incident?" I stand up and grab my coat, not waiting for his answer. I wish I hadn't worn the stupid dress. "I get that what happened to us was bad. It was, and there is no denying it or taking that from you or me or Em. But there are always people who have it worse. You were right. Your advice was right. I can't rot in that old dirty house. I will never be okay with what happened. I can't say the words or think about the things that happened, without wishing it were me that didn't make it out. But I did. And maybe my hard life in an orphanage, where I was taught not to feel sorry for myself, was the easier environment to be able to heal in. You need to listen the next time Dr. Bradley tells you to be grateful. I'm slowly getting there. I'm grateful to you for every-thing you have done for me." I walk to the elevator, a bit confused about everything. He had seemed so over it all, but my fears of his clinging to it by working so hard to save me are confirmed.

He jogs to where I am and grabs my hand. "Wait." He spins me to face him. He moves his mouth like he wants to say something. Instead, he brushes his hand along my face, tracing my jawline. I'm breathing out of my mouth and thinking things I have only seen on Netflix in the foreign-movie section. I don't even know what to think, but his touch does something.

His eyes burn. "You're so much stronger than I am. I see that now. Maybe I didn't need to save you, maybe I need you to save me." He lowers his face and brushes his lips against mine. The kiss is like a teaser, but he won't give me more. I let him tease me for a minute and then I reach up and pull his face down on mine. I grip to him for dear life.

Then, like I've hit the on switch, he shoves me back into the door of the elevator. His hands are on either side of me, pinning me into the wall.

He stops and bites his lip. His breath is in my face. He licks his lips and shakes his head. "You're right. I'm not like you. I can't be grateful like you are. I talk the talk, but I can't get past the fact I never saved her." He pushes the elevator button next to my arm. "I never saved you both."

"You saved me." My inhalation is heavy, but not for the usual reasons.

"But I couldn't find you for so long." He lowers again, kissing me with meaning and desperation.

He runs his hand up my dress, tracing a line on my bare thigh. His fingers brush up and onto the back of my leg. His fingers slip into my panties, gripping my ass cheek. He squeezes, making a gasp leave my lips. He kisses harder, making me moan into his mouth.

He stops kissing, but his lips stay touching mine, lightly like a feather would. "I'm bad for you, Sarah. I won't ever be the gentleman you need."

"Maybe I don't want gentle. I've had gentle for so long. Kid gloves. And I'm tired of them."

He pulls something from his dress pants and presses it into my hand. "And that is my fault."

The elevator opens. He lifts me into his arms, shoving his tongue into my mouth, sucking mine. He moans with me. I feel him taking steps. He places me down gently inside the elevator and steps back.

His blue eyes are almost black in the dim light. A soft and defeated smile crosses his lips. "Forgive me." He wipes his mouth and steps back. The doors close on him.

The image of him standing in the doorway of the elevator, in his silver dress shirt and dark-gray dress pants wiping me off his lips, is the sexiest and most devastating thing I've ever seen.

I feel like I'm having a heart attack. My hand is shaking. I lift it to my face to see what the crumpled piece of paper is.

I drop my coat and smooth the paper. The elevator stops and the doors open, but I stand and look at the name on it.

Sebastian Hollinger and an address.

I look up to see the front desk guy leaning across the desk, looking at me.

Eli kissed me like that and then handed me a piece of paper with the name of another man on it? A man I didn't need help finding.

My lips curl into a sneer as I push the ten again.

My eyes narrow.

Heat is pouring off my hands.

When the elevator door dings I walk out into the apartment. He's standing in the dark, leaning against the window and looking down to where my car is parked.

"Leave." His voice is edgy and dangerous. He sounds the way he did on the phone, when I just knew him as a benefactor and not a person.

I crumple the piece of paper and throw it at him. "I have his cell number. I don't need this. You know I do. You answered him when he sent me messages."

It bounces off one of the windows and lands on the dark hardwood floor. I walk toward him when he ignores me. I shove his back. He flexes and braces for the impact and spins and points at me. "He's the right guy for you, Sarah. You don't want to start this fight." He's angry.

"You want me to be pissed at myself like you are? You want me to take years to talk about my feelings and slowly crawl out of that fucking hole?" I point at him. "When you pulled that trigger at eleven, you were twice the man you are now."

He vibrates. "Get out," he growls through his teeth.

I arch an eyebrow at him. "You mad?"

He licks his lips. "Yup." He gives me my usual answer.

I laugh and take a step back. "Good."

He walks to me, scooping me up in his arms. I wrap my legs around him. His mouth crashes into my lips. His tongue is searching for mine. My hands rake through his hair. He slams me into the elevator door and pushes the button. His teeth scrape against my lip.

I cry out and grab a fistful of his hair and pull his head back. He laughs. It's dark and menacing. He crushes me harder into the door. I squeeze tighter with my legs. My dress is pulled up to my chest. His erection is popping out the top of his pants, pressing between my legs and onto my bare stomach. He thrusts, rubbing himself against me. His hands cup my ass, kneading and squeezing to the point I'm certain my cheeks are bright red.

The door dings.

He steps in with me. He presses the button for the lobby and rams my back into the steel wall inside the elevator.

I groan.

It's exhilarating to have him pressing me so hard into the wall. I squeeze tighter with my legs. He cries out in my mouth.

His hands are searching the back of my underwear. He's tugging them hard. They cut into my leg on the opposite side of where he pulls. I wince. He grabs them with his other hand and rips them. My eyes widen.

The door dings. I glance at the foyer. We are on the wrong side of the elevator for the front desk douche to see us. Eli's left hand slips back and cups my ass, holding me up. I feel his right hand fumbling in the front of his pants. I hear the zipper of his pants as he sucks and kisses my neck. I moan and press the ten again. The doors close. He's licking up and down my throat.

He growls in my ear. His heavy breathing is making me hot and sweaty. I'm sitting on the handle on the wall, loosening my grip on him so he can get his fumbling fingers between my legs. I'm wet, soaked, so his fingers slip inside me with ease. My wind is lost in the pressure of his fingers in me. I can only get out tiny spurts of air as he thrusts rapidly, but only for a moment. Just long enough to make me delirious. His hand is between my legs again, not inside me. He rubs the head of his erection in my opening and pushes in with one rough thrust.

I cry out, partially in pain and partially in ecstasy. Somehow they have become the same thing to me. The pain makes the pleasure heighten.

The zipper from his pants rubs against the bottom of my thigh as he pumps into me wildly. His face is lost in my hair and neck. He's kissing and moaning. The back of my head is being thumped into the steel wall of the elevator repeatedly. The pain of it makes me come alive suddenly, like it's freeing me.

My legs are losing their grip, but his thrusts are pinning me to the wall. I lose a boot and cry out simultaneously. I'm putty. I'm feeble and losing all the control I've held for so long. Memories of him blindfolding me and paddling my feet flash in my mind. I cry out harder. The images of the paddle make me wetter. My hands are clawing at his shirt. I'm grasping his neck as I grip his erection and convulse. The paddle and the pain are making me come. They make me free of the things I've used to confine myself. It feels as if I've grown wings.

My body spasms.

He grunts and moans, "Goddamn, Sarah." His words are almost blended in one long gasp.

He pumps with uneven jerks. His grip loosens. I open my eyes and watch his face. His mouth opens as he cries out. I bite his lower lip and pull. He moans loudly.

I want to bite harder but I don't.

I want more of him. I want to hurt him the way he hurts me.

I don't feel better.

I'm still a bit pissed.

He steps back and pulls himself out of me. I slide down his body. He blushes and tucks himself back in his pants.

The door dings. I glance out and realize we are at the foyer again. A lady is standing there looking at us. She's holding a small shivering dog and they both look horrified. I follow her gaze to my shredded panties lying on the floor of the elevator.

The doors close again as I pull my dress down and pick up my boot. I press the ten again.

I'm still out of breath and horribly shocked. I pick up my coat and pull it on. The doors open. He doesn't walk inside. I look at his apartment and then the floor again. He stands with his back to me, he's heaving still too.

He seems so large standing in front of the doors as they close. The elevator moves again. He bends and picks my underwear up and puts them in the pocket of his pants. I scowl and feel weird about him taking them. He doesn't talk.

The door dings. The lady is still standing there, but now she gives me a disgusted look as I step off the elevator. I'm halfway across the foyer with flaming red cheeks, both sets, when he grabs me. He drags me until we are outside the building. He pulls me alongside to an alley. We are standing in the snow. My thighs feel slippery and cold.

He trembles but I don't think it's from the cold.

He looks like he wants to say things. The air is frozen and making steam out of his breath. His blue eyes are sweet again. His dark hair is getting coated in flakes. I look down and wait for it—the rejection I know is coming. He doesn't say anything. I'm cold and I don't want to talk about it. I don't know what to think about anything.

I stand on my tiptoes and press my mouth to his. It's soft and sweet. I whisper into his lips, "It was nice seeing you, Eli." I step back and walk away. He doesn't say anything. I cross the street and try to not have a panic attack about the fact that I have semen between my thighs, running down them, and I'm in a cotton dress. In the snow.

"I hate winter," I mutter and knock on the steamy windows of the car.

Stuart leaps out quickly. He blushes and looks at me. His mouth breaks into a grin. I roll my eyes and climb in.

"Was he mean to you?" Shell asks still looking pissed.

I don't know how to answer the question without actually saying we might have hurt each other. So I don't look at her. She'll know and kill him. Either way, I don't want to deal with it.

❧ 16 ❧

I pace her office, looking out the window. "Does the winter ever end here?"

She chuckles and sips her water. "It does—in the spring. We have four full seasons here. It's lovely."

I look back at her and sigh. "If you say so."

"Sarah, I want to talk about them. I want to know what you're willing to give into."

I bite my lip and cross my arms, wrapping them around me. I swallow and nod, "My birthday. I turn twenty. I think I can do it."

She nods. "I agree. I think you can too. I just need to hear you say it all aloud. What's holding you back?"

My nostrils flare. "What if they have an idea of what I should be and I'm not?" She doesn't know about the darkness.

"You were their child. They gave birth to you and raised you for nearly three years. You were their baby. They will love you, no matter what has happened to you and no matter the outcomes of those situations."

I hear her words. I honestly do. But I cannot force myself to believe.

"How do I let them in?" I whisper.

"Slowly. The first time you meet them cut it short after a couple hours, or even an hour. Then the next time, a few more hours and slowly get there. If this were an adoption you would have dates where you meet and then get used to each other. But it isn't. These are your people. They already love you. You just need to remember."

I glance back out the window and wish for the nerves and expectations I've placed on myself to go away.

"Have you seen Mr. Adams?"

I try to hear in her tone whether she thinks I have seen him or not.

I narrow my eyes but don't turn around. "No." I don't know what to say. I don't want to talk about seeing him and the dirty things we did. I don't need that sentence to be released in a room with this much light and judgment in it.

"Is he texting you?"

I glance back and nod. "Of course. You know what he's like." He is texting me. Nonstop. He's driving me insane with it.

Her stare is uncomfortable but I hold it. She is searching me for something. I hate being evaluated.

I cross the room. "Thanks, Doc."

In the elevator I can't help but pray he's standing at the bottom like last time.

I'm disappointed he isn't when I get to the main floor and go out to the car.

When I get back to my room I sit and stare at the phone. I don't know what to say to him. I imagine he feels the same. Shell doesn't seem to suspect. I'm glad I never told her. I don't know how to say that I needed him. I needed something. He made the touching and feeling a good thing. It was dirty in a way I allowed. Like I controlled the filth that was all over me.

"So, are you phoning Sebastian or am I?" She leans in the doorway.

I glance up and smile. "He's picking me up in an hour." Something I am actually dreading. It's my way of forcing myself to move on and be the girl I want to be.

"Birthday plans?" She closes the door and pulls off her coat.

My phone vibrates. I glance at it and blush. *Hi.*

I shake my head and look back at her. "I have something I need to talk to you about—my birthday actually." I take a deep breath. "I want to meet them on my birthday, and I want you to come with me. I need you."

I glance up at her mouth-agape stare. I nod.

"Your family?" She sits on the end of the bed. "You want to meet them? You only found out your birthday was coming up like a few weeks ago, and you already want to meet them?"

I nod again.

"How? Go to Chicago?"

I shake my head. "Eli will take care of it."

She reaches forward. "I'm so excited and proud of you. That's awesome." She doesn't sound like she is either of those things.

"Thanks. I'm scared, like shit-my-pants scared. But let's be real, I need this. I need the new leaf to include them. I just want it to all be real and done. I have a family."

She laughs. "You have a family. Well, you always had mine, but now our family is bigger."

My phone vibrates again.

My cheeks light up, burning from the heat in them. I lick my lips and glance at the text.

Hi.

He keeps sending it. He wants to talk but doesn't say anything. A grin creeps across my lips when I think about his fingers and the handle of the elevator. My breath is uneven when my mind fills with the distorted image of us in the brushed stainless steel of the elevator wall.

"So is Eli going to fly them over on the company jet?"

I laugh and blush and trace my fingers over his constant *Hi's*. "I don't know. Maybe. I guess."

"Oh my God." Shell is still staring at me, analyzing. "Did you have sex with him?"

I'm pulled out of my strange haze. It takes me a second to realize I'm blushing and sweating. I swallow and shake my head. "No."

She sits on the bed and lifts my face. "Did you have sex? We are talking about your family and you are blushing and sweating?"

"It's not what you think." Boy oh boy, is it not. She couldn't even come close to comprehending. I don't comprehend it.

I bite my lip and look up at her through my lashes. She looks like she's stalling—processing.

My phone vibrates.

Hi.

She is pointing at the phone and stuttering, "Th-Th-The night we went there, y-y-you and him—you went upstairs and—oh my God." Her fingers are resting on her lips. My phone vibrates. "I thought you would show up and make him tell you things—answers. I didn't think you would just give it all up. Not to him." A disgusted look crosses her face. "Him? He isn't worthy of something like that! He paddled your feet! He made you shit in a cell."

I can't explain it. I shake my head blankly and clutch the phone. "It's like you said, we're both so screwed up; I don't know what happened."

Her face is slowly becoming more horrified. "Has he called you? Has he tried to see you since? Is this becoming a thing or did he use you?"

"No. Just texting me."

She sits back. "You gave him that, your virginity, and he hasn't called?"

I shove my feelings down my throat, choking on them. "It isn't what you think. You can't understand."

"You've been the queen of walls and barriers and the word 'NO' and you GAVE it to HIM? No work? No dinner and a movie? To say the least, he owes you that!"

I snap, "He's paying my tuition and yours and everything else. I think he bought me dinner already. It isn't like that."

Her nose wrinkles and I can tell it's involuntary. "So you're working for your meals now?"

The emptiness creeps up inside me. "I guess so. Yours too." I get up and grab my coat and walk out. I never believed she would understand, but I also never imagined she would call me a whore. My boots hit the stairs with near violence.

"Em, wait. Sarah. Shit," She calls after me. I pound the stairs, pulling on my coat and mitts. She grabs my coat and pulls. I jerk free and step out into the snowstorm.

"Sarah." I stop. I like it when she says my name. I turn. Tears are streaming down her cheeks. She shakes her head. "I had no right."

I shout, "No! No, you didn't! You've slept with a dozen guys! You've had sex in like seven states!"

A guy walks past us. He nods at Michelle. She scowls and grabs my arm, dragging me to the path. We stand under the street lamp. "Dude."

I shake my head. "No. You don't have any right to judge me for anything. I have had random weird sex once, with a guy I technically have known my whole life. I am trying *desperately* to get rid of something I've formed in my head. So I can understand sex and sexuality and desire. Without the lonely coming and taking it all back. I sort of slipped and lost my virginity. I'm nearly twenty years old; it isn't like I'm doing anything reckless. I'm an adult, he's an adult. If it happened once and that's it, then so be it. We have a weird relationship anyway." I hold my fingers up to make an inch. "I am this close to losing it all and ending up in a ball in the snow. I am on the edge of something and it's going to be amazing or it's going to be horrid. Either way, I am free of the disgusting feelings I've had. For now. Maybe they'll come back and paralyze me and this will be it. This small moment in my life will be the joy I once had."

"I never thought of it like that."

"Because you see the broken girl. You see me. If anyone does, it's you. But I need you to see the changes and help me through them, not doubt every step I take."

"I'm sorry, Sarah."

I nod, sniffling and shaking. "I need you more than ever. I'm meeting my parents. I might have brothers and sisters I don't remember. I have normal right there waiting for me, and I can't get past all the dark and scary. Instead of fearing it now, I like it. I like feeling afraid of him. Do you know how screwed up I feel? Like the old disgusting bits of me like the bad things." The confession crumbles from my lips, dropping in broken breaths and gasps.

"Don't. There's nothing wrong with liking the dark and being afraid. You used to be afraid of the silliest things. This is the first time you've been genuinely afraid of the right thing." She sniffles and wraps her arms around me. She's shivering and clutching me. "And you're right. I don't understand and I know I never will. Dude, I'm super sorry. I'm excited about your birthday, really excited. And I'm scared."

"Me too." I hug her back. "I'm sorry I said you had sex with like a dozen guys in like seven states and shit."

She laughs into my hair. "It's true. We are taking you to the doctor tomorrow. You need to go on the pill. Being sexually active changes some things."

"I'm not sexually active. I had it once by accident." I grimace.

"It only takes one time to get pregnant."

"Oh God. I never even thought."

She shakes her head. "You're probably fine, but I'm going to give you a pack of my pills to start taking tonight. 'Cause, dude, no one wants to be that college girl. And you need condoms. You can't be getting shit from him or anyone else. Whoever you decide to have sex with has to wear a condom. You don't know where he's been."

"No, I don't. I don't even know him. We had this thing, and I don't know what it means. And he's texting but not saying anything."

"You're both just damaged and screwed-up and shit. So y'all don't know how to just be a boy and a girl."

I give her a look.

She closes her mouth and blushes. "You know what I mean?"

"No. But I think what you might mean is true. It's like we met at the screwed-up kidnap victims' camp. But in truth, I think if I really look hard, I have always seen him as my hero. When I was a kid he was the one who saved me. I thought he left me behind because I had killed her. Then I blocked it all out, and when I found out I had a benefactor, I have to admit I saw him as my hero again. I didn't know it was him, but that's what I saw. Until he kidnapped me. Then I had to try to ignore the disturbing thoughts I had previously about him—thoughts I can't sort out in my head. I can't even kid myself about them. Even if I wanted to. I like the fact he is who he is. I wish I didn't."

She tries to hide her disapproval. "You know you can't like, have a relationship with him, right?"

"Right. Of course. I do see that we're more like survivors of the same plane crash and drawn to each other through disaster." I lower my voice, "How I see him is not how I see Sebastian." It's true but in my heart of hearts, I know Sebastian is the right man for the normal girl I want to be.

She pulls back. "This is so weird. I never imagined we'd be having the safe-sex talk and the boyfriend talk, and the conflicted-heart talk. I've just always had you one way; I need to change my mind about you. I need to see Sarah."

That hurts me in a good way but my eyes still water. "Thanks."

She kisses my cheek softly and grips my face. "I love you."

"Me too."

A man's voice interrupts us, "Are you cheating on me already?" I glance up at Sebastian on the path to Speare Hall. I step back and squeeze Michelle's hand as she whispers and waves at Sebastian. "We cool?"

"Always. See ya in a bit," I whisper back.

"Text me lots, kay?"

I nod and pull away.

She grins. "You crazy kids have fun." She crosses her thin arms and wipes her eyes. "Damn snow always makes me cry. Don't let me forget to get that stuff for you either, Sarah." She emphasizes my name and makes me feel awkward, like she's my mom.

I laugh nervously. Sebastian looks confused and slightly frightened.

"Hey," I say and can't stop myself from feeling weird around him.

He takes my mitt in his and pulls me along the path gently. "Hey."

I tug my hand free and stop in my tracks. "We need to talk first."

He nods and looks up at the snow falling on us. "Can we just get out of the snow?"

"No. I need to say this now. Before."

He looks worried. His eyes are dark brown, as if the hazel is gone even though it may be a trick of the light. "Okay." His voice is hesitant.

I look at him and hug myself. I step back and point to the path. "Maybe we should walk." I don't want to see his face as I say it.

He nods. He looks terrified.

"So, I know Shell told you some of the stuff that was going on, but she didn't tell you everything." I look back at the dorms. "She didn't know everything."

He gulps.

I wrap my arms around myself and close my eyes. "I was taken when I was two, just about three." The story finds its way out of me, in an efficient and tidy way. I leave out the torture and some of the obvious horrors. They are like rocks that I don't want to lift and let anyone else look under. The creepy things that live under them will crawl out and chase me around.

I don't look at him. "And when he revealed who I was and who he was—that he was Emalyn's brother, I thought I might die. It was all a form of therapy, the whole thing. I know Dr. Bradley spoke to the police when you and Shell called them. She explained the whole thing, and that I was a patient who was in deep therapy and isolation. She told me that I had actually signed the consent form for the entire thing in the beginning. I just didn't read the fine print." I switch between looking at the snow, the cars driving by, and the building behind him. "So that's it." I finish talking and shiver. My face is frozen and my hair is soaked from the snow. I tremble, part hypothermia and part anxiety.

In the sounds of the traffic and snow falling and my own rapid heartbeat, I think I can hear him stepping back emotionally. I don't blame him though.

He doesn't move, but it feels like he couldn't be farther away. After a second he pulls out a bottle of hand sani from his pocket. "So, I don't need this anymore?"

I laugh. It's filled with relief and tears.

He wraps his arms around me and kisses the top of my head. "I'm so glad. My hands are so chapped."

I cry harder and laugh at the end of it. He laughs too, and I swear for a small moment I hear a sob in there.

"I'm so sorry, Em."

"Sarah," I whisper.

He pulls me back. "I like Sarah better anyway." He presses his warm lips into my forehead and takes my mitt in his again. "But I can't actually feel my legs so can we go now?"

I nod.

I don't offer him a way out. I don't tell him he can leave and let me go home. It's not like the first date. He's become part of the baggage I now carry. I have a morbid curiosity to see where it goes.

"So can we eat at a normal restaurant?"

I nod. "I haven't done it yet—been in crowds and eaten at a regular place." His eyes light up and the hazel flashes under the streetlight. "So a first?"

I smile. "A first."

❧ 17 ❧

The restaurant is busy. The waitresses look like they might be selling something beyond food.

I cut my piece of chicken and try to keep calm. I've cut everything on my plate into tiny pieces. My stomach doesn't like restaurants yet. Not this kind. The noise of everyone else is disturbing and annoying.

"Stop."

I look up at him and frown. "What?"

He laughs. "Stop. I see it still. Your eyes are darting around the room like you're plotting something, and you look like I'm forcing you to eat liver."

I drop the cutlery and shiver.

He leans forward and touches my hands. I like that. "Not everything is going to change all at once."

"I know." I pull my hands away and rest them in my lap and try not to feel failure in the meal. "I'm disappointed in myself. I hoped I would be able to do it. I think I've been all talk all week, acting like nothing bothers me, but slowing down and seeing it, I am bothered still."

He nods at the blonde waitress. She comes over grinning at him.

"Can we get our bill please?" he says. She looks at our full plates and frowns. "Is everything okay?"

He shakes his head. "It's fine. We just need to leave." He squeezes my hands. "You okay?"

I sigh. "I'm just bummed. I want to be better."

He sits back. "Em—" he winces and pauses, "—Sarah. Sorry. You need to give things time. It's been a couple weeks since school started again. You spent the winter break in therapy. I'm pretty sure you are doing amazing, compared to other people in your situation. I mean, come on. Let yourself take a pause on judgments. You've just remembered things most people haven't seen in a horror movie."

I stand up. The bill isn't there but I can't stay. "I need to wait outside." I grab my jacket and walk out.

My heart is racing. My tongue is numb. I grip my cell phone. When I burst through the front door of the restaurant, before the valet can even get the door, I'm huffing in air. My hand is shaking. I hate the way he makes me feel. I pull my phone out.

I smile when I see the ten *Hi* messages and text back. *I need you* and walk to the awning. I stand there and take deep breaths.

My phone vibrates. I smile when I see it. *I think I need you too.*

Sebastian walks out doing up his pea coat. "You okay?"

I shake my head. "I don't think I can do this." I point between us. "I'm sorry. I didn't mean to lead you on. I just can't do this. I'm never going to be this girl."

In the distance I hear the car and when I look back, Stuart has the SUV parked illegally across the street. His favorite way to park.

I step in and kiss Sebastian's cheek. I savor the smell of him for a moment. "Goodnight." I turn and leave before he can say anything. I jump into the SUV and bury my face in my hands. I'm not crying. I'm terrified. I don't know of what.

Stuart drives. He knows not to talk. He's seen worse than this.

The SUV stops outside Eli's building. I look up. "He asked you to bring me here?"

He shakes his head. "He said you needed to be picked up."

"You brought me here?"

He climbs out and opens the door. "I did. You don't look like you can do Michelle or alone. I know what that feels like. When I met Eli, I was boxing for real. For money to pay for drugs." He grabs my hand and squeezes. "I get it."

"Thanks, Stuart."

"Nothing to thank me for. I'll wait here if you want."

I look down and blush. "Nah, you go home. Or my place or wherever the hell you two go."

"She still isn't talking to me."

"She's Italian. You gotta go for the grand gesture. Huge." I turn and run across the street and through the open door.

"Good evening, miss."

I nod at the valet and run to the elevator.

"Uhm, miss." I look at the front desk guy. He blushes and shakes his head, "Never mind." My cheeks flush.

I press the button and step inside. When the doors close my insides feel like they're riding a rollercoaster. I'm making a mistake and I don't care. My heart is racing, and I'm thinking about a million things but really it's only one thing.

I can barely swallow when the door dings. I jump when the doors open and he's standing there. His face is dark. His eyes are dark. He grabs my hand and pulls me off the elevator. He doesn't kiss me. He drags me into the dark apartment.

My boots thump along as we almost run through the apartment.

He opens a metal door and storms inside, with me hot on his heels. Candles are lit, but in the dim light I can see what it is.

My skin shivers as I look around.

It's a warm room with the light of a fireplace flickering off the paddles along the wall. The bed is huge—four posts of dark thick wood with a railing like it should be a canopy, but he doesn't have one there. A strap hangs off one of the posts.

He lifts my chin, exploring my eyes before speaking, "Some people don't deserve good things. They don't deserve them. Those people are unlovable and unchangeable. And while I want you," his words turn to a desperate whisper, "I know that I can't ever have you. This is why. Can't you see that?" He looks around and all I see is shame. "This is what I want you for."

"You don't scare me," I whisper, but I know I can't hide the horror on my face. It takes a second for the shock to sink in. I tremble seeing the paddles. I wonder if one of them is the one he hit me with. My feet cramp up, remembering the pain and the fear and hidden pleasure that make me want to vomit.

"I scare you."

I shake my head but he can see the lie.

"You like being scared." He closes the door. The hollow sound of it clicking echoes. The firelight licks his face. I see him the way I imagined he would be when he was just a benefactor. He's rich and scary and cold. But I know it's an act. Deep down he's a scared little boy.

He takes a step toward me. His voice is gruff and cruel. He spits when he talks and points around the dark room. "You texted me, Sarah. You needed me. This is me, unfortunately. This is what I have to offer. I don't have anything else to give you."

My fingers are unsteady when I lift them to the zipper on my coat and pull down slowly, watching his gaze. I let it slip off my shoulders, challenging him with my gaze. I'm terrified and excited. It's the first time I've felt anything since the last time he touched me.

"You sure you want to play this game?"

I nod, swallowing the rocky lump in my throat.

He steps back and sits in the chair in the corner with his legs spread, like before. "Undress."

I take a deep breath and pull my shirt off, dropping it to the floor next to my jacket. I slip off my boots. I'm wearing the bandeau, which I've grown fond of. I hold his burning gaze when I unzip my pants and wiggle my way out of them. I'm standing in my bandeau and panties.

I shiver, and not from the cold. The crackle of the fire and my racing heart fill the air.

"Go to the bed."

I turn my back on him and walk to the bed slowly. I don't know what to expect. I put my hands on the bed. Before I get a chance to crawl up on it, his body is against mine. He's got me pinned with his arms around me. He grabs my hands and lifts them up in the air. I grip the railing on the top of the bed.

"Don't move those hands," he whispers into my nape. I nod and lick my lips. I'm on my tiptoes. My breath is catching and coming out in spurts of rough air. His hands run down my arms. I shiver when his lips brush the back of my neck. He sweeps my hair to one side, kissing down my shoulder blade. Heat and nerves battle low in my belly as his hands grip my hips, pulling me back to him.

"Don't let go of that railing, Sarah." His words are growled between kisses and licks. I hear the menacing threat in them.

I wince when he nibbles my back. His hands are rubbing and lightly gripping my stomach. He doesn't touch anything I want him to.

His lips reach my panties. His fingers trace the fabric along my butt. It tickles and makes me squirm, but I don't move my hands. He is the man from the room, with the paddle and the cocky smile, who felt no remorse. I fear him in a way that excites me. It's like having the control because I said yes. I am his because I chose it. I made this happen. I am not a victim of it.

His fingers dip into my underwear, trailing their way around my waist. He stands and leans against me, like he is trying to make me let go of the railing. But I am obedient if I am anything. A lifetime of obedience can't be changed overnight. I grip it for dear life and anticipation of where it will all go.

In the dim light I see his movements making shadows on the wall across from me.

A blindfold is pulled over my head. The darkness is familiar. He moves around me and sits on the bed. I think I'm standing between his legs. The heat of him is around the front of me and the heat of the fire is behind me. I'm shivering, but I'm not cold in any way. He feels so large, like he's all around me, encompassing me.

Something brushes against my right nipple. I gasp. I think it's his finger tracing my nipple through the rough lace of the bandeau.

I falter in my ability to stand on my tiptoes. He thumbs my nipple until it sticks out. Then his other hand finds my other nipple. He's flicking and lightly squeezing both of them. He does it in a pattern that resonates throughout my body. I'm squeezing my thighs together and biting my lips. His mouth caresses my stomach. He kisses and trails his tongue up my abdomen. He flips the bandeau down and I moan loudly. I don't even know why.

His mouth clamps down on my nipple as his fingers continue the pinching and tugging of the other. He sucks and licks in a swirling motion. My stomach tightens. I don't know what's happening but I'm getting lost in it all.

"Are you going to come for me, Sarah? Before I even touch your pussy?" His voice is warm against my wet nipple.

I moan louder and squeeze my thighs so tight that I lose my grip.

"Come for me, baby." He sucks harder and tugs on my nipple. I orgasm. I let go of the railing, twitching and crying out. I'm gripping his shoulders and head.

Immediately, he's off the bed. My face is shoved into the soft blankets. I'm still confused and breathing heavily. I can barely keep my mouth closed.

"I told you to keep your hands there." He's pressed against me. One of his hands is holding me against the bed, dragging up and down my back. He steps back. I lie there and wait, breathing into the bedding.

He walks across the room, making his shoes slap heavily against the floor. My eyes try blinking against the blindfold. I don't know what to expect. I'm terrified about the paddles. My feet are clenching the floor in desperate protests.

His hand touches my ass cheek again. I whimper.

I jump when he rubs something cold against me. It's wide and I have no idea what to expect.

"If you struggle, I will hit you harder." His voice is ice. I'm clutching the blanket and breathing into it. My jaw is trembling with terror and a perverse idea of where this is going.

His hand creeps along my underwear to my belly. He presses and then suddenly something connects with my skin. I scream. It stings but shocks more. It's gone and then his hand presses into my stomach again and the metal cracks me on the ass cheek. I've squirmed slightly. He pulls my hips, arching my back more.

"Touch your toes together," he growls at me. I do it quickly. He pulls my butt back farther. The third strike hurts a bit, but the vibration of the impact against my groin makes my scream become more of a moan. I never saw that coming. The smacks mellow out but come more frequently. My stomach is tightening again with every vibration the striking creates. Each smack vibrates against me inside my underwear .

I feel like I need to move in a thousand different ways but can't. He slows down the rhythm.

"Faster," I mutter breathlessly into the blanket.

He chuckles. "No, no, no. You've had an orgasm. You don't get another one." The next hit is hard. It stings. I wince and suck my breath.

"That's my girl." The next hit is the same. My butt starts to go numb to the heat of the room but still stings. The paddle drops. It makes the same sound it did when he dropped it from paddling my feet.

His zipper is pulled roughly. My underwear are ripped down. They scrape the front of my thighs and calves.

He's between my thighs again. His erection is seeking out the moisture. He rubs it up and down my slit and then thrusts into me with a grunt. I cry out as he pulls my hips back.

I'm almost off the ground. He rocks into me several times hard and fast. His body pounds mine. I'm building up again from the pause in the spankings. He orgasms before I can.

He grunts and finishes using me. He pulls back. I'm holding the bed, spent but frustrated. I am close to tears. I don't even know why.

My ass is on fire—it matches my cheeks. My jaw trembles. He leaves the room before I can even comprehend what's happened.

His semen is dripping down my thigh again. I feel dirty, but it's soothed by a sickening, depraved happiness. I chose this.

The pain in my heart is making me happy on a level I never want to explore.

My arms and legs are weak. I feel like I've done one of my harder runs. I stand up and fight my legs from buckling. I look around for my underwear but they're gone, again. I pull on my jeans and shirt. A tear slips from my eye as I get my boots on. I wipe it away and grab my coat. When I get to the door, my hand almost refuses to grab the handle.

I look back at the room. It isn't how I had imagined the night panning out. In a place in my heart, larger than I want to admit to, I had imagined he couldn't get enough of me. I had imagined those ten texts were him reaching out. Not him checking to make sure I was alive, so he could use me for a few minutes.

His mixed signals are epic and worthy of a young girl's. My heart breaks when I think about leaving Sebastian for this. I know he would never treat me this way. He is the right choice. He is the normal I want.

This room is a darkness and a sickness and an underworld that I want no part of. The excitement and the forbidden desires are there, but they are chased down with a bitter feeling that I can't forgive him for. A feeling he has made me want.

I pull my phone out and text Sebastian with trembling fingers.

Meet me tomorrow at my dorm. I won't have this number anymore.

You sure? His response is instant. Like he was waiting for me.

I need you to help me become the girl I want to be. 8 pm my dorm. Goodnight.

He doesn't respond. I put the phone on the bed and walk to the elevator. I can hear the water in the kitchen.

I press the button.

I'm frozen.

It isn't the lonely.

It's so much worse.

It's emptiness, but it's also like a world war inside me. I want to run to him. I want to kiss him and attack him and slap him. I want him to hold me.

I suddenly understand exactly what Shell was talking about. He's the grumpy guy at the bar, and I want to fix him. I smile at my first attempt at normal girl problems.

Thankfully, I have that explanation and just an ounce of self-respect left. It reminds me that while I want him to want me, I don't want to force him to do it. It doesn't feel like too much to expect or too much to ask for.

"Don't leave," he speaks softly behind me. The elevator opens. I don't move. I can't.

I also can't face him. My ass is on fire. My jeans are making my cheeks sting. I begged him to humiliate me for a little bit of pain. Pain I somehow wanted.

I can't look at him when I say it, "I don't want your money anymore. Or anything. I'll make it work on my own." I step in as the door is closing. I hear him leap and press the button, but I press the M and collapse against the wall. I'm a sobbing wreck when the elevator moves.

It dings and I miss it somehow. The door closes. I don't push any buttons. I curl into a ball in the corner. It opens again. Feet step in. Matte leather shoes with squared tips and dark-gray dress pants. A button pushes. I want to kick his feet out from under him, but I'm frozen in terror. Not of him, but of me. Me and the dark places I will allow myself to be taken.

He bends down and picks me up off the floor. He holds me to his chest and kisses the top of my head. He walks into the apartment when the doors open again. It's dark and warm, but I've never been in a colder room.

He carries me to a room. He flicks on a light. It's a huge master bathroom. He turns on the shower. I flinch. He pulls my coat out of my hands and lifts my arms in the air. He pulls my shirt and bandeau off.

"No. Please don't," I whisper. He undoes my jeans and pulls them down. He kneels and removes my boots and jeans. He kisses the front of my thigh once.

He stands.

His eyes look dead. Like how mine used to look, before he beat the ever-loving hell out of me and woke me up.

He looks at me expectantly. I reach up and undo the buttons of his dress shirt. What is underneath is so different from what's on the outside. He's always dressed like he's attending meetings all day.

But underneath he has a huge cross tattoo done in Celtic-looking artwork. The banding is thick and winding. The top of the cross starts just under his left pec and goes all the way to his hipbone. The intersecting line of the cross spans the bottom of his entire left ribcage.

A name is delicately sketched onto the cross in the very middle. I trace it with my fingertips. The name doesn't belong to me and it doesn't feel like it's mine. For the first time in my life, the name of the dead doesn't belong to me.

I pull his shirt off and notice the scars along his bicep. They run thick and deep. When I touch them they slow my stroke like a speed bump would. I undo his zipper slowly and gently and slide his pants past his groin and knees. I drop to my knee and lift his feet to remove his shoes and socks. There is a huge scar on his left thigh. It's massive. I can see the staple marks. Like Frankenstein would have. His body is hard but not chiseled or sculpted the way Sebastian's is. It's meaty though.

"Where did you get these scars?"

"I was hard on myself as a kid."

I leave it at that but run my finger along it until he stops my hand and lifts me off the ground. The bathroom is humid and filled with steam from the shower.

He steps in and pulls me to him. He presses my head against his cross. Her cross. Our cross.

❧ 18 ❧

The shower was steamy and relaxing. It feels like he let me in by allowing me to see his scars and tattoos, all seven. They're not all huge like the cross, but they're bigger than I would have imagined.

When we get into the bed I notice he has something on his back ribcage. Getting closer I see it's a quote. I peel back the covers of the blankets he has wrapped us both in and look at it.

If you prick us do we not bleed?

If you tickle us do we not laugh?

If you poison us do we not die?

And if you wrong us, shall we not revenge?

It's Shakespeare. I remember it from lit. I brush my hands across the words and wonder if he will ever find peace. His hand moves like a snake and snatches mine. He pulls it up and turns his face and kisses the back of it. "Go to sleep."

I shake my head. "I can't. Someone got me all worked up and now I'm kind of buzzing."

A grin plays upon his lips. "You came. In case you forgot."

"I forgot. I think you should remind me how it felt, jog my memory."

He shakes his head. "I think I like you, how you are now." He opens his eyes and looks at me. "Do you want me?"

I fight the pathetic face I know I'm wearing. I nod.

"What do you say?" He's being cocky. He wants me to beg.

My natural instinct is to fight against him when he's being that way. Acting submissive is not a natural state for me. It's there from the torture. I don't fear him anymore and have a harder time submitting to his attitude. I rip my arm from him and climb from the bed.

I smirk and walk to his closet. I pull a pair of jogging pants and a t-shirt from the shelves of the huge walk-in. I walk out and pull my long hair into a bun and tuck the ends in to make it stay. It won't but it gives me something to do with my hands, beyond scratching his eyes out.

"Where are you going? In my clothes no less?"

"You won't miss them. You don't wear anything but Armani. I'm pretty sure these are from Old Navy. You probably didn't even know you had them."

He snorts. "Get back here." His tone is the one from the chair. I shake my head and break into a run. I grab my jacket and boots and bolt for the stairs. I unlock the door to the stairs and pull it open fast. I can see him running in his boxers. I fly down the stairs barefoot and out into the lobby. I can hear the elevator. I've played this game before. I tug on my boots and run out the front door as the valet opens it. My boots slip a bit in the snow. Uggs have no grip in snow. I haul on my coat and let the fresh air wash me clean of the shame I'm battling.

"Sarah," he shouts, barefoot from the awning.

I look back and wave. "Goodbye, Eli. It was nice seeing you again." I shout into the blizzard.

"Wait for me. Give me one minute. Please," he yells back and then he's gone. He sounds angry and demanding, but he said please and he never says that. It makes butterflies in my stomach.

I pull my hood up and tug on my mitts. His jogging pants are warmer than my jeans, but I still don't wait long. I turn and start to walk. I hear him come jogging up beside me. I glance back and sigh. He looks sexy in his hoodie and sweats. "I like casual Eli. That's a brilliant change in you." His face drops a bit. It makes me smile to see him offended. "Don't get me wrong, I like the suits and dress pants and groomed thing you have going on, but this is nice too."

"What are you doing?" he asks, looking intimidating.

"I want pancakes."

"I'll make you pancakes."

I laugh and turn around to walk backward. "I don't want your pancakes. I want normal pancakes. Not head-game pancakes. Not maybe I'll make you happy or maybe I'll scare the shit out of you. You know?"

He squints. "You're awfully playful and free suddenly. Where is the girl from the elevator?" His tone is mocking, and I assume he means to inflict pain and embarrassment.

I jam my mitts into my pockets and shrug. "She's in here. I think there are a few of us in here. But she and I both are onto you. We see your ploy."

He laughs. "Ha. You think you do." He does something I don't expect. "When I was a kid I used to do this all the time. My dad would take us to our cabin in Aspen, and I would do anything to not be with them. When Emalyn was gone they canceled their divorce. They stayed together, hating each other and drinking. I would stand out on the deck and catch snowflakes until I was nearly frozen solid." He tilts his head back and lets the snow fall on his tongue.

I watch him for a moment and wonder if we're both friggin' bipolar. It feels like it.

I don't last long watching him, before I grab his coat and plant my lips on his. I suck his tongue and kiss him with everything I have. I slide against him, tugging my mitts off and climbing him like a tree. His hands wrap around me and carry me to the wall of the building we are beside. He thumps my back into the bricks. We make out like there is no need for air or food. Just as he puts me down and starts dragging me back to his place, I dig my heels in.

"No."

He looks back at me. "You want this."

"No, I don't."

He grins. "I can make you."

I laugh nervously and jerk my hand free. "I want the you that tilts his head back and eats the snow. I want the you that holds me and snuggles into me. I want him, but you hardly ever show him to me. I see a glimpse of him and then it's you that's back." I point disappointedly. "I want the sweet guy who puts his hand out for me."

His eyes fight something. His lips tighten. "He's in here too. I think they're a few of us." He lets go of my hand and walks away. I hate him as much as I'm suddenly and overwhelmingly addicted to him. How do I always end up as the bad guy with him? First, I was too feeble and too quiet and too broken. Now I'm too smart-assed and too playful.

I snarl and turn to walk home. I make it a few blocks when an exhausted-looking Stuart pulls up.

"Get in, you pain in the ass."

I glance at him and roll my eyes. "It's like a few blocks." I point.

"If you get raped in one block, I'm a dead man."

I mutter rebuttals but climb in the front seat next to him.

"I heard that," he mutters and drives.

"I hate him."

His lips wriggle back and forth. "I know. I also know you all can't live without each other. You saved each other when you were kids, and it isn't any different now. You just gotta find a way to save each other again."

I look straight ahead and let my filter turn down all my arguments. When we get to the dorms I stumble up the steps and feel lost in too many ways to process. I'm exhausted.

When I hit the sheets I sleep instantly.

I wake to Michelle humming and glance at the clock with a grimace. She frowns at me. "Dude, when did you get home?"

The light is blinding, and I can barely get my eyes open. "Booooo. Stop being cheerful and humming."

She sits on my bed and bounces it. I grumble and pull the covers up.

"Did you make the crawl of shame?"

I open one eye and peak from the covers like a hermit crab. "What?"

She pulls back the covers and plucks my t-shirt. "What is this?"

Pressing my lips together, I swallow and stretch and moan a little. "My—" I clear my throat, "—uhm, t-shirt."

There's no way to avoid her eyes or the inquisitive brow. I make duck lips and watch her arch her eyebrows and shake her head, pointing at my shirt and waggling her finger. "Nuh uh. No. I know all your dirty, skeezy little orphan clothes and this shit isn't yours." She bats her eyelashes blankly. "Spill bitch."

"It's nothing." I roll onto my side and try to imagine the words I would use to describe it. There are none.

"Fine. Keep your secrets. Just say it was Sebastian. I want details eventually; I kind of have an idea how it goes anyway." She closes her eyes and grinds her hips on my bed. "Oh. Yeah I got some visuals for that one."

I shove her and laugh. "You're so nasty."

"Was it Sebastian?" Her green eyes narrow.

My heart is racing and I force a nod, but she immediately knows it's a lie. "No. What have you done? Did you wreck it with Sebastian?"

I shake my head. "I don't know. Maybe. I'm seeing him tonight to try to fix things with us."

"Sweet Jesus. Somebody lost her V-Card and went wild with it." She looks around. "Where is your phone?"

"Why?"

She grins. "'Cause Catholic Girls Gone Wild is gonna be calling. Dating two guys at once is the minimum requirement for the show."

I roll my eyes. "I left my phone at his house. I told Eli I don't want anything from him. I am going to go to financial aid today and apply for a loan for summer semester."

Her perfectly arched eyebrows knit. "Huh? You humped him and wore his shit home, so he can't pay for your schooling anymore?"

I cover my eyes and moan. "Noooooo. Don't say humped. So nasty." Who am I to call anything sexual, nasty? I open my eyes and bite my lip.

"Dude, did you take those pills I gave you?"

I nod.

"Good. Did you use a condom? You don't want to be having sex without protection. You don't know where Eli has been."

My heart burns when I think about his room. He has that for a reason. He uses it on other girls. He didn't build it over Christmas for us. This is a thing for him—a way of life. I fight a gag.

"For reals, are you done with Eli or not? Stringing dudes on is wrong. Even I don't do two at a time."

"No. I don't want to see him again." I shake my head again. "I don't know. No. I don't know. I just want to sleep longer and then go to financial aid. I have a paper due next week and I haven't even started. I'm meeting Sebastian tonight. I know that much."

Her eyes twinkle. "Wanna take this new found awesome-sauce you have and try going to a bar again?"

I'm about to shove her right off the bed and say no, but I don't. I stop and think. I nod once. If I can get blindfolded and spanked, I can try a bar again.

She squeals and butt-hops on my bed. "We can double. I'll ask Vince to come."

"Who?"

Her eyes widen in delight. "Rebound boy. I love me some rebound boy."

"What about Stuart?" I think about what he said earlier. I like Stuart. I feel loyal to him.

"What about Sebastian?" She mocks me.

"Dick."

She sticks her tongue out and leaves for class. I stare up at the stark white of the ceiling. The images I never saw because of the blindfold, but can imagine, flood the empty space in my mind. His hands holding me and the silver flash of metal spanking me. I squeeze my thighs together and sigh. I need closure. I need to not want him.

I get up and pull on my own yoga pants that Shell said I needed and a lime-green hoodie. I slip on my Uggs and my white down coat. I turn the lock and walk out of the room. I'm partway down the stairs when I think I see him.

My insides tighten to the point of cramping. I can't get air.

Last night I joked and laughed and called him crazy, and then he broke my heart a little. Today, seeing Eli makes me want to cry, but the tears are trapped in my chest making it tight. I feel like I had a heart attack.

I stop and watch him looking like Business Eli in his pea coat and dress pants, while he's talking to someone. His dark hair is in the faux-hawk. He's pointing with a leather glove at my building and shaking his head. I grimace and watch him. His blue eyes look intense and angry. It makes my stomach twinge.

I creep to the door and push it softly and pull my hood up. I hurry to the path to the left, instead of toward the sidewalk where he is.

His voice speaking to the man like he's a subordinate reminds me of how he talks to me. "I don't care what the problem is with it, it's how I want it. Change the policy." The arrogance in his voice makes me shudder.

I hustle along the sidewalk, through the paths made by other people's footsteps. The wind is cold and bitter.

I climb the steps of the building and walk to the financial aid office. I walk in and smile at the secretary. She is older with brown hair and a mom look. She isn't trendy like Dr. Bradley. She's just a mom. Cuddly and soft.

"Hi, sweetie," she says. I like her instantly.

I have a seat and smile. "Hi."

"Can I help you?"

I nod. "I hope so. Here's my student ID. I need to discuss a student loan for next semester and beyond that."

She smiles. "Grants and scholarships running out?"

I cross my arms. "Something like that."

She takes the card and pulls on glasses. "Let's see what we have here." She puts my number in. She frowns. "Honey, you have paid your tuition up to the end of your degree. There is a note on the account that if you choose to stay on for your masters or doctorate, we are to contact your guardian, a Mr. Elijah Adams." She squints. "Does that sound right?"

"Something like that." I sigh, defeated.

She hands me back the ID. She looks bug eyed with the glasses on. I take it back and stand up, crushed. "Thanks."

I'm sure she thinks I'm nuts. I walk back out into the cold and look in the direction of my building.

I don't have anything without him. I need a job. I walk to my dorm, sneaking past the sidewalk where he was but he isn't there anymore.

I climb the stairs and wonder what to do about my financial situation. I'm muddled and distracted from plotting through my heavy disappointment when I open the door. It's how I miss the man on my bed. I close the door and stop when I see the shoes. They're the ones that kicked me in the parking lot. They make the breath in my throat hitch. He kicked me with those shoes.

I press my back against the door and let my eyes travel up his pants slowly.

He looks moody when he cocks his eyebrow and holds my phone up. "You forgot something last night."

"Why did you pay all my tuition for the next four years?"

He ignores me. "Stop being a pain in the ass. Do you know how hard it is to track you without the cell phone? Stuart and I literally have to follow you everywhere you go. It's annoying. Luckily, I had a meeting here today so I could return it."

"I don't want any more help from you. I don't want money or stuff or Stuart driving my ass around."

He stands up and fixes his coat. He walks to the door and bends to kiss my cheek. "Are you angry?" he asks in a soft voice. His words brush against my skin, making me shiver.

I nod.

"Good." He takes my hand and opens the door to the dorm. "I have something I want to show you, and I sort of need you angry for it." He pulls me from the dorm. My stomach flutters with excitement.

I let him drag me but I mutter, "I want those damned shoes burned."

He laughs. "Deal."

"I still can't believe you kicked me."

"I didn't want to. I needed you to believe."

I glance at him as we leave the dorms. "Keep telling yourself that."

He grins his cocky, shitty grin. "Keep telling yourself the paddle doesn't turn you on."

I blush and hate that he knows so much about me. Hearing the word "paddle" makes my cheeks feel like they are on fire—both sets.

🌟 19 🌟

His hand doesn't leave mine, not even in the SUV. Stuart pulls up to the curb of a dodgy-looking building. His eyes meet mine, and I sense worry coming off him as we climb out. I notice Stuart doesn't get out and open the door for Eli. Eli's grip on my hand tightens as we walk up to an unmarked building. I glance to the right, contemplating how fast I could make it in Uggs slipping and sliding down the road before he caught me.

I'm filled with a disturbing fear.

He wants me angry.

He wants to show me something.

I have no idea what it could be, but the last time I agreed to something I ended up being tortured and beaten. I understand why Dr. Bradley wanted it done, but I don't think I'm strong enough to do it again. I know I'm not.

I see a bulky guy walking up to the door. He's beaming when he sees Eli. "Adams, yo. You're back." They slap hands like they grew up in the same hood. I'm officially freaking out. The guy eyes me up. He nods at me.

Eli points to me. "This is Sarah Mastermen."

I've never heard of that girl, except in the article. It feels weird to be her.

"Sarah, this is Angelo. He's a lightweight champ."

I eye him up and down, swallowing hard. Is he going to hurt me?

He's a beast. He doesn't look like a lightweight. Angelo grins. "I can strip weight off like a mutha."

Strip weight like a mutha?

I nod and smile like my Spanish teacher always told me to do when I was lost in class.

Angelo gets the door for us as though he wants to open the door for Eli.

They both watch me, waiting for me to go in. I walk nervously into the room.

It's gray: gray walls, gray floors, a gray feeling. The air is warm and heady.

I clutch my coat. Then I hear it. Grunts and slaps.

I gulp, holding my shaking hands and fighting the tremble trying to take over.

"You're safe." Eli's whisper on my neck and his hand on the small of my back are warm, like he's trying to relax me. He guides me through to a room with benches. Angelo watches me, grinning and shaking his head. He starts taping up his hands and stripping clothes off.

Eli is doing the same. Seeing him down to a tight white undershirt is a distraction from the feeling I might pee my pants any second. I can see his tats through it.

Angelo is even more so a distraction. His abs are sculpted and ridged. I feel the blush glowing on my cheeks and glance down at the floor. Angelo leaves the room and winks at me. "See you out there, Tinkerbell. Unless you chicken out. I understand if you're too scared to do this."

He thinks I'm scared because of whatever this place is. He doesn't know why. I look back at Eli. "Tinkerbell?"

He smiles. "You do kind of look like her. Big blue eyes and light-yellow blonde hair. I can see it." He hands me a bag and nods toward the corner. "Go put this on."

I snatch the bag and stalk off. I fling the changing room door open and sit on the bench inside the small closet-like room. I look at myself in the mirror. I only see me. I almost wish for a second I could see her still. I would do anything to see the dead-fish eyes. I would do anything to not be alone in my head. It feels like every doubt echoes in there now.

I pull out the things in the bag and look at them all. It's workout gear. Yoga pants, runners, and a sports bra. He wants me to exercise with him?

I sigh a relief-filled breath and start to drag my clothes off. Everything from the bag fits perfectly, including the runners. I jump when he bangs on the door. "Let's go, Tink."

"Fuck you, Eli." My response startles me, but I'm on edge from what I thought this might be.

The changing room is silent. His response is clearly not a good one, but I am getting past the point of caring.

I fling the door open, stuffing my things in the bag.

His face is red and his square jaw is tight. "Do I ever speak to you that way?"

"Let's not discuss the things you do to me."

He looks at me bitterly as I walk to the elevator. I hate myself for wishing the Eli with the paddle was the one here. At least if he was using me for sex we might both be in a good mood.

I shoulder past him and walk through the doors Angelo went through. I'm in a long hallway. I hear the door swing again when he walks through it. He shoulders me back and turns. "In this place, you get what you give."

"Well then, let's play. I have some serious shit I'd love to give back to you."

He licks his lips and fights a grin. The dimple distracts me for a second.

He nods and walks through another door at the end of the hall. The noise blasts into the hallway from the door. I slow down and fight my stomach gnawing feeling. I push through and gulp.

The room is so much more than I expected.

It's several rings, wrestling or boxing rings. There is music playing somewhere from a shitty sound system and guys grunting everywhere. I see a girl with man muscles and grimace.

"Don't look so horrified. She's a pro female boxer."

"Heavy weight?"

"No." He laughs and shoves me along. His fingers bite into my skin. I pull away. He looks at me and the red marks on my arm. "Sorry. I get pretty hyped in here."

My arms wrap around me. It's involuntary.

I've boxed in gym class. I actually liked it. It was fun to hit things and people, but I haven't done it in years and never with guys like this. Eli who has to be six two and two-twenty is not a big guy here. He's not even average. He's lean. Everyone else is a beast of sorts.

Everyone knows him, from the old guys who look like bikers, to the young guys who look like UFC champs. People wave to him and pound his knuckles.

He strolls over to the far corner where an older man is talking to some younger guys. They're skinny and more my size. I realize they're more like twelve, as we get closer.

I sigh, realizing he's going to make me take self-defense classes with little boys. I wonder if maybe they're Catholic too, and chuckle in my head at my joke.

I stop chuckling, reminding myself how sane people don't laugh at their own jokes inside their heads. They tell them aloud and laugh.

I look at the crowd and straight away my filter shuts that one down.

The older man smiles at me. "You must be Sarah." He claps his hands and beams at me.

I force my lips to turn up and be polite. He has enough joy inside him for us both. He's old but still sparkly eyed and feisty.

"I'm Lance, in case Eli there hasn't told you, and this is beginners' boxing."

The boys look at me, appraising me.

Hands grip my shoulders. "You boys go easy on Tinkerbell here, okay?" Angelo squeezes me. "You still have a chance to run away, Tink." He slaps me on the ass and walks off laughing. My eyes are wide and horrified.

Lance laughs. "If that's gonna offend you, Tink, you're gonna need to toughen up. Or take a seat on the pine over there."

Fire burns in my eyes when I glance at Eli. He is pressing his lips together. He looks like he's about to burst.

Lance claps his hands again. "Three laps around the gym. Fast. I want a quick warm-up."

I stretch my legs and flex everything. When Lance blows his whistle I jolt past Eli.

I could kill him.

I think of the millions of things I want to say to him. How I don't want to obey him and be under his thumb. The things get less and less important as my legs finish their stretch and I kick it into high gear.

I'm lapping the kids and Lance.

As I lap Eli I laugh. "Still can't catch me, huh?" I shoulder him and keep running. I hear his pace pick up, but I have loads of room left in my legs to stretch out. I kick it up. He doesn't stand a chance. I finish my last lap and start stretching.

Lance comes in next; he beats Eli and the kids. I eye up Eli as he comes in next. He gives me a death glare but I shrug it off. "Somebody let an old man outrun him."

"In the ring, Tink." Lance points at me.

"Lance—uhm—sir. My name is Sarah." I sigh.

He waves me off. "We all have nicknames here. I'll never remember Sarah. But with your hair in that bun, you look like Tinkerbell."

I look back at Eli who is still sucking wind. "What's his nickname?"

Lance looks confused. "That's Eli. We don't nickname him."

I point at Angelo kicking the crap out of a guy in the ring next to us. "Him?"

"Angelo."

"What's his real name?" I ask and pull myself into the ring.

"Angelo?" He says it like I'm the dumb one. I'm exasperated, but I climb in the stupid ring. It feels funny when I walk. I bounce and hop and get why boxers can spring around so easily when they fight on TV.

The kids start to filter in. Lance throws tape at me. "Tape up."

Eli saunters over and takes the tape. He wraps my hands. They feel funny. He sticks the tape in his pocket and winks at me. "For later."

My right eye twitches. He laughs and walks away.

The kids and I stretch, practice air boxing, and practice some more. My shoulders and arms are burning. A couple times I feel like I might pass out. I'm the one wheezing and sucking air now. I haven't done an exercise like this one in ages.

Eli has left. I look around for him and catch the cross tat in the far corner. He's naked from the waist up and fighting a beast of a man. Eli is fast. I wouldn't have even known it was him, if it weren't for the huge cross. He fights with severity and passion.

"He's good, huh?"

I glance over at the kid next to me and nod. I look around at the fighters and sigh. "Kinda scary. These guys are all good."

He hits my butt with his glove and nods. "We'll be that good one day, Tink."

I glance at Lance and shoot daggers with my eyes, but he just grins at me.

"Okay, first up for sparing. Tink and Brandon."

I look around to see a kid grinning and thanking his lucky stars he gets to beat on a girl.

Brandon is taller than I am and not nearly as skinny as I would like him to be. I purse my lips and wince. "Can't I have that kid?" I point to a scrawny kid in the corner whose face matches mine.

Lance rolls his bright twinkly eyes. "Tink. He's eleven. Brandon is fourteen. He's closer in age to you."

Brandon has a shit-eating grin. I want to make him eat it. I know what's more realistic though. I'm going to get beaten up by a little boy. Lance straps my helmet on and knocks it. "Ouch."

"That's so you know how it feels." He slides a guard in my mouth. I start to panic and gag. "Shith hurtsh." I point with my glove at the guard in my mouth that he touched. Is it clean?

He ignores me. I try to forget about the fingers that touched my mouth guard. I am not that girl anymore. I'm stronger than that.

"Thtupid mouth guard gives me a lithp," I mutter.

He grabs my heavy-ass gloved hand and drags me to the middle of the ring. Brandon looks like he's king of the hill. I just want to kick him in the pills and end it.

"Clean fight, no kicking in the junk, no biting, and no kissing, Brandon." I look horrified and Brandon's face is beet red. He snickers and nods at the smug-ass kid behind me.

"Mitts in."

I put my mitts in and Brandon pounds my hands. My skinny arms drop. The gloves weigh a ton.

Lance throws a hand up. "Fight!" he shouts. I step back immediately. Brandon swings wildly. I turtle and cry out, "Ow, you little thit. Thtop it. Let me have a chanthe."

His fists pummel me. I realize after a bit he isn't hitting that hard. Eli hits harder with a paddle.

"COME ON, TINK!" Lance is screaming like a madman.

I swing out once but the gloves weigh a serious ton. Brandon connects when I swing and knocks me in the eye. I stagger back as the kids groan. Brandon stops hitting.

I see red. It takes me a second to get my eyes to stop seeing stars. I jump up and fly at him. I'm screaming like a savage. Only I'm not punching. I'm swatting like a girl. He screams and turtles as I lose it.

Hands grab me. I'm kicking and shouting. Lance is holding me back. He's laughing so hard he's shaking me. The boys are laughing. Except Brandon. He looks pissed. My eye is swelling. I'm still like a savage animal. I'm snarling and snapping like a rabid dog.

It's chaos.

Lance is shaking me and pinning my arms and screaming at me, or Brandon. Brandon comes at me. He pulls back his arm. I see the fist closing in on me and I duck. My arms come free from Lance. I tackle Brandon to the ground and pin him there. The boys are cheering and laughing.

I'm swinging like a girl, hitting over and over like the kid on *A Christmas Story*. He's screaming, but it isn't the pain he's screaming about. It takes me a minute to realize that red spit is pouring from my mouth guard. I lift my glove to my mouth, disgusted. "Oh my God, I'm tho thorrry." He is trying to shield himself from the spit I'm shooting everywhere when I talk. I scream and jump off, "I'm thorrry."

He flinches and scrambles to his feet, wiping blood and spittle from his face, arms, and chest. I gag, even though it's mine.

Lance has taken a knee. Angelo and Eli are both watching, leaning against each other and nearly crying.

I'm the only one not laughing.

My eye hurts. I shake my hands at Lance. "I want out."

He laughs, harder. I'm trapped in the stupid gloves, bleeding and swelling, and poor Brandon is far worse for wear. He's completely covered in my spit.

❧ 20 ❧

"**I**f he hit you, you can tell me." I glance at Shell in the mirror and scowl. "For reals, it was a fourteen-year-old little shit. I blame Eli, but it was a little boy who hit me."

Her arms are crossed. She pulls her phone out and texts. "I just don't see why you didn't leave."

"Because they called me Tinkerbell and made fun of me. All the women there looked like dudes. I was the only girl with girlie arms. I had to try. What would you have done if they called you Tinkerbell?"

She laughs. "You know, you do look like Tinkerbell. In tenth grade the theater teacher really wanted to cast you as Tinkerbell, but I convinced her you would never do it."

Horror is spread across my face in the mirror. She puts her hands up defensively and goes to her side of the room. I dust the huge bruise under my eye with my powder concealer, but nothing seems to be working. I sigh. "Sebastian is going to be meeting me here in twenty minutes, and I look like a victim of domestic violence. He's gonna look like a monster if we go anywhere."

She laughs. "Dude, no one is gonna think that."

I arch an eyebrow at her in the mirror.

"Okay they will, but screw them. Who cares? You're *Million Dollar*

Baby."

I roll my eyes. "I was so *Million Dollar Baby*. It wasn't even funny. I was a natural, let me tell you."

She laughs at the sarcasm dripping off each word. She gets up and applies makeup to my eye. She steps back and nods. "There. No one will even see it." She slumps back onto her bed.

I inspect the job she has done and nod. "I was the worst boxer— ever—to grace the rings of that club. Or any—" I'm interrupted by a noise. I look around. "Do you hear that?"

"It's your phone." She doesn't look up from playing with hers.

I frown. "I gave it back."

Her eyebrows raise but her tone is nonchalant, "Yeah, huge shocker —he managed to sneak it back to you. The guy's a creepy ninja."

Standing up and crossing the room I mutter, "It's a dick move if he did." I squeeze the pockets of my coat but nothing. Hearing it again, I glance at my Ugg as a sneer crosses my face. I tilt the boot back and the iPhone falls out into my hand.

"Sneaky Sneakerton," I whisper and turn it over.

I need to see you tonight.

I shake my head and text him back. *No. I have a date with Sebastian.* My stomach twinges, imagining what he'll do to me if I see him. How much further into the darkness he will pull me. Or how much further I will let him.

Where are you going?

I purse my lips and ask Shell, "Where are we going tonight?"

She doesn't look up. "Liquor Store."

"That's a bar?" Doesn't sound like a bar.

She nods and keeps playing with her phone.

Liquor Store . . .

No. They have a mechanical bull. Think about how classy that is.

I roll my eyes and mock his right to call anything classy. I put the phone in my pocket. The warmth of it is a comfort. It vibrates more. He's calling. I ignore it. I pull on my coat and boots.

"You can't wear that." She glances up and points at the boots. I look down and shake my head. "It's freezing out there. I'm wearing boots."

She gets up and passes me a pair of ballet flats. "Wear these at least. With the boots, dude, they won't even let you in."

I snatch them and put them on. My feet are cold in our warm room. She opens the door and grins at me. I am fighting an army of butterflies in my stomach. I don't even want to face him, but I know I need to. I need to face my fears more often.

When we get outside, Sebastian is mulling around the front of the building with a guy I've never met. I assume he's Vince.

When Sebastian's hazel eyes meet mine, I can see the hesitation in them. It doesn't surprise me. I can't blame him at all.

He looks like he did the first date, casual. I like this look better. He's mellow and comfortable. It reminds me of Audrey Tautou, lazy kisses, and ice cream.

Shell smirks. "Vince, Sebastian, and my BFF Em—er—Sarah."

"Emersarah, that's a strang—interesting name."

"It's Sarah." I laugh. Sebastian raises his eyebrows and watches me. He offers me a hand, looking at Shell. "We've introduced ourselves already."

Vince looks smug and Italian, of course. She has no intention of dating him longer than she needs to, in order to make Stuart suffer. She hates Italian men.

I roll my eyes and take Sebastian's hand. Vince grabs her butt and kisses her neck.

My eyes dart nervously for the SUV.

"Can we get a ride, Sarah?" Shell asks sweetly.

I look at her, horrified, and shake my head. "No. Absolutely not." I get her loyalty to me, but I won't torture Stuart. Not even if he tortured me.

Sebastian points. "I drove over. I can get us there." I smile at him and ignore the constant vibration in my pocket.

We walk to the car, and I feel as though I have lost my ability to have a conversation. The guilt is heavy and uncomfortable. I hate how close we are to Shell and Vince, but I need to get it off my chest. I squeeze his arm. "I'm sorry. I'm an emotional moron."

He squeezes back. "It's all adjustments. Tiny adjustments. So what's the plan? I thought we were going to talk?"

"Shell wants to double date. New guy. She doesn't like going alone with new guys. I don't like it when she does either."

He nods. "Yeah, God forbid you both end up kidnapped this year."

I try to see if there was any humor in his voice or if it was all bitterness. I shake it off and smile. "Anyway, I was thinking why not. Why not just do something normal? You're normal and I want to be normal and bars and dancing are normal."

He laughs. "You and the normal. You have got to get past that."

Vince interrupts us with an excited question, "Dude, is this you?" He points at the small silver SUV-type car Sebastian is leading us to.

I see him in a new light when he grins and presses the unlock button. I glance at Shell, but she looks confused like I am. It's a car. Apparently, it might not be just a car. Not the way Vince is laughing and nodding approvingly. "Wow. Awesome."

I'm lost. Maybe it's some kind of special car.

Sebastian opens the passenger door for me. The inside is leather and smells new. I frown. "You decided against the hybrid for this?"

He walks around and sits inside smirking as Vince leans forward. "This is the 2013 Porsche Cayenne. It's a hybrid. Dude, this is a sweet ride." It's like listening to people speak another language.

Sebastian shrugs. "It's awesome and badass, but it's good for the environment. It's not a Cayman. But I figured with the way winter is here and back in Maine, this was the better choice. Besides, I can always buy a Cayman next year." He sounds like he's gloating a bit. It's weird seeing him be this way. He's always so humble and normal.

I smile. "You got the hybrid?" I like that.

He nods. "I wasn't sure if you remembered that boring talk we had, but I did. I went out after I left and bought it."

I look ahead. "I remember. It's a nice car."

"Thanks." He looks in the rearview at Shell and Vince. "Where are we going?"

"Where do you want to go? You're twenty-one. We're not. We kind of wanted to go to Liquor Store."

His lip twitches. "Vince? You probably know better than I do. I don't go out much."

Vince nods. "Yeah. Let's do Rain or Liquor Store."

Sebastian puts the car in drive and nods. "Liquor Store it is." He handles the snow and wind like a pro. The car is very nice. I can't help but get excited. He's normal, squeaky clean, and responsible. Shell would call him vanilla. I like vanilla. You know what you're getting into with it. You can add anything to it. It doesn't spank you and make you like it.

My phone vibrates and I fight the sick fact I like the control. I glance over at Sebastian and know it'll never be a power struggle with him. It'll be a partnership.

When we get to the bar I see it's exactly like Eli said it would be. It's not seedy but it's also not classy. Sebastian looks around and drinks from his beer. I nudge him. "So are you horribly rich?"

He glances at me and takes another swig.

"I've been meaning to talk to you about all of this."

I feel my walls starting to build as my emotions lay the foundation bricks. For some reason he makes me nervous in a bad way.

He shakes his head. "I'm not a student at the college. I never was."

The next layer of bricks is mortared and dry. My wall is going up fast.

He grabs my hand. "No—stop. Don't look at me like that. You assumed I was in school. I could tell you were—different, so I never corrected you. I didn't want to scare you off." He says it in an ever so slightly patronizing tone.

I don't like that. I remind myself it might be that I'm pissed and being jaded, like I do with Shell. I swallow the anger and let him finish.

"My company is doing work for the school. We are helping them design a new intranet. I own a company. My family lives in Maine. I'm a fisherman's son. Regular guy."

I scowl. "How old are you?"

"Twenty-six."

I nod and think. "Why were you using the gym like a student?"

He blushes. "The dean told me I could use the facilities whenever I wanted."

"Twenty-six," I say slowly. My brain is trying to wrap around it all. My twentieth birthday is soon. He's six years older than I am. Eli is five years older. It's not creepy older, but I still feel off about the lying.

I can't breathe very well processing it all. He takes another drink and suddenly I realize he's drinking too fast. "You're driving, right?" I ask.

He shakes his head. "No. I had someone come and get the car and put it in the parking under my building. I have a ride coming to get us later."

I don't know how I feel. I don't know where to put everything.

"Are you pissed?" He watches my face.

"About the car or the lies?"

He laughs. He looks at me and shakes his head. "I never told you I went to the school. I have never lied to you."

I point at him but my words get stuck. I sigh. "You knew I thought you went to school. I asked you how things were and you knew I meant classes. You knew."

"I did, but you seemed really comfortable with that idea, and all I wanted was for you to be comfortable."

"I need to go to the bathroom." I walk away, before he grabs my arm and drags me to a corner to explain.

I glare at Shell. She runs off the dance floor, following me to the bathroom.

I almost wish we'd brought the paper bags, just in case of a moment like this. I feel like I don't know him at all. I hate that.

"What?"

I cross my arms and look at myself in the mirror. "I do look like Tinkerbell."

She laughs. "You did not interrupt my rubbing against Vincent's massive erection for this conversation."

I give her my best pathetic-orphan face. "Sebastian doesn't go to our school."

"I don't understand."

"He's like twenty-six and owns a company and he's super successful."

"Are you complaining?"

"He lied, Shell."

Her jaw drops. "How in the fuck do you keep scoring the hotties with the wallets. Damn. Girl, Vince doesn't even have a car. Sebastian has a job already. He owns his shit. Vince wants to be a gym teacher and Stuart is a chauffeur. Your chauffeur."

My face is red. I grimace. I have no defense. She doesn't see how much all those things are just things to me. They don't belong in the world that I do, so I don't notice them the same way she does. I don't place value on them. "He lied," I mutter again.

She throws her hands in the air. "OH MY GOD! HE LIED! YES, LET'S STRING HIM UP FOR TRYING TO CODDLE THE ORPHAN!" She turns to leave but looks back at me. "This is crackers, dick. You don't want to date him. You want to date Eli. Poor Sebastian doesn't stand a chance. You'll find something wrong with him, no matter what. Like Pinterest says, 'Look at that bitch, eating her crackers like she owns the place and shit.' This is crackers." She storms out.

I look at my reflection and force myself to think about it. I want to end it and just walk away. It'll be his fault. I can make a clean break if he lied and he's to blame. I'd be able to walk away from the commitment and intimacy, and still be free from the baggage I bring.

I nod at myself. "She's right." I walk out of the bathroom and stalk across the bar. It's one of those moments where you need a killer song and a hot pair of boots to stomp across the bar with, to make the scene complete.

Unfortunately, the song is lame and I'm wearing ballet flats. I don't let that take away from the strength and fearlessness I am exuding; it's fake, but I can fake it till I make it. His eyes widen when he sees me come across the bar at him. He sets down his drink, preparing.

But I do the unexpected. I grab his face and pull it down on mine. I suck him in with my kiss. His arms wrap around me, lifting me. My chest is crushed against his. His hands cup my ass, squeezing harder than I would have imagined him capable of. I moan into his mouth. His hands knead and massage.

He lets me go and I slide down his torso. He licks his lips and looks past me. "What the hell was in that bathroom?"

I laugh. "Common sense. I was in short supply."

"You okay?"

"I'm not breakable. Stop coddling me because I'm an orphan. I know I was insane before, but I have learned I am not breakable."

He puts his hands in the air. "I swear, never again. In fact, it's a bit of a relief. I can finally start acting like the asshole I am around you." I laugh. His eyes sparkle like Santa and his manners are impeccable. He's perfect.

My thoughts are broken by the sound of shouts and cheering.

"Oh shit," he mutters. I spin and gasp. Michelle is on the bull in her bra and jeans. My hands are hovering at my mouth in horror. I still can't touch my fingers to my lips in a public place, but it's flu season and that's common sense.

Michelle is bucking and riding the bull. Her fuchsia bra is bouncing up and down.

"Oh my God."

He's laughing. I can feel the vibration. "Wow." She is getting sloppy and laughing. Vince is cheering her on.

My face is red. I rip my phone out and send a text.

Maybe you should get Stuart to come get Shell.

Call her Michelle. No. Stuart's hurt. I'm not doing that to him. We need to talk.

No. I'm hurt. I'm not doing that to me.

I pocket my phone. "We should take her home."

He looks at my pocket. "Who was that?"

Pursing my lips, I sigh. "That was my benefactor. I haven't been honest either. But we need to leave and take that with us." I point at her.

He laughs. "She's having fun. Mellow out. The bull rides are free, and you win a prize if you take your shirt off."

His arm is against the wall, trapping me in. "Spill."

I close my eyes and just get it out, "The guy who was there when I was little, the one who saved me—he's my benefactor. He takes care of me." I open one eye and watch his face. The loud music and raucousness being caused by Shell are annoying. I wish we were alone for this moment.

He looks like he's processing. He drinks a swig of beer. "Okay. I'm an adult who owns a company and you're a benefactor-having orphan. Do you moonlight as a superhero?"

I shake my head.

He blinks a couple times and looks down at me. "Anything else?"

I chew my lip, shaking my head. I'm not telling him the rest. We will cross the dirty-bitch bridge if he spanks me and gets a surprising reaction.

He bends and brushes his face against mine. "Was it him you were texting on all our dates and all the time?"

I nod and wait.

"Is it strictly financial? The two of you?"

I shake my head. "No. We're—uh—close." I don't know how to tell him that we have PTSD sex and he spanks me, but that there is no relationship beyond misplaced intimacy and a bizarre friendship.

"Like siblings?"

"Uhhhhh, no."

He pauses and thinks some more. He's killing me with his processing. He stands up straight again and drinks another big gulp before he talks. "Okay. It's weird, and I don't know that I can ever understand. But I'm going to just trust you and assume that if you and I get together it's just you and I."

I don't have any response for him. I don't know what we are.

Shell gets off the bull and grabs Vince. She plants a huge kiss on his lips and the bar erupts in a cheer. I smile. I don't have a choice. Even if she's insane, I love her so much. I love her freedom. Nothing weighs more than a feather would in her mind.

She pulls on her shirt and grins at me. She nods at the bull. Immediately, my cheeks are hot. I shake my head and pray she isn't going to make a scene. She sees me shut it down and laughs in a way only she can. People are dancing and forgetting about the gorgeous topless girl who just rode the bull like a pro.

"Let me know when you're ready to go."

I force a smile across my face. I know it doesn't reach my eyes. "Let's dance."

He looks at the dance floor and nods. "You sure?"

I grab his beer and put it on the bar and drag him to the dance floor. I happen to love the song playing. It's "Don't You Worry Child" by Swedish House Mafia, and it's amazing. We dance without touching but then the next song comes on, "Scream and Shout" by Britney and will.i.am. My hips start to bounce on their own.

I understand the phrase booty pop. I'm popping mine. A trickle of sweat tickles its way down my back as the crowd of people surrounds me. It makes me nervous but we move together. We pause together. The music controls us all like marionettes. Hands grip at my hips, pulling me into him.

I glance back at Sebastian. His eyes are on fire. It makes me smile. My nerves get worse, but it isn't the crowd. It's the hands pulling me backward, into his groin. He grinds me against him to the beat. My arms are in the air. I wanna scream and shout too. I want him to make me scream and shout.

The slow part of the song hits. I reach back and grip my arms around his neck. His hands wrap around me, sliding against my belly but still pulling me into him. It's me moving my hips, grinding against him. The beat picks up again. I pull away and dance. It's fun. The girl next to me bumps into me. I recoil, but let it go. My throat is thick with nerves, terror, and the anticipation that is coming from the look in his eyes. I can see that he wants me.

It's the greatest panic attack I've ever had. He's not the most amazing dancer but he's there. His hands are in the air, making him look seven feet tall. He looks normal. Being at the bar with him is normal. It feels freeing until I catch myself looking at his shoulders and thinking about holding them while he's pinning me to a wall. He may be normal but I may never be.

He catches my glance and laughs, shaking his head. The song blends into Olly Murs, "Troublemaker." I love this song. He points at me and mouths, "You are this girl."

I open my mouth offended, "Hey." He pulls me closer. The song is awesome, just not sexy like "Scream and Shout" was, but it's fun. I glance at Shell and Vince dancing. He's an amazing dancer.

"Want to go?" Sebastian whispers into my neck. I pause a moment to give the decision a fair amount of debate. *Will I actually be able to sleep with him? No.*

I shake my head. "No." He looks disappointed, but he's too kind to let the look stay there.

✥ 21 ✥

I finish proofing my essay and click save. I close my laptop and sit with the feelings I'm having. I don't have a decision made. I don't have a choice I want more than the other. But I'm not dating both. So I will wait it out. I nod at myself, like a crazy woman. I've spent the entire day avoiding Sebastian's attempts at getting me to come over. I know what he wants, and I don't know if I can do it. Not so soon after doing it with Eli. I'm not like Shell.

I pick up my phone. It's vibrated nonstop. There are tons of messages and voicemails.

The newest text is from Eli. *Meet me now.*

Instead of giving the request thought I get up, pull on my coat, and run down the stairs. When I cross the street to where Stuart stands outside the SUV, I notice he looks different. Less of everything—confidence, life, energy, and even muscle mass. His lean, gorgeous glow is replaced with something sad and empty.

The snow falls on our heads. The sounds surrounding us are plenty, but it feels like I can hear the snow falling in our little world where it's just he and I on the sidewalk. I touch his coat sleeve and smile. "She's trying to make you jealous. That says something. If she didn't want you jealous, she wouldn't be flaunting him about."

His eyes flinch. "I just messed up so bad. I should have told her about it. I should have just made her more than him."

I shake my head. "It was authentic with her being scared. She is a terrible actress. Terrible. I would have seen through her act. I wouldn't have feared for my life and felt like I had lost everything. I wouldn't have died inside, knowing they were hurting you."

He looks me in the eyes, showing me his pain. "I am so sorry. I swear I will never do anything like that again."

"Don't be." I shake my head. "It worked. Crazy as it sounds, it worked. You said that, remember? I would look back one day and see it had worked. Do you know how hard it was to live with the lonely? Every day was the biggest disappointment. Every day those eyes haunted me but I couldn't place them. The curtain in my mind was more like a steel wall. You saved me, Stuart. And she will come around when she sees that it was necessary."

He opens the door. "Thanks."

I lean in on my tiptoes and kiss his cheek. "Thank you. You always will be the hands in the dark that saved me from the lonely." I climb in and wait.

He drives us in silence.

My jaw clenches seeing Eli's building. My palms are sweating, but when he opens the door I climb out. My body works against me. It's on autopilot. It wants him, more than anything.

I slowly cross to the foyer and press the button. When the doors open he's standing inside. He holds a hand out the elevator doors. I put my hand in his. He squeezes and pulls me inside. The doors close. The silence is thick and painful.

"I'm sorry," he says, maybe to me, maybe to the elevator. I don't look at him. I look at our bizarre reflections in the brushed metal. I smile, remembering what it looked like when we were crawling all over each other.

The elevator dings and he pulls me inside. He walks me to the living room I guarantee no one ever sits in but me. He doesn't let go. He sits and drags me with him. We sit on the dark-burgundy leather in silence. It doesn't feel like empty silence. It's filled with all the things we won't ever say to each other. We don't talk like normal people. Normal couples. There will never be anything normal between us.

I glance at the snow on my boots and frown. "I should take my shoes off."

"No." He says it brusquely.

I flinch. He sighs and speaks, still not looking at me, "What do you want?"

"What?" I turn and face him, adjusting how I sit so I can see him. He looks different. I don't have an answer because I don't understand the question. I just pray he speaks again so I don't have to.

"What do you want, Sarah?"

I shake my head. "What do you mean?" My voice is timid and small. My stomach is in my throat.

"I mean in life, in general. What do you want?"

I think he's about to say he won't spank me anymore. He won't touch me anymore. His grip on my hand is firm and intense. I want us so close we are like one person again. I want his skin against mine. "I want you," I whisper. It's ballsy and I've never been ballsy.

He nods. "You want the things I can offer? You can live without the others?"

My mind halts—the others? Does he mean the wishes I made a thousand times for normalcy? The normal I have craved for so long? Can I live without it? "No. I want both." I need to choose me.

He shakes his head. "There's no both. There's what's here and what's out there."

"Why do you want me? You have all that stuff down that hallway for a reason. You have all those things for a reason. You obviously didn't get them to be with me. You've had them for a while. I doubt you're in desperate need of girls to submit to you." I don't mention the fact his capabilities as a lover are outstanding and intense, like a roller-coaster would be.

"It's not something I care to discuss or explain."

I hate his walls more than I hate my own. I jerk my hand away. He flexes his, like he's letting blood back in after gripping mine so hard. I stand up. "Well then, I guess we're done with this. Why don't you call the doc for me?" I stomp away. I push the elevator button. I hear him get up. He wants me angry. He wants me to play along. He wants me to get pissed and end up bent over his dirty fucking bed. I am angry, but not in the way that he wants. I'm sick of him. I tap the button like always. He's standing behind me. I can feel the heat of him towering over me.

He's going to rush me into the elevator and strip my clothes off. I'm shaking with fury that's so close to the surface, my blood is bubbling.

My fists are clenched.

The elevator comes. I take a deep breath and step in. I turn and face him. He doesn't move.

"Why did you even want me to come over?" I ask and hold the door. I don't know why I'm bothering, but he's making me so angry.

His eyes flicker. "I followed you and watched you last night. You were having fun and being free and you looked normal. I wanted to see it up close."

I step back and let the doors close. His hand shoots in and stops the door. My skin crawls. His face is hard and smug like the man in the chair. "I want you to pick me."

My back is pressed against the cold steel wall. "And live a half life?"

His eyes flicker. He's getting angry. He looks like a monster. "I can give you everything."

I grip the steel shelf that left bruises on my butt and thighs. "Except the one thing I want. I want you. Can you give me yourself the way I've been able to give myself? I don't have any dark corners left. You've invaded them all. But then you talked like you were healed too. But you aren't."

"I want to be enough for you. I want it too." He pulls his hand back and the elevator closes. I could cry on the floor. I know he would come and get me. He would hold me and comfort me. In some ways, he desires me to be that weak girl who needs him to protect her.

Instead, I storm across the foyer and out into the cold wind and snow.

"Dr. Bradley's, please," I mutter and climb inside the SUV.

Stuart drives and lets me stew. He doesn't speak. I'm grateful.

I jump out, almost running for her building. I'm near tears when I open the door and tap the shit out of the elevator button.

I feel like something is chasing me, and if the elevator doesn't get there, it will get me.

The door opens. She's inside. She looks confused but trying to be pleasant.

"Sarah? We don't have an appointment today."

I jump inside and take huge breaths. I didn't realize I was holding my breath.

"Are you feeling all right?"

I shake my head. "I need you." I've never said those words before. We ride up to her office and I hustle into my chair. I slump in it and then I'm up. I'm pacing.

"He has me driven insane. He wants to be with me, but then he won't let me in. He won't be with me. He'll have sex with me." I pause and look at her. "No—he'll fuck me. He'll fuck me and make me crazy, but he's always got the control. I never get any. He doesn't relinquish an ounce of it. Is this still part of the game to make me better? I feel like I'm getting worse. You should really take this part out." I feel sick, imagining him with the other female patients. I sit again and cup my face in my hands. My breath is lost and erratic.

She walks across the room and sits quietly. She watches me. Her eyes are scaring me. "You have been having sexual relations with Mr. Adams? Actual sex?"

I look up, mouth agape. "How did you not clue into that? I've been strung out. Even when he was just the benefactor—even then." I can't finish the rest of the sentence.

"As a protector and a torturer. Not as a lover. Not a real one. The goal was to push you to the brink and make you walk the rest of the way."

She has never let me see behind the curtain before. It feels like *The Wizard of Oz,* and I'm just now seeing the little man and disappointment is everywhere. There is no Wizard. There is only the plan that was clearly hatched by a couple people who don't have a clue what they're doing.

"So you had no part in the seduction of the poor orphan?"

She crosses her arms. She is losing the control. He's taken it from her as well. Or maybe this time it's me that's taken it. "I would have strongly discouraged anything between you two. He sees you as his little sister in a lot of ways."

That makes me almost vomit. I breathe it back.

"He saved you. You replaced her in his heart. His protective instincts are brotherly. He is still very sick and needs a lot of care. He has never made it as far as you have, ever. His control issues have remained firm and rigid. Saving you has been the only mission in his life, since he found you. Before that it was all about finding you. He maintained your existence, even when the rest of us believed you to be a creation of his mind. Even finding you though, he has not come alive again. All he cares about is saving you, like he never did for his sister. He does nothing for himself."

Images are flashing behind my eyes. The boxing ring felt like we were friends. Siblings no, but it felt like friends. The texts have never been anything more than that, if I was lucky. I'm nearly gagging. My hands are shaking. *How did I miss it?*

"Did he punish you, sexually?"

My eyes betray me and answer her question.

She nods. "He has a thing with that. He was punishing you as Emalyn, for dying and making him a failure."

I wish I were the one who had died.

She sighs and continues, "Not to mention, how you feel about him. He saved you. You will never see the man, only the hero. You will forgive him his flaws too easily. I imagine that was what you were feeling. Not true lust. I honestly didn't think you were capable of true lust. This is progress for you, even if it's twisted and bizarre. Considering the dirty house and all."

I'm up and walking to the elevator.

"You need to stay away from him until I can help him," she calls after me.

I feel sick and dirty. My finger taps the button in a disturbing panic. My fingertip goes numb.

The elevator opens. I step in and fight the tears. I run across the parking lot, away from the SUV. Stuart doesn't see me. His head is down. I run hard and fast. My boots are killing my feet, but I run until I can't. Then I pull out my cell phone and call him. I'm frozen and pacing on the sidewalk.

"Yes." His tone is cold.

"You think of me as your sister? You've fucked me, imagining I'm your sister?"

"What? What are you talking about?"

"Dr. Bradley, she told me that you think of me as the sister who died. That you've replaced me in your heart as your sister and you love me like a sister. You protect me like her and you punish me because you're angry with her for dying." I'm huffing and puffing and blowing steam in an angry circle.

"You told Dr. Bradley about us? What we did at my house?" His voice is still cold.

"ANSWER ME, FOR FUCK'S SAKE! DID YOU FUCK ME AND THINK ABOUT YOUR SISTER?"

My ear is pressed into the phone but I know he's gone. He's hung up on me, again. My tears are blocking my throat up. I'm wheezing and pacing. My heart is broken into a thousand pieces. I crouch on the ground and sit on my heels.

"Sarah?" I look up. Stuart is pulled over to the side of the road. I laugh. I laugh hard and psychotically.

He's parked illegally and running across the street. He grabs my arm and lifts me. "What happened?" He looks concerned, but I just laugh.

He takes my cell from my gripped hand and dials.

"Meet me at the place I always park. She's upset." He hangs up.

I laugh harder.

He's called Eli. Eli who has made me dirty, and yet somehow has broken my heart in it all.

Stuart helps me across the street and into the SUV. He drives fast. He pulls up in front of the dorms. Michelle is there. She looks worried.

Stuart opens the door for me but I get out on my own. "I'm fine," I say. I don't want them to know. Even here, on the cusp of madness, I protect Eli.

Michelle looks at Stuart with daggers but he shakes his head. "I don't know."

"They just keep fucking with me. They won't let it go." I turn and grab Stuart's coat. "Thank you for everything. Don't be offended if I don't want a ride or to see you. Please."

He shakes his head. "I get it."

Michelle puts a hand out for me. I look at it. I shake my head. "I can walk alone." I hug myself and trek across the road and the snow-covered grass.

My dorm is a haven. It's the only place I feel safe, with or without Shell. I curl into my bed and turn on the TV. Shell comes into the room, watching me.

"I'm fine," I say and turn on the Xbox.

"You're clearly not fine. Spill." She sits in the way of the TV. I stare past her. I can't let her see inside me. I can't let her see what's in there and what I have allowed to happen. What sick fetish filth I have let overcome me.

My jaw trembles slightly. I know she can see me. She is the only one.

"He doesn't love me," I whisper.

"It's more than that? I can tell."

"He really sees me as his sister."

She pauses and takes it in. "What do you mean?"

I can't pull the words back. I've let them out. I'm panicking about the fact she's processing them and I hate the things I have allowed. The things she will see any second when she puts it all together. She will see me for the weak girl I am. But in the end I need someone. Someone I can process it with.

"Sarah, what do you mean?" she presses me.

I keep my eyes covered and continue, "He wanted me to be his sister; he sees me as her. When he saved me it was like he saved her. But when he punished me, he was really punishing her. I am her." My head is twitching.

In my peripheral I see her face. It's filled with the disgust I knew it would be. "Sick bastard," she whispers.

I close my eyes but feel her weight on the bed. She wraps around me and kisses my forehead. "Forget him, withdraw from school, and stop taking his money. This isn't worth it. You were better off with the lonely."

"I know."

"I'm going to go kill him now. So I'll be back and we can talk about this then."

I grip her arms and shake my head. "No. Don't leave."

"I need him to bleed and suffer."

I shake my head. "I let him do it. I let him punish me like I was her." I've said too much.

Her fingers dig into my arms. "What? You mean, the therapy thing? I told you that doctor is a quack. I knew it."

Tears seep through my squeezed lids. "It's so much worse than that. When we had sex I let him spank me and be rough and punish me. I let him hurt me and be rough with me." My voice has become nothing but a shell of what it once was. I don't have the bravery to talk to her aloud.

"He hurt you? Sexually?"

I suck my breath and nod. "I liked it. So much is wrong with me." I'm heaving and shaking.

She holds me. "Wait—so you—liked being dominated? Dude, everyone likes that. We all like a guy who wants to be in charge."

I shake my head. "I liked being spanked and told what to do." I'm so ashamed, but I'm grateful I can't see through the blinding tears.

She pulls me back sharply. My eyes jerk open. She's smiling and fighting a giggle. "Everyone likes that."

I can't speak anymore.

"I love being spanked. I don't like to talk about it. I don't ever want to discuss it again, but you need to see. Everyone likes it. Those smutty books sell because women wish their husbands had half the balls the men in those books do."

I stop. I think she's telling the truth, but I doubt its validity.

"You aren't a freak." Humor is spreading across her face. "Women enjoy a paddling and a spanking and some biting. We all like safe games in a relationship where we are safe to be the submissive or the domi-nant one. Women like that. I read those books, and I wish I could meet a guy like that—a bad boy. A guy who spanks me is a common fantasy."

I swallow. It doesn't lessen the pain.

"He is the bad boy. The player. The rough-and-tough sex freak. The one we all want but then we don't. We want the sweet boy who will run to the store in the middle of night and get us ice cream and hold our hair when we puke."

"I don't see him in the rough-and-tough sex way. I think he would get me ice cream."

She shakes her head. "No, you love him. You won't ever see any of his flaws. Love is blind and you fell in love with the fantasy."

"I'm not in love. I don't love anything except you. And my fantasy is the normal I've always wanted. I don't have the same fantasy as the rest of you. I don't want a bad boy. I want a normal guy."

"Okay." She stops gripping my arms and relaxes a bit. "There is no normal. I wish you could see that. You are normal. Normal is being screwed up, but being able to work with it and appear calm. My family had too many kids; I never got attention. Now I'm an attention-seeking whore. I get that. I probably have daddy issues, but I work with it. I have fun with it. Why not? Why not just embrace the inner freak. So, you like bondage and spankings. Jesus. At least you don't like being peed on or having things shoved in your bum, 'cause seriously, Dr. Oz says those muscles can relax and stop holding the poop in."

I laugh at her serious face when she says poop.

She pulls me in and hugs me again. "Dude, I'm exhausted, thinking about the year you've had. You left the orphanage. You came to school, got abducted, fell in love with two completely opposite boys, and conquered the lonely. Now you've learned you got some freakiness in ya. Well, so what? It's not so bad." She sighs. "Can we just finish the year, screw Eli? Well, not screw Eli, but forget him. He wants you to be his sister, then be that. Be his sister that hates him or could give a shit about him. That's how I feel about my brothers. Pieces of shit. Done."

I nod against her. "Okay."

Her forehead rests against mine. "Are we still on for your birthday though? 'Cause we can bail. Your family will get it."

I shake my head. "I need it."

"Okay. I'm in for whatever you are. What movie we watching tonight?"

"*Amelie*," I say. She sighs. She hates subtitles.

"I'll go get some chocolate. Lord knows I could use some." She stands up and looks at me. "You know, there isn't a single thing wrong with you. Not one. There isn't anybody who deserves love and respect like you do." She leaves the room and I let her words be true. I push the power button on the phone to turn it off and leave it alone.

❄ 22 ❄

Class was boring. Walking down the path I take a deep breath of fresh air, grateful to be out in it. The snow is still falling but I don't care.

"Does winter ever end here?"

I laugh at Shell and shake my head. "I know, right?" I nudge her. "You sure you want to do this?" I ask.

She nods. "I guess so, huh? Can't make you go alone and be the only skinny girl who sucks ass."

I laugh. We walk over to the bus stop. Stuart watches us. I can see the look in his eyes, but I don't meet them. We climb onto the bus. I see her watching him out the window. She misses him. "Just call him."

She looks at me. "What?" She knows what.

"Just call him. He's the best guy in the whole world. Trust me. I'm not a trusting person. I trust him."

She raises an eyebrow. "You are the worst judge of character ever."

"True. I'm friends with you."

She laughs and nudges me. "Let's just get this embarrassment over with."

The bus ride is loud and gross. My OCD is not gone. Clearly. I'm thinking about just throwing out my pants when we get off, and hate the feel of my hand on the rail in front of me.

"We need a car, dude." I sigh.

She nods. "Yeah. This is gross."

My eyes are fixed. I can't look around me at the people on the bus. I'll never eat again. Someone coughs and clears their throat. My eyes widen.

"I see you," Shell whispers into me. I shake my head. "No, you don't."

"It's okay. Just do it. I want some too."

The hand sani is out of my pocket and I'm dumping the cool liquid on both of us before I've taken a breath. The smell of the cinnamon and gingerbread man is soothing. I slosh it around on my hands. I take deep breaths and just feel the tingly sensation. It calms me.

I'm losing it. Shell leans in again.

"Wanna hear about the first time I ever got spanked?" she whispers, almost silently. The shock of her sentence stops my panic attack.

"Remember two years ago when I went on the senior class trip with Angela, Jessica, and Brianna?"

I nod, keeping my eyes shut.

"Well, we spent all our money on clothes and shit. It was our last night in Austria. We wanted to get drunk but we had no cash. So we decided to look for a mark. Someone who would buy us drinks all night long. We were sitting in this bar downtown, about a block from our hotel. We couldn't decide on who to use. The guys in the bar were young and hot, but they all had pretty girls or just didn't look interested. Then, in walks this guy. He was in a pilot's uniform and looked like fucking James Bond. He was so beautiful and sexy and confident. He strolls up to the bar and orders a drink. I point and say, 'Him.'"

I smile. I can see it so clearly.

"So the girls are like, 'No way, he's too posh' and shit. But you know me. So I walk up, right next to him, and climb on a stool. I get on my knees and lean across the bar. I almost stick my ass right in his face. The bartender comes over and I say, 'You got any Rolling Stones?' The bartender looks confused and turns and changes the music. I totally pick the Stones 'cause they're sexy and older, like

Bond. I figure he's like thirty-five or forty. Anyway, 'Paint It Black' starts playing. I slink off the barstool and go sit down. Brianna smirks and swears there is no way he's coming over. But I am the master. He strolls over with a tray of shots and we get trashed with him."

I laugh. "You are ballsy."

"I am ballsy. So the night progressed. We got so drunk and had a ton of fun and did a ton of dancing. Pretty soon everyone wanted in on the action. But I was having fun with Mr. Bond. He and I snuck off to his hotel room. We made out in the elevator. He ripped my skirt."

I'm starting to feel the scene with her. Her breathing picks up slightly as she tells it.

"So we got in the room. He undressed and damn. Hot. Oh my God hot. We were getting it on hard, and then suddenly he pushed me down on the bed, and I felt this hard slap on my ass. Not what I was expecting. At all. Needless to say, it went well. I almost died of humiliation and the bizarre love I had for that moment. Anyway, I left and that's the first time I ever got spanked."

I smirk. "Did you tell the girls?"

"Some of it. What I never told them was that after we finished, he put a ring on his wedding ring finger. My stomach almost dropped, dude. I was so upset. I literally like almost cried. I said, 'You're married?' and he says, 'Yeah, of course I am. I have kids older than you. I'm fifty-six years old.'"

I open my eyes and shoot a look at her. "What? Oh my God, you were eighteen. That's disgusting."

Her face is beet red and pained. "Yeah. Fifty-six. I've had sex, and I mean nasty, spank-my-nipples dirty sex, with an old man. A man who was ten years older than my dad. It was humiliating, and I have never told a single person that story. No one ever knew. I let him use me, and you know what? It's still the best sex I have ever had." She sighs. "Senior-citizen sex. So humiliating."

I lean in and hug her and kiss her cheek. "Thank you."

She shrugs. "You're my bitch. I would take a bullet for you. I just want you to know that I get it. I know what it feels like to be crushed and upset when someone gets something from you."

I see her in a new light. But we don't get to talk about it because the bus stops and we're outside the gym. We climb off in silence.

"You don't think less of me now, do you?" she asks as we trudge through the snow to the front entrance. I glance at her. "No. More."

She grins. "Ditto. I never imagined you had the balls to do half the shit you've done."

We walk in and I start to feel my nerves getting the best of me. I think about her walking out of the hotel. I imagine she made the same face I did leaving his apartment. I see how strong she is and how much I admire and want to be her, and suddenly it's there. I am like her. I am strong like her. He can't break me. I see the point he was trying to make. His one act won't ruin all the strength I have inside me.

We walk down the hall, and I feel like I'm in one of those movies where the underdogs come and kick ass.

I wish that I could say that was how it happened.

We walk out into the gym, smiling at Lance.

"He looks like Santa, but like boxing Santa," Shell whispers. I laugh and nod. "Twinkle eyes."

The boys are there. Brandon eyeballs me. I nod at him.

"Ready for warm-up ladies?" Lance asks, in a voice filled with joy.

I point. "This is Michelle."

Lance nods. "Mickey and Tink. I like it."

Michelle looks lost. "What just happened?" I shake my head at her. It's impossible to explain any of them.

Lance shouts, "Three laps slackers. Let's go."

We start to run. I leave Michelle in the dust. My legs can't help but beat the little turds in the running. They'll be kicking my ass in rings in an hour anyway. I lap her and a few of the other boys.

I run harder, letting my legs open up and push it.

The air is blowing by me. I finish the lap and bend over to suck wind for a second.

"Someone hasn't been running much, huh, Tink?" My ass gets a hard slap. I grin and stand up to face the beast.

"Angelo, you wanna race?"

His face splits into the cockiest smile ever. "Only if you let me slap you around afterward."

I take a step into his face. "Done."

He lifts an eyebrow. "Ready?"

I nod. We line up. He smells good. He says go. I take off like a rocket. My legs are warm from the three laps. He's grunting behind me, but I push it harder and pull away.

"GO TINK!" Lance screams as I pass the first lap. I run my ass off and finish before he's even halfway on his last lap.

He comes in, winded and wheezing. "Goddamn, you are fast."

I nod, sucking wind hard. My throat hates me.

"I'm gonna make you pay, Tinkerbell."

I laugh. "We fight when I say."

He stops, red faced and scowls. "What? No way."

I pace and nod again. "Yeah. You just said after. You never speci-fied. I want to choose when we fight."

He laughs and shakes his crimson face. "Cheater, cheater!"

I laugh, bending forward to catch my breath. I stand up straight and start my high knees. I need to stretch my legs out.

"Seriously?" He sounds a little annoyed.

"Yup."

He sighs and walks away. "Fine. But your ass is grass."

I laugh and look at Michelle. She makes a face and nods at his back as he's walking away from us. "Wow. Angelo?"

"Yup."

She grins and shouts after him, "Hey, Angelo."

He turns back around and smirks at her. "Yeah?"

"Can my ass be grass too?"

He laughs and gives her a thumbs up. "Done!"

She runs after him. She flirts and twirls her hair and lifts her leg in the air behind her playfully.

My breath is just starting to come around when Lance yells at me, "Tink, get your ass over here and tape up."

I leave Shell in terrible hands and turn for the ring and the ever-impatient Lance.

When I turn around he's there.

I stop breathing for a minute, I swear. My stomach aches and tenses. He's sweaty and wearing his white t-shirt. I can see his tats through the wet shirt. He's got on thick jogging pants and a stare that could knock me over. My jaw clenches as I walk past him.

Lance points at Eli. "He's got the other tape." He turns and starts taping some of the boys.

I walk up and put my hands out. I look him in the eyes daringly.

"We need to talk," he says softly as he tapes up my hands.

"Talk."

He smirks. "You know what I mean."

"Talk, Brother," I repeat.

He tapes them roughly but maintains the right amount of pressure. "I need to see you. I need to explain some things."

I laugh, but it's not mine. It belongs to this bitch who sometimes likes to come out of my throat and say shit I'm not entirely sure I mean. "Screw you, Eli. I have nothing but that to say to you. I have no desire to see you. I came here because I seriously liked the idea of being able to fight. I like the idea that if some asshole tried to pin me, I might stand a chance at defending myself." My eyes bear down on him. "I won't ever be the victim again." It's a lie and false bravado and probably see-through, but I don't care. I brush past him, shouldering him roughly.

"He's not doing it right, Lance," I say and put my hands out. Lance looks at the tape job and then past me. "What the hell is this, Adams? Jesus. My retriever does a better job than this." He tapes my hands up, cussing away.

I hear the light pitter-patter of Michelle's shoes behind me. "Hey. Oh my God, he is so hot. What do we do now?" Lance makes a face at me.

I smile and nod at him as I answer her, "Get him to tape up your hands. Then the little boys beat us up."

She grimaces. "This isn't as fun as I thought it was going to be."

I laugh, but it's still bitter. "Just wait till one of the assholes hits you in the face."

"Who was that Hotty McNaughty in the white t-shirt with the tats? That is a smexy boy. Smexy, smexy boy." She follows him around with her gaze.

I swallow my fears. "Stop making up words. That's Eli." I say it like she should know.

She looks at me and then back at him. "Dayum. I didn't make up smexy or dayum. Google it. It's slang for I almost peed my pants when I saw him. I mean he's still evil and damaged and shit, but wow. Maybe the damaged is part of the appeal. Yikes." She turns her head and follows him around the gym with her gaze.

I shake my head. "The damaged is the appeal. I have to work a million times harder than with any other normal guy, to get an ounce of anything out of him. But somehow it makes it worth so much more when I do get something."

Finally, she points and nods. "That explains so many things. Ouch. For reals? What the hell? Is that legal? He is too hot and too bad boy and he boxes. Sweet baby Jesus."

"You're rambling." I laugh and shake my head.

She looks savagely in his direction. "I don't know how to box, but I would like to kick the crap out of him." I would believe her, but she licks her lips and won't stop staring at him.

"Yeah well, prepare for the little boys before you go beating up the big boys." I shove her lightly, mostly to get her to stop looking at him. It's making me look at him.

Of course, it turns out she is way better at boxing than I am. She manages some good shots and even wins her fight. She is jumping and loving it. I think she uses her hatred of Eli as a fuel. She fights like a psycho.

I still suck. But between my date with doom, aka Angelo, and my hate, I manage to do a bit better.

23

"Dude, you're going back again? It's like seven a.m.," she whines.

"Yeah. I need to practice, like every day. And I need to blow off my crazies before we see them."

She sits cross-legged in her pajamas and watches me. "Why did you agree to fight Angelo? He's going to wipe the floor with you." She blushes. "So far he's been wiping the floor with me."

I roll my eyes. "Gross." It's not gross. I want details, but I'd never let her know that.

There is a knock at our door. I frown and turn around as she gets up and gets it. My face lightens.

"Happy birthday." It's Sebastian and a bouquet of daises.

"How did you even get daisies?" I frown.

Shell smiles sweetly. "Oh my God, that's your favorite flower."

"How did you know?"

He shrugs. "Gotta keep my secrets. Lord knows, you have yours."

I laugh and take the flowers and kiss his cheek. "Thank you."

"I wanted to make sure I got here before you left. Will you have dinner with me tonight?"

I grab my bag. "Walk me out." I turn back to Shell and nod. "See you after."

She has the doe-eyed expression she gets when we talk about Sebastian. Which we do a lot. She has always been voting for him to win. Always.

He takes the bag from me. "Where are you going? I had imagined I would be waking you and then taking you for breakfast."

My cheeks flush. "Boxing."

"Wow. That is not the answer I expected. Can I drive you there?" My insides flip out.

"Yes, please. Save me from the bus. I still have attacks on the bus."

He grimaces. "Oh God. I have attacks on the bus and I don't have OCD."

I laugh as he gets the door. "So, boxing?"

We walk out into the cold air. I snug my jacket around me and nod. "Yeah. New thing. Trying to feel stronger. You know?"

"I do. I boxed a lot when I was a kid. Our town didn't have a real gym. Just a boxing gym. So you could take boxing or be lazy. I started getting fat, like all kids who are geeky and smart and sitting in front of the computer all day. One day my dad put me in. Said I was getting too chunky. I was addicted to it, right off the bat. I played World of Warcraft and Diablo and PlayStation, so I liked the combat aspect."

I look at his thick shoulders and get it. They're huge from the boxing. "I've noticed I'm liking it too. I feel less angry and out of control. I don't ever win any fights, in fact I suck. But it's like I'm there and present for the whole thing. I'm not daydreaming and imagining and wishing. I'm just fighting for something. Sanity maybe. It's like a rush to be rid of everything and just focus on one thing. I'm not anyone, just a girl in the ring."

"Wow, that's the most you've ever shared with me."

I nudge him. "Shut up."

He opens the door to the fancy car. I love the clean smell. I squeak into the leather seat and sigh.

"You love this car, don't you?"

I nod. "I do. It's so nice and clean and quiet."

"Do you want it?"

I turn my head sharply. "What? No!" Disgust has crossed my face. I can't fight it. "Why does everyone think that just 'cause I grew up an orphan, they have to give everything to me? Like—am I so pathetic?"

His face turns red. "I'm sorry. I never meant to offend you. At all."

I close my eyes and mutter, "Sorry. I've been having outbursts like that one a lot." I hate it but it seems natural. It's almost like it's the girl I might have been, had I not been taken, slowly finding her way inside me and taking control.

His hands rest on mine. "I don't place the same value on money that you might," he says softly.

I open my eyes and nod. "I know. I'm sorry."

"I just think you should have a car, freedom. Not a driver. It's weird."

"I know it's weird."

"Has he offered to buy you a car or does he only want you under his thumb with his driver?"

I give him a harsh stare. "No. He doesn't want me learning in the city."

He looks hurt. "Why does he get to give you money and not me? I love you. I want to be with you, completely. I want you. Baggage and all. But I don't want some other guy's girl."

I frown and swallow hard. He's said something no one but Shell has ever said to me. I don't know what to say. I grab my bag and open the car door. "I'm sorry." I climb out, but he's out the door in a shot. He walks around and pins me to the car. His lips crash on mine. His tongue is searching, savagely. His hands rake my back and butt. I moan into his mouth.

He opens the car door wide again and shoves me in. I'm panting as he closes the door and walks around. He starts the car and puts it into drive.

"I'm tired of your running away. We are finishing this goddamned conversation before I explode and kill someone." He's angry. Vicious. I've never been more attracted to him.

He pulls into underground parking. We have sat in the awkward silence for the entire drive.

He parks and gets out. He flings open my door and drags me out of the car. He's not speaking. I don't know what to think, but I like the determination in his eyes.

He presses the elevator button with savagery, like I do, like he too is scared of whatever is behind us. The second we're inside and the door is closed, I jump him. I wrap my arms around him and kiss him like I'm trying to kill him. When we get to his floor, he carries me to the door of the penthouse. He fumbles with the key. I laugh into his mouth as he curses.

He flings open the door, banging it into the wall. He grabs the door and slams it shut. He drops me to my feet and looks at me.

I'm breathing heavily.

He pulls his sweater off. His muscles are pronounced and trembling. I reach out and run my fingers down the front of him. There is a small amount of hair on his chest.

The silence isn't awkward anymore. It's full of sexual tension. He grabs my hand and places it over his beating heart and holds it there. It's like he's giving it to me maybe. I pull off my shirt and do the same with his hand over my sports bra. I want it to be him in my heart. My gesture might not mean the same to him, but it means a lot to me.

He yanks me in, pressing our chests together. He bends and kisses my neck. His body is exploding with heat. He pulls me to the bedroom I was always running from. He shoves me back on the bed and reaches down for my yoga pants, pulling them off.

I grimace at my granny panties. "They're comfier for boxing."

He smiles when he sees them. He undoes his pants and pulls them off as I pull my sports bra over my head, with the usual amount of difficulty. It isn't sexy. It's horrible and almost dislocates my shoulder every time.

He bends and licks up my calf. I shudder and lie back. He's rubbing up my legs softly, kneading and massaging, licking and kissing. I start to get lost in it. Lightly, his fingers brush my soft cotton underwear.

I gasp.

The anticipation and delicate touches are worse than anything I've ever experienced. He drags his fingers up and down my underwear. I'm slowly spreading my legs, begging him to just touch me—just let me out of my misery.

His finger loops into the middle of the underwear and brushes up and down my lips. He doesn't talk but I hear a packet. A condom. I'm grateful he's in control enough to make a smart choice.

He kisses the sides of my thigh softly. I'm clutching the blankets. He drags my underwear down with his looped finger. I help him and kick them off. He slides up my thighs again. He's trying to kill me I think.

Before I know what to expect, warmth drags up and down my slit. I cry out, before I can stop myself. The warmth of his mouth crashes onto me. He sucks my clit, making me jerk and grab at the bed.

He licks and sucks slowly. One of his huge fingers touches me. He pushes it in slowly, just dipping it in a couple times. It's enough. It's all I need. He sucks my clit and I orgasm. He feels me tighten and pumps his fingers in and out of me.

I'm in a frenzy. He slides his fingers out and I feel him moving around. I shiver when I feel the warmth of his mouth hovering over my nipple. He rubs his erection up and down my slit.

As he delicately pushes himself inside me, his mouth crashes onto my nipple. He sucks and pushes and I'm lost. It's slow and intense. Everything he does is like he's paying homage to my body. Worshipping at the temple that is me. His hands caress my arms. His kisses land on my neck and chest. When his mouth meets my face I'm hungry for him. His strokes inside me are still slow and methodical. He makes complete strokes, fully in and out. I'm moving against him, trying to make the pace quicken. Deep down, I know it's that I want him to take me. Fuck me. I want him wild and out of control. I want to feel the freedom I get from the loss of everything.

But he isn't. He's in control.

I'm opening my legs, wrapping them around him, but he maintains his control. I don't look at him. I can't. He's seeing me exposed. He's seeing the need I am exposing myself to.

His body is fully sliding against mine. His hands are gripping me, holding me. It's sweet and soft.

"Fuck me," I whisper. It's desperate. I have a need.

"I am," he says softly.

I open my eyes. "Hard."

He sits up and lifts my legs in the air and pounds me.

"Like this? You want this? Goddamn. You feel so good." I like it when he talks.

His body slamming into mine is ecstasy. I get lost in the thrusts and the pressure. He bends forward, pushing my legs almost to my head. His thrusts are slapping his body against mine. I orgasm a second time, forcing his orgasm. He cries out into my legs and finishes. He unravels my legs and collapses onto me. I grunt with the exhale as he does.

"Am I squishing you?" he asks.

I lick my lips. "In a good way."

"Holy shit, Sarah." He's breathing into my hair.

I laugh. "Yeah."

"I think I almost had a heart attack." He pulls out and climbs off me. "I'm not even kidding. That was maniacal and I feel like I used you."

"I used you back. Don't worry."

He shakes his head. "You're different than I ever imagined you would be. In every way." He tosses the condom in the garbage and pulls on his boxers and collapses next to me, bouncing on the bed slightly. "From the girl I met in the gym, to the girl who had the attack at Chicken Lou's, to the girl who threw up in my garbage can, to this. You have come so far. That therapy really worked."

I shiver and crawl under the blankets. "I don't want to talk about it."

He blushes. "Sorry. You're just surprising me. In a good way." He traces his fingers up and down my arm. "What should we do now, birthday girl? God you're so beautiful."

I shrug. Mostly out of discomfort. Why is he talking and touching so much?

He makes a face, like he's inspired and stands up. "Be right back."

He leaves the bedroom. I wrap the blankets tightly around me and fight the feelings away.

He comes back in after a minute and crawls into the blankets with me.

"You know I was thinking, why don't we go somewhere this week?"

I frown. "What?"

"Well, I have a job going on in Los Angeles. I need to go there this weekend. You could come with me."

I look at him and hate myself. "No. I need to train and I have school."

He kisses my cheek. "Okay. I won't push it. It took almost the whole damned year to get you to here. We can take it slowly." I press my face into his cheek.

He strokes my hair out of my face. "How's the whole semester looking?"

I grimace. "Bad. I think I'm failing creative writing. Not good for a journalism wannabe."

He laughs. "How the hell do you fail creative writing?"

I move my head to look at him with daggers in my eyes. "It's harder than you think, smarty pants. The prof hates me. She wants us to rewrite everything a minimum of fifty times. Which I think is insane. It's poetry. It's the fruit of the moment. You know?"

His eyes sparkle and look greener than I've ever seen them. "I do not."

I laugh and shove him. "A poem is based on the emotions you have at that moment. If you rewrite it, then you're taking away the raw emotion you were having and replace it with something that's not authentic to that moment."

His eyes widen. "Well, well. Look who is deeper than a puddle."

I open my mouth in offense. "Hurtful."

He rolls his eyes. "You never let me in."

A buzzer interrupts my pout. He jumps up, dragging on his pants and running from the room.

I sit up and wait. He comes back after a couple minutes with two trays. He places them down. They are silver trays with steaming pancakes, sausages, bacon, eggs, fruit, and coffee in to-go cups. I smile. On one plate the pancakes have "Happy Birthday Sarah" written on them. I sit back on the bed and pull the blankets up to cover myself. He places the tray down. "I figured since you didn't want to go to breakfast, we could just have it here."

I smile at him. "Thank you. You're so sweet."

He grins and climbs on the bed to eat his. "I don't feel sweet after earlier."

I roll my eyes. He gets my hint that I don't want to discuss it—ever.

"Can we do dinner tonight though?"

I shake my head. "I can't. I have to go meet my real parents tonight. It was my goal for my twentieth birthday."

He looks worried. "Who's going with you?"

I eat my bite and fight the fact my appetite is going quickly. "Shell. I just want her there."

He nods but I can see the look in his eyes.

"She's like my security blanket from childhood, you know?"

"How did you two meet?"

I shove the memory down and shake my head. I push away the food and give myself a minute.

"You okay?"

I take a breath. "Just a sec." Sometimes memories make me feel dirty. I lower my heart rate with breaths and being grateful.

I open my eyes and look at the breakfast again. "We were at the pool. The orphans were allowed to go swimming. These mean girls from the town bullied me. They were making fun of me for my haircut and my old, faded bathing suit. So I ran away and hid in a corner. I had a thing for corners."

I could cry from the shame that's still there, but I don't. I just talk quietly, "Shell just came up and sat beside me. She was so pretty. Her bathing suit was new, bright green with black polka dots. She looked like a dark-haired Barbie. She asked me random questions and didn't care that I didn't want to answer them. She forced me to be her friend. Then this girl came over and was making fun of me, calling me a lesbian. I sat there, calm and quiet. I wouldn't cry for anyone. Shell stood up and punched her in the face. The girl ran off crying and told the nuns that I hit her."

"Oh my God."

I nod once. "They came to get mad at me and make me go back to the bus. But Shell went and got her mom who went all 'crazy Italian' on the nuns. She said if her daughter said she hit the little bitch, then she did it and not me. Then she yelled that they deserved it for calling me a lesbian. The nuns were pissed. The other girls got thrown out of the pool. She was the first person who ever stood up for me." But my brain points out the lie in the statement. *Besides Eli.*

He grabs my hands. "I'm sorry I made you remember that."

I shake my head. "No. It's not a bad memory. It's good. I need to focus on the good part of it. A girl who was popular and well liked, picked me. She has always picked me."

He tries to make himself smile but he can't. "It was all so hard, wasn't it? Every minute?"

I look at him. "No. Nothing is ever all bad. I had amazing moments."

He looks confused. "Between the bullying and beatings, mean nuns, hand washing, OCD, and anxiety?"

"The nuns weren't mean. They were efficient." I see myself in his eyes for a second and feel a little bit sorry for myself, but my brain shuts it down fast. "And I could have died like Emalyn."

He nods once and pushes his breakfast away. "That's very true."

❧ 24 ❧

I cross the grounds holding her hand. "You slept with him?"

I nod. "I feel horrible. Like a slut. I actually thought about Eli, which is so gross. He thinks I'm his sister and—" I shudder.

"I highly doubt he thinks you're his sister. I saw the way he looks at you. That doctor is a whack job, I am telling you." She nudges me. "Besides, Eli's not the kind of guy you forget easily. Dirty-talking, bum-spanking, panty-stealing, bad boys are hard to come by."

I laugh, it's nervous laughter. Seeing the SUV is making me nervous.

"Did you blow the crazies off with your sexy workout at Sebastian's?"

"No." I shake my head. "I think they're worse. I feel sick and gross and I miss Eli, but I'm terrified he's going to know I did it with Sebastian. It's going to hurt him and I hate that. I should like it but I don't."

She snorts. "Girl, please. That man probably already knows. I swear he has you GPS'd. And not wanting to hurt him isn't a bad thing. Look how you feel after he hurt you."

"And I feel bad for Sebastian. He was giving me his whole heart, and I left there not wanting it. I am so fucked up. My family isn't going to want me, Shell. I'm such a mess," I say as we get to the SUV.

"They will love you. Trust me. It's impossible to not love you." She nudges me again.

Stuart opens the door. "You okay, Sarah?"

I shake my head.

"We'll be there for you the entire time." His voice is steady. He doesn't even steal a glance at Shell. He is there for me. He always was.

Shell pushes me inside the SUV. I sit and try not to feel like vomiting.

I don't know how I feel about the fact Eli had them fly here. He will be part of the whole thing. He is the whole thing. He's organized it all and made it happen.

Stuart speaks in the rearview, "They're staying at the Hotel Commonwealth. It's nice. They have the suite, so we can sit in private and meet them."

I start to panic. My head fills with a million different bad things. "What if they don't like me? What if I'm not the way they imagined?" Shell pulls a paper bag from her purse and holds it out.

"You're not in the orphanage, tard. These people gave birth to you. They're yours, your parents. They'll love you, no matter what. Mine love me through all the bullshit."

My hands shake when I take the paper bag. I'm shaking so hard I can't get the edges open. She takes it and opens it. "Calm. Deep breaths." I grip the bag, tearing it, and start to cry.

She pulls a second bag out. It makes me laugh, but it's a sobbing laugh. She holds the bag up to my face. I dig my hand into my pocket and grip the gingerbread hand sani. My body is clenching and aching. I'm huffing the bag, but I can't get calm.

Stuart pulls up to a red awning outside a beautiful building. My hands are shaking. The SUV door opens. His hand is there. I'm instantly grateful for him. I close my eyes and take it. He pulls me into him and instantly everything is better. His touch takes away all the sharp edges and makes them soft and safe.

"Eli! Leave her alone! She doesn't want to see you!" Shell is shouting and scrambling after us, but I'm gripping to him.

"Don't be strong and brave for them. Be you. They expect nothing," he whispers into my ear, wrapping his body around mine. No amount of hate or disgust I harbor for him, can steal the fact that he is my savior. Always was.

He brings me to a fancy white door. I see the women's washroom sign as we walk through and he locks the door. He sits me on the counter and brushes my hair away. His icy-blue eyes are hard and focused.

"They don't have any expectations. They never even had hope until I confirmed who you were. Be you. You're sweet. We both know that." He isn't soothing. He's an asshole. But I believe him.

I nod and sniffle. "I'm scared."

He leans in and kisses my forehead. "I am too. But you have me, even if you don't want me. I'm here. I'll always be here." He pulls a handkerchief from his pocket and puts it up to my face. I shy away, horrified. "Is that clean?"

He laughs. "Yes. Fresh from the laundry. Just let me wipe your eyes." He wipes my eyes softly. "When this is over, you and I need to have a very serious conversation. I don't want to take away from the specialness of what you're about to do, so we'll just put that on the back burner. Just focus on this moment now. It's hard. I know that. You're amazing and they are lovely people. Trust me."

I flinch when he says it, but I nod. "I do." And I do. There is no one I trust like I do him. Sister or no, I trust him with my safety. Sometimes I still think it's Stockholm.

He puts a hand out. I take it and let him lead me. I'm gripping my sani and him. It's more than I have ever needed.

Shell is in the reception area of the hotel. Stuart is close to her.

She looks at Eli but speaks to me, "You okay, Sarah?"

I nod and squeeze him. He bends into me and whispers, "You ready to do this?"

I grip him and my sani tight. "Yup."

Shell smiles sweetly. "They're going to love you. Like we do."

Tears threaten my eyes again. "You're already more than any orphan could ask for." My words tremble out of me. Eli holds me and pulls me closer to him. I numb myself to him and all of it. I take a breath and nod. "Let's go." He leads me to the elevators. I blush when we step inside. I stand too close and need too much. I can't stop it.

The elevator stops with silence. No ding. No bell. Eli clenches my hand as Shell leans in and kisses me.

We step off and walk down a short hall where Eli knocks on a fancy white door. I feel like I might throw up.

I don't want to be a freak. I want them to see me as a normal girl. I hold my breath and wait. My eyesight starts to narrow. I take a deep breath.

The door opens, making me cringe a bit. I hold it back.

A tall man with gray hair, a gray mustache, and sparkly blue eyes answers. His hand comes up to his mouth. His face trembles. A woman comes and stands beside him. She has blonde hair like me and blue eyes that immediately fill with tears. They are both incredibly clean people.

She leans into the man and starts to sob. I see movement behind them.

She reaches forward and grabs me. Eli holds my hand, but the woman trembles and grips me with shaking strength. The hall and room are completely silent. None of us make a sound. Everything is quiet. The man wraps around me. I'm sobbing. I can't see anything, but as long as I can feel his hand I'm okay. I don't know what to say.

"You look just like my mother," she whispers into my hair.

The space around me becomes dark. I grip his hand for the life of me. I can't see. I can smell them and deep inside I know it. I know the smell. It's gingerbread cookies and warm hugs and a black and white cat.

Eli speaks softly, "Let's just step inside."

The man heaves slightly and when he steps back I can see light again. There are others. Boys. My age, or close to it. They're huge. Tall and strong looking. One has dark hair like Eli and the other has blond hair, like me. I can see it immediately. I belong with them. We match.

The man tries to talk but he can't. I can't either. One of the boys is crying. He points. "Dad, Mom, Jake, Lyle." He points to himself. He's Lyle. I look into his eyes and watch it happen. He remembers me. I see it.

They drag me into the hotel room. I drag Eli with me. The mom grabs Eli and attacks him with hugs and savage kisses. They look painful.

"Thank you, thank you, thank you. You dear boy. Thank you." Her voice is broken. He looks stoic throughout the assault.

I look back at Shell. She's crying into Stuart who has red eyes and a quivering jaw.

The dad grabs me, forcefully. I flinch. He stops his assault and moves slowly, "Sorry, Sarah. I just—well—we never imagined. We hoped."

I can see it in his eyes. He's normal. They're normal. He's wearing a sweater and a polo shirt and she's has on a blouse. The people who wore sweaters and blouses were the ones you wanted at the orphanage. I always wanted a sweater and a blouse. But they all knew who I was. No one wants that kid. God knows what's already been done to that kid or what she'll do to the kids already in your house.

But I don't have to worry about that anymore. This sweater and blouse are mine.

I let go of Eli's hand and let my dad wrap his arms around me. He folds around me, like he's making up for lost time. My mom stops mauling Eli and joins our embrace. Her hug is the gingerbread where his is the cat that I remember.

"Sarah, do you remember us?"

My lips feel dry and chapped and too thick to speak, but I manage, "I remember gingerbread cookies and skating on a pond and hot cocoa and a black and white cat."

Apparently, it is enough. They cry and nod their heads. "The pond is at my mother's farmhouse. Your grandma."

"I don't have anything else to give. I wish I did," I say softly.

They hug harder. Jake and Lyle join in again. They eat me up, and I don't know what to do with it all.

I turn my head and lean into my father's chest. I open my eyes to see Eli watching me. He smiles. It's almost sweet.

My brothers leave my embrace and grab at him. They pull him in and pat him.

"Come and sit, Sarah. We have so much to talk about." My mother points to the huge sitting area. I look at Shell and Stuart and hold a hand out. Shell rushes and grabs me.

"This is Michelle. She has been my family since I was eight."

My mom grabs her and holds her close. They cry together. "Thank you, Michelle. Thank you."

Michelle shakes her head in quick jerks.

I nod at Stuart. "This is Stuart. He helped me remember everything that happened. And he keeps me safe." My mother's arm shoots out. She drags him in.

We cry for some time before I actually manage to sit in a chair. Eli sits beside me, holding my hand.

"I'm Helen, if you don't want to call me mom just yet. Your dad's name is Roger." She fumbles with a book beside her. "This is yours." She passes it to me. It's thick and heavy and soft pink. I put it in my lap and lean into Eli. He opens to the first page for me. Instantly the tears are there again. A wisp of white-blonde hair is taped to the edge of the book.

"You had almost none, so chubby and bald compared to your brothers. But we managed to get a bit for the baby book." She sounds lost suddenly, like the book has transported her back.

I lightly brush my fingers over the fine hair. I turn the page and see the announcement in the paper. The piece of paper looks old and tarnished.

"Happy birthday, baby," Helen says softly. My brother Lyle reaches over and puts a hand on her shoulder. She lifts her hand to his.

"You were the baby. Lyle is twenty-three and Jake is twenty-five. They were five and seven when you were taken." Her words break inside her mouth and fall out in jumbled pieces. I get what she means though.

As I turn the pages I notice how worn they are. I can almost feel the grease of fingers that lingered too long and tears that fell too often, from eyes lost staring at the pages. Each page is another stage: a baby sitting up or crawling or walking. Golden locks and big blue eyes. Eli is so tight to me, I'm certain he is the only thing stopping it from feeling like a dream.

"We searched—for so long. About five years ago we had that built."

She points. I turn the page and see it. It's them. And me. My tomb. My headstone and monument. They buried me. I drag my fingers along the photo.

"We just thought—well, we gave up. For that we are so sorry."

I shake my head. "I gave up too."

She is crying into her hands. I wonder if it's guilt or relief. I hate that they feel bad. But I can see it in their eyes.

"We would like for you to come home with us."

My skin crawls. Eli senses me tensing and puts a huge hand on my thigh. It looks massive there. I nod and mentally slap myself. "I can come."

"You should bring your friends of course. We have plenty of room."

I look up. "When?"

"Easter? We would love it if you came for Easter."

It is much more time than I would expect. I agree. "Can we visit again though?" I don't want them to leave me. I'm terrified I will leave the suite, and they will dissolve into the ash I had imagined them to be.

"I was thinking perhaps I could host breakfast tomorrow. We can have it catered here in one of the small meeting rooms. I have the staff on standby with the idea." Eli pats my leg.

My mother's face lights up. "Yes." She looks back at my father and brothers. They nod.

I turn the next page and can't do anymore. I close the book and smile at them, my perfect-orphan fake smile. "Thank you for meeting with us. You are the best birthday present I have ever gotten." Which is true. I never knew my birthday before Eli told me when it was.

My father walks to me and offers me his hand. I put mine in it, hesitantly. He lifts me up and wraps his arms around me. "You are the greatest gift any of us could ever have."

Eli stands beside me, hovering as usual. "We should be going. It's no doubt overload for everyone."

I close my eyes and breathe my father in. I move on to my mother and do the same thing.

My brothers hug me at the same time. We are strangers and complicated, but I would take it over anything in the entire world. It is an amazing and terrifying feeling to have them. My greatest fear is that they will be taken away again. I want to stay longer, but I know it was supposed to be a short visit and then gradually they would get longer.

We hug and kiss and they touch me a thousand times. They squeeze me and hold me and walk us to the elevator. I am a mess but Michelle and Stuart look ready for death. They're holding back something I don't think I want to see. Eli presses the button as my father shakes his hand and looks at me as they talk. He leaves his side and hugs me once more. He whispers into my ear, "I already approve of your boyfriend, if you don't mind me saying." He says softly, "He saved you, cared for you, brought you home, and has supported you. I approve."

I pull back, confused. I look at Eli who just stares at me. "Thanks, Ro—Dad," I say. He tears up again.

Finally, we are in the elevator, silent and stunned as the doors close on my weeping family. Michelle collapses into Stuart and howls. She tries apologizing, but I can't understand her. She grips to me and him and looks like she might faint.

"I'm gonna take her home," Stuart whispers. I nod. I have a feeling I will be spending the evening the same way.

Eli steps off the elevator and holds his hand out for me. I take it and let him bring me to his car. I've never driven with him before. He has an SUV that matches the one Stuart drives.

We drive in silence until I need an answer. "What did he say to you at the elevator?" I look straight ahead when I ask.

"He thanked me for being there for you, even as a boy, when he could not protect you himself. He told me that I had his permission to love you and that he wished he had been able to give it when we were younger."

My eyes tear up again. He drives out of the city. I don't know where we're going. I don't care. I'm just dreading the conversation we have to have.

"I feel so vulnerable having them again. Like I have something to lose." My voice is sad and small, just above a whisper.

"What happens if you lost them all tomorrow? Would that take away from the joy and the love you got from them there at the suite?"

I watch his face for a moment and then shake my head.

"Sarah that feeling is forever. It doesn't shrink or grow. It's just there. It exists. It's yours and no one can take that." He sounds so smart for someone so broken. I realize he's good at helping me but terrible at helping himself.

I look back out the window. I'm exhausted and can't think about it. I curl into the window and let my visions of her eyes, his lips, her hair, and their smells fill me up. They are me. I know this to be true.

❧ 25 ❧

I wake, blinking and squinting. I'm sleeping in a bright room. The curtains aren't drawn. The view from the windows is beautiful. White frothy waves and a snow-covered beach. The ocean and sky are both gray, like they're cold and unfeeling.

I look around the beige and white room. It's plain but classic: eyelet lace and wainscoting, but the blanket is expensive and the bed is incredibly comfortable.

At the far side of the massive room, Eli is sleeping on a huge couch. I step off the bed and pick up my boots and coat. I look at him and shake my head. He is so beautiful and chaotic. I hate but appreciate his attempt at being my brother and sleeping on the couch. Not that it changes how I feel. I'm disgusted and sickened at how I feel about him.

I sneak from the room, closing the door slightly. The hallway is huge, grand even; large paintings line the sand-colored walls. I tiptoe down the wide staircase into a large foyer. I pull on my boots and coat and open the front door.

The front of the house is remarkable. I walk around, stunned by the yard. It's exactly the sort of place I have dreamt of my whole life. I zip my coat and pull my fur-lined hood over my head.

I need to be outside, in case he's got plans to trap me in there and torture me again.

The wind and snow feel colder here at the sea. I crunch through the dry snow to the beach. The waves are violent and white with the snow swirls getting lost in them.

I feel too many things, but mostly I feel like the snow. I feel like I'm getting lost in the water. It's so big and violent, and I can't separate myself from it once I let it take me in. My phone vibrates. I pull it out and grin.

Hope it went well. I miss you. Can I see you today?

I text back. *It was amazing. I remember them a tiny bit. I remember the way they smell. I'm with them today again. I will text you.*

He makes a sad face. I laugh.

"You seeing him again today?"

I spin, seeing Eli. He's standing against a large log with only his t-shirt and pants on. I frown. "You'll freeze. Where is your coat?"

He shakes his head and walks toward me. "Don't change the subject."

I look down at my phone and nod. "I don't know."

"You plan on just seeing both of us? Use me when you need me and be with him the rest of the time?"

I look up, shocked but desperate to keep the hurt from my face. "No."

He's cold; I can see it, but he still walks to me and pulls me into him. "You want me, Sarah."

I don't know what to say. There are so many things between us that feel gross and horrid, and I don't want to, but I have to make them bigger. I shove him slightly. "I don't want to."

"You have to know." He takes my hand and presses his warm lips into the top of it. "I love you. Not because you're my replacement for my sister. That is the most repulsive and abhorrent thing I have ever been accused of. My dead sister?" I see how hurt he is, but I can't shake the nastiness of it all.

"I never want to talk about this again."

"I don't either but I have to tell you. She is obsessed with me. I didn't know."

"Did you sleep with her?"

He presses his lips together. He doesn't have to talk for me to know the answer.

"Gross." I grimace. "What is wrong with you? Why would you sleep with your therapist? Did you take her to that room? Is that how she knows you like to punish girls?"

He shakes his head, but I am stuck in my sick feelings. His voice is desperate, "It happened once, two years ago. It was a mistake. I was drunk in the bar, after I found you. I was celebrating."

I shake my head and cover my ears. "WHAT THE FUCK? I DON'T WANT TO KNOW THIS SHIT! JESUS!"

I run up the beach. He's almost got me, but when my legs reach the grass and snow I take off. I run past the house and up the driveway. I don't know what I'm doing. I just need to be away from him. I run until I'm so disgusted I can't breathe. I slow to a walk and pace.

I pull my phone out and call Shell. "I need you," I say softly. I'm out of breath.

"Where are you? Are you okay?"

I shake my head and sniffle. "I'm fine. I just—I don't know. I need a ride to the hotel where my parents are."

"Go to maps on your phone and look up current location and map it to my place. I'll text you the address here. I'll start heading out to the car. Me and Stuart will come get you."

"Okay." I do as she says. I'm frozen when they show up half an hour later.

"Get in the front seat with the heater," she says when they arrive. I jump in and put my frozen hands on the heater.

"What the hell is going on?"

I shake my head. "Nothing. Just drama." I glance back at her.

"You okay?"

I shake my head. "No."

She puts a hand on my shoulder. "Jesus. You're frozen."

"Yup." My phone is going nuts in my pocket.

"Don't tell him you picked me up."

Stuart gives me a sideways glance. "He doesn't know? Shit."

Shell squeezes my shoulders. "Okay. Do you want to talk about it?"

I shake my head and look down at my phone, which is nonstop ringing.

We ride in silence to the hotel.

I walk into the lobby, exhausted and in the same clothes as the day before.

"Can I help you?" a lady at the front desk asks us as we arrive.

"She's with me." I flinch when I hear his deep voice. I cringe and turn.

"Very good, Mr. Adams," the lady says. He offers me a hand. I walk past him and mutter, "Not now." Shell and Stuart walk with me down a hall.

He walks fast and grabs my hand. He drags me down a different hallway. He stops and grabs my arms. "You ever scare me like that again, and I will make sure you don't ever forget to let me know where you are. You don't run off." The anger in his eyes makes the man in the chair and the cell look like Santa.

I gulp and shove him back. "You are not the boss of me."

He grabs my hand again and pulls me into a room. Everyone is there already. Shell and Stuart and my family.

My mother smiles and I forget everything else. I don't have to force the smile across my lips.

The men stand as I get in my chair.

"Good morning, honey." She grabs my hand and squeezes. She looks at Eli. "Morning, Eli, honey." I hate that she uses the same pet name for him and me.

"Did you sleep well?" my dad asks. I smile and nod. "I did."

My mom squeezes my hand again. "I slept like I haven't slept in a hundred years." She laughs and I know the sound. It's distant but I remember it. Like wind chimes I once heard but will remember every time I hear them.

I laugh and nod. "I know that feeling." I remember her voice. I like that.

We eat breakfast and laugh and hug. She pours my coffee and he smiles when he passes me the butter. My brothers bicker and make fun of me with Shell. I feel like I'm at Shell's but these are mine. I belong.

Hours later, sitting in the car with Stuart driving, I'm lost in what to do. I refused to go back with Eli, and he wasn't bold enough to drag me to his car in front of my dad and brothers. I have a dad and brothers. Protection of my own.

"They are so awesome." Shell smiles at me.

I glance up and nod. "Awesome."

Stuart looks at me in the rearview. "I love them, dude. So amazing. Your mom is demanding we all come for Easter. Is that cool?"

"It is. I want you guys there too."

Shell narrows her eyes. "What did Eli do? You looked ready to murder him."

I shake my head. "The usual shit. You know Eli."

Stuart nods but Shell shakes her head. "I don't actually."

"Well, you're not missing much."

Stuart laughs. "Oh, you're missing a lot. It's just whether you want to see what all you're missing."

I look behind us and see him. He's so close I can see the cold anger in his eyes. It makes me nervous.

Stuart looks at me. "He says I have to take you to his place."

I look back and give him the finger. I send a message to Sebastian quickly.

Meet me at front entrance of the Mandarin Oriental building in ten minutes, please.

Okay. You all right? He texts me back too quickly. Like he was waiting for my message. It hurts but I need him.

Yup.

I hate what I'm about to do. I'm selfish sometimes. It's self-preservation, and I am better at it than I imagined.

We pull up in front of the building. I dash from the SUV and run across the road to the white Porsche parked out front. I jump in and point. "Just drive, please."

My phone rings. I glance at it and sigh.

"What's going on? Are you all right?" Sebastian looks confused.

I shake my head. "No. I needed to talk to you." I look at him as the engine revs. "Can you take me to the dorms?"

He looks angry and I don't blame him. He sighs and turns up a road. "Are you breaking up with me?"

"It's not that I'm breaking up with you. I'm freeing you from the insanity that's me." I turn and face him. "You told me you didn't want some other guy's girl."

He licks his lips and nods. I hate what I am about to do to him.

I clear my throat and speak softly, "Fourteen years ago a boy held his hand out for me. He rescued me from my prison. I have never gotten past it. No matter what I do, or where I go, all I see is his hand. His fucked-up, bizarre, damaged hand." I stop and listen to myself. I shake my head. "I realize I'm not even making sense. But let me just say this: no matter what happens in this world, I will always be that guy's girl. I've made him so big in my mind that I can't even move around in there. It's not that I can even be with him. I just won't ever be without him. I'll never be whole without him."

He frowns. "This is insanity. You're going on the emotions of your family and the feelings that are overwhelming you. You need to distance yourself and find your true feelings."

"From both of you," I whisper.

He looks at me with the greenest hazel eyes ever and the most broken look on his face. I force myself to look at him and see every ounce of pain. He stops the car and looks down. "Yesterday was amazing. I don't even know what to say about it all. But I think I'm out of patience, Sarah. I won't be back or waiting around. I think I've gone as far as I can, waiting for you to get better. I can't believe you called me for this."

"I know. I wanted to do it face to face." I want to tell him I'll never be better. This is better. But I don't want to prolong the conversation. I just want out of the car.

He looks at me and smiles bitterly. "I'm leaving Boston. I'm going to Los Angeles for work, and I don't know when I will be back."

"Okay."

He leans over and kisses my cheek so softly it barely touches. "Take care of yourself."

"I will. You too."

He looks back at the steering wheel. I climb out, hating myself.

My brain hurts.

I storm up the steps to my building and to my room. I open the door and collapse on the bed. I grab the remote and switch on the TV. I don't think I'll ever be able to watch *Amelie* again. I turn on a vampire movie and hang with my people—the stupid girls who always pick the monster.

The next day I'm walking across the path to my dorm when my phone vibrates.

I pull it out of my pocket and answer it with anger worthy of the annoyance of him calling every five minutes. "WHAT!" I snap.

His voice is desperate. All the anger is gone. "You have to see this isn't about you. She wants you and me under her thumb. I haven't had a session with her since it happened. She isn't my therapist. It isn't even a big deal. You slept with that Sebastian fellow on your birthday, and I never brought it up. I haven't been with anyone since I found you. I swear to God. I haven't slept with anyone since I found you. Except of course that very night when Dr. Bradley and I had our moment of drunken mistaken attraction."

"YOU LET ME GO THERE! YOU LET HER TREAT ME! YOU TWO FUCKING TORTURED ME IN A CELL! YOU FUCKED A WOMAN YOU LET TORTURE ME!" I forget I'm in the middle of the path on campus. "THEN YOU FUCKED ME TOO!"

"SHE IS THE BEST, SARAH. FOR FUCK'S SAKE!" he screams and swears. He's mad. I hang up, slightly panicking. He is never that mad.

I run to my dorm and pack my bag. I'm opening the door when Shell walks in. She frowns. "What's happened?"

"I need to go box. I just need it." She sees my face and texts Stuart and grabs her bag too. She loops her arm through mine and walks with me down the stairs. "Tell Shell-Shell what's wrong."

I shake my head. "I just need a time-out from reality."

"Did you and Eli hash things out?" she asks.

I look at her like she is crazy. "Hash out what? He slept with our therapist and let her treat me. She loves him or is obsessed with him and lied about his feelings for me. She told me he liked me because he'd mentally made me his sister."

"I did tell you she was a whack job. I also told you he doesn't think you are his sister. You need to start paying me for therapy. I'm way better than she is." She holds my arm tight and walks me across the campus to the SUV.

"I just feel like an idiot."

She stops just shy of it and looks at me. "You know I'm the biggest Sebastian fan—ever. I have long wished you would beat this thing you have with Eli and marry Sebastian. I was thinking senior year, in Chicago. Let your mom and my mom plan everything so we can listen to them bicker about how you're actually Italian from my side of the family."

I laugh weakly.

She shakes her head. "I don't think that anymore. I have never been Team Eli, but after watching him with you, I am all Team Eli. I am one-hundred-percent Eli. He is so in love with you. He took care of you and forced you out of survival-orphan mode. He has spent his entire life either looking for you or figuring out the way to help you. He has no one, Sarah. No one. His parents are ridiculous and his therapist is a tart. He hasn't had girlfriends or anything. I have grilled Stuart like a mutha. That boy has literally spent his life devoted to you. All you. Not his sister. Not replacing you with her. Just you. He had the tombstone made for Emalyn. He was the one who started the Emalyn Adams Foundation for victims of child abuse. Stuart said he did that to get closure. There is a whole other Eli we don't know."

I slump. "Well, shit."

She sighs. "I know, right? All that badass and tattoos, *and* he's a fucking score. It's so not fair." She grins. I nudge her and walk to the car.

I smirk at Stuart. "Thanks for coming."

He nods at Shell. "I was already here."

I grimace and climb in. We drive over to the gym.

I look out the window, processing everything she said. It sounds true. In my heart, which is blind to his faults, it feels right. He loves me. I know he does. God, I hope he does. I hate the control he has, but at the same time, I'm so grateful he has it. He has me and everything else taken care of. In a twisted way, loaded with codependency, I love that about him. I trust him.

We pull into the gym parking lot. I climb out on my own and point at Stuart. "Stop." He backs off and laughs.

I shoulder my bag and walk up to the doors. I don't feel like boxing suddenly. I feel like closing up and refusing the entire world so I can sit and ponder the shit I don't want to deal with.

My phone vibrates.

Where are you?

I look at it and rub my thumb over the screen where the snow is falling. I shake my head muttering, "God, I hate Boston in the winter. I hate snow."

Shell laughs. "Oh my God, me too. I just want to go to Cuba for like two weeks and lay on a beach."

Stuart smirks. "Spring break?"

She grins. "For real?"

He nods and pulls her into his embrace. I walk inside, leaving them making out in the goddamned snow.

I tape up my hands and walk slowly out to the rings.

He's here.

I shake my head. "Do you have a GPS tracker on me?" I ask.

He laughs but it doesn't reach his eyes. "I do."

I cross my arms. "What? What do you want to say?"

He turns and walks away. I follow. He's still got the control. He climbs into a ring. I look around and see the gym is empty of other people. I climb into the ring with him.

He brings over gloves and pulls them on my hands, delicately. More so than he has ever been.

He speaks softly, still confidently though, "She is the best. She was the only one who believed that you could be rescued and I needed you." His eyes are wide and filled with tears. "I needed you." His vulnerability scares me. He walks slowly to get his gloves and slides his hands into them. "No one believed me about you—that I didn't invent you. No one saw me as a hero. No one but you, and for that belief in me that you had, I let you down. I left you sleeping in that barn, thinking it would be better if you didn't have to see the police. I was protecting you even then. You have never, nor will you ever, be my sister. I know I'm messed up, and I am insane in so many different ways, but the fact you could believe me capable of such a horrific thing —" he looks at me as a single tear leaks from his icy-blue eye, "—it kills me inside." His statement and his face break my heart. Somehow I'm the bad guy again.

His lip trembles, making his voice unsteady, "You have always been the girl who took my hand and trusted me to save her. The girl who saved my sister from a fate worse than any. The girl whose sadness matched my own. The girl whose face has haunted me my entire life. You saw Emalyn's eyes, well I saw yours. You are the bravest girl I have ever known."

I'm trembling and scared as he draws closer.

"I have thought of no one but you for fourteen years. I can't have a regular relationship. It isn't you I'm punishing, it's me. I don't deserve the kindness of love. I failed her and you. I should have fought harder and saved you both. I never should have left you. I'm so sorry. I never should have left you. You ended up there because of me."

I am a sobbing mess. The kaleidoscopes have taken my eyes. The angles and shapes that make my world harsh and sharp have taken over my eyes. I step forward, grabbing his hands. "You saved me. You saved me from the dirty house, and you saved me from being a dysfunctional waitress spinster for the rest of my life." I reach up and run my hands across his cheeks, taking his tears. "I see you," I whisper.

He wraps around me and we become one. Our skin is so close that in the crease between us, I feel a spark that could light up the entire world.

I hold him and caress him, and for the first time I see him. His hatred for himself is stronger than any feeling he could possibly ever have. He will always be the broken mess he is. I get the feelings of self-preservation Sebastian had when he left me. I get it. I could walk now and choose survival.

But I don't. I hold him closer and choose him. The hard work and constant frustration is worth the moments like this one, where I get to see inside. Even if it's just for a moment. I hate that we are both so damaged.

I hold him and know that without him there never was survival.

But that doesn't mean I need to self-destruct. I know what I have to do, for us both.

He shakes and sobs into me, and I have a bad feeling it's the first time he has truly let himself cry. My back hurts from the pressure and weight of him, but I hold him tightly until he's ready to stand up on his own again.

We grip to each other, like we did when we were little.

He looks at me and shakes his head. "I'm sorry. I just panicked. I don't know what to do without you. I don't know what I am without you."

"We can't be two broken things and have a relationship."

He frowns.

I rise on my toes and kiss his lips softly. "I don't want anyone but you. But at the same time, I don't want to be the china doll you glued back together. I don't want to look whole from a distance, but when you get close enough you can see all the cracks."

He runs a gloved hand down my cheek. "The cracks make us who we are."

I shake my head. "We can be more than this. But it feels like we need to be healthier for ourselves. I need to be better for me and you need to for you. If you can't love you and I can't love me, then we will never truly love each other."

He looks stressed and confused. "You don't want to be with me?"

I kiss his frozen lips again. "I do. But not like this. I don't want to need you to make me whole. My whole life I've wanted normal. I don't care about that anymore. Shell is right, there is no normal. But with us there is a danger that we will let this consume us. We won't ever get better if we don't let go of each other and find ourselves."

He kisses me back after a minute of my gentle pecks brushing his lips. "You're so much stronger than I am. I can't do this without you."

I grin. "You need like a year with some hard-ass nuns and you'll feel better. Trust me."

He laughs and shakes his head. "I need you."

"I need you too. When we don't need each other anymore and just want each other, we can try again."

He grips me. I can feel his hands trembling. "I can't be without you."

I nestle my face into his hard chest and nod. "Yes, you can. You just have to trust me. If you trust me to take care of myself, you'll see."

"What if I lose you again?"

I smile and listen to his rapid heartbeat. "You found me once, you'll find me again." My own heart is breaking. I don't want to be strong. I want him to drag me back into the changing room and punish me for such thoughts. I want to be weak and succumb to his every whim. But I don't.

"It doesn't feel like it right now, but this is me choosing you," I whisper.

He holds me tighter. "You're right, it doesn't feel like it now."

I close my eyes and feel the right path before me. "It will."

He pulls back. "Are we going to box then?"

I laugh. "I need all the help I can get, and we both already look beat up."

❧ 26 ❧

I tremble as she wraps the tape. She looks at me and smiles. "You got this."

I laugh. "I've got an ass whooping coming. That's what I've got."

She smirks. "Yup. But you look sexy in your t-shirt." I glance down and laugh. The Tinkerbell tee is exactly what I needed. When Lance gave it to me I almost killed him. But then watching him hand out the t-shirts to the Lost Boys made me feel better.

I hop back and forth and try to loosen up.

"Okay, if you panic, kick him in the balls and run. We both know Eli won't let anything happen to you."

I nod.

"Or Lyle and Jake."

I nod again. She sanitizes her hands and slides the guard into my mouth.

"Ready?"

I shake my head.

She laughs and drags me out to the rings. My brothers smile at me, but I can see they're scared. I grin my mouth guard at them. Jake laughs and shakes his head. Lyle doesn't laugh. He watches me and then looks to the door where Angelo walks out.

He grins at me and points his glove. "My turn."

I laugh. I have a secret weapon he doesn't know about. I look around for the only face I really need to see. His icy-blue eyes meet mine from a doorway. He's leaning with his arms crossed. He looks deadly sexy. I have to focus the blood in my body. I force my eyes away from his. We've been hanging out like regular people, but it's been painful.

I climb into the ring and start to hop around. I move my neck around and roll my shoulders. Angelo is doing the same. I smirk at the boys all wearing their *Lost Boys* t-shirts that Lance made for them. They're cheering, even Brandon, the little shit.

Lance steps in. "Clean fighting. No cheating. No biting. No kicking. No kissing, Angelo."

I grin.

Angelo holds a mitt up. "If you gotta kish me, I get it."

I narrow my eyes and hold my mitts up. He knocks them with his. We step back and get ready. Lance throws his arms down. "FIGHT!"

Angelo comes hard and fast. Thankfully, I can tell he's holding back, but if he hits me it's going to hurt. His right connects with my arm, but grazes off. He frowns. I grin. He hits with the left, but I move and it grazes off again.

He's confused and underestimating me. I take advantage of it and hit him in the jaw. His head barely moves. He laughs and comes at me.

I turtle as his shots connect. They still hurt, even though they glance off my arms.

"Tink, you got shomeshing you want to tell me about? Like a magical forshfield thatsh prtotecting you?"

I hit him with my pathetic swipes. He laughs. I attack harder, making his laugh get louder.

He swings at me, connecting with my face. I fall back. Luckily, it too glances off.

"TINK!" He jumps and grabs me. I'm laughing now instead of him. I rub my glove against my face. His gloves drop. He looks scared. "Can we be done now? I didn't even hit that hard and my shots aren't connecting, but this is stressing me out."

I laugh and nod. The cocky bastard is gone and replaced by this pussycat. He looks at my face and frowns. He looks at his glove and shakes his head. "Cheater, cheater."

I laugh. I'm sure I have a very glittery face.

He looks at Shell who waves at him, holding the bottle of glitter body oil.

He holds up his sparkly gloves. "How did I mish thish?"

Lyle and Jake are there beside me, lifting me up. Protective isn't the right way to describe them. They moved to Boston the week after my birthday and we had planned family outings every second day until they finally got us to agree to move in with them. They even joined my boxing club. They're out of control. But I like it.

"You okay?" Lyle asks and glares at Angelo. Jake pulls off my gloves. I drop the guard into my hand and grimace. Lyle makes the same face. He has a thing with germs. It warms my heart.

I look around the gym for Eli, but he isn't there. He's gone.

"We have to leave for Easter. You ready?" Lyle asks. I nod.

"Is Eli coming?" Jake looks around the gym.

"Not sure," I say.

Jake looks worried. "You guys are still cool, right?"

I blush. "Yup."

Lance comes up smirking. "You went down like a sack of potatoes, Tink. We gotta work on your ducking."

Brandon scoffs. "She lasted ten times longer than I thought she would, and she hit him."

I glance at Angelo and wink. "Race when I get back?"

He nods. "Then we start working on that plan of yours."

"Thanks, Angelo."

He nods at me. "Get that girl to call me again. She's not returning any of my texts."

I look at Shell, talking to the Lost Boys and shake my head. "She's off the market, dude."

"Bummer. Have a good Easter, Tink."

"You too."

I get cleaned up, staring at my phone the entire time.

We leave the gym. Stuart is standing at the SUV, looking at his watch. "Come on!" He's waving his arms, motioning for us to get in. He drives like a madman.

"We're gonna miss him if we don't hurry."

I lean over the seat between him and Jake. "What?"

Stuart glances at me. "Seat belt."

I growl. "Where is he going? Is he coming with us?"

He shakes his head and gulps.

I sit back and look at Shell. She looks upset. She knows and hasn't told me. My stomach is in a ball. He's leaving for somewhere without me? I've made a mistake. I was trying to be stronger than I am. He's leaving me. He's choosing survival over me. Like I did.

Stuart pulls up to the departures entrance. "We'll get your shit, just run." I leap over Lyle and run into the airport.

I pull my phone out and text while I run.

Where r u?

I run faster until I get to the check-in area and then I'm not sure which way to go. I am standing, looking at the departure gates screen when my phone vibrates.

Please text like an adult. R U? Really?

I start to laugh.

Look behind you.

I turn and smile. He's standing against a pillar with posters of missing kids. It's weirdly ironic and delightful.

I leap at him. His arms wrap around me, pulling me into him. I tilt my face up. He kisses and holds me like we are paused.

I melt into him.

"Where are you going?" I ask against his mouth.

"To live with some mean-ass nuns for a while."

I laugh into his face and cry. "A year?"

He kisses my forehead and grins. "You said it was what I needed. I don't think it'll be a year. A few months though. I can't take too long from work."

I pull back and look at him. "I didn't think you'd take me seriously."

He arches a dark eyebrow. "I take everything you say seriously. Well, when you speak like an adult."

I bite my lip. I'm panicking inside. "Are you calling my bluff? I don't want you to go. I want to come or you to stay."

He laughs and grabs my hands. "Sarah, I need this. I need to see with the perspective you have. There are people who have it worse, and I need to be grateful for what I have. You were right. My environment wasn't a great way to grow up after everything else."

"Where are you going?"

"South America."

I laugh. "Armani in South America?"

He laughs and squeezes me. "I went to a strange store called Cabela and bought all the beige and khaki I could find."

I laugh and rest my head against his chest again. "What if we lose each other?"

He kisses the top of my head. "I will always find you."

I smile and close my eyes and make myself feel everything about the moment. I'm going to need it.

"I never imagined you would take my advice. I'm twenty. What do I know?"

He pulls my face back. "A lot. Now, stay close to your brothers and please, for the love of God, don't go out without them. Stay in Boston or Chicago with family and friends. Keep training with Angelo and don't let him kiss you, he'll suck your whole damned face in." I make a face. He laughs. "I knew a girl who dated him."

"I'm going to miss you." The tears are there before I can stop them.

He brushes them away. "I need this. I need to stop myself from obsessing about where you are at every moment. I need to trust you."

I shake my head. "You don't have anything to prove. You don't need to be a hero there. You are my hero already. You can learn to trust me here. I'm fine, I swear."

He shakes his head. "I'm not. You were right."

I hate being right. I hate this moment. I hate that I see he needs this.

He cocks an eyebrow. "Behave yourself, and I expect FaceTime dates frequently." He chooses to ignore my hero comment. "They're going to call my flight, and I haven't even gotten through security."

I grip him. "Don't leave me."

He kisses my lips. "Never again. This isn't me leaving you. This is me choosing you." He throws my words back at me.

He kisses me once more and then pushes off. He leaves and doesn't look back. I fight the urge to run after him.

I grip my phone and watch him until I can't see him anymore. Then I send a text. *I'm grateful for you.*

I hear footsteps and turn to see the rest of them have caught up to me. Shell grips my shoulders. "You okay?"

I slump and shake my head. "My heart just left for South America."

Lyle and Jake join the hug. I'm squished in amongst them all. It's not enough, but it's more than I could have ever asked for.

Jake grips my arm. "Millionaires, what can you do? They're all crazy. You can be sad on the plane. Come on, time to go."

We fly home. I'm heartbroken and excited simultaneously.

Home.

It's a weird word for me. I have not seen the house since I left it to go to the hospital. Apparently, I was wearing pink pajamas and clutching a bear with a pink ribbon. The bear was my favorite toy.

Dad is at the airport when we get there. He hugs me hard, like he's going to break my back.

We leave for the car, hugging and sniffling. Evidently, that's my family's thing. We cry and hug a lot. But the sweetness of it is better than anything I've ever experienced.

Chicago is amazing. We—yes we. I have a we—we live on the outskirts, in a suburb. I look around nervously as we drive into a community. He drives the rented minivan up a street that takes my breath away.

"You sure we have enough room at the house?" I ask.

Dad nods. "Plenty of room."

We drive into a neighborhood like I have never seen before. It's like out of a movie. The houses are massive; they're not mansions but are huge. Each one has a private driveway and a huge yard. We pull into one with bricks and bushes, and windows with the white shutters

I always dreamt of. I will lose my mind if I let myself realize this was all sitting here waiting for me. I was suffering and dying inside and this was here.

I fight off the trembling fear and wish he were with me to see it and help me be grateful. Seeing it is like seeing the finish line in a race I was certain would kill me.

She is at the front door smiling, looking like a mom. She has a sweater on with the ruffled edges of a blouse sticking out the collar. My face splits into a smile when I see her. Her blonde hair shines in the brightness of the spring day. It glistens.

We get out of the van with stretches and nudges. Jake shoves me and Lyle shoves him. I grin at them both and wish I could have known them when we were little. Not that it's too late. It isn't. It's just hard not to daydream about how fantastic it would have been to be wrestled and attacked, with love and brotherly affection. Jake grabs my head and bends me forward. He grips my head and gives me a fake back-breaker. I flip him the way Lance showed me. He's on his back, laughing and shaking his head.

"You know better than to give her an inch." Lyle crosses his arms.

They both know better. They spar with me all the time. Not that I'm good, but I'm getting better and I cheat.

We've been play fighting in the ring for two months. It's been a good way to get to know each other. Moving into a condo all together last week was an even better way. Shell and I jumped at the chance. No more communal showers or crappy kitchen. Plus it stopped them from coming to the dorms every other minute. They're worse than Eli when it comes to surveillance and protection. I seriously believe some of the other students think I'm protected by the Secret Service.

Mom shouts, "Get in here you guys." The boys jump up and grab our bags. They don't carry mine but they take Shell's.

I stand there affronted by it until Shell beams. "My brothers do the same thing to me."

I like that.

I grab my bag but Dad grabs it and wraps an arm around me. "Welcome home, Sarah."

"Thanks, Dad."

I have sworn I won't cry. We've been talking every day on Face-Time and text, but I think I will have that vow broken before Mom even gets a hug in.

I climb the steps and a huge weight lifts from my shoulders. Mom grabs me and pulls me into her. The house smells like gingerbread, and at the top of the hardwood stairs I see a black and white cat. She looks so old I can hardly stand it.

My mouth is hanging open.

"Kitty, or as you referred to her, Titty, is eighteen. Well, she'll be eighteen in a couple months. She was tiny when you—well, she was tiny then. It's crazy she's still with us," Dad says and looks at Mom. I walk past them and hold my hand out. The black and white cat rubs against my fingers. I pick her up and smell her neck fur. She smells the same. I swear she does. She begins to purr right away as I grip her, probably too hard, but I can't help it. I also can't help but wonder if she stayed alive because she knew I was out there.

Mom grabs my arm and leads me up the stairs. She takes me to a room and opens the door. It's cold and stale inside. It's a small girl's room. Ponies and rainbows and a small bed with a Strawberry Short-cake blanket make the room cluttered and homey. It doesn't look like they have changed a single thing since the day I left. I stroke Kitty and wonder how hard it must have been to have such a constant reminder.

My vow is broken instantly.

It took me a lot of years to find my way, but I am home.

27

His face is dirty and tired, but I've never been more in love with him. He points with the child at the screen. It fuzzes out, but then I can see them again. She is beautiful and frightened.

I wave with my family behind me. We wave.

"We miss you, Son," Dad shouts.

Eli grins, his icy-blue eyes kill me. "Her name is Arielle. She's seven. We saved her. The river near their home flooded. They were trapped." He doesn't say anything else. He doesn't need to. I get the gist of it.

I laugh. "Hi Arielle!" I wave. She looks frightened. "Your name is very pretty." She bats her eyelashes and looks down. I look back at him. "Did your khakis get wet?"

His eyes flash something. I see it in his face. It's a flash of something I've seen before. It's terror. "They did." He licks his lips.

I feel the fear cross my own face. "You be safe."

He nods and swallows. "We're being careful."

"I mean it. You've been there four days. How can you be so careless so quickly?"

His lips are playful again. "Yes, Mother."

My mom leans over me. "She's right, Eli. Be safe. We miss you, honey."

I love it. They love him. They don't really know him, not the dark and scary parts, but then again they don't know those places in me. Only he does. Only he has seen the darkness. Only he embraces the darkness inside me and turns it into love and light. The things that happened to make us dark and scary are our little secret.

"We better go. She needs to get back with the other kids." His eyes meet mine.

He points at me. "No. Behave. No crying. I miss you. Go torture that cat of yours. She's had too many years of peace." He waves and the screen freezes. His blue eyes and her hand extended to him are all that is left of the picture.

I'm brokenhearted but I'm home. I let them be enough. My mom squeezes my shoulders and my brother hits me in the arm. "Want a beer?"

I laugh and nod. "Yup. Please." I need one. I finally get that feeling of needing something, even if it's just a little.

He passes it to me and sits across from me at the table. His blue eyes are worried and distant. I look at him and take a drink. "You okay?" I ask in a hushed tone.

He shakes his head. "No. I think having you here is making it all real. For years I pretended it was a sad story on a show I had watched and not my life at all." He smiles. "You're here and real, and as annoying as I imagined you would be."

I roll my eyes. "Moving into an apartment with me and Shell wasn't real enough? I washed your boxers last week."

He looks at me. "I may live with you until you're eighty. I can't let you out of my sight."

"The more comfortable we all get, the meaner I will get." I glance at Shell who nods. "It's true. Sometimes she's kinda shitty. She has survival-orphan syndrome moments still."

The room is silent except for my laugh. Shell's face is white, but I'm killing myself laughing. Slowly smiles spread. "Too soon?" she asks quietly.

I shake my head.

Lyle nods. "Yeah."

I laugh harder and mutter, "Survival-orphan syndrome. It's so true." I take another drink of my beer and grimace. "I still don't love the taste of this."

Jake takes it and drinks it. I almost have a stroke, but I laugh when I see the horrified look on Lyle's face.

Dad brings me a glass of red wine. "Try this maybe. It's what your mother and I drink."

I take the warm glass and already dread putting it up to my lips. I feel my throat thicken but take a deep breath. I tilt the glass and take a drink. The wine is bitter and I shiver. Instantly, I hate it, but want more. My taste buds love it. The rest of me hates it.

I take a second drink. I nod. "This I can do."

Shell smirks. "My mom is gonna love this."

In the middle of the conversation, Mom interrupts us, "Lyle, why don't you and Jake take Michelle and Stuart and show them around town." Lyle looks like he's about to argue but he doesn't. She stands up and everyone follows him out of the kitchen slowly. Mom sits at the table where Lyle was. She puts her hands out and touches mine. Hers are so clean and soft. Her skin is ivory.

"Honey, I need to know. I need to know how it was. I know they don't want to know, and I'm sure you don't want to talk about it. But there is something inside me that can't let go until I've properly understood it."

I shake my head. "It's okay." I look at the table. I can't look at her and talk. I've worked so hard to push it all down and find the normal inside me.

I grip the glass.

"Baby, if you'd rather talk about it later, that's okay. I just want you to know that at some point I need to know." Her soft voice is soothing.

"How much do you know?"

She shakes her head. "Not much. Eli explained that you were kept at a place you called the dirty house. That's where he met you. I've obviously looked up the Spicers on Google."

I feel sick for her. I'm scared she's asking me, to torture herself but

I talk anyway, "It wasn't bad for me. I have limited memories of the dirty house. I remember the hole. They had a hole dug. It was round and dirty, and it had a thick board on top for a lid. The smallest amount of light could get through. When Randy was edgy, she put me in the hole. Only she could put kids in and take them out. The hole was off limits to him. I was off limits. If he got angry or edgy, I was put in there. Laura would tell me it was for my own protection. My memories are choppy, but I know he never molested me or anything like that." I don't tell her about the things I saw. I can spare her that.

She sighs and wipes away her silent tears. "When your child goes missing, you fear the worst. For you to be with the worst, well I assumed you suffered."

I shake my head. "No. It was just dirty and gross. They were bad people but not to me. I was like a daughter to her so she protected me."

"What about the orphanage?"

I can meet her eyes and free her from this. I smile. "It was amazing in comparison. I learned a million things I needed in life. I learned to be strong and to be grateful. They didn't have time to love us, but they never hurt us. It was easy, once I learned how to live there."

She squeezes my hand and drops her face to the table. Her back shakes and jerks with the sobs. I squeeze back. "Mom," I say softly. I rub her back the way Shell rubs mine and let her sob until she can't anymore.

She lifts her face. "I'm sorry." She sniffles and wipes her eyes. "I just am so relieved. I don't know how it happened and how it worked, but you seem so normal. I need to thank those nuns one day." I almost grimace when she says it.

Instead, I grin and fight back my own tears. I jump out of the chair and wrap my arms around her.

"I prayed every day we would find you, but I was terrified of what we would find. I'm so grateful."

I close my eyes. "Me too."

"You needed teeth out. It was routine but we were so stressed. The enamel hadn't been good on your teeth. I breastfed you at night. I didn't know it would rot your teeth. They were just going to take out two and then fill the rest. They don't do dental work on two-year-olds without anesthesia, not even ones that are about to turn three any day. They put you to sleep for it." Her voice is muffled and sad, "We went and sat in the waiting room. I paced and gripped the bear. We'd brought the bear. Lyle and Jake were being naughty. I was so tired and just wanted it over with. But you never came out of that recovery room. The doctor came to tell us you were fine, and it had been routine and normal and you were sleeping the drugs off. You would wake soon. But we never saw you again. Not until Eli came to us. He had a photo and a story. I doubted it all until I saw the photo." She reaches into her back pocket and pulls out a photo of me, taken at a bit of a distance. It's wrinkled and worn. I imagine she has held it to her face a thousand times.

"I thought I had died and gone to heaven that day. When he told us we couldn't see you yet, and you had been traumatized and needed time to resurface—well, I thought I was going to murder him right then and there. I couldn't believe that smug little shit was keeping you from me. After seventeen years, I was dying to see you. But your father agreed that it was better to try to pull you out of the fake world you had created."

I pulled back and nodded. "It was for the best. It didn't feel like it at the time, but it was."

She wipes my hair away, and I wonder if we look the same—red nose and puffy eyes.

"You are so lucky to have each other. I've never actually seen a man love a woman as much as he loves you, Sarah. I love your father and he loves me. We have survived a lot of things, but I know in my heart of hearts our love is not as intense as yours."

I laugh. If only she knew. I shake my head. "He's just an intense person. Trust me, I don't think I'm capable of half the love he is. But I can laugh and have fun, where as he can't. He isn't fun. Not in the way Jake and Lyle are. He's intense in everything."

She smiles. "He's been through so much. His guilt over losing you, when he went for the police, has been unbearable."

"He didn't lose me. I assumed he had run off, hating me for

shooting her." The words sting on my tongue. It's the first time I've said it without bawling like a baby.

She kisses my forehead. "I don't ever like imagining it all."

I hug her again and melt into her.

We fly back to Boston the next day. Mom packs us food for the plane and food for our apartment. She hugged me so hard I thought I might die. She gushes about coming to Boston and helping us decorate our new place.

On the plane I'm nestled between my brothers. I'm certain they booked the flights with the seats confirmed this way. They're smothering me, but I'm cool with it. I'm certain eventually I will smother them back, with a pillow. But it won't be today, well maybe. Jake is laying his head on my shoulder and mouth breathing. I look at Lyle, scowling. "Gross," I whisper.

He looks horrified. "That's why I put you in the middle. I've done my share of car and plane rides."

I laugh and hang my mouth open. "Hurtful. I thought you put me in the middle 'cause you wanted to be the big brother and protect me from sitting by strangers."

He nudges me. "Whatever."

I smile and love him. We are soul mates. I pull out some hand sani and offer it to him. He puts his hands out. I squirt his and then do my own. We rub our hands together, the exact same way.

"Dad's obsessed with it too."

I laugh.

"Hey, so Shell was saying you dated Sebastian Hollinger?"

I nod. "Yeah. You know him?" I love that he calls her Shell.

He raises his eyebrows. "Uh, yeah. Everyone knows him. Quite the success story there. His dad is a fisherman or something in Maine. We were in school at the same time at MIT."

I wrinkle my nose involuntarily. "He hates me."

He raises an eyebrow. "Ended badly?"

I nod. "Yeah. I came back from meeting you guys for the first time, at the end of February. It was before Eli and I had decided we wanted to be together. I decided I just needed to be single. I told Sebastian I was taking myself off the market to do some self-discovery. He was pissed. He felt like I had led him on, I think."

He frowns. "What a wanker. Wait—did you lead him on?"

I bite my lip and nod.

He looks disappointed. "How could you?"

I shrug. "I wanted him to be the one. He's normal, sweet, and kind. He's awesome and safe. But no matter how hard I tried to make it work, it didn't. He always saw the sad little orphan. I think he liked that I was broken. Eli thinks I'm the stronger one. I like that. Plus we have a spark."

He rolls his eyes. "Girls. You're so fickle. The right one. The magical kiss. The special someone. The spark. It all equates to the same thing—bullshit. You have your minds made up when you meet us. Forcing yourself to love us for who we are is ridiculous."

I raise my eyebrows. "Coming from the guy who hasn't dated since twelfth grade. Jake told me."

His face flushes like mine does. "That's not true. I dated at college. I've just put myself into my work. He's one to talk anyway; he bloody well works for me now."

I laugh at his red face. He wrinkles his nose and sneers. "You're still a little brat."

I stick my tongue out.

But behind it all, I know their lives were stunted because of our situation. I was taken and everything else was hard. I'm grateful for them.

❦ 28 ❦

I take a deep breath and grip her hand. I look down and nod. "Do it."

She rings the bell.

A man in a suit answers the door.

"Hello. How may I help you?" He has an English accent and reminds me of Niles on *The Nanny*. I love Netflix.

"We called about meeting with the Adams family." Shell snickers. I fight a grin. "Uhm—Michelle and Sarah."

His eyes light up. "Of course. Yes. Please come in. They're expecting you."

My heart is in my throat. He opens the door more and we walk in. The home is posh and overly fancy. I feel like I'm at a hotel I can't afford.

He leads us to a study where a thin woman in a white pantsuit is waiting for us. A man is across the room doing some kind of paperwork. They are both older and worn looking, but in a rich sort of way.

The woman in the pantsuit turns as we are announced. "Miss Mastermen and Miss Monkton to see you."

I still feel weird being a Mastermen.

"Thank you, Franklin. We'll take tea in the sitting room." She rushes at me and puts her hands out. "You must be Sarah." Her eyes are icy blue like Eli's. Her smile is cold and distant. She never fully warms up, I don't think.

I nod. "I am Mrs. Adams. Thank you for seeing me."

She shakes her head. "Gloria. Please call me Gloria."

His father stands and offers me his hand. "And call me Dick." Michelle snorts.

I shake his huge warm hand. "It's nice to meet you both. This is my friend Michelle."

She waves. "Hi."

They look phony and cold when they greet her. "Hello." They almost talk like they too have accents. They enunciate everything. Mrs. Adams' blue eyes sparkle. "We were so pleased when you called." I see a flash of pain or something in her eyes.

I nod. "I was scared you wouldn't want to see me."

She shakes her head. "We never blamed you, dear child—never."

His father smirks. "We were actually quite grateful you existed at all. Poor Eli was considered quite mad for some time."

It hurts me inside, but I fight it and shake my head. "It was me." The words are breathy and soft.

His father's response is not one I expected. He grabs my chin and points my face at his. "You saved her. You freed her."

I'm not strong enough for it. I don't want their forgiveness. I want a clean conscience. I have confessed and wish to be absolved by God, not them.

Her lip quivers. She puts a hand up to her mouth. "Forgive me. I'm just so grateful you are here." She wraps her arms around me. I'm stunned. Even more stunned when his arms find their way around me as well. It isn't easy to be forgiven.

"Tea is served."

I've never been grateful for that statement before, but I am now. We sniffle and wipe and make our way into the sitting room, following behind Franklin. It too feels like the set of an Austen movie. Floral and fancy with gilded frames and sculptures, and chairs that feel like they haven't been broken in yet, regardless of being a hundred years old.

I sit and take the tea on a plate with a cookie. I don't know what

I'm supposed to do with it. I stare down at the black tea and dread drinking it.

Shell holds hers up. "Can I get some cream and sugar, please?"

Franklin looks appalled. "It's got honey and lemon in it. It's Earl Grey."

I stir the cup and try not to let the smell get near my face or I risk gagging. It reminds me of the cell a bit.

"Have you heard from Eli?" his mother asks casually, as if we hadn't all just cried.

I nod. "A couple weeks ago. He was in a village, building houses with missionaries and then they were going to be leaving with some doctors from Doctors Without Borders. They were vaccinating and stuff in a remote area."

She sighs. "I don't like this. I know he's fond of you, always has been. When he was in the center he used to write you these letters. It was quite sad. Anyway, surely you must be able to get him to come home?"

My mouth waters as I catch a whiff of the tea and shake my head. "No." I swallow. "I don't think so. He's pretty bent on finding himself."

His dad scoffs. "It's that damned Dr. Bradley, no doubt, that put this foolish notion into his head. Her pseudo science almost lost him several times. She has those theories about pushing people to the brink. Crazy woman."

"Yes." I raise my eyebrows. I don't know how to tell them it was me that made him want to do this.

Michelle sips the tea loudly before speaking, "I'm sure he's fine. It's good to go get dirty sometimes. Makes you appreciate everything else more. He's only been gone a couple months. He'll be fine."

His parents look disturbed for a microsecond and then smile and nod.

I look at them hesitantly. "Have you heard from Dr. Bradley at all?"

His mother scoffs. "Hmph, she won't darken our doorway anytime soon. That woman is dangerous. Franklin has had her removed from the property. Right before he left, Eli came to us and told us an alarming tale of his recovery with her. She is insane. I blame her entirely for his want to be in South America. He's so bent on proving himself."

His father agrees, "Yes. We have told him time and time again how proud of him we are. Someone like him cannot expect a full life and a full recovery. He is doing well for someone like him." He nods at me. "As are you."

My blood is boiling. It's no wonder he was so dependent on Dr. Bradley, or that he was so easily swayed by her and eventually used by her. I had been stuck on the words "the center" but the last sentence has me there. I stand with the teacup trembling in my hands. "Well, thank you for tea and for meeting with us. We should be going though."

Michelle is mid sip when she stands and hands the cup and saucer to Franklin who is standing at the ready. "Have a lovely day." I want to say life. I want to practice my boxing moves. I want to scream my face off. I take deep breaths and storm to the front door. Michelle is jogging to catch up to me.

We walk out into the cool spring air, and I know what I have to do, beyond forget I ever met those people.

I get her to drive us to the airport.

I phone Lyle. "Hey."

He sounds funny. "Hey."

"I need you to book me a flight."

Michelle looks at me like I'm nuts.

❧ 29 ❧

The heat of the day is unbearable to my cold Boston skin. I know it isn't any hotter than a New Mexico summer day, but it feels like it's scorching me. The jeep I'm in has no roof. I'm holding a rag over my face to keep the sand out of my lungs. I am underprepared and completely moronic. I see this now.

We drive until we get to a small village. The people stare at me. I'm scared and in desperate need of hand sanitizer. I don't like the feeling of being watched. I get that my blonde hair is intriguing, but I'm uncomfortable. I'm not strong enough for this.

My driver climbs out. He's one of the drivers for the Doctors Without Borders. He picked me up from the airport that I call a patch of grass with a shack on it. Lyle and Stuart arranged everything for me.

He looks back at me as he walks up to the village. I watch him speaking to a man. The man looks at me and makes a face. The driver looks back. My breathing is starting to make my chest rise and fall rapidly. I can feel the panic. Something is wrong.

He comes back with a look on his face. A look I'm not sure I can handle.

He shakes his head. "They left here about a week ago and went into a remote part of the jungle. There was a sickness there."

"Okay, well let's go there then."

He shakes his head. "Everyone is on quarantine. No one is allowed in or out. They are calling it a plague."

My hand dives into my shorts pocket and grabs at my sani. I dump it into my palm and spread it around. He watches me.

"You okay?"

I shake my head. "I want to go to him."

He gets in the jeep. "No. We go to the closest village, but if they don't have news, we leave."

I'm desperate and sick. Eli's going to die teaching me to be grateful for the time we spent together, instead of always judging us for it. I'm almost crying, but I know the sand will be brutal if I cry. I could chant that I am grateful. I am. The weird things we like to do to each other can't make me feel bad when he's possibly dying right now.

I look up at the clear sky and clasp my hands. I have not prayed since they made me last time at church in twelfth grade.

"Watch, oh Lord, with those who wake or watch or weep tonight and give your angels and saints charge over those who sleep. Tend your sick ones, oh Lord Christ. Rest your weary ones. Bless your dying ones. Soothe your suffering ones. Pity your afflicted ones. And all for your love's sake. Amen." I close my eyes and open my heart. I pray he can see it. He has kept me safe. Up to this point a million things could have happened differently, but I see the miracle of it all. I see the help I've received. I don't see it the way the church does, but I still see it.

"You a nun?"

I glance at him as he drives. "No, I went to Catholic school." I lie. I don't want him to see the poor orphan. She doesn't really exist anyway. I never was an orphan.

He drives back into the small town where I have a room.

I see him immediately. He looks different. More tanned but as though there is less of something. It isn't anger. He has tons of that on his face. He's walking to the jeep, irate. At first I think it's a mirage, but then I realize it isn't. He's far too mad to be a mirage.

"What the hell are you doing here?" His voice is low and growled.

I look at the driver. "Thanks."

He looks scared. "That him then?"

I nod. "Yup."

"Good luck, miss." His words could make me laugh, but I'm feeling too many things.

Eli rips the door open and offers me his hand. I take it and swallow. The touch is a million times better than I thought it would be, but I'm still scared.

He drags me to the small hotel. He climbs the stairs and produces a key. I'm not even slightly surprised when he opens the door to my room.

"Corrupt Third World countries," I mutter. He closes the door and presses his back into it.

I want to jump on him but I have a slight twinge in my belly. He looks savagely angry. "What did I say when I left?" His words are calm, the scary kind.

I bite my lip.

His eyes flicker to mine but I shy away from them. "I said don't go anywhere without your brothers or Stuart and not to leave Chicago or Boston. Did you misunderstand my words?"

I take a breath and a step forward on my tiptoes and press my sandy, salty lips against him. He doesn't kiss back. I speak into his lips. "You are not the boss of me. If you can gallivant throughout South America, then so can I."

He has me in his arms suddenly. "You scared me," he whispers.

"Ditto."

He pulls me back. "We are leaving in an hour. I have flights booked."

I frown. "You're leaving the missionaries?"

He shakes his head. "Not exactly. We never made it to our last destination. There is a sickness here. All non-residents are being sent home unless they have medical experience. I do not. Pack your bags. We leave as soon as possible. I don't want you here with this."

I want to pull his clothes off, but the idea of the sand and the dirt is a huge turn off.

I kiss his lips once more and pack my stuff. I give him a sideways look. "I went to your parents' house. I confessed it was me."

He looks concerned. "They knew that already. Why?"

"I need absolution from God for my sin."

He rolls his eyes. "You don't get to pick and choose how religious you are. You never go to church. Why need absolution over that? It wasn't your fault."

I grab my stuff and walk to him. "I just needed to." I don't tell him I believe in God. I completely believe in God.

"Were they cruel to you?" His eyes are hard.

I almost flinch. "God, no. They were perfectly polite. Hugged me once even."

Shock lifts his eyebrows up before he can catch himself.

"They told me about the center."

He swallows. "Did they?" His eyes cool off again.

I nod. I put a hand out. It's so creamy white against his dark face. "I needed to hold you and make sure you were okay."

He kisses my palm, almost making me gag. He smiles. "I have you. I'll always be okay."

My lips tremble when I get the words out, "I need you to know I was wrong. You don't need to live here and be grateful because it was so cushy and easy for you growing up."

His mouth twitches.

"My life was easier than yours. There is no doubt. Those nuns loved me way more than those people loved you, and that is saying a lot, but I still think it was easier than just not being touched." I'm scared he's going to shut me out. I'm pushing his limits. I can see that.

He licks his lips and shakes his head. "It doesn't matter. I am grateful. I see what we have, and I found you and I trust that you're going to be okay. Coming here made me see that."

"I love you, Eli. Whatever we like or don't like to do to each other is okay."

He shakes his head. "I don't want to talk about it."

I nod gratefully. I don't want to talk about it either.

He kisses my lips softly. "I am grateful for you."

I nod and open the door. He grabs my arm and pulls me into his embrace. I close my eyes and it's perfection. The kiss is needy and desperate, but it's closed mouth. It's the words we don't say. Words like I needed you more than anything in the entire world and here you are.

It's the sentences neither of us can say. Neither of us likes grand gestures or big words. But the kiss says it all. The desperate tremble of the fear upon his lips against mine speaks volumes, compared to the words we may or may not be able to say.

When the silence breaks he whispers, "Let's go home."

EPILOGUE

I don't know where he is. It was his stupid idea to move in together. I look out over the snow through the window and grimace at the first snowfall of the year. I can't help but wonder where he is. I rode the elevator alone, carried the groceries to the kitchen by myself, and put them away.

I sat on the couch for ten minutes, waiting for him to attack me savagely, but he never graced me with his presence. I sit down and tap my finger against the sofa and remind myself of Dr. Bradley. I stop and look around, sighing in annoyance. I get up and walk down the hallway to have a bath. I hear something that makes me stop. It's in the bedroom at the far end of the hall. The one I made him put a lock on.

My heart pounds. Excitement and terror take up equal amounts of space. The hair on my head even tingles. I shudder and slip my boots off. I tiptoe to the end of the hallway to the large door. I swallow.

I close my eyes and turn the knob. It's locked. I drop to my knees as a new terror begins to creep in. What if he isn't alone? Is that a possibility that I have not even considered out of foolish naivety and blind trust? I place my fingers around the cold knob and peer into the keyhole on the wooden door. He insisted on it being an old-fashioned key, an intricate-looking one that would look like it belonged on the boudoir of a man and his mistress. I roll my eyes, thinking about the way he had said it, all pretentious and ridiculous.

Now, however, I'm grateful he's a snobby bastard. I'm trying desperately to control my breathing as my mother's words about him loving me more than anything in the world are flashing through my mind. I blink in front of the keyhole.

I jump and scream when I see his eye, also peeking through the hole.

The door is unlocked and opened. He has the wickedly cocky smile.

"Spying on me? Really? Are you so insecure?"

I frown. He's in that mood. I want to argue; I know what that will entail.

He steps to the side, leaving me just enough room to enter. I walk past him with my head high in the air. He loosens his tie and rolls his sleeves up. I catch a glimpse of his tats and scars. I lick my lips and forget about the bath. He closes the door, grinning.

He walks to the corner and sits in his chair.

He's in luck. I had planned on us having savage sex in the living room. Mostly because he refuses to do it anywhere but a bed, but I've been working on my seduction. Today I came prepared.

I unzip my jacket and let it drop to the floor. It's the only sound in the room. I pull my ponytail out and shake my head back and forth. Walking closer to the bed I undo one button on my blouse. I turn and face him as I slowly get the others. His mouth opens when he sees what's underneath. He's shocked. I like that.

I bite my lip and shoulder out of the blouse. I'm wearing a strapless white bustier with a lot of push-up. Maintaining eye contact with him, I undo my jeans. I turn around and pull them down, bending over completely. I have on ruffled white underwear that match the bustier. His head tilts slightly as he watches, making a sliver of a smile grace my lips. I stand up and turn around.

He looks flabbergasted. I have a small mental dance party and turn around. I bend over the bed and wait for it.

When I hear him get up I brace for the hand on my ass. He's hasty from the unexpected aspects of this and has not grabbed a paddle or hairbrush from the wall.

What I get surprises me. His warm lips press against my left ass cheek. His hands slide up and down my thigh. It's nice.

I'm about to beg—he likes it when I beg—when he pulls his face away and his hand makes contact with my right cheek.

I moan into the bedding.

"You like that, don't you? You thought I was going to go easy on you because you wore pretty underwear?" He slaps in the same spot. I writhe and mouth breathe into the blankets. "What you didn't know, is I like you in your cotton underwear. I like you that way."

I do know that. I know how he feels about slutty underwear. I grin as his hand makes contact once more.

"If you want to dress that way. I can treat you that way."

I bury my face to hide the smile crossing my lips as I hear the buckle of his pants. He spreads my legs with his and slides my underwear to the side. His fingers slide up and down me, soaking in the moisture. He plunges a finger in, making a gasp rip from my parted lips. His body bends over mine as his finger plunges in and out. He grabs my shoulder and pulls me back a bit, arching my back more. He's pumping in and out and I'm clawing at the bed. I pull away before I orgasm, making him chuckle.

"Not the orgasm you want, baby?"

I shake my head.

He rips the panties off me, making me a bit sad momentarily. They cost a small fortune and matched the bustier.

He's between my thighs and pulling my butt into him. He rubs himself up and down me, before slipping only the tip in. I try to push back to get more, but he doesn't let me. He slowly enters, but not roughly.

"You will come when I let you," he growls. He bends and kisses my back softly. He knows how much I hate soft, slow sex. I clench my jaw.

He rams me once hard and fast. I cry out but then he slows again. He's driving me insane with the inconsistent thrusts. I'm ready to knock him out and ride him my way. He slides his hand up my back, massaging and rubbing. He is thrusting slowly and evenly. His hand slides up the back of my head. He grabs a fistful of hair, right in the sweet spot and pulls my head back. Then he starts to buck, the right way. He's slamming me and pulling my hair like a savage. I'm crying out and clenching him. I orgasm as he growls. "You like it that way, don't you?"

He moans as my clenching and squeezing forces his orgasm. He collapses on my back and kisses it softly.

We roll up into the bed and lie there for a minute, trying to catch our breath.

He strokes my head and looks at me. "What time are you going to the rings?"

I smirk. There is no weird pillow talk and no pretending we're soft delicate people. No apologies, limits yes, but no shame.

I glance up at him. "I'm meeting Angelo at seven. We're going to try to get as many places involved as we can. The program is looking like it will go ahead. Self-defense classes for free for every girl on Saturday afternoons. Angelo is cool with teaching it, as long as he gets to kick my ass the whole time."

He arches an eyebrow. "Yeah, that's realistic. Stuart picking you up?"

I nod. "Yah. He's taking me driving later with Jake." I roll my eyes. "They are so mean to me about my shit-ass driving."

He laughs and kisses my forehead. "You suck, that's why."

I shove him but he grins harder. "Hey, I watched you take driving lessons in New Mexico. I saw what was happening there. Why do you think I hired Stuart when you moved here? That driver's ed guy said you had been trying for years and the church finally said no more. You cost a fortune."

I furrow my brow. "Hurtful."

His face softens. He kisses my face again. I climb out of the bed and shrug on my robe. I pass him his. He stands and I trace my fingers along the cross on his left side. I bend forward and gently kiss her name. I walk to the door and offer him my hand. He takes it, kissing it, and letting me lead him for a change.

THE END

Check out the companion novel, The Lost Boy, for Eli's version of the events you have just read. It's the behind-the-scenes rendition of The Lonely.

About Me

I believe growing up in a really small town gives a person a little advantage when it comes to the imagination. You need one or you go mad.

Needless to say, mine saved me. After it got me into trouble first, that is. That's the problem with a vivid imagination, all the lies you tell.

According to my age, I am meant to be a responsible adult, but it isn't going well at all. I would still head off to Hogwarts tomorrow and I suspect there isn't a single wardrobe I haven't crept into, hoping to find the door to Narnia. And don't even get me started on the King's Road, I get lost.

Fortunately, I am an international bestseller so I have wormed my way into a quirky or eccentric category.

Thank God for that.

I am happily married with two daughters.

I have two giant dogs, two savage cats, and a penchant for a glass of red.

I am represented by Natalie Lakosil from the Bradford Literary Agency and am published traditionally with Montlake Romance and Skyscape Publishing.

https://www.tarabrownauthor.com

http://TaraBrown22.blogspot.com

 facebook.com/TaraBrownAuthor

twitter.com/TaraBrown22

instagram.com/tarabrown_author